The DUKE'S Holiday

— Book One of the Regency Romp Trilogy —

The
DUKE'S
Holiday

— Book One of the Regency Romp Trilogy —

MAGGIE
FENTON

Montlake
Romance

Text copyright © 2015 Margaret Cooke

Published by Montlake Romance, Seattle

www.apub.com

Amazon, the Amazon logo, and Montlake Romance are trademarks of Amazon.com, Inc., or its affiliates.

ISBN-13: 9781477828021
ISBN-10: 1477828028

Cover design by Kim Killion
Library of Congress Control Number: 2014955193

Printed in the United States of America

Dedicated to my mom, who kept pestering me about publishing "that cute Duke of Mumford story." Thanks for supporting me in all of my artistic endeavors. I may even let you read the whole thing this time, Mom, even the naughty bits . . . well, maybe not. They're pretty naughty, and you're . . . well, you're my mom.

"When one is in town one amuses oneself. When one is in the country one amuses other people."

—Oscar Wilde, *The Importance of Being Earnest*, Act 1

Chapter One

LORD CYRIL Halbert Algernon Monk, the eleventh Duke of Montford, got drunk for the first and only time in his life at the tender age of twelve. His best mate, Sebastian Sherbrook, managed to procure a bottle of blue ruin from a stable hand for a sum of money they later found out to be outrageous—a crown indeed!—and the two of them, curious as only twelve-year-old boys can be on the subject of vice, hid in a copse of elderberry bushes outside their dormitory at Harrow during the winter holidays (as neither had families to go home to), drank down the whole bottle like it was water, and scoffed to each other how little effect it had on them.

Five minutes later, they were *in* the elderberry bushes, not just hiding amongst them. And eventually his lunch and Sebastian's lunch were also in the elderberry bushes, and *on his new boots*. But for the brief euphoria before that terrible, messy fall, the experience was an unmitigated disaster.

Yet he had an explanation at long last for the one thing in his life his usually agile brain could not seem to take in. Namely, why his parents, who had been two rational, fairly perceptive people—or so he'd been told—had given him not one, not two, but three perfectly dreadful names. The sort of names that made a little boy shipped off to Harrow at eight years old an easy target for his peers. For, until that point in time, he had been raised by a team of solicitors, tutors, and house servants, and had been obeyed like a petty despot since he'd learned to speak in sentences.

Harrow was indeed a rude awakening. In that first year he was tripped, teased, pinched, punched, and the butt of countless schoolyard jokes, most of them taking the form of the ever-popular limerick.

His parents, he decided, had been drunk when it had come time to name him. It was the only thing that made sense.

That revelation—and the sad state of his boots—was enough to convince him of the myriad dangers of alcohol. He was never drunk again. He was no teetotaler by any means, but he knew his limit when out with his more reckless mates. He knew he'd had enough when any of his names started to sound good to him. When that happened, he put down his glass, stepped away from the decanter, and called it a night.

The only good thing to have come out of his parents dying tragically when he was four was inheriting the title and availing himself of a name that was blessedly un-ridiculous. Having no immediate family left, there was no one to call him by his given names. He was His Grace to servants and strangers and just plain Montford to his circle of intimates.

No one had dared utter Cyril, Halbert, Algernon, or even Monk to his face since his second year at Harrow when he had given Evelyn Leighton, Viscount Marlowe, aforementioned bully, a drubbing so fierce that molars, spit, and blood had been flung about the schoolyard in a ten-foot radius. It was the one time in his life he had not fainted at the sight of blood, so distraught was he.

Never mind Marlowe was twice his size and a year older. Never mind he'd been suspended for the rest of the term, banished to one of his guardian's country estates, without the company of anyone but the staff. Something inside of him had burst after one of Marlowe's infamous cuffs to his neck and an uninspired limerick that rhymed Algernon with hard-on. He'd jumped upon Marlowe in a frenzied whirl of arms and legs, spouting a litany of curses so foul even Sebastian, already world-weary at age ten, had gasped in astonishment. He'd had to be pulled off of Marlowe's stunned, nearly unconscious form by the combined efforts of two instructors.

No one had teased him after that.

And that drubbing had won Marlowe's heart, it seemed, for from that day forward, Marlowe had decided to be his bosom friend. The sick bastard.

By Cambridge, with Sherbrook and Marlowe by his side—not to mention having sprouted up to an impressive six foot two inches tall—he was no longer teased. He was Montford, one of the wealthiest, most powerful aristocrats in the kingdom, even at eighteen. Of course, behind his back, some braver souls—including Sherbrook and Marlowe—labeled him The Monk, because of some of his more peculiar personal habits that could not be hidden behind any title.

He had always been fastidious, what could he say?

For instance, he liked his boots shined until they were like mirrors. And when his boots weren't on his feet, he liked them to be lined up in the wardrobe, heels precisely aligned. He had his valet, Coombes, arrange his jackets and waistcoats by color—black, gray, blue, green, et cetera—and his breeches by category—a drawer for riding, a drawer for morning, one for afternoon, and one for evening. And he liked his cravats starched, ironed, and tied just so. If he spotted, felt, or suspected a wrinkle, he had Coombes fetch a fresh one immediately. He invariably went through half a dozen breeches by the end of the day—twice that if he'd been out riding about his estates or fencing at his club.

He'd given up on Coombes shaving him just to spare himself the anguish of discovering a stray hair midmorning and Coombes's inevitable tears when his error was pointed out. He therefore shaved himself. And after he was done with his morning ablutions, he made sure that all of his brushes, razors, strops, and bottles—square, not round—were lined up on the table at perfect ninety-degree angles.

And then there was his desk. His desk was his haven. A more orderly desk in London could not be found. His inkwells, paperweights, blotters, and ducal seal sat in a neat, even row at the top center, precisely three inches from the edge. His stationery sat directly in front of his chair, so meticulously stacked it looked like a single, thick rectangle.

He allowed his man-of-affairs, Stevenage, to sort his correspondence into tidy piles, the bottom right-hand corners aligned. When Stevenage had taken the position after the retirement of Stevenage the Elder—for he had inherited his job in much the same way Montford had inherited the dukedom—the man had taken it upon himself to align the correspondence just so, revealing a love of detail and order that spoke directly to Montford's heart.

Stevenage, suffering from the same obsessive affliction as his employer, was more than happy to put the duke's correspondence into pristine piles. A pile for estate affairs. A pile for banking receipts. Another for House of Lords business. Another for his personal correspondence. Another for the social invitations he wanted to accept (a very short pile). Another for the social invitations he *didn't* want to accept but was obliged to (a rather large pile). And another labeled Miscellaneous—correspondence that, like the oversized books in his library he'd banished to a far corner, defied categorization and utterly nettled him.

The Miscellaneous pile—*That Pile*—nettled Stevenage as well. Montford often caught his man-of-affairs glancing at it as nervously as he himself did when he thought no one else was looking. Stevenage was, if at all possible, even more concerned with the order of things than Montford himself.

And Stevenage was, on this particular morning, looking *extremely* concerned when Montford entered the library to take up the morning business. His man-of-affairs was, as usual, immaculately dressed in stiff, unrelenting black superfine, the kind that only solicitors and undertakers seemed to wear, his cravat simply but neatly tied, his steely gray hair combed and pomaded, and his gold spectacles as unsmudged as ever. But the brown eyes behind the spectacles were a little . . . well, *wild*, and the man kept glancing over to *That Pile* on the desk.

Montford knew something was dreadfully wrong when Stevenage tugged upon his cravat, disordering it ever so slightly.

"What's wrong?" Montford demanded.

"I don't know how it happened, Your Grace . . . how it was over-looked. Indeed I do not know . . ." Stevenage trailed off into incoherence, a first for the usually acute man.

Montford sat down at his desk and braced himself, then noticed an opened letter clinging perilously to the cliff's edge of *That Pile*, as if it had been dropped there, willy-nilly, by his man-of-affairs. Or had sprung to life of its own accord like some pernicious barnacle, uncaring of the chaos it caused.

Montford sucked in a breath and told himself to remain calm. "Remain calm, Stevenage, and tell me the problem."

"Aloysius Honeywell is dead, Your Grace."

Hmm.

Well, this wasn't exactly *bad* news. He'd been waiting for years for Aloysius Honeywell to kick off, hadn't he? "And what's the problem?"

"Well, er . . . it appears . . . Your Grace . . . that he has been dead for . . . er, some time."

"Some time."

"A year."

Montford jumped to his feet. He sat back down. Then he jumped up again, strode to the window, and looked out onto the busy Mayfair street below, trying to get his head around the news.

Dead. For a year.

It seemed that even in death, Aloysius Honeywell—a man who had been the bane of Montford's well-ordered little kingdom since Montford had assumed the full reins of his title—had thumbed his nose at him. Montford's only consolation was that Aloysius Honeywell's given name was even worse than his own.

Not that he had ever met Honeywell. Not that Honeywell knew he was a bane to a duke . . . No, scratch that. Honeywell knew *exactly* how much his existence vexed Montford. He knew as well how little Montford could do to be rid of him, however much he taunted and teased in his haphazard reports sent down from Yorkshire. The Honeywells had been a thorn in the side of the Montford dukes for nearly two centuries now, ever since one of Montford's illustrious female ancestors had unwisely married into that family of . . . of . . .

What *were* the Honeywells? Merchants? Confidence men? Fairy people?

At the very least, they were upstarts.

Mushrooms.

Or they had been two hundred years ago, when they'd swindled a long-ago duke into a contract so convoluted no team of solicitors since then had been able to extricate the dukedom from its grasp. The contract had allowed the Honeywells to become the proprietary tenants of one of the ducal estates in Yorkshire for as long as the Honeywells endured. And the Honeywells had endured.

And endured.

And to add insult to injury, they made ale. *Blech.* They used acres and acres of prime farmland to cultivate their wheat and barley for their foul plebeian brew. Honeywell Ale. It was, sadly, ubiquitous in every pub north of London. Or at least it was ubiquitous when it was available, which was *not very often*, as it was made in small quantities. There was invariably a rush on the pubs when the yearly shipments were sent out.

Sherbrook and Marlowe stockpiled the stuff, the traitorous bastards.

Needless to say, Honeywell Ale did not turn a sizeable profit. The ten percent that went to the duchy each year was a pittance, hardly worth the effort of a receipt. All that prime farmland, wasted. It was enough to make Montford want to cry. And he hadn't cried since he was four years old. He liked seeing his holdings prosper, his investments blossom. It pained him to have this one glaring, gaping blot upon his record of success.

But if Honeywell was dead . . . and since Honeywell had no sons, that meant . . .

What did that mean? And why had he not been informed?

"A year?" Montford asked, turning back to his man-of-affairs with a glower that sent Stevenage's fingers back to his cravat. Montford pointed toward the letter. "Who is that from? What does it say?"

"It is from the president of Dunkirk Brewing Company. A Mr. Lightfoot. It seems he wants to purchase Honeywell Ale—that is, Rylestone Hall and the rest of the estate, now that Mr. Honeywell has . . . er, passed on."

Now that was vaguely interesting. Dunkirk was the largest brewing concern in Yorkshire. As profitable as Honeywell Ale was not.

"What the devil could he want with Rylestone?" Montford muttered.

"Apparently, the land is in close proximity to Mr. Lightfoot's own property. He wants to expand the business."

Montford's interest in the letter and its proposal began to wane. It was all very well and good for Mr. Lightfoot to want to build his business, but Montford did not see how this could be of benefit to *him*. He didn't give a jot about Lightfoot or his desire to become an ale impresario. And he certainly had no intention of selling Rylestone Hall after it was finally the dukedom's again.

"Who the devil has been writing to us, then, Stevenage? If Honeywell's been dead a year, who's been sending us those damned reports?" He gestured, rather impatiently, toward a gargantuan rosewood bureau set against a far wall, in which all of his old correspondence sat neatly filed.

"I . . . don't know, Your Grace. That's just it, I don't know," Stevenage said bleakly.

"Well, don't stand there like an idiot," Montford grumbled. "Fetch me the last report that devil sent me."

Stevenage scurried over to the bureau. Several minutes passed, in which Montford returned to his seat and began thrumming his nails against the desktop with impatience. At last, a squeak came from the direction of the bureau, and Stevenage held up an envelope as if he'd pulled a prize fish from the river.

"Well, come on, man, haven't got all day," Montford grumbled, which of course was a lie. He hadn't anything to do that day, as his affairs were, as usual, neatly tidied away. Except, of course, for the matter of Aloysius Honeywell.

Stevenage placed the envelope into Montford's outstretched hand. Montford unfolded it neatly before him and squinted down at the convoluted text.

To His Grace the Duke of Montford,

Concerning His Grace's inquiries in his last letter in regards to the profit margin versus expenditure of the brewery and how the former might be increased over the latter. It is, frankly, the least of my worries at the moment, but it was So Good of His Grace to Be Concerned. Honeywell Ale holds itself to a high standard, which, alas, often means setting itself above margins and expenditures and other mercantile interests. I am sure His Grace, if anybody, understands the need to Set Oneself Above. Of course, if His Grace is suffering financially, my family, owing to our long association with the esteemed Dukes of Montford, would be more than willing to aid you in your time of need. We do not have any ready cash at hand, but if His Grace would be so kind as to accept in lieu two barrels of our special reserve ale to keep His Grace watered during a Difficult Time.

Regards,
A. Honeywell

Montford wasn't any less irked by the letter now than he had been six months ago upon its receipt. It read just like countless other letters he'd received from his tormentor. He would have known the uneven shape and slope of those letters anywhere. The script was as flowing and untidy as usual, all jerks and loops and blots. All the lines were written on a slightly downward slant that made him dizzy. The last sentence—if one could call such a poorly written string of words a sentence—even had the audacity to curve around the edge of the page, the author having run out of room. *Difficult Time* dangled along the edge like a deflated balloon, cramped and flattened but unmistakably capitalized, unmistakably insolent.

A. Honeywell.

Lightfoot claimed Honeywell was dead, but he wouldn't put it past Aloysius Honeywell's ghost returning to earth just so he might pen a snide letter to Montford. But unless he had suddenly stepped into the lead in one of those dreadful gothic novels Sherbrook was always toting about, Montford was quite sure no ghost had been involved. That meant whoever had been writing to him for the past decade was someone other than Aloysius Honeywell. *Or* the past few letters had been written by a master forger.

However, Montford doubted the latter. He was firmly convinced Michelangelo himself could not reproduce the studied anarchy of A. Honeywell's writing. Which led him back to the question of the morning:

Who the devil was A. Honeywell?

"Stevenage," Montford murmured, folding up the letter carefully. "Someone is bamming us."

"Who would dare to bam *you*, Your Grace?" Stevenage breathed, sounding as affronted as Louis XVI must have felt when he learned how his head was going to spend its last few moments on earth.

To give the loyal servant some credit, Stevenage's horrified reaction was only a slightly exaggerated version of what a less high-strung man would have done, given the same news. For who indeed would dare to cross the Duke of Montford?

No one in his right mind, obviously.

No one except a Honeywell.

And that was only because they thought they could hide behind that damnable contract. Only because they thought they were immune to being crushed under his ducal heel. Which couldn't be further from the truth, now that the Honeywell line was at an end. Only a direct male heir could fulfill the terms of the contract. And Aloysius had none, which meant the estate . . .

Reverted back to the dukedom.

After two hundred long years, Rylestone Hall and environs were his once more, to dispose of as he wished.

Montford could have jumped for joy had he not thought it would mar the creases in his breeches. And he couldn't celebrate just yet. It was one thing to learn someone was dead from a third party, another altogether to have direct proof. Ocular evidence. Montford wouldn't rest easy until he was assured of Aloysius's current resting place—which he hoped was six feet under a rocky patch of Yorkshire dirt.

And as for the author of this little deceit . . .

"Stevenage, I want you to pay a visit to Rylestone Hall."

Stevenage's eyes went as wide as saucers. It was not in Montford's habit to send Stevenage on journeys of such magnitude, delegating his business outside of London to a Montford steward already on site. In fact, it was not in Montford's habit to let Stevenage out of the library before nightfall—unless the man had to use the chamber pot, of course, though even then Montford had to be well-convinced of the necessity.

He would go to Yorkshire himself—he was vexed enough by this mess to overcome his aversion to traveling—but he couldn't leave London right now. Lords was still in session for the next few weeks, and then he was getting married. It was to be the biggest society wedding of the year. Obviously. He was Montford. An affair of that magnitude required careful planning and an endless parade of luncheons, dinner parties, musicales, and balls, all guaranteed to irritate the hell out of him.

He did *not* do well in crowds. But he did not have a choice but to play the doting bridegroom, if he was to wed the inestimable Lady Araminta Carlisle, society darling, perfect future Duchess of Montford. Appearances were everything with the *ton*. And with Araminta. And of course with Montford. Which was why he'd chosen the flawless paragon for his duchess. Yet Montford just wished for the whole blasted business to be over and the requisite heir and a spare produced so that his life could return to normal. Propagating the ducal line was turning out to be the most inconvenient duty he'd had to undertake yet in his role as Montford.

Stevenage nodded vigorously. "O . . . of course, sir."

"I want proof of that man's death. Certificates, et cetera. A trip to the gravesite. That sort of thing."

Stevenage went from incredulous to horrified in the blink of an eye. "Your Grace, you don't want me to . . . dear heavens, you don't think I should actually . . ."

"Out with it, man!"

". . . *dig up the body!*" Stevenage concluded, winded.

Good God, did Stevenage actually think he would stoop so low as to demand such a thing? Montford was appalled.

Then he cocked his head to the side and thought about it for a moment. *That wouldn't be such a bad idea, actually.*

Stevenage must have read the drift of Montford's thoughts, for he backed up a step and crossed his arms over his chest in a rare gesture of defiance. "Your Grace, you know I would take a bullet for you if I could, but I draw the line at . . . at . . . gravedigging!"

Montford cleared his throat and waved one arm through the air in what he hoped was a convincingly dismissive gesture. "Of course I don't want you to dig up his grave. That would be . . ." *Thorough? Conclusive?* ". . . wrong. A rubbing of the headstone is probably enough."

Stevenage's shoulders sagged in relief.

"And while you're up there, I want you to figure out who's behind this little charade."

Stevenage nodded, looking more like his old self. "With pleasure, Your Grace."

"And you might as well take an inventory of the estate. Somehow I don't think this is the first time the Honeywells have pulled the wool over our eyes."

Stevenage nodded solemnly. "I understand there are gypsies in their lineage," he offered, as if that explained it all.

"Hadn't heard that one," Montford said. He sat back in his chair, pinching the bridge of his nose, feeling a headache coming on.

Stevenage stared at him, blinking. Montford began to wonder why the man was still standing there.

"Well?"

Stevenage jumped at Montford's tone. "Do you mean you want me to go *now*, Your Grace?"

"As soon as possible. I want this matter sorted. I'm getting married soon, and I don't want any loose ends hanging over me. It will be chaotic enough around here."

Stevenage gathered up the errant letters cluttering the desk and began bowing his way out of the room.

"Oh, and Stevenage?"

"Yes, Your Grace?"

"I want detailed reports. Every day."

"Naturally," Stevenage said, as if this needn't have been asked. "I would dream of no less."

Then Stevenage was gone, and Montford was alone in his library with nothing to do until he had to be at the House of Lords. In three hours. He thrummed his fingers on the desktop for a while, but when he saw how he smudged the surface, he brought out his handkerchief and wiped it clean.

And, as he was doing this, he wished that the Honeywells could be removed from his life as effortlessly as his fingerprints from a desktop.

⚊⚊ ⚌✦⚌ ⚊⚊

BUT HAVING that wish come true was clearly too easy, for it appeared Stevenage did, in fact, dream of something less than what he promised in the matter of progress reports.

In the two weeks since Stevenage's departure, Stevenage had sent precisely one letter to Montford. It appeared to have been written the day of Stevenage's arrival in Yorkshire, was all of five sentences long, and did nothing to assuage Montford's already frazzled nerves.

When Stevenage wrote progress reports, he accounted for nearly every minute of the day's business in cold, clinical detail, rather like the prose one would find in a medical compendium. Stevenage's letters were usually five pages long at the bare minimum, not five sentences. And they hardly ever contained adjectives.

And never, *ever*, did they contain emotion.

But this odd note—Stevenage's normally immaculate script slanting slightly to the right as if dashed off in a passionate rush—was all emotion. And chock-full of adjectives. It was alarming.

Your Grace, it read, *I have confirmed that Aloysius Honeywell is dead. But it is, alas, the only thing I can say for certain in regards to that family. They are all as mad as March hares, I avow, although Miss Honeywell suggested that I am the mad one. I haven't located A. Honeywell yet, as there are so many of them, but I beg you to consider recalling me to London posthaste. The Honeywells are quite unsettling indeed. Stevenage.*

Montford had written back immediately for Stevenage to stay put and get to the bottom of the Honeywells' schemes. He wanted no unpleasant business hanging over him when he was married.

But Stevenage sent no reply, and a week and a half passed without Montford hearing from his man-of-affairs at all. Montford sent a barrage of letters, each one more mystified than the last. The final one sent northward was merely one sentence long:

What in the hell is going on up there?

Which summed up the problem quite nicely, Montford thought.

But when still he received no reply, Montford began to worry that something dire had happened to Stevenage. Or rather, that the Honeywells had *made* something dire happen to his man-of-affairs. Stevenage had called them unsettling in his letter, which, at first, Montford had assumed pertained to aspects of character that usually unsettled his man-of-affairs. Like disorganization. Loud laughter. Poor hygiene. But the more Montford thought about it—in truth, obsessed over it—the more he began to fear that something more sinister than poor hygiene was going on up north.

For Montford could not imagine anything short of death keeping Stevenage from his usual perfection.

It would be most inconvenient if Stevenage turned up murdered by the Honeywells. But at least Montford would have the satisfaction of seeing one of their clan hanged, if that were the case.

Montford decided to wait it out for a day or two more. After that, he was prepared to take drastic action, even if it meant getting into a carriage and driving up to Rylestone himself, weak stomach be damned.

Meanwhile, Somewhere in Yorkshire ...

EVERYONE WHO knew and loved the Honeywell clan—and their numbers were legion in Rylestone Green—bemoaned the fact that Astrid Honeywell had not been born a man. For as soon as she was old enough to walk and talk, everyone agreed she would have made Aloysius a splendid son.

Everyone, that is, except Astrid herself. Aside from the obvious advantages being Aloysius's heir would have given her family—and the fact that the Honeywells could thereby poleax the Montfords for at least another generation—Astrid was glad she was not a man. For she had discovered at an early age that men were morons. Even her father, whom she had adored with all of her heart, had been a prize idiot. Especially after a few pints of Honeywell Reserve.

Astrid often wondered how in the hell women had allowed men to rule the world. Men were physically stronger, granted, and were thus quite good at getting what they wanted with their fists. But women were, by and large, so much *smarter* than men. It seemed an easy enough thing to outwit the male sex despite their brawn. Astrid did it every day.

But Astrid knew her questions were rhetorical at best. She knew precisely why women were chattel and men their keepers.

Because most women filled their brainboxes with so many trifles they could not navigate their thoughts around them, a conspiracy perpetrated by milliners, dressmakers, clergymen, the marriage institution, and novel writers. It was rather like owning a grand palace, then filling only a small front parlor of it from floor to ceiling with meaningless bric-a-brac, gewgaws, and fribbles, with nary a decent chair to sit upon, and then leaving the rest of the rooms to molder with cobwebs and damp.

Women could, Astrid had to grudgingly agree, be quite as idiotic as men.

But that was only because men had made them so with their petty despotism and paternalistic property laws.

Fortunately, Aloysius's male failings had not extended to the matter of his daughters' education. He'd been wise enough—or unwise enough, depending on how one looked at it—to believe in equal education for the sexes. He'd been a self-proclaimed progressive, but most people had just called him endearingly eccentric, as they did all the Honeywells. Whatever the case, due to old Aloysius's eccentricity, the Honeywell girls were quite possibly the best educated females in Yorkshire.

Or the worst—again, depending on how one looked at it.

Astrid and her sisters knew very little in the way of feminine accomplishments, the sort of subjects taught at expensive finishing schools for ladies. Things like pouring tea, making idle conversation, embroidering pillows and handkerchiefs, and dabbing at watercolors were baffling endeavors to them. The forthright Honeywells never made idle conversation, and they never *dabbed* at anything. And who, Astrid had always wondered, needed to be instructed on how to pour tea, for heaven's sake? She did it all the time quite easily enough without having studied it in school.

The Honeywell girls knew Latin and Greek, European languages and history, philosophy and economics, and even a smattering of biology (scandalous indeed). Alice, Astrid's younger sister by three years, excelled at maths, of all things, and helped Astrid keep the estate books in order. Ardyce and Antonia, the two youngest, liked to chatter to each other in ancient Greek and reenact scenes from Homeric epics in the stable yard. Astrid, unsurprisingly, enjoyed spouting political theory the most, and had firm opinions on the matter of women's place in society. She was a bluestocking and proud of it.

No, she was quite glad she had not been born a man. Yet she thought the primogeniture laws in this country—written by men to benefit men—were absurd and downright antediluvian. Because she didn't have a rather inconvenient piece of equipment dangling between her legs (oh, and the Honeywells were *not* delicate flowers regarding anatomy), she was denied her father's legacy; and because of this, the Honeywell family was going to be denied the home they had lived in for more than two hundred years.

Never mind the fact that she had run the brewery, the farm, and the estate single-handedly since her father's first stroke when she was fourteen years old. Never mind that her staff, employees, and the tenants—with a few notable exceptions, of course—respected and obeyed her quite as if she had been a man. Never mind Rylestone Hall and all of its tenants prospered under her stewardship. One had only to cross over the property line into the next county to see how badly off most tenant farmers had it at the hands of their bumbling aristocratic overlords.

And that was another thing. Astrid thought the aristocracy was equally as idiotic as the male species. No wonder most of the country's inhabitants were starving; because the Upper Ten Thousand hoarded the profits from their estates to build enormous houses, throw elaborate balls, and buy new hats at the drop of . . . well, a hat. Not to mention wage ridiculous wars with neighboring countries. It was a wonder England's lower classes didn't take a page from the French, storm Whitehall—or better yet the sublime banality of Almack's—and drag off the Prince Regent and his cronies to *madame la guillotine*. Astrid was quite sure the world would be a better place.

One only had to look to Rylestone as an example. It was a true democracy, free of any inbred titled fop's unwelcome interference. Or at least she strived for it to be. Most of the tenants couldn't seem to wrap their heads around the idea of majority rule and ended up asking Astrid what to do anyway. Monarchism had become a bad habit not easily broken. But she tried. And she distributed the profits from the estate from a common bank, keeping no more for her family than anyone else.

It had been this way in her father's time, and in his father's time

(Honeywells had always been radically, if not successfully, progressive), and the system worked. The only flaw in it was Montford.

Montford was an entity, unseen and unheard, but always there, hovering over them like the Old Testament God. To her knowledge, no Honeywell had actually seen a Montford since the seventeenth century. The centuries-old feud connecting the Honeywells with the Montford dukedom was as impenetrable as a storm cloud. But some things were clear.

The Norman-ish Montfords had stolen Rylestone from the Saxon-ish Honeywells. The Honeywells had promptly stolen it back. This went on for some years. Back and forth, back and forth. Then another Montford sent into the Honeywells' midst a Trojan horse in the form of a Montford female. Astrid's ancestor had signed a devilish contract in order to be allowed take the woman to wife.

Apparently, she had been quite a catch.

And that marriage had marked the Honeywells' doom. Of course, they'd managed to postpone it for two hundred years, but still. She had bought herself an extra year simply by conveniently forgetting to inform Montford of her father's death. The only reason His Grace knew now was because of that blasted Mr. Lightfoot.

But something would come to her, she was sure. What she needed was time.

And stalling was one of her fortes.

Poor Mr. Stevenage had never stood a chance against her family.

Astrid crept into the front hall of the castle in the early morning light a fortnight after the strange little man's arrival and intercepted Stevenage's latest letter from London, as she had all of his correspondence. Glancing around to make sure she was alone, she hastily ripped open the note and scanned its contents.

What in the hell is going on up there? M.

Astrid's lips curled at the edges in a sly grin, and one eyebrow lifted in an expression that an onlooker would have likely termed devilish.

"What indeed, you bloody piker?" she murmured, crumpling the letter in her fist and heading for the nearest available open flame. "You'll have to send someone worthy next time around. Not that it would do you any good. We aren't going anywhere."

Though inside she was not nearly so sanguine. Trouble was coming to Rylestone Hall. It was only a matter of time. But one thing she knew for certain: Rylestone belonged to the Honeywells, not Montford, no matter what any trifling contract said.

Chapter Two

Back in London . . .

MONTFORD WAS supposed to have gone somewhere that evening. A ball, he believed it was, at the Duke of Belmont's. He had, at his last tedious morning call to Araminta, promised to lead his fiancée out for the first waltz. The prospect had filled neither Araminta nor Montford with anything resembling anticipation. He was merely doing his duty, and so was Araminta, with her usual glacial poise. But now, it seemed, he would fail in that duty this particular night. Which was quite horrifying.

He never failed in his duties.

Never.

But this damned Honeywell business was cutting up his peace.

Montford couldn't explain why it had unsettled him so much, or why he was presently sitting behind his desk in the library, staring vacantly into the fireplace at ten o'clock at night. Yet the truth of the matter was that, loath as he was to admit it, he had felt poised on the edge of a precipice ever since he had formally asked for Lady Araminta's hand, and the Honeywell business had given him the final push.

Montford did not believe he had made a mistake regarding his choice of duchess. He had carefully selected Araminta out of all of the eligible women in the kingdom. No one had her impeccable bloodlines, her poise, or her tidiness. She seemed intelligent enough, so he did not have to worry about his offspring being lack-witted. And she did not natter on as most females did, and had no bad habits, as far as he knew, that would annoy him overmuch. And even if she did, he owned seventeen residences, all of them big enough so that he never even had to see his wife if he so chose.

Oh, and Araminta was thought to be quite beautiful. He supposed he found her attractive enough in a purely theoretical way, rather in the way he found Grecian marbles attractive. But he took no great pleasure in her beauty and felt no stirrings of lust when he kissed her.

Which was precisely why he had chosen her, he supposed. It would not do for him to lust after his own wife. Or, God forbid, fall in love with her. Such a thing was the height of bourgeois. Not to mention thoroughly, utterly impossible for Montford. He did not love anyone.

He had done exactly what he was supposed to have done by courting Araminta. And it was inexplicable to him why he should now be at sixes and sevens. No, not inexplicable. Inconvenient to be bothered at this juncture in his life with this impossible restlessness.

He was a formal man. A cold man. He would not deny this. He was the living embodiment of an eight-hundred-year-old duchy. He *was* Montford. But sometimes—not often, but sometimes (usually right after he'd tossed back a port or two and right before his given names began to sound good in his head)—he longed to be just a man with a simple name, not a title that conjured up ancestral ghosts, coats of arms, grand estates, and duty, duty, duty.

But then he would quickly come to his senses. He could not very well shirk said duty simply because he was plagued by emotions and sentiments in his rare, weaker moments. Someone had to steer the helm, pay the bills, and run the country. Who else was going to do it? Sherbrook? Marlowe?

Now *there* was a laugh.

As if his thoughts had summoned up the devils in question, his butler knocked on the door and announced two visitors. Montford had no difficulty figuring out who they were, for the two men strode into the room on Stallings's heels, as was their custom, before Stallings was able to get out their names. It had become something of a running joke, if such a thing existed under Montford's roof. Stallings always tried to announce them properly, and Sherbrook and Marlowe always interrupted him before he could, one or the other of them slapping the old codger familiarly on the back and sending him on his way.

Which Marlowe did now with a sturdy thwack that made Stallings hop in place and yelp involuntarily.

"Steady on, old thing," Marlowe drawled, dropping his considerable frame onto a chaise lounge by the fire, sending his evening hat tumbling over the side. "'Twas only a love pat. Fetch us some of them little sandwiches, will you, Stallings? And maybe them biscuits your little frog man makes down there, what with the little knickknacks in them. I'm famished."

Marlowe was always famished.

And he never asked for permission to order food from Montford's kitchens—food that Montford's French chef, Pierre, was always offended to have to prepare. Marlowe's favorites, sandwiches filled with "knick-knacks," and meat pies, did not qualify as worthy of Pierre's talents.

"Very good, your lordship," Stallings responded, recovering his gravitas and bowing out the door.

"What the blazes are you up to, Montford?" Sherbrook demanded, pulling off his elegant gloves before prowling over to the sideboard and pouring them a round of drinks. "Looked for you at White's and Belmont's."

Montford grunted, in no mood to explain himself.

"'Twas a damned crush," Marlowe added. "And a crushing bore. Me sister drug us there. I believe she is trying to turn us respectable." Marlowe belched and scratched his arse, illustrating just how onerous a task her sister had set for herself. "Give us a tipple, Sherbrook."

Sherbrook obliged by placing a snifter of port in Marlowe's outstretched paw. He put one in front of Montford as well. Montford took a reluctant sip, one eye glued to Marlowe's precarious hold on his glass. As Marlowe settled his rump more snugly into the chaise, port sloshed over his fingers and down his sleeve.

Montford rolled his eyes and wondered not for the first time how it came to be that his two best friends were perhaps the slovenliest pair of malingerers in the country.

At least *Marlowe* was, with his rumpled clothes, slight paunch, shaggy black mane, and permanent state of intoxication. Sherbrook was a bit harder to categorize. He was always smartly enough turned out . . .

All right, so Sherbrook was a bit of a man-milliner, as evidenced by his current attire. He was at that moment wearing a pink waistcoat embroidered with silver thread and a matching coat cut to his elegant form like a second skin, Brussels lace spilling out of the sleeves. All of his fingers were encircled with bejeweled rings, and not one, not two, but . . . *five?* gold-chained watch fobs crisscrossed his abdomen. He wore the encrustation of lace and gold and jewels with a lackadaisical elegance no other English gentleman had yet matched, though they had tried.

And he always managed to convey the impression from his dashed-off cravat and carefully mussed hair of having just tumbled out of bed. The ladies were mad for Sherbrook.

Less so for Marlowe, who had the ruddy complexion and slightly bloated abdomen of a dedicated sot. He cared nothing for his wardrobe and would as soon—and often did—go out in public in his dressing gown and a pair of sandals he had acquired on a trip to Greece, his toes hanging out for the entire world to see. Marlowe prized comfort above all else.

But it was universally agreed by both sexes that the gentlemen in question were the worst libertines in England. Worse than Byron and his cronies, who were mere featherweights in comparison. The pair of them had failed out of Cambridge, and after a Particular Incident involving Sherbrook's contemptible uncle and Marlowe's fist (which was referenced among the three friends as a deed better left unexplained), the pair, with Montford's help, promptly bought commissions in the army, and gambled, wenched, and brawled their way through Spain and Portugal.

After they were simultaneously injured at Badajoz and decamped to London as War Heroes, no gaming hell, racetrack, brothel, or any other den of iniquity had been spared their attentions. They only occasionally set their unwilling Hessians in respectable venues, having been dragged there by Montford or Marlowe's long-suffering sister, the Countess of Brinderley.

Despite their reputations, Marlowe and Sherbrook were beloved by the *ton*, which didn't surprise Montford, since he knew they were the source of society's juiciest gossip. Marlowe was sought after for his genial, slightly inebriated good humor and his instinctive knowledge of horseflesh. And the ladies collectively swooned at Sherbrook's feet, as he was regarded as the Singlemost Beautiful Man in London.

This was according to the *Times*.

That same publication had often wondered over Montford's unerring association with the two rogues, as His Grace was—also according to the *Times*—a Pillar of Moral and Sartorial Rectitude and a Creature Not Quite Flesh and Blood. Montford was equally baffled over his friendships, but it had been the case that ever since their days at Harrow, he, Sherbrook, and Marlowe had been inseparable. He supposed he was cast rather in the role of older brother, extricating the two of them from various scrapes, urging caution at the gaming tables, and exhorting them to *please, for the love of God, make sure the wench is clean before you stick it there.* That sort of thing.

When he'd migrated to London after Cambridge (*he* had not flunked out), Marlowe and Sherbrook had greeted him with open arms, and had urged him to "cut a dash" with them. Which meant gaming, wenching, and racing his way through the Season. But while his best friends had become the Worst Libertines in London, somehow he had not qualified for such a lofty sobriquet.

After all, *someone* had to keep a level head in order to rescue Marlowe and Sherbrook from the worst of their excesses, scare off whoever was spoiling for a fight with them, and carry them to their beds when they lost the ability to stand.

Montford was Montford, and that was precisely Montford's problem at the moment, as he sat behind his desk, sipping his port and bleakly watching his friends loaf about the room, feeling as if his head might explode at any moment.

Stallings returned bearing a tea tray laden with sandwiches and biscuits. Marlowe was roused from his dozing long enough to make short shrift of the food, then fell back against the chaise lounge, closed his eyes, and took up his port. In that order.

"You're even less fun than usual," Sebastian said fondly, perching on the edge of the desk and molesting the box full of quills, knocking it out of its parallel alignment with the desk edge.

Montford gritted his teeth and tried to ignore Sebastian's deliberate goad. Sebastian knew precisely how much he was bothering him. They'd roomed together at Harrow, after all. "Some of us have important business to attend to, Sherbrook," he muttered.

"Last time I checked, the House of Lords was recessed."

"Last time I checked, I had a dukedom to manage," Montford retorted.

"You have old Stevenage for that." Sebastian craned his neck around the room. "Where *is* your shadow? Don't tell me you pack him up in one of your drawers at the end of the day."

Marlowe, who had begun to drowse with his snifter of port balanced precariously on his burgeoning gut, started awake. "Drawers?" he blustered, looking wildly around the room, only just catching his port before it sloshed onto the upholstery. "Never wear the blasted things. Chafe like the devil, what," he declared before dropping back into his stupor.

Sebastian grimaced. "Didn't need to know *that*." He turned back to Montford, who was trying very hard not to visualize what Marlowe was *not* wearing beneath his extremely snug breeches. "I do hope you allow Stevenage out of this room sometimes," Sebastian continued playfully.

"Clearly I do, as he's not here," Montford sniffed.

"I am speechless." Sebastian paused, took up one of the feathers, and began twirling it in his fingers. "Well, what have you done with him?"

"He's in Yorkshire on business."

"You don't sound very sure of that."

"I've not heard from him in a fortnight."

He must have sounded strange, because Sebastian dropped the quill into his lap and blinked in surprise. "You're really worried, aren't you?"

"It's very unlike him not to keep me informed."

"Yes, one would expect an itemized accounting of every minute of his trip," he said dryly. "This is Stevenage we're talking about. A man even more meticulous than you. And where in blazes did you send him? Yorkshire? Nothing but bloody sheep in Yorkshire last time I checked."

"I sent him to sort out some business on one of my estates."

"Aren't *we* vague tonight. As you have so many damned estates, it would help if you were more specific."

Montford did not want to be more specific. He knew exactly how Sebastian would react if he brought up Honeywell. God knew how Sebastian had ferreted out the story of the Montfords and the Honeywells. God knew how Sebastian came to know most of the things he did. One wouldn't suspect from glancing at the self-avowed model of indolence currently perched on the edge of his desk that behind that bored, cynical face dwelled a very acute thinking organ. Sebastian was quick. Quicker than Montford had ever been. And he had the memory of an elephant.

Especially in regards to matters pertaining to the pursuit of pleasure. Like Honeywell Ale.

"What are you hiding?" Sebastian asked, eyes narrowing.

Damn. He supposed Sebastian would find out eventually. "Aloysius Honeywell is dead."

"Honeywell . . . wouldn't mind one, if you have one on hand," Marlowe murmured, roused by the possibility of more beverages.

"Gads, Marlowe, you sot. He said Honeywell is dead!" Sebastian exclaimed, rising from the desk.

Marlowe's florid face went white as a sheet. He jumped to his feet in a flash—faster than Montford had seen him move in years—and this time he was so distraught he forgot about his port. The glass tumbled down his gut and landed on the Persian carpet.

The sound that emerged from Montford's throat was *not* a whimper, but it was damned close.

Marlowe blotted the front of his stained waistcoat to no real effect and bent over to retrieve his snifter. "Awful sorry, Montford," he muttered.

"Don't worry. I'll buy a new one," he said through his gritted teeth, feeling a headache come on.

"Yes, well . . ." Marlowe drifted off and furrowed his brow in an obvious attempt to recover his train of thought. It came back in a horrible rush. "Honeywell's dead!" he blustered with a passion Montford would have appreciated in his apology about the carpet. "Don't tell me the brewery has folded! I don't think I could bear it."

"Of course the brewery's not going to fold," Sebastian scoffed. He turned to Montford, looking a bit apprehensive himself. "It's not, is it?"

Montford shrugged, and because he couldn't stand it another second, he marched over to the spill, armed with a handkerchief, and began to blot up the port on the carpet. "Honeywell had no male heir. The property reverts back to the dukedom," he said.

"But you won't . . . surely you won't shut it down," Marlowe cried. "Montford! You wouldn't be so cruel!"

"Aloysius Honeywell died a year ago. Clearly someone is still producing that swill you call ale. You are in no danger of dying of thirst."

"Oh," said Marlowe, who, seeing that the crisis had been averted, shrugged and returned to his seat—after pouring himself a new glass of port.

"Oh," echoed Sherbrook, who furrowed his brow. "A year, you say. How peculiar. It's not like you to let a detail like that go, Montford."

"I didn't. I didn't know he was dead until two weeks ago."

Sherbrook cocked an eyebrow. "Indeed. I wager that one has been sticking in your craw."

"You have no idea."

"So what are you going to do?"

"I haven't decided."

"You aren't going to shut down the brewery, are you?" Sherbrook asked again, pitching his voice so as not to distress the slumbering Marlowe again.

"It is hardly profitable."

Sherbrook shook his head and threw up his hands in exasperation. "That's everything to you, isn't it? Profit?"

"Not everything. But damned near close." *Someone* had to keep his two friends in beverages and meat pies.

"At least you're honest."

"See here, Sherbrook, you know how the Montfords despise the Honeywells."

"May I point out you've never even met a Honeywell?"

"Yes, well, be that as it may, Rylestone is my responsibility, and I will be damned before I let it continue to be so grossly mismanaged. The tenants must be starving, considering what I've seen of the returns on the estate."

"But the *ale*! Montford, it's the best ale in the kingdom!" Sherbrook wheedled, the plight of the tenants completely beside the point, as far as he was concerned.

Montford sighed and rubbed his forehead. "I honestly don't know what I'll do. With Stevenage out of touch, I am feeling . . . disjointed."

Sebastian nodded his head decisively. "What you need is a good holiday."

Montford snorted. A holiday indeed. "Dukes do not take holidays."

Sebastian gave him an arch look. "Really, Montford. You can be so tiresome sometimes. You're a mortal man, same as the rest of us. And if you ask me, you need to loosen that cravat of yours a little before you strangle on it."

"Hear, hear," Marlowe seconded, apparently more alert to the proceedings than his posture indicated.

"I didn't ask you," Montford growled. "Or you," he added in Marlowe's direction.

Sebastian rolled his eyes.

"Besides, there's no time for a . . . holiday, what with the wedding in a month," Montford finished.

Sherbrook's face darkened, as it always did when the subject of Montford's upcoming nuptials was mentioned. "That's another thing, Monty. Lady Araminta? Are you *quite* sure?"

"Of course I'm quite sure. She'll make the perfect duchess."

Sherbrook shuddered. "Aye, if duchesses were carved out of stone and encased in ice. Lady Araminta is a cold-blooded, heartless, self-centered Bath miss."

Montford took no offense at Sherbrook's words. He accepted Sherbrook's opinion on the matter of his fiancée and family, because it happened to be his own. "I thought that was her sister," he said dryly.

Sherbrook's eyes narrowed. "What? Lady *Katherine*? My beloved auntie?" He snorted. "You're right. Ten times worse than her sister. Never have I met such utter conceit, such utter frigidness—"

"I was unaware you had conversed with her," Montford interposed.

Sherbrook stopped up short, looking extremely put out. "Well, I haven't, but I *have* met her. We've *been* introduced." As if that explained it.

Montford was the one to roll his eyes this time.

Sherbrook began to pace in front of the fireplace. "The Carlisle sisters are the most high-in-the-instep, vapid, insipid, frigid *paragons* to have ever lived." He turned on Montford, fists clenched. "She makes me want to take her by the shoulders and shake some life into her. And if I didn't fear that I would turn to stone merely by touching her, I would—"

"Are we speaking of Lady Araminta or her sister?" Montford interjected.

Sherbrook stopped pacing and blinked. "What?"

"You said *she*. That you wanted to take her by the shoulders and—"

"Yes, yes, I know what I said," Sherbrook bit out. He glanced around the room with a haunted expression, then stalked over to the desk and retrieved his port, swallowing its contents in one thirsty gulp.

Montford suspected that Sherbrook had no idea what he had said, or what he had meant. And he knew as well that Sherbrook was referring to Lady Katherine, not her sister. Sherbrook had taken an immediate and bone-thorough dislike of the Marchioness of Manwaring, his estranged uncle's new wife, upon their first encounter at a ball some years ago. And Montford knew that the feeling was mutual.

"Oh, bugger it," Sebastian muttered after throwing back his drink. "Enough about bloody females."

"Hear, hear," Marlowe chimed in.

Sebastian saluted Marlowe with his empty snifter, then turned back to Montford. "I know you hate traveling, Montford, but you just might have to go to Yorkshire."

Montford more than hated traveling. He physically abhorred it. "Not a chance."

"It sounds just the thing."

Montford grew suspicious. "Why do I not trust you in this moment?"

Sebastian quirked his lips. "Well, it seems to me you need to clear your head. And Yorkshire, what with all of the countryside and sheep and such, seems a good place to do it in. I hear the air in Yorkshire is lovely this time of year."

"No doubt reeks of manure."

"You can take some of that pent-up anger out on these Honeywells. Turn them out of house and home. Shut down the brewery."

"I shall never speak to him if he does," Marlowe threatened from the chaise. "Tell him, Sherry. If he shuts down the brewery, I shall cease to be his friend."

"Maybe you could at least spare the brewery," Sebastian said with a wink. "Unless you wish to alienate the entire male half of the country."

Montford snorted. "How can anyone drink that twaddle?"

"Have you ever had a pint?"

"Well, no, but . . ."

"Do not judge, then. Now where was I? Oh yes, hurl your thunderbolts at the Honeywells. Spare the brewery. Take in the fresh air. And perhaps come to your senses about this atrocity at the end of the month . . ."

"You mean my wedding," he said flatly.

"What other atrocity were you planning?"

"I can think of several at the moment, involving you and that beached whale over there and the business end of my—"

Sebastian chuckled and wriggled his eyebrows suggestively. "I just love it when you flirt, Your Grace."

"I should burn down the brewery for that comment alone." He strode toward the door.

"Where're you going?" Marlowe cried, sitting up.

To bash my head in. "To bed."

"You are such a bloody stuffed shirt, Monty," Marlowe replied laconically.

"I've told you, don't call me that."

"Or what? You'll break my nose again?"

"Don't tempt me."

"Pleasant dreams," Sebastian called, long after Montford slammed the door behind him.

Their conversations often ended this way. And Montford knew that when he came down in the morning, he'd find his sideboard emptied of its stock, evidence of the fun his friends had had in his absence and at his expense.

Usually, Montford never begrudged his friends their fun. He knew for a fact that both of them were perpetually skirting dun territory and bumbled their way through life dining at their friends' tables and drinking their liquor. He didn't mind it when they took advantage of his largesse, for they never asked for loans or importuned him in any other way . . . well, besides wheedling sandwiches from his cook and drinking his port. But tonight he was seriously considering taking them by their collars and kicking them out on their arses.

Which was insane. They were his best friends, after all. His *only* friends, now that he thought about it.

And this realization made him feel even worse. His only friends in the world were a pair of leeches who used him for his sandwiches and sideboard, and who would not even do that should he deprive them of their goddamned ale.

His life, he thought bleakly as he trudged up the grand marble staircase in the cavernous gilded foyer, was as empty as his house.

Maybe he *did* need a holiday.

Chapter Three

In Which the Duke Ventures Forth into the Wild

BESIDES HIS sundry well-documented compulsive behaviors, Montford's inner demons manifested themselves in two distinct aversions: riding in carriages and the sight of blood. He couldn't explain these phobias any more than he could explain why he hated to let different foods touch each other on his dinner plate. But he had become an expert at disguising his fears, for it would never do to let people discover that the Duke of Montford tended to vomit in coaches and faint when he got scratched.

He avoided extended journeys that would require a carriage and rode his mount when at all possible. When he was fencing, a sport at which he excelled, he made sure his foil never came loose, thus avoiding nicking his opponent. And if *he* was nicked, which was not often, and usually only at Sebastian's expert hand, he never looked down at the wound. Fortunately, only one of the duels in which he had stood second for Marlowe had ended in bloodshed, when his friend had taken a ball to his shoulder. No one noticed his light-headedness, however, in the drama that had followed.

Nonetheless, three days after speaking to his friends, Montford arrived at Rylestone Hall after an excruciatingly long and messy journey northward. His agitation over the situation had at last overcome his aversion to travel, and he'd decided to put up with a miserable few days traveling rather than let this Honeywell business go unresolved.

As he couldn't abide putting up at a vermin-infested roadside inn, and as he owned no other residences between London and Rylestone, he had made his driver stop only long enough for him to vomit, for Coombes to retie his cravat, or for the horses to be changed out. The journey, even at such a rate, should have only lasted two days, but on the second day one of the horses went lame, and it had taken the entire afternoon for a replacement to be located.

On the third day, by his calculations, which were always precise, he should have been on the estate by midmorning. But Rylestone proved as elusive as an oasis in the desert. The Yorkshire dales were hardly made of sand, but they certainly qualified as wilderness to Montford, who had little love of pastoral life. He had to suppress a shudder every time he looked out the window and saw beyond him nothing but endless stretches of farmland and timber forests, interspersed by the occasional cow or sheep. It all looked unbearably rustic . . . and *dirty*.

By noon, it was clear that they were lost, and he ordered his driver to stop in the nearest village to ask directions. The village, which looked to have more ovine occupants than human, proved to be little help to them. Clearly, the human occupants of the village were as little impressed by the ducal crest upon his carriage as the livestock, and they were unwilling to offer much assistance. The directions they finally wrenched out of one man, who had just tumbled out of the village tavern three sheets to the wind, were spoken in a thick Northern brogue that was as unintelligible as Chinese to Montford's ears.

Newcomb, his driver, more exhausted from the journey than Montford—as drivers could not sleep—sent the man on his way with a few shillings, and turned to Montford, who leaned out of the carriage window, weak from the traveling sickness.

Coombes cowered back in his seat, handkerchief covering his sensitive nose, eyes widened on the fragrant patch of mud in which the driver stood.

"What the devil did he say?" Montford demanded.

"Haven't a clue, Your Grace. But he made some gestures with his hands I think I can make some sense of." Newcomb's brow furrowed. "That or he was insulting me."

"Let's pray it is the former."

"East, I think he meant," Newcomb said, shrugging in the manner of one who was simply too weary to care much where they were going any longer. Then he climbed back on the perch and whipped the team to a trot, putting them on a muddy road that looked like every other muddy road they had taken in Yorkshire.

A few minutes later, Montford made Newcomb pull over so that he could lean out of the window and retch for the fifty-first time in forty-eight hours, even though there was nothing in his stomach.

When Montford managed to pull himself back in the carriage, Coombes stared at Montford's less-than immaculate cravat with a faintly accusing expression.

"Don't say anything," Montford growled. "We may restore ourselves to rights when we arrive."

Coombes looked extremely doubtful about that. "But Your Grace," he said in a whisper, as if afraid of being overheard by the carriage walls, "I don't think they *bathe* this far north."

Montford bit back a retort to this ridiculous statement, but it was a ridiculous statement that reflected Montford's own fears. Who knew what dreadful fate awaited them at Rylestone Hall? Outside privies? Garderobes? He shuddered.

He half expected to find poor Stevenage done in, or at the very least mired in the thick Yorkshire mud, put there by a vengeful Honeywell.

He was beginning to doubt his own judgment in undergoing this journey alone with naught but Newcomb and Coombes, but he always traveled light when he had to, thinking the fewer who were privy to his weak stomach the better. Newcomb was a solid enough man—an ex-boxer from Liverpool, and extremely loyal to Montford. Montford didn't doubt Coombes's loyalty either, but unless it had to do with waistcoats, cologne, or bootblack, the man was completely at sea.

Montford had expected to sweep into Rylestone Hall and have everyone under its roof kowtowing to his will. Even the Prince Regent tended to follow his directives. But in this case he was not so sure. The farther they journeyed, the farther removed he felt from the civilized world. Rylestone Hall was more remote than he had assumed, certainly more remote than any of his other estates—besides the one on the Isle of Mull he had *no intention* of ever visiting.

It would take days to reach something even resembling a city. And if it was so difficult for him to locate the Hall, how in blazes would anyone else find it, should something befall him?

Dear God, he was *not* paranoid, he had to remind himself. He didn't *actually* think anything sinister had befallen Stevenage—well, he hadn't much more than the tiniest of niggling suspicions. But judging from the welcome he had received from the few human inhabitants of this godforsaken wilderness, he didn't think he would have a warm reception at Rylestone Hall.

Not that he expected one. But as the Duke of Montford, he preferred a certain amount of deference. Even from Honeywells.

Somehow he thought *that* would not be forthcoming. He wondered if the inhabitants of this remote section of the world even realized they were the Crown's subjects.

Montford's mood momentarily lightened when at last, late in the afternoon, they rounded a bend in the lane and saw something other than fields and sheep in the distance. It was an old gray castle, settled strategically on a hillside and surrounded by gardens and orchards. It looked like something out of Mr. Constable's paintings, with the slanting sun bathing the gray, slightly crumbling walls in a warm-honey glow, the trees in the orchard heavy with fruit, the garden tangled with late-summer blooms.

Montford's stomach clenched with an unfamiliar, uncomfortably warm feeling, and for once it was not the preface to a bout of vomiting. The castle looked like some place out of a fairy tale, to be honest. The sort of place families lived in, for instance. Perfect, picturesque, slightly ramshackle, and quaint. The sort of place the Duke of Montford would never visit willingly. He did not *do* ramshackle and quaint. He prayed that this wasn't Rylestone Hall, while at the same time some small, hidden part of him he refused to acknowledge hoped to God it was.

He leaned out of the window and ordered Newcomb to proceed, keeping his wary eyes fixed on the approaching castle. And as they grew closer, he found himself becoming more and more disoriented. Something was off about the castle, and he couldn't figure out quite what. He was perfectly aware of its crumbling edifices and the seemingly haphazard, slightly overgrown quality of the gardens in front. These were imperfections he had noted and dismissed with an annoyed toss of his head. But something more fundamental was wrong with the castle, which was making his head spin and his palms sweat, as if the ground beneath him were tilting . . .

"Coombes, the castle is crooked," he declared.

Coombes studied the castle, pulled out his handkerchief, and wiped his brow, which had broken out in a very untidy sweat. "I do believe you're right, Your Grace. Good heavens. We aren't staying *there*, are we?" the man practically howled.

"Calm down, Coombes," Montford said, feeling anything but calm himself. He couldn't take his eyes off the castle, especially the north tower, which listed dangerously toward the south tower, like an old woman's back, defying all the laws of Newtonian theory. It was like looking at a grisly road accident or a hideous facial disfigurement. One just couldn't look away.

Now he truly wished with all of his heart for this to be someplace other than his final destination. Although he knew deep down that they had arrived at Rylestone Hall. Who but the Honeywells would live in a crooked castle?

They pulled up to the castle keep and waited for several minutes for someone to greet them, as was customary. When that didn't happen, Montford ordered Newcomb to knock on the large, pitted oak door. No one answered except a flurry of squawking crows, who seemed to have a nest in the battlements above.

Newcomb turned to him and shrugged.

"For the love of . . ." Montford muttered, throwing open the carriage door and stepping down the stairs, right into a mud puddle that came up to his ankles. He looked down at his boots, looked up at Newcomb, who was very wisely *not* smiling, and cursed.

He stalked up the stone steps to stand beside his driver and pounded on the door. And pounded and pounded until the oak frame shuddered and the crows squawked another protest.

"Perhaps no one is at home?" Newcomb suggested, which was obviously not the case, for a cacophony of sounds arose from behind the door, many of them human. *Someone* was at home. *Someone* was avoiding answering.

He began to knock again, despairing over the stains to his gloves.

At last, when he was about to throw up his hands in defeat, the door groaned inward. He looked down and found himself staring at a small child. Seven or eight at the most, with shaggy brown hair, a dirty face, and an even dirtier outfit that resembled a Roman toga. It was impossible to tell if the child was a boy or a girl. He—or she—stared up at him with wide eyes.

"Is this Rylestone Hall?" he demanded gruffly.

The child just gawked at him blankly.

"Where are your parents, child?" he asked. "Or a servant?"

The child shook its head.

"An adult, then. I am looking for a Mr. Stevenage. Or an A. Honeywell. Do you know either of them?"

The child nodded a bit warily.

"Then this *is* Rylestone Hall," he said.

The child looked reluctant, but it nodded.

At last, they were getting somewhere. He would have been relieved, had he not just discovered he was in possession of a crooked castle.

He began to ask the child something else, but when he looked down, the child was gone. He cursed again and turned to Newcomb.

His driver just sighed, took off his hat, and ran his hands through his hair, which was so dusty from the road it stood up on end. "What do we do now, Your Grace?"

"I haven't the foggiest," he said in all honesty.

"May I suggest you go inside, Your Grace? And perhaps I, and Mr. Coombes, of course"—he rolled his eyes—"could attempt to find a stable? The team is quite tired."

"Fine. Send in Coombes later. I have no idea what lies on the other side, but I should like some time. I don't want Coombes fainting on me."

"Of course, Your Grace."

Montford sighed and stepped past the oak door into the dim corridor. He traced the path of the toga-clad child into another corridor off to the right, then found himself in a parlor cluttered with shabby furniture, books, and the sort of meaningless paraphernalia—porcelain statues, decorative vases filled with flowers, and collections of enameled gewgaws strewn haphazardly across tabletops—that made him want to blow his head off.

He strode past one massively untidy table, stopped, and backed up, unable to bear it. He rearranged a collection of small snuffboxes so that they all lined up precisely with the edges of the table, equidistant from each other. His pulse calmed, and he continued on his way, stopping at a desk and glancing down at the book that lay facedown in the center, opened to the middle. His eyebrow flew up at the title on the spine.

Sir Thomas More's *Utopia*. Not the sort of book he would have expected to find in a room with an enameled snuffbox collection. He picked up the book and was startled when another smaller volume fell out from between its pages.

He rather guiltily recognized the volume at once, having just received a copy from Sherbrook a few months ago. Christopher Essex's latest collection of poetry, so shockingly scandalous it made Lord Byron's seem like nursery rhymes. But he did not own every single one of Essex's banned publications because he was in the least titillated by the contents. Not at all. He just thought Essex's wit was considerably better than other poets of the day.

But whoever was reading this volume clearly was doing so on the sly and for pure titillation. *Thomas More indeed!*

He put the books down as he'd found them—or rather, he lined them up parallel to the desk—and started out of the room. He nearly jumped out of his skin at the sight that greeted him. For there, standing in the doorway, was the ghost of Marie Antoinette. Or what appeared to be that unfortunate lady at first glance, attired in an elaborately gilded, old-fashioned, slightly shabby paneled ball gown that might have been worn at the court of Versailles, with a tall powdered white wig nearly half of the lady's height, studded with bows, fake fruit, and fowl, perched upon her head. But the woman was quite real, and quite ancient, the thick layers of lead paint and rouge cracking along the deep wrinkles lining her face.

When she saw him, she let out a shriek, causing her wig to list slightly to the right, picked up the sides of her elaborate gown, and fled the room.

Montford stared after her, dumbfounded.

Then he started after her.

"Madam!" he called, passing back into the corridor.

But the old woman had disappeared as thoroughly as the child had done.

He wandered aimlessly about the keep, searching for some signs of humanity but finding none. At last, he came to a conservatory of sorts, as disordered as the front parlor had been, and crowded with potted plants and children's toys. He picked his way over the mess until he stood at a pair of French doors leading out into an overgrown courtyard, with a fountain set in the middle featuring a statue of Poseidon.

The fountain didn't work. Shocking.

But it seemed to be inhabited. By two children. One he recognized as the child from before. The other looked older, but just as dirty and genderless. They seemed to be engaged in some sort of playacting and were hitting each other with sticks while running around the fountain.

He stepped outside and called to them. They turned, dropped their sticks at the sight of him, and fled into the rosebushes. Montford strode to catch up with them, and cursed when he rounded the bushes and found no one. He cast his head to the heavens in exasperation, which turned out to be a bad idea, for he found himself staring up at the north tower.

He staggered back, suddenly seasick, and lowered his glance.

Just then, he heard a noise in the distance. It sounded like a human voice. His spirits rose considerably, until he heard the noise that followed, which didn't sound human at all. It was more a squeal, or a snort. A noise only an extremely dirty creature could make.

Having no choice, he followed the direction of the sounds around the side of the castle, until he came to what appeared to be the stable yard, with a largish vegetable garden stretching off to one side. The sounds seemed to be rising from the garden, and at last he saw a human head bob up, then disappear back over a wall, muttering a curse.

Montford looked despairingly across the expanse of mud separating him from the garden, then down at his boots, and began to walk. Extremely carefully. Through the mud.

He arrived at the wall and peered over it. His eyes widened at the sight. It was a lad in a floppy hat, dressed in breeches and a jerkin caked with mud, and tugging on a rope attached to the most enormous pig Montford had ever seen.

Granted, he didn't think he had ever *seen* a pig, aside from the one gracing the banquet table at Christmas, but he was *quite* certain it was the largest pig in the world. It was at least four times larger than the lad who was vainly tugging on the rope around its neck, and it was likely to grow even larger, given the mouthful of cabbage it was enjoying from the garden's bounty.

The lad cursed and tugged and made no headway at all with the animal, other than an occasional snort.

Montford decided to end the farce and put the lad to better use. "You there, boy," he called out. "Stop this nonsense at once and go fetch me someone in charge."

The lad, startled by his voice, slipped in the mud and fell on his backside, the floppy hat tumbling into the cabbage. He turned to face Montford and pushed his hair out of his eyes, scowling belligerently.

That was when Montford realized that the lad wasn't a lad at all. The lad was a . . . a female! The slanting light of the late afternoon cut across the garden in that moment, catching in the woman's hair, making it blaze the furious red and orange tones of a bonfire. He had never seen hair that color, so off-puttingly red, falling in wavy, haphazard abundance from uncertain moorings at the back.

Her brows were off-putting as well, thick and lustrous and almost black, compared to her blazing hair. So were her lips, too full and wide for her to ever be considered truly pretty, even had she not been covered in freckles. And mud.

He gazed at her, even dizzier than he had felt when staring up at the tower.

There was something about this female, something he could not quite put his finger on, that was completely . . . well, wrong. Askew.

Never mind she was dressed like a stable hand, or had hair the color of fire, or that her skin was riddled with freckles (blech!), or even that she was covered in mud. He felt the same impulse he had felt when confronted by that collection of enameled snuffboxes: the need to line something up before he screamed.

His hands clenched into fists at his side.

What *was* it?

The female's eyes went wide at the sight of him, and she hopped to her feet, mud flying. He somehow managed to notice—though he knew not why—that she was a head shorter than he was, and that beneath the mud-encrusted lad's clothes she was quite . . . quite . . . well, *curved*.

So curved that he wondered how he had ever mistaken her back-side for a lad's.

A pang, hot and shattering, passed through his body, as if someone had just hit a Chinese gong inside his breeches. Which made no sense. He didn't like short redheads. He didn't like short redheads with curves. He most decidedly did *not* like short redheads with curves *in trousers*.

He liked blondes. Immaculate, begowned, bejeweled blondes with willowy bodies.

Good God, why was it suddenly so hot? It was nearly October, for Christ's sake. For the first time in his life, he wanted to tug at his cravat.

"You . . . er, girl," he said, "I'm looking for a Mr. Stevenage."

The redhead's gaze narrowed, and something like shrewd assessment replaced her initial shock. Her brow cocked on one side, and she crossed her arms over her chest, which consequently pushed her breasts upward and *outward*, sending another inconvenient jolt shooting through his nether regions.

Montford was so completely caught off balance he had to grip the wall to stay upright. No one had ever dared to treat him with such utter disregard for his station. Granted, she did not know who he was, but it was obvious from his attire that he was *mountains* above her in class and station. Good God, she was in a garden with a giant pig! How much more disgustingly plebeian could one get? "Very well, I wish to speak to A. Honeywell."

Her brow rose even higher. "Do you, indeed? And which *A.* Honeywell would that be, for there are five who answer to that name."

He was going to be sick. Again. Five? "I shall speak to whoever is in charge, insolent chit," he retorted.

The girl's face turned as red as her hair, and she gave him a venomous look before turning away from him to take up her rope once more, ignoring him completely.

"You there, girl! I will not be ignored," he bellowed.

She snorted indelicately and tugged on her rope. Her anger seemed to have given her extra strength, for at last she made some headway with the pig, who trotted a few paces in her direction.

"I wish to speak to Stevenage. I know you've done something with him," he insisted.

She passed by him at the wall, pulling the pig toward the gate a few paces away. She rolled her eyes as she passed, and the scent of sweat, hay, and lavender followed in her wake, startling him.

He trailed her, furious, but still slightly dizzy from looking at her. "I am the Duke of Montford. I happen to own this lopsided pile of stones and everything in it. I demand to see A. Honeywell."

The girl rounded on him, clearly furious. "*You* own this lopsided pile? Says what? A two-hundred-year-old piece of parchment?" The girl snorted, unlocked the gate, and began to pull the reluctant pig through it. "The Honeywells built this lopsided pile with their bare hands in the year of our Lord nine hundred and ninety-six. And the Montfords have attempted to steal it from us since the Invasion. Lying, bloody thieving Norman upstarts!" she scoffed contemptuously, marching past him. "Just because my ancestor couldn't keep it in his breeches and had to have *your* ancestor for a wife—tainting our pristine Saxon bloodlines, by the by—I will be *triple* damned if we lose our home to the likes of *you.*"

Montford was further disoriented by the redhead's outburst. She was dressed like a stable hand, had the perfect diction of a blue blood, and cursed like a sailor.

She was, of course, a Honeywell.

"Are *you* A. Honeywell, then?"

"I am *an* A. Honeywell," she said cryptically, stopping in front of him and glancing up at his face challengingly.

In that moment, several things happened. He realized why she made him dizzy, he found Stevenage, and the pig decided to start moving. Really moving.

She made him dizzy because, as he stared down at her face from this short distance, he could better see her eyes, which were large, rimmed with soot-colored lashes, and . . .

Two different colors. One was brown and the other was blue, sky blue.

He had to clench his hands at his sides in order not to reach out and try to erase such a glaring imperfection. Logic told him he could not do so merely by shaking her shoulders, but he was tempted to try.

Before he could do so, the door to the barn across the yard swung open, and a couple spilled out of it, laughing and stumbling in the muck. He couldn't manage to turn away from the redhead's uncanny countenance, but out of the corner of his eye, he noted a rather buxom woman, breasts spilling out the top of her dress, straw-colored hair pinned loosely back from a middle-aged but pleasant-looking face, laughing and tugging on the arm of a man.

The man, dressed like a peasant, was chuckling, attempting to steal a kiss from the woman, and weaving slightly on his feet, hiccupping with every other step. But something about the man's wiry frame, steel-gray hair, and spectacles, which were sitting slightly askew his beakish nose, distracted Montford from the redhead's unearthly eyes.

It was . . .

No, it couldn't be.

Could it?

"Stevenage?" he called out, his voice mirroring his inner turmoil.

The man froze, looked up from the woman's bosom, and turned as white as a sheet.

"Your—*hic*—Grace—*hic*?" Stevenage attempted a courtly bow, but staggered back and fell on his rump.

Montford turned back to the redhead. "What have you done to my man-of-affairs?" he roared.

But before she could answer, the pig grew impatient and began running across the yard, yanking the rope from the redhead's hands.

And as the pig passed by Montford, it decided to bash its hock against his legs, causing him to stumble backward and land with a thwack in a puddle of mud that reached his navel.

Montford was too shocked to do anything other than sit there, staring around the stable yard and wondering if he had fallen into his worst nightmare.

Or the seventh circle of hell.

Chapter Four

In Which the Duke Takes up Residence in a Lopsided Castle

ALL HELL had broken loose in the yard. Petunia took off at a gallop, knocking the Duke of Montford into the biggest mud slick in the county, Art and Ant burst out of the shrubbery, chanting in Greek and hitting each other with their makeshift swords, Alice and Aunt Anabel appeared at the door to the kitchens, and two men Astrid didn't recognize—one large and muscled and dressed in travel-stained livery, the other thin and consumptive and dressed like a peacock—burst from the stables, chased by Charlie and Mick, the stable hands, who were wielding, respectively, a pitchfork and a hammer.

Everyone came to a halt at the sight of the Duke of Montford sitting in the mud, looking, for all intents and purposes, ready to do murder.

Ready to murder *her.*

She took an involuntary step backward at the icy glint in his silver eyes. "COOMBES!" Montford roared.

The consumptive peacock jumped, squeaked, and started forward, tiptoeing across the muddy expanse. The duke staggered to his feet. The peacock reached his side, produced a bit of lace from a pocket, and started to dab ineffectually at the duke's mud-soaked breeches.

The duke gave a pained groan. "Will you please refrain from dabbing at my *arse*, Coombes," he bit out, swatting away the man.

And because she couldn't have stopped herself had a gun been pointed at her head, Astrid let out the laugh she had been attempting to quell ever since the duke, in all of his sartorial splendor, had landed on that aforementioned arse in the mud.

The duke caught his breath and glared at her in indignation. Then he looked over her shoulder toward Stevenage and shouted his name.

She followed his glance and discovered that Stevenage was now attempting to hide behind Flora. At the sound of his name, poor Stevenage's courage fled him completely, and he turned and ran out of the stable yard as if chased by the devil, hiccupping along the way.

The duke looked aghast at his man-of-affairs's desertion. He turned his steely eyes back to her and attempted to speak, but Petunia squealed and began charging in their direction once again. The duke looked at the pig, and something resembling terror flashed across his face. Petunia rushed past them and back into the garden.

Astrid groaned. Her cabbages! Her prize cabbages! "Charlie! Mick! See to Petunia," she ordered. The two stable hands rushed toward the garden. "Flora, why don't you show our guest to a room so that he might"—she glanced down at the duke's lower portion, dripping with mud—"repair himself."

Flora nodded.

Astrid turned to the duke. "If that suits His Grace, of course."

"It does," he snapped, then began to walk toward the castle, his boots squelching in the mud. He gave Art and Ant, who were doubled over in giggles, a quelling look as he passed by them, which sobered the girls completely. They scurried to Astrid's side and attempted to hide behind her legs.

When the duke and the peacock had disappeared inside, Astrid let out a groan and turned to Alice, who had come out into the yard, a look of sheer panic contorting her pretty features. "Oh, Astrid! What are we to do?"

Astrid wished that she knew. She had not planned on this particular development.

She caught the glance of the burly man in livery who was staring at her speculatively. Montford's driver. After a moment, he just shrugged and disappeared into the stables, as if none of what had occurred was of the slightest concern to him.

Astrid sighed.

She had known from nearly the first moment she had seen him standing over the garden wall that the Duke of Montford had come to call, like some villain out of a fairy tale. He was towering, lean, but nevertheless powerfully built beneath his splendid, princely clothing, and he seemed to occupy the space around him as if he owned it. As if, in fact, he owned the very air he breathed—or at the very least, as if the air he breathed should feel humbled that he was allowing it to pass into his exalted lungs. His dark hair was close-cropped and tamed into perfect submission, his features so blindingly perfect and completely glacial they could have been hewn out of marble, and his eyes—silver overlaid with ice—bored into her with an intelligence and probity that had quite literally taken the breath from her body.

She had never seen anything like him before. His coat alone, black silk tailored in stark lines that emphasized the strength of the body beneath, had clearly cost more than her and her sisters' wardrobes combined. His starched cravat, with a single, giant ruby nestled in its crisp folds, was whiter than snow. His perfectly manicured hand settled atop the wall, smooth and unsullied by anything so plebian as manual labor, was adorned by an enormous gold signet ring on his long index finger, topped by a crest studded by another gargantuan ruby. The only signs that he was flesh and blood were the dark circles under his eyes and a slight pallor to his complexion, suggesting a long, difficult journey.

He was ridiculously imposing. Arrogant. As beautiful as an ice sculpture. And so completely trussed, groomed, and buttoned up that Astrid had the overwhelming desire to run up to him and rip the cravat from his neck.

She'd hated him immediately. Even before he had called her an insolent chit.

And she knew that he was going to prove a nearly insurmountable obstacle.

She turned to Alice. "Hide the book," she said.

Alice, who had never been the sharpest tool in the box when it came to anything other than her wardrobe, looked perplexed. "What book?"

"The estate book," she bit out.

Alice's eyes widened in understanding. "Oh, that book. Where shall I hide it?"

Astrid sighed. "In the last place the Duke of Montford would find it, obviously."

Alice nodded and hurried inside, past a confused-looking Aunt Anabel, whose wig was sitting slightly askew on her head.

"Astrid," Ant said uncertainly, pulling at her trousers. "What are we to do?"

She looked down at her younger sisters. "Why, carry on as you were, of course." Then an idea began to form in her head. She smiled at the pair of ruffians. "In fact, I give you permission to act as naughtily as you possibly can while our houseguest remains."

They looked startled for a moment, then understanding blossomed across their impish faces, and they grinned cunningly. They ran off into the gardens, whispering to each other, no doubt fomenting something very naughty indeed.

Astrid nodded to herself. "Right then," she said, straightening her shirt. "Into the fray."

If the duke survived the night, he would be a very lucky man indeed.

Or more formidable than the combined forces of the Honeywells. And *no one* was more formidable than that, even if he happened to be more powerful than the Prince Regent himself.

"Aunt Anabel," she said, taking her by the arm and guiding her inside, "how would you like to have tea with a duke?"

"Why, that would be lovely, my dear." She glanced around her, perplexed. "What duke?"

⚜

BY THE time Montford managed to wash, have his trunks hauled from the carriage, and have fresh clothes procured, the sun was going down, and any vestige of patience he had was lost. The journey had been a nightmare. His *arrival* had been a nightmare. He hardly remembered why he had come and was beginning to wonder how he was ever going to get back to London. He didn't think he could stand to ever set foot in a carriage again. It would take days—weeks—*months!*—for his nerves and stomach to recover. Now he was stuck here. In a crooked castle. With pigs. And Honeywells.

Coombes's hands were trembling so violently it took ten tries before he managed a proper cravat. When Coombes attempted to brush the lint from his jacket, Montford's patience snapped. "Leave it."

"But sir, I—"

He fixed Coombes with a glower that had once cowed the whole of Parliament into passing an unpopular bill—damn those smug Whig upstarts—and Coombes backed away, the brush falling from his hands.

A knock sounded on the door, and the blowsy woman called Flora peeked inside. She seemed more sensible than the rest of the household and gave him an uncertain curtsy. "Yer Grace, Miss Honeywell and . . .

ah, Miss Honeywell kindly requests your presence in the parlor. Erm . . . Yer Grace." She bobbed a curtsy again.

He gifted her with a hard stare. She turned and fled.

He rounded on Coombes, who was *still* trembling. "Make yourself useful and try to find Stevenage."

Coombes's eyes widened to saucers. "Your *Grace*!" he whined.

Montford cocked an eyebrow. Coombes lowered his head in despair. "Yes, Your Grace."

With a growl, Montford strode outside the bedroom and down a corridor. Only when he reached a wall with no exit did he realize he hadn't a damned clue where he was going. He turned around and began in the opposite way. Eventually he came to a stairwell that looked somewhat familiar and descended to the bottom floor.

After several wrong turns and a dozen muttered oaths, he finally reached an open door with light beyond it. He looked around the edge of the door and found himself staring into the cluttered parlor he had entered earlier in the day. A fire was lit in the grate, and the old-fashioned wall sconces blazed with light, casting flickering shadows around the room.

Two women sat by the fire. One was the old woman with the enormous French pompadour. The other was initially unfamiliar, dressed in a shabby-looking gown that must have once been green. It was modestly cut but looked ill-fitting and a shade too small on the woman's rounded, voluptuous body. He hadn't the foggiest clue why such an ugly garment should make him sizzle with heat and could only assume that it was due to starvation. He'd not eaten since breakfast, and all of that meal was strewn about the roadside running south.

But then the woman rose to her feet, and the fire caught in her blood-red hair, which was haphazardly wound and pinned in a crooked bun at the nape of her neck. Recognition flooded through him. The pig-woman from the garden. Of course. She seemed to be in charge around this godforsaken place.

She graced him with a perfectly executed curtsy, which niggled him, because he somehow knew she was mocking him. "Your Grace. How lovely for you to join us."

The old woman didn't bother to rise but peered at him through a quizzing glass. "Is *this* a duke, then, Astrid?" the woman inquired in a stage whisper.

"Yes, Aunt," the woman answered, never looking away from him, her lips curving into an enigmatic smile, her mismatched eyes dancing with deviltry, daring him to set down an old lady.

The old woman bobbed up and down in her seat with delight. "Oh, what fun!" she exclaimed. She gestured toward the duke. "Well, come here, young man, and let's have a look at you."

Montford found his legs moving forward of their own accord. The old woman leaned forward in her seat and gave him a once-over with her monocle. Her gaze paused right in the vicinity of his nether regions. Then she dropped her quizzing glance and turned to the other woman. "He looks like a *man* to me, gel."

"My good woman—" he began, clenching his fists.

"Your Grace, please have a seat. You must be exhausted after your . . . ordeal," the younger woman cut in, indicating a rather threadbare settee near the fire.

Montford was suddenly too tired to protest, and he crossed the room and sat down stiffly.

The redhead settled in the seat across from him. "I am Miss Honeywell. And this is my aunt, Miss Honeywell," she said, inclining her head toward the old woman. "We are honored, of course, that you have deigned to grace us with your illustrious presence. Tea? Biscuit?" She gestured toward the table in front of them.

Oh God, she was mocking him all over the bloody place. The little . . . "Miss Honeywell—" he began.

"However," she interjected, ignoring him completely and reaching for the teapot, "I am sure it was completely *unnecessary* for His Grace to come all this way over a misunderstanding that could have been easily rectified by post."

He watched in horror as she commenced to pour the tea without the slightest delicacy over the table, managing to get more onto the surrounding saucers and tray than the actual cups.

Clearly she'd not gone to a finishing school where ladies were taught the proper way to handle a teapot.

"Do you take sugar, Your Grace? No? Milk? Of course you do." She upturned a pitcher of milk over the edge of the cup until the liquid sloshed over the top. Then she stirred it halfheartedly, tossed the spoon aside, and rose to hand him the offending cup.

He took it in hand because he was certain she would let it drop on his lap if he didn't. He took a deep, calming breath and returned to the subject at hand. "Miss Honeywell, I am sure I don't know what you mean, as I am quite certain the post does not reach you."

"Oh, but it does," she assured him.

"Since I have sent nearly two dozen letters to this address in the past fortnight without a response, I am sure it does not."

She gazed at him innocently and sipped her tea. "But *I* have received no letters from Your Grace. Perhaps they were misdirected."

"I did not send them to *you*. I sent them to Stevenage."

"That would explain it," she said, though, really, it explained nothing.

"Madam, the Royal Mail aside, I see no misunderstanding between us. The terms of the contract are quite clear, to my mind."

"Contract?" she asked, looking perplexed. She dropped four cubes of sugar into another cup and poured it to the brim with milk. She stirred it neatly and handed it over to the old woman. "Biscuit, Aunt?"

"Why, yes. Two. Young man, you *must* have a biscuit," the old woman stated. "They are quite simply delicious. Astrid makes them herself." She beamed at the younger woman.

"No, thank you." He refused to be distracted, despite his gnawing hunger. "Miss Honeywell, you know quite well what contract I speak of, as you yourself made reference to it earlier in the day."

"I do not recall having made reference to any contract. Wouldn't you like a biscuit? You must be famished after the journey. Your long, *unnecessary* journey. They are quite good, and I do make them myself. An old recipe from my Scotch grandmother." She stuck the tray of biscuits under his nose.

He began to wave it away, but the smell of butter and sugar and vanilla wafted to his nostrils, causing his empty stomach to protest in agony. He took one with a great show of reluctance and bit into it.

And was immediately transported to heaven.

The crumbs melted on his tongue in a symphony of sweet, buttered perfection. He barely suppressed a groan, closed his eyes, and leaned back against the seat, his body suddenly boneless.

He forgot everything, including who he was, until the biscuit was devoured. Then he opened his eyes and found the redhead regarding him with a quizzical expression. He straightened, reality crashing down on his shoulders. Damn. She was good. "Miss Honeywell, I shall not be sidetracked. I am here to—"

"Astrid!" came a strident call from the hallway, cutting him off. Another female entered the room in a rush. He vaguely recognized her from the yard and knew immediately it was another Honeywell. Clearly a near relation to the redhead, but younger, taller, with hair more auburn than red, and prettier, dressed in a becoming muslin gown. Her eyes widened when she noticed him, and she skidded to a halt.

Miss Honeywell rose. The courtesy pounded into him since the cradle demanded that he rise as well.

"Your Grace, may I present my sister, Miss Alice Honeywell," Miss Honeywell said.

Miss Alice curtsied prettily and not at all mockingly. He approved of her immediately.

"What is it, Alice?" Miss Honeywell asked.

"It's Petunia. He's in the cabbage again."

"Well, set Charlie on him, or Mick."

"I would, but they've gone to the brewery with . . . er . . ." Alice glanced nervously at him. "Roddy."

As he hadn't a clue as to what they were talking about, he wondered why Alice was so nervous.

Miss Honeywell looked perturbed. "Well, damn and blast . . . I mean, heavens. What a muddle. Find Ant and Art, then, and set them to it."

Alice grimaced. "If I could find them, I would."

Miss Honeywell set down her teacup in consternation. "I'll not wrangle with that pig another moment. You know he hates me and eats my cabbage to spite me."

"Madam, your pig is named Petunia?" he interjected.

All eyes swung to him.

"Why, yes," she said.

"And he is a male . . . er, pig?"

"Why, yes." Miss Honeywell blinked, as if he were silly for even asking.

"I've landed in Bedlam," he muttered. Then he reached down and took up another biscuit.

"Well, what about the coachman?" Miss Honeywell said, turning toward him. "Your driver, or whatever it is you call him. Would you think that he would be willing to assist us?"

He barked out a hysterical half laugh and bit into his biscuit. He was light-headed with hunger, bone-tired from casting up his accounts for three days solid, and surrounded by lunatics, his only consolation a biscuit. *And* he was having a conversation about livestock. "Of course. I am sure Newcomb would like nothing better than to assist you, Miss Alice," he said archly.

"Well, then it's settled," Miss Honeywell said. "Find Mr. Newcomb and see if he will lend a hand."

Alice nodded and scurried to the door. She hesitated at the threshold, turned, and curtsied in his direction before exiting.

"Now, where were we?" Miss Honeywell asked, swinging her attention back in his direction.

"I believe you were attempting to gammon me, Miss Honeywell."

"Gammon you!" she breathed, her color heightening in affront. "I am sure I don't know what you mean."

"Gammon. As in make a fool of," he clarified.

"I should not think such a thing possible, Your Grace. You are clearly not a fool."

He could not tell by her dry tone whether she was mocking him or not, but he decided to err on the side of caution and assume she was.

He set down his biscuit—reluctantly, as he was quite ravenous now—and gifted her with his frostiest expression.

She did not so much as flinch under his gaze. Which did not seem possible, as everyone, even Sherbrook on occasion, flinched at that look.

And then her brassy hair had the effrontery to begin to fall out of its bun a strand at a time, then in ever larger clumps, until half of it was dangling down her back and the other half remained pinned in place, giving her a lopsided look that made him seriously consider howling.

She was just so completely wrong on so many levels it quite astounded him that the gods had allowed such a creature to exist. It seemed a fundamental crime against nature.

But Miss Honeywell did not seemed bothered in the slightest by the atrocity taking place on her head.

"Miss Honeywell," he began.

She cocked a brow.

"Miss Honeywell, your *hair*." It came out as a pained groan.

She reached up, patted the side of her bun that had not fallen down, and furrowed her brow. "What about my hair?"

"It is . . ."

She drew herself up to her full height, which put her no farther than his collarbone, and fixed him with a stare of pure feminine outrage. "What is wrong with my hair?"

"It is red . . ."

"Hardly a sin."

"And it is falling down."

She crossed her arms over her breasts, completely ignoring her hair, and gave him a superior look. "I shall excuse your behavior because of your long journey. Surely, when you are well rested, you shall recover your gentlemanly manners and realize that one does not remark upon a lady's person, no matter what the state of her hair."

That was when he made his worst mistake of the evening. He snorted and said disbelievingly, "*Lady*?"

She froze, her jaw jutting out, her mismatched eyes glinting with a fire that had nothing to do with the flames in the grate. Something inside of him wilted.

She stalked toward him, and he looked nervously about the room, though his rational mind—what was left of it—told him he would find nothing to aid him against the approaching harridan. He glanced at Aunt Anabel, but she had dozed off into her teacup, her wig halfway down her forehead.

"I'll have you know, Lord High and Mighty Montford, that I am more lady than you are a gentleman. Storming into my household, threatening to throw us out on our noses—"

"I have done no such—"

"—my poor aunt in her dotage, who has known no other home, and four unmarried ladies, with nowhere else to go but the workhouse. It is cruel and inhuman, but what else should I expect from a Montford? And how dare you question my . . . my upbringing? I am every inch the lady. I am the daughter of a gentleman, *sirrah*, and a lady. My mother was the daughter of an earl, as a matter of fact. And Honeywells owned this land centuries before your barbarian ancestors crossed the seas wielding their cudgels and *cutting up our peace*."

By the end of her tirade, she was inches from him, poking her finger into his chest. Which was quite insupportable, really. The last person who had poked him—Marlowe—had wound up with a broken nose.

"I beg your pardon. I must have been confused by the trousers you were wearing earlier. And the pig. And all of the swearing. Perhaps this is how *ladies* behave in Yorkshire?" he bit out, heat flooding his veins, his head throbbing.

He seized her hand to shove it away, which was his second mistake of the evening, because when his skin touched her skin, he felt as if lightning had shot from the heavens, through the crooked castle walls, and right into the place that they were joined, ricocheting through the rest of his body without pity.

He nearly swooned. Like a besotted London chit in a too-tight corset.

"Your Grace," Miss Honeywell whispered. "Montford."

He opened his eyes. She was looking at him with the same befuddled and slightly panicked intensity that he was feeling. Then he looked down and realized he was squeezing her hand so tightly his knuckles were white.

He dropped her hand and stepped back. "Miss Honeywell."

"Your Grace."

"I am tired. And hungry. And about three seconds away from throttling someone. I would like a bed. And some food." *And a wall to bash my head against.* "If, of course, it is not too much to ask."

She looked as if it was entirely too much to ask. "No, certainly not. We can continue our delightful conversation tomorrow morning. Before you *leave*."

He laughed without humor, realizing that at this moment, despite the mud and the shrewish woman before him, wrangling with this nest of vipers was slightly more appealing than hopping back into the carriage.

He would look into acquiring a mount. Perhaps riding back to London—despite the mud and the threat of rain and highwaymen—might be the best way put an end to his ill-advised jaunt. But in the meanwhile, he was going to fix the muddle at Rylestone and get the Honeywells out of his Miscellaneous Pile for good. "Oh, I am not leaving, Miss Honeywell. As much as we both might wish otherwise, I am staying here until we come to an understanding."

She gave him an arch look. "Then I am afraid, Your Grace, that you'll be staying until, oh, say, *hell freezes over*."

Aunt Anabel started awake with a snort, her wig snapping back into place. "Astrid, my dear, really. Do mind your tongue. We have a duke hereabouts."

He was standing right in front of the old lady, not *hereabouts*, but he wasn't about to quibble with her sound advice. "Yes, Astrid, do mind your tongue," he murmured.

Miss Honeywell shot him a fulminating look, turned on her heel, and marched from the room.

He followed in her wake, and it took every ounce of his remaining self-control not to seize her by the shoulders and pin her hair back into place before . . . before . . .

Good God. He must be thoroughly done in. Because for a moment, he'd had the strangest desire to kiss Miss Honeywell senseless.

He shuddered in revulsion and pinched himself, in case this was some horrible nightmare after all.

But he didn't wake up.

Chapter Five

In Which the Duke Enjoys Rylestone Hall's Amenities

THE INMATES of Rylestone Hall were used to waking at dawn. But usually they were coaxed from pleasant dreams by the vocal gymnastics of Chanticleer IV, proud descendant of Chanticleer I, Aloysius Honeywell's prize cock. They were not so used to waking up to blood-curdling screams, however.

Astrid, who had *not* had pleasant dreams, and who had, in fact, spent most of the night dreaming about being chased by a twenty-foot-tall monster resembling the Duke of Montford during the village's upcoming annual Harvest Festival's foot-and-ale-race, came awake with a start, followed by a thud.

It took her a moment to realize she had tumbled off her bed onto the floor. She stared at the ceiling, where the early morning light was beginning to chase away the shadows, and tried to figure out what was wrong. Aside from the fact that the Duke of Montford had spent the night two doors down from her. *And* aside from the fact that she had not murdered him in his sleep as she had originally planned to do.

Then the scream came again. High-pitched and very human. Astrid bolted to her feet and pulled on her dressing gown, then flew out of her door. She skidded to a halt at the scene before her. The peacock—Coombes—stood in the corridor two doors down in a nightshirt and head stocking, covered in the contents of the slop bucket intended for Petunia. Flora was attempting to dislodge a root vegetable of some kind from behind his ear as the man spluttered unintelligibly, spitting out bits of last night's stew.

Astrid knew immediately from the upturned bucket rolling at their feet and the giggles drifting from the bedroom across the hall what had happened. It was a standard trick in Ant and Art's repertoire, balancing a bucket on top of the door of an unsuspecting mark.

"I presume they missed their intended target," came a dry voice beyond Coombes.

The duke stood in the doorway to his bedroom, trussed up in a rich velvet robe the color of brandy, arms crossed, an eyebrow arched.

"Your Grace," spluttered Coombes, blinking bits of carrots out of his eyes, "this is insupportable. Unholy."

"Quite," he agreed, his mouth set in a grim line.

It was not at all appropriate for Astrid to laugh. She covered her mouth with her fist to keep the giggles contained.

"Antonia, Ardyce!" she managed to bite out behind her hand. "Come out here at once."

"But you said—"

"At once," she repeated, hoping she sounded convincingly stern.

After a moment, the two criminals reluctantly dragged their feet into the corridor, heads bowed.

She faced them, hands on her hips. "You heard Mr. Coombes. Your little trick is insupportable and unholy."

"Don't forget misdirected," inserted the duke dryly.

"Yes, that too. Montford was not even hit by residual . . . er, splatter. Now go down to the kitchens and fetch something to clean up the mess you've caused."

"But *Astrid*, you *said*—" Ardyce began.

She raised an eyebrow, silencing the girl. "Go now. Later you can apologize to our guests."

"Yes, Astrid," they said in unison, looking suitably cowed.

As they passed by her, she winked at them. She couldn't resist. Their spirits rose considerably, and they took off at a dash.

She turned to Coombes, wondering what to do with the poor man.

"I think I'd best take him out in the yard, miss," Flora said. "Throw a couple of buckets from the well over him."

Coombes looked even more horrified.

"Yes, I think that's probably the only thing for it," Astrid said. "I am sorry, Mr. Coombes."

"No, she's not," the duke observed casually from his place by the door.

"Well, come on, Mr. Coombes. We'll have you sorted soon enough," Flora said, taking him by the sleeve and pulling him down the hall.

Coombes was too stunned to do anything but follow, casting wild looks toward his employer.

When they were gone, Astrid tiptoed around the spill and picked up the empty bucket.

"Am I to expect this every morning?" came the duke's voice over her shoulder.

She straightened and turned toward him. "Certainly not. As you are leaving today anyway," she said lightly.

"No, I am not."

"Then I cannot say for sure what you can expect in the future."

"Those brats should be thrashed," he intoned.

Her blood began to boil. She put her fists on her hips in order to emphasize the set-down she was about to deliver. "Why, you arrogant, insufferable—"

"*You*, Miss Honeywell," he interrupted, "should be thrashed." At the end, his words slowed, his voice lowered, and so did his gaze. "*Thoroughly*," he added in an undertone.

Something shifted on his stony countenance, barely perceptible. A flex of his rigid jaw, a slight darkening in his eyes that turned them from silver to something approaching a storm cloud. His gaze seemed frozen on her body. More precisely, her chest. She glanced down and saw that her dressing gown had come completely open, and that her night rail was unbuttoned, revealing an amount of cleavage that would have been indecent even in a brothel.

It had been an unusually hot night.

She felt the blush rise from her toes and swiftly reach her hairline.

She slowly looked back up at the duke, whose grim lips had parted slightly and whose eyes had grown heavy-lidded. For the first time, with his hair still mussed from sleep, his features imperceptibly softened, he appeared *almost* human. And very much a man. An extremely handsome, tall, powerful . . . *handsome* man.

Something strange and warm and entirely unrelated to the blush unfurled like a summer bloom in the vicinity of her abdomen, and her heart began to hammer against her ribcage. She began to pant as if she had run a mile.

She snatched her dressing gown together and scowled at him.

He seemed to snap out of whatever spell her breasts wove, and stepped back.

"You, sir, are no gentleman," she said in a breathless rush.

"You, madam, are no lady," he retorted in kind. He slammed the door to the bedroom in her face.

Astrid stood a moment staring at it.

Then she ran to her bedroom and slammed her door. She opened it and slammed it again, just to emphasize her point.

AFTER HER morning ablutions and a quick conference with Flora and the house staff concerning what to do with their guests (coddle and stall, for the moment), Astrid grabbed a crust of bread and a hunk of cheese and stole out of the castle to meet with the estate manager down at the brewery to discuss this latest wrench in their plans.

The brewery was located closer to the fields on the banks of the Ryle, about a quarter mile's walk from the castle. Her grandfather, considered quite industrious for a Honeywell, had moved the brewery away from the main house half a century ago and renovated the gristmill next door, doubling the output of grain and ale for the estate.

Aloysius Honeywell, however, had been less of a businessman than his father and more of a run-of-the-mill Honeywell (i.e., idealistic and valuing things like beauty and truth over profit margins). He had concerned himself more with the romance of being a brewer. Which meant he spent a great deal of time tasting Honeywell Ale. Aloysius had not been precisely a drunkard . . . well, perhaps that was exactly what he had been. But he'd had his uses. It was generally acknowledged that Aloysius had done for the taste of Honeywell Ale what his father had done for the business of selling it.

Thankfully, Astrid had inherited her work ethic from her grandfather, and she had spent the past ten years turning the estate around. She was not about to let the duke stick his nose into her business or have her tenants begin to panic, especially now, during harvest. But Astrid was extremely worried, now that the initial shock of the duke's appearance had faded, for one false move on her part could spell certain doom to not only her family but also to the rest of the tenants, the farm, and the brewery. For she knew it was in the duke's power to throw them all out on their heads if he so chose, no matter how much she wanted to believe otherwise.

She walked inside the granary just as a group of workmen were leaving for the fields to take in the last of the wheat. She could tell from the way they avoided meeting her eye that they knew about the duke's visit.

Hiram McConnell, the estate manager, greeted her grimly in his small office, puffing on his pipe and pushing away his ledgers. He was a large, brawny Scot approaching middle age, who had been hired by her father many years ago, and who was as much responsible for keeping the estate afloat and flourishing as Astrid.

He didn't even have to speak for Astrid to know what he was thinking. Astrid had known him all of her life, and in many ways he had been more a father to her than Aloysius. He was a plainspoken ex-Presbyterian, whose moral compass never needed recalibration. He believed first and foremost in the power of truth-telling. Such a practice had worked out well in his own life, and nothing exasperated him more than the Honeywell tendency to skirt around, evade, pick apart, and remake the truth.

He had certainly not approved when Astrid had decided to "forget" to tell Montford about her father's death. He had thought it best for Astrid to come clean with the duke and attempt to reach some sort of rational compromise with him. Hiram couldn't believe the duke would simply kick her and her family off the land.

Then again, Hiram tended to believe that all people were inherently good. He had been certain, for instance, that Napoleon must have had *someone's* best interest at heart when he turned Europe on its head.

Astrid did not want to disillusion the poor man, but not telling the duke about her father's death was hardly the worst of her sins when it came to Montford.

"Well, lass, what are we to do?" Hiram said, getting straight to the point.

"Proceed as if nothing is amiss," she said with more confidence than she felt. "It is harvest time, and we cannot think of anything but getting in the crop."

"Aye, we'll see to the crop, and the business. But to my mind, ye must start thinking about what *ye* will do. And yer family. Ye've the wee ones to think of."

"Hiram—"

"Aloysius is dead, lass. Yer ten times the manager yer da was, but that doesn't make ye a man, now does it?"

"Which is an unfair, ridiculous—"

"Yes, yes, I know. But it is the way of the world. According to the law of the land, the Duke of Montford has the right to put ye out on the street if he so chooses, and there is nary a court what could change that."

"Rylestone hall belongs to the Honeywells, Hiram," she retorted.

"It belongs to the duke, lass. It always has. Yer family's been there on sufferance, far as I can tell."

She looked at him askance, for Hiram had never been so harsh with her before. "And to think I came here this morning for a bit of sympathy. You can't imagine the sort of pigheaded, arrogant, preening stuffed shirt the duke is."

Hiram crossed his arms and shook his head in that stoic way of his that always presaged a lecture. "I'll not sugarcoat it for ye, Astrid. Not now. Ye bought yerself some time with yer little omission—he could prosecute ye for that, by the way."

She huffed.

Hiram raised an eyebrow. "Indeed he could. And I only pray ye haven't been a party to any more half-cocked swindles."

"Swindles! Hiram!" she scoffed, attempting outrage when what she felt like doing was squirming. She was once again glad Hiram had never learned that, owing to creative Honeywell bookkeeping, the tithe given to Montford was not exactly what it was supposed to be. He probably would have turned back to his Presbyterian roots had he known what sinners he worked for. And if this decades-old practice was found out by the duke, she was glad that none of the blame would fall on Hiram's shoulders.

It would all fall on hers.

Which was a sobering thought. Nearly as sobering as Hiram's admonishing look at the moment. He did have a way of making her feel about ten years old. "Don't forget, I've known yer family for longer than ye've been alive. What ye need to start doing is thinking about Ardyce and Antonia."

"Don't you dare say I should . . . I should what, Hiram?" she cried, feeling even worse than when she had started from the house.

"To my mind ye've three options, and ye're not going to like any of them."

She sighed and slumped against a wooden bench, covering her face with her hands. "I suppose you better tell me," she muttered.

"One, ye can march back up to the Hall, fall on bended knee, and beg the duke's pardon for all of the faffing about and see if he might be agreeable to letting ye stay on. 'Tis yer home, after all, an' it's not as if he needs another castle. I'm sure he already has one or two."

She guffawed. "Sooner would pigs fly than a Honeywell would beg a Montford for anything!"

Hiram gave her a droll look. "I figured that. The next option is for ye to marry Sir Wesley."

"Cousin Wesley! Have you gone quite insane?" she cried. "You know that is impossible."

"He's in love with ye," Hiram pointed out.

"Blech. Don't make me throw up. I have no intention of marrying anyone, *especially* cousin Wesley. I'd sooner marry Aunt Anabel's pompadour."

"He's considered a good catch, and handsome enough."

"He's silly—"

"He's a baron." Hiram's brows wiggled comically.

"An insolvent, silly baron with a fishwife of a mother—"

"Your *aunt*—"

"Who hates me," she groaned. In truth she was hardly surprised by Hiram's suggestion. Marriage to her cousin would be an easy solution to most of her problems, for at least then she and the girls would not be homeless, if it came to being tossed out of Rylestone. And they could still live nearby, at Benwick Grange.

But it was quite impossible.

"Besides which, Alice is in love with him," she murmured.

Hiram sighed. "There is that. It would be helpful if the lad figured that one out and started courting the correct lass."

"He's never been the brightest half penny, has he?"

Hiram chuckled. They sat in companionable silence while Hiram tapped the end of his pipe and loaded it with fresh tobacco.

"Well, and what's the third choice?" she demanded.

"Yer auntie."

"Lady Emily?" she sniffed. Wesley's odious mother. Pompous, arrogant windbag who had always despised her sister's family.

"She has a responsibility to ye, whether she likes it or not. Ye should go to her. Yer a lady, Astrid, and so are yer sisters. The missus and I would take ye all in if it come to that, but I think ye and I both know that ain't what's best."

"I'm not a lady," she argued, though, ironically, it was the exact opposite of what she had argued last night. "I mean . . . you know what I mean."

Hiram shook his head. "Ye're educated, lass, and got blue in yer veins. Ye know that means something, much as ye try and pretend ye're one of us."

"But I am one of you!" she cried.

Hiram just stared at her with a faintly wistful expression and puffed on his pipe. "An idealist, just like yer da."

"Hardly," she snorted.

He leaned forward, and his countenance hardened. He took his pipe out of his mouth and pointed it at her. "Yer da was allowed his funny ways because of his last name, lass. Don't think it's any different with you. The way ye run the business, the way ye act and dress and spout your opinions. The lads listen to ye and put up with yer ways because ye're a Honeywell, and the last of the lot at that. If ye weren't, do ye know what ye'd be called?"

"A common tart, I suppose," she retorted.

Hiram's brow darkened. "Nay, worse than that," he said in a low voice. "And so ye see ye ain't one of us and never will be. You'll go to Lady Emily and have her do right by ye, find some fine gentleman for you and yer sisters to marry. And don't tell me she won't, if only to get rid of the lot of ye. I think she'd wrestle the moon if it meant keeping ye from marrying her son."

She stood up, quite at the end of her tether. "Thank you very much for ruining my morning."

Hiram inclined his head as if accepting a compliment.

"I see you're going to be no help."

"I'll always help ye lass, but only if ye start helping yerself."

"That is exactly what I am trying to do," she bit off in exasperation.

She scowled at him for a moment longer, turned on her heel, and left the room.

"Please refrain from murdering the duke, lass," Hiram called. "I wouldn't want to see ye hanged."

"They're more likely to throw me a parade," she retorted.

"I can't wait to meet him. Oh, and lass?"

"What?"

"If ye see that weasel Roddy around abouts, send him here, won't ye?"

"Certainly."

Astrid stalked out of the granary and began tearing down the path leading back to the Hall, fuming. Of course, he had the good sense to give her the dose of cold, hard reality that she needed, but she did not want to listen to him. She did not want to acknowledge that things were so hopeless. That she must face the fact—fact? *Fact?*—that she was going to lose Rylestone Hall. That she was going to have to give up the reins of the estate, the farm, the brewery. It was just too horrifying to accept.

Marriage? To Wesley? Unconscionable. And the mere thought of turning to Aunt Emily for anything, even a table scrap, left her innards in knots.

But Hiram was, of course, right. He was always right. The Honeywells were gentry, and no matter how much she wanted to believe otherwise, the country they lived in was defined by class hierarchies.

She had Antonia and Ardyce to think of. And even Alice, if Wesley didn't come to his senses and realize he was in love with the girl.

What were they going to do?

She picked up a stick alongside the path and began thwacking the weeds off to the sides in angry, bitter strokes.

At least Hiram had left unspoken the other alternative that was even more unpalatable, which was marriage to Mr. Lightfoot. He had proposed, and she had rejected him now, *twice*. She was certain he had written to the duke in retaliation for her continued stubbornness. Mr. Lightfoot couldn't grasp how she could possibly refuse his suit.

Aside from the fact that she loathed him.

Aside from the fact that he had cheated her father in order to start his company.

Aside from the fact that he wanted to marry her only because of some vendetta he still carried against her family. Either that or he was just insane, as Astrid had long suspected.

Mr. Lightfoot assumed because he was rich that she would follow along with his schemes. He was rather like the duke in that regard.

Although where Mr. Lightfoot was portly and starting to go bald, the Duke of Montford was as fit as they came and possessed a splendid head of hair that was the precise color of chestnuts bathed in an early morning dew . . .

Astrid stumbled to a stop and stomped her foot on the ground.

She would *not* compare Montford's hair to chestnuts. Or his eyes to stormy seas.

And she would *not* imagine any part of his anatomy covered in early morning dew.

She slapped the stick as hard as she could against an old oak tree, and the stick shattered.

"Psst. Pssssst!"

She spun around, trying to locate the sound.

"Miss Astrid!" came an anxious whisper from behind a neighboring beech tree.

"Who's there?" she demanded.

A head poked around the tree tentatively, reminding Astrid of a turtle. Stevenage—or Roddy, as he was called now—pushed up his bent spectacles on his nose and peered up and down the path.

"It's me, Roddy. Is . . . er . . . *he's* not with you, is he?"

"Who, His Bloody Grace? No."

Roddy winced, as if afraid her colorful appellation was in danger of being overheard by the despot in question.

"Mr. McConnell is looking for you," she said.

"I was on my way. Just wanted to avoid . . . well, running into *him*."

"You'll have to face him sometime, Roddy, as you still technically work for him."

Roddy looked abashed and nervous, and Astrid sighed in resignation. It had taken the duke all of twelve hours to undo the past two weeks' worth of progress with Roderick Stevenage. The poor man had been wound up tighter than an E string on a violin right before it snapped when he'd first arrived at Rylestone. He'd talked exclusively about crazy things like terms of contract and property laws and inventories, made lists ten pages long, and jumped every time he saw Aunt Anabel's wig. He'd been distraught when all the laborious reports he sent to the duke received no response and began to accuse them of all manner of perfidy (which, of course, was quite accurate).

After Ant and Art ruined most of the man's extremely morose wardrobe by cutting his clothing up to use as costumes in their production of *Agamemnon*, Astrid thought the man was going to spontaneously combust. But the men down at the brewery forced some brew down his throat, Flora took a shine to him, and Roddy had begun to emerge, shocking them all.

Roddy liked ale. Roddy *loved* Flora. Roddy, in fact, planned on never returning to London or his employer.

"I know," Roddy replied bleakly. "I just can't believe His Grace has come here."

"Can you not?"

Roddy gave her a dry look. "I know the duke better than most. He despises traveling. So that means he must be *extremely* put out at your family to have made the journey." His face paled. "Oh, and *me*. He must be put out at *me*!"

"I think he thought we had murdered you, which is why he came."

"Murdered . . ." Roddy looked baffled.

She decided to enlighten the poor man. "Roddy, you must know I intercepted every report you sent to the duke, and every letter he wrote to you. He must have been very worried not to hear from you."

The Stevenage of a week ago would have keeled over at this news, but the Roddy of the present moment looked startled for a moment before allowing a slow, appreciative grin to spread across his face. "I guess I must have known it all along, Miss Astrid. You're a canny piece of work."

She returned his grin. "Thank you, Mr. Stevenage. But after yesterday, I would have to agree that he is now officially put out with you. But don't worry, we won't let him hurt you."

Roddy looked despondent. "Oh, he'd not hurt me. I mean, he would not physically harm me, he's not like that."

"That's good to know."

"But to see the disappointment on his face, the disapproval . . . oh, Miss Astrid! Did I tell you about the time His Grace made a roomful of ladies weep by just looking at them? He is quite the master of the cutting look."

"It is only if you care what he thinks that such looks could affect you."

Roddy sighed miserably, his shoulders sagging. "That's just it, Miss Astrid, I do care what he thinks."

"What? Still? But you are so happy here, Roddy. You're not thinking of returning?" Meaning, *You aren't thinking of turning traitor on us now, are you?*

"Of course not. Flora and I . . . well . . ." Roddy cleared his throat and blushed, suddenly bashful. "Well, quite frankly, Flora's the best thing that's ever happened to me. That and coming here. It's like . . . I don't know. For the first time in my life I am actually living. And it feels wonderful. Oh, I'd not go back, Miss Astrid, not for all the tea in China." His expression grew wistful. "But I can't help but feeling . . . Miss Astrid, I've known the duke since he was in leading strings. My father was his father's man-of-affairs, and my grandfather was his grandfather's man-of-affairs . . ."

"Family loyalty. I understand."

Roddy shook his head. "No, it's more than that." Roddy looked on the verge of saying more, but then seemed to think better of it. "Anyway, I suppose my business with His Grace is my business, and I shall have to face up to it eventually. I'll not burden you with it."

"That's quite all right."

"I don't know what *you're* going to do."

"Neither do I, but something shall come to me. Look how well I handled you."

Roddy chuckled at this and then grew sober, more sober than she'd seen him in a week. "Don't think you can do the same with Montford. You thought *I* was a stuffed shirt." He exhaled deeply. "His Grace is the most remote man to walk the earth."

This struck a chord in Astrid. Not so much what Roddy had said—she had garnered as much from two seconds of the duke's frosty company—but the way he had said it, with such deep, nearly tender despair. She realized in that moment that Roddy loved the duke. Something she would not have thought humanly possible for anyone. She had thought Roddy feared the duke, held him in awe, but she would have never guessed the truth.

"And it's not his fault," Roddy continued, reading her thoughts. "The way he is . . . well, you'll think me ridiculous for saying it, but he deserves our pity."

She snorted. "Pity! What? By all accounts he is the richest, most powerful man in the kingdom. Pity him indeed."

"He did not choose to be who he is, you know. He was but four when he inherited the title after the tragedy."

Astrid did *not* want to be interested in Roddy's revelations, but she was. Very interested. "What tragedy?" she couldn't help but prompt.

"Why, the accident that took his parents' lives. A carriage accident." Roddy shivered. "Very gruesome. Killed everyone except for His Grace. They were on their way northward to a summer estate in Scotland. No one found them for two days. My father was one of the party that came upon the wreckage. He found the child in . . ." Roddy trailed off, his eyes unfocusing, his features bunching up into a grimace of revulsion. After a long pause, he seemed to come back to himself. He shrugged his shoulders as if attempting to dislodge an unwelcome memory. "Well, suffice to say the boy was in very bad condition. We all thought he would go the way of his parents, and that it wouldn't have been such a bad thing in the end, if you know what I mean."

Astrid didn't know what he meant at all, but the tale had left a hollow feeling in her gut. Clearly, the accident had been an unspeakable horror, and for the child to have been left alive on his own for two days . . . with the corpses of his parents . . .

Astrid shivered, despite the morning's unseasonable warmth.

Roddy looked suddenly thoughtful, as if he'd just realized something. "I suppose that is why he doesn't like to travel," he said, more to himself than her.

"Well, yes, I suppose that would do it," she murmured.

"But it's a fine thing he survived, though I wouldn't wish his upbringing on my worst enemy. Not that he *had* an upbringing. He was Montford before he could read, and he's been Montford ever since. And he'll crush you, Miss Astrid, if you try to play fast and loose with him."

Astrid bristled, coming back to her senses. "I've already done so. He doesn't frighten me."

"Yes, well . . ."

"*Miss Honeywell!*"

Roddy froze, and so did she, at the sound of a booming voice coming up from the path leading from the Hall.

"*Stevenage!*"

Roddy's face drained of color, and he turned on his heels and ran into the shrubbery, his courage once more fleeing in the presence of his soon-to-be ex-employer.

"Coward," she hissed.

"Miss Honeywell!" the duke intoned, closer now, and sounding even more displeased than usual.

She turned around and pasted a false smile on her face. The duke strode up to her side, outfitted in a gray cutaway jacket and fawn breeches tucked into high Hessian boots, their glossy surface marred by the mud from the path, the only aspect of his person not perfectly in order. She marveled at the crisp, unwrinkled fabrics, the starch of his collar, the spotless gleam of his top hat and silver-tipped walking cane.

She raised a hand unconsciously toward her head, and only by great effort forestalled her fingers from attempting to put her hair to order. She had, of course, forgotten her bonnet in her haste this morning, and she could feel the damp, curling tendrils of her hair beginning to sag out of its pins in the back.

She did not care what she looked like. Not one jot.

If only he did not look so blasted . . . perfect.

And if only Roddy had not told her that blasted story. How was she supposed to think straight about anything now?

"Miss Honeywell, was that Stevenage who just hied off into the shrubbery?"

"What? Who? Oh, was there someone?" She glanced around her, looking perplexed.

"Yes, there was . . . oh, for the love of . . . never mind." He stabbed his cane into the ground and glared at her.

She met his glare with one of her own and told herself not to think of the last time she had been in his company. When he had stared at her breasts.

Too late. She cursed inwardly as she felt the blush creep over her cheeks. She hated being a redhead. "Your Grace. Did you want something? Directions, perhaps, back to London?"

"I am not going anywhere."

"I would have thought Ant and Art had quite convinced you that it would be in your best interest."

"Ant and Art." Something twitched in his jaw. "Your *sisters*, I presume."

"Yes. Antonia and Ardyce."

"They shall not run me off."

"Damn. I mean, fiddlesticks."

His jaw twitched again.

"Nevertheless, if you deem it necessary to stay in the area, you should be more comfortable at the Thirsty Boar," she said breezily.

He looked at her as if she had grown a tail.

"The coaching inn in the village," she elucidated.

His eyes grew wide as saucers, and he blinked once, twice. Apparently she had grown hooves, wings, and a snout to accompany her tail, from the look on his face.

"Good God, no," he breathed, as if she had suggested he dig a hole to China. "I never stay at coaching inns."

"Then is this your first time out of London?" she persisted.

"Of course not."

"Then how have you not had to put up at a coaching inn?"

"Madam," he said in that haughty, condescending ducal tone she had already grown to hate. "I own thirty-seven properties in England alone. I hardly need to stay at a coaching inn when I can sleep in my own bed."

"How very convenient for you to have so many beds." She paused. "Have you thought that you might be inconveniencing *us* to stay at Rylestone Hall?"

"I am sure it is no inconvenience," he said in that superior tone.

She snorted. "Have you thought that we might not *want* you to stay at Rylestone, Montford?"

"Of course. But that is beside the point. I own it."

"Ha! Do you indeed?"

She picked up her skirts and started past him.

"Which is precisely why I am here," he continued, falling into step beside her.

"If you own thirty-seven properties, what need do you have for this one?"

"Again, beside the point. It is the principle of the thing."

She shot him a fierce glare. "Rylestone Hall is our home. The Honeywells have managed this estate for centuries."

"And made an appalling hash of it. The Hall is crooked, madam, if you haven't noticed."

"The towers need some work, granted . . ."

"And I can't imagine the state of the tenant farms. Or the poor sods under your shoddy management."

She stopped up short and turned to give him an earful. But he was not expecting her sudden movement, so he kept on walking, right into her. She collided with a solid pillar of manly and sartorial excellence, her nose smashing against the ruffled perfection of his cravat. She inhaled the scent of him—clean linen, a hint of sandalwood—and felt the splendid heat emanating from his body. Something deep inside of her melted, turning her insides to mush. She had the oddest desire to reach up and bury her fingers in the folds of his jacket and push herself closer, ever closer, into his warm, hard body.

She jumped away with an abruptness that left her teetering dizzily on jelly-like legs.

He jumped away as well with a sharp intake of breath.

"Miss Honeywell . . ."

His voice was soft, as it had been this morning in the corridor.

She looked up and met his startled glance. His brows were arched, his mouth slacked, and his silver eyes bored into her own as if divining her soul.

Her insides melted all over again. She licked her lips unconsciously.

His gaze dropped briefly to her lips, and his eyes darkened to an opaque, satiny gray. Then he glanced back to her eyes, looking as baffled as she felt. "Miss Honeywell," he repeated. "Your eyes . . ."

"Yes?"

"Your eyes . . . *don't match.*"

The last two words were little more than a pained whisper.

She crashed back to herself with a thud, her body suddenly cold and rigid. His observation was a blatant accusation. He seemed disgusted—horrified, really—by her eyes. And who could blame him? They were uncanny and off-putting to most people. Some even thought she was cursed. But it was not as if she could help her hideous appearance, any more than he could help being so damned beautiful.

She had thought herself beyond the point of being wounded by comments about her looks. But her vanity was struck very low indeed in that moment. "I am sorry to offend you, Your Grace," she ground out, stalking ahead, not wanting him to see how he had affected her.

She heard him groan behind her and lengthen his stride to catch up with her. "Miss Honeywell, wait."

He put a hand on her arm. She felt it as keenly as one felt a bee sting, even though his glove and the fabric of her dress stood between their flesh. She tried to shrug him off, but he held on tenaciously until she was forced to stop. But she didn't look up at him. She couldn't.

Her eyes felt hot and wet, and she tried to convince herself it was an allergy.

"I am sorry, I didn't mean . . ."

"I know exactly what you meant. You don't have to explain. I am quite used to rude comments from you," she said in a surprisingly even voice, considering her inner turmoil.

He was silent for a long while, and she was forced to listen to the rhythm of his breathing above her. It was as uneven as her own. He still held on to her arm, as if afraid she would slip away if he didn't, which was probably true.

"You make it very hard for a man, Miss Honeywell."

She didn't know what he meant, yet at the same time she knew precisely what he meant, and she didn't like the implication of that at all. She wanted no insight into him, and she certainly didn't want him to know *her* at all.

"Please, let me go," she whispered, her voice breaking.

His hand fell away. He backed up a pace or two. He began smoothing out his cravat, tucking and folding with a nearly obsessive intensity. "Miss Honeywell, this is ridiculous. I do not want to insult you. Indeed, I do not even want to *be* here."

"And yet you are. And yet you intend to stay."

"I want to know what the bloody hell is going on. You've already lied about your father—"

"I never lied. I simply forgot to inform you."

He raised an eyebrow, looking smug. "Ah, so then it *was* you. You are *A.* Honeywell. You are the blasted letter writer who's plagued me for years."

"Of course I am. Who did you think was in charge around here?" she demanded.

He held up a hand in a gesture of pure defeat. "Madam, to be perfectly honest, I've had a great deal to sort out in the past four days. Carriages. Mud. Lame horses. Hysterical valets. *Mud.* Pigs. And you. *You,* Miss Honeywell, are quite a lot to sort out. As you refuse to give me a straight answer to anything, it is all I can do not to throttle you," he said in a dry, level voice. "I am . . . unused . . . to such treatment."

"Clearly."

"However, if you would start cooperating, I promise to refrain from throttling you," he finished, flicking invisible lint from his sleeves and looking as if this offer of conciliation should solve all of their problems.

And for some bizarre reason, all of her anger at him and all of her hurt feelings over the incident with her eyes drained out of her in that moment. He looked, facing her in the lane, wearing an expression of such smug arrogance, precisely like a ten-year-old boy determined to have his way.

Which made the ten-year-old girl inside of her dig her heels in.

Roddy had warned her not to grouse the duke. But she was already in too deep. She was now quite glad she had run into his chest rather than contradict his assumption about the condition of the estate. For if he discovered the truth—that it was flourishing, not languishing— then he was bound to figure out that her family had been bilking the dukedom for generations.

Or, at least, that was how *he* would see it. To Astrid's mind and the minds of her forebears, however, no laws were being broken.

Again, the duke was bound to see things in a different light, and Astrid did not want to spend the rest of her life in Newgate. Who would take care of her sisters, or the brewery, or the tenants?

She would not panic. Not now.

She wasn't any closer to figuring out what to do with the duke or the muddle between them, but she wasn't about to let him have the upper hand. The only thing to do at the moment was stall, evade, and so flummox the duke that he never had a chance to get his bearings long enough to discover the truth.

And lord knew the duke could use some flummoxing. She had never seen such a stiff collar or rigid spine or tense jaw. She wondered how he did not shatter under the weight of such self-importance. He was wound even tighter than Roddy had been.

The most remote man to walk the earth.

She raised her eyes to his and considered Roddy's assessment as she saw the duke . . . no, actually saw *him*, for the first time. Not Montford. Not her loathed nemesis. Not a stuffed shirt in shiny boots. But *him*, the man beneath, the one who reminded her of a ten-year-old boy, the one who had stolen a look at her breasts this morning and eaten one of her biscuits last night with such an expression of surprised ecstasy Astrid had nearly dropped her tea in her lap. The man who kept peeking out at the world behind that dour, icy demeanor.

She realized Roddy was quite wrong. Montford was not the most remote man to walk the earth. He was the loneliest man . . . no, the *saddest* man she had ever met, and he was so coiled up in himself he didn't even realize he was miserable.

Her heart swelled in her chest, and he was no longer a ten-year-old bully, but a child of four, alone on the side of a highway, tears streaking down a face covered in dirt and dried blood. She could picture him in her mind as clearly as if she had been there. She wanted to reach out to him, take him in her arms and soothe his hurt, take away his pain, kiss away his tears . . .

Damn Roddy for telling her such a heartrending tale. Damn him for making Montford . . . *human* to her.

But once Astrid's heart swelled like that, there was no turning back. She would never let anyone know the truth—that beneath her prickly tongue and bluestocking tendencies she was a sentimental fool. She had always been a sap when it came to wounded animals, teary-eyed little boys, and lost causes. It never failed that she wanted to take broken creatures under her wing and fix them, even though most of her projects eventually found a way to, either literally or figuratively, bite the hand that fed them. But she never stopped trying.

Montford, to her mind, fit all three categories, especially the last one. If ever there was a lost cause, it was the perfect, odious man standing before her now.

What was she thinking? She would be a fool to try to rescue him from himself.

An utter fool.

But damned if she wasn't going to try anyway.

His brow furrowed. "Why are you smiling like that, Miss Honeywell?"

"Am I? Well, I suppose it is because you think I am going to cooperate."

"I take it you're not."

"No indeed, Montford. For where would be the fun in that?"

He looked as if she had spoken a foreign language, not made a declaration of war, which, unbeknownst to him, she had.

She stuck out her tongue, turned, picked up her skirts, and ran all the way back to the Hall.

Chapter Six

In Which Montford Is Confronted by a Pastoral Utopia

MONTFORD COULDN'T quite believe what had happened moments ago. No one had ever done such a thing to him. It was outrageous. Inexplicable.

The bloody woman had stuck her tongue out at him.

If she thought he was going to chase after her, thereby losing what little dignity remained to him, she was quite mistaken. He would *not* run like some common swain in pursuit of that red-haired virago.

Although that was what his legs itched to do, quite regardless of his resolve.

Damn that woman to bloody hell, but she was a . . . a . . .

Handful.

A strumpet.

Worse. He suspected she was a bluestocking. The horror. He couldn't think of anything more tiresome than a woman who pretended to be a man. As if he couldn't see very well that she was female, what with all of that hair. And the dress (she had foregone the trousers today, thank God). And the breasts.

The very full, very round breasts he had had the misfortune to glimpse in more or less full glory this morning. Yes, the night rail had covered at least half of those glorious mounds, but no, the night rail had *not* done its job properly, for the hallway had been cold, and the early morning light drifting through the windows had rendered the thin fabric a moot point at best. Those breasts were a . . . a . . .

Handful.

And he had found himself struggling with the memory of them the entire time he'd been attempting to converse with her just now. It had not helped when he had run into her and the very same appendages he had been trying so hard not to think about had smashed up against his chest. Now he had not only the memory of how they looked, but also how they felt—soft, nubile—to plague him. Not to mention the scent of her rising up off her hair—hay, lavender, *woman*—and lingering in his nose long after the fact.

His body—a traitor to all Montfords past—had quickened with an unmistakable animal lust.

He wanted her, he realized with alarm. He wanted this woman, who was so wrong, so utterly *flawed* and *incorrect*, more than he'd ever wanted a woman before. For a split second, when they had been body to body, he'd imagined himself dragging her off the path, pinning her to the ground, and taking her right there in the shrubbery, like some animal. He had more than imagined it. He had *considered* it.

He had clearly gone insane.

Taking firm control of his wandering libido, Montford managed to restrain himself from running after Miss Honeywell. Instead, he walked in the direction of Rylestone Green in an effort to clear his head. Despite the mud and the general disorder of the natural world, the walk into the village was pleasant. The sky was as blue as Miss Honeywell's right eye and mild for early October in Yorkshire. Had he been any less of a prude, he would have unbuttoned his jacket and loosened his cravat to accommodate the heat. But he was not. And he was not any less disturbed by the mud on his Hessians than he had been yesterday.

But he could not deny that the air was fresh and clean and faintly sweet-smelling, a far cry from London's polluted atmosphere. It was amazing how good it felt to simply breathe in the pristine air. He could get used to rural life—if something was done to eliminate the . . . well, *ruralness*.

He passed by a field of grazing sheep, and two of them wandered onto the road directly in front of him. Montford jumped back, catching his hat in his hands before it could pop off his head. "Good God," he muttered.

He detoured around the intruders, careful to let no part of his clothing graze their puffy, dirty white wool. He nearly jumped out of his skin when one of them *baaahed* in the general direction of his privates.

At length, he reached the village. The sight of it filled Montford with the same uncomfortably warm feeling he'd had when he'd first seen the castle. It looked too perfect, the long, wide green that provided the village with half its name leading up to the steps of an old Norman chapel. The green was well tended and dominated by an ancient elm, under which frolicked a handful of young children playing hoops and chasing their pets. The main street was cobbled and bustling with local traffic, the shop fronts freshly painted and immaculately polished. The citizens of the village looked as prosperous and quaint as the village itself. A veritable pastoral idyll.

It was a far cry from the other shabby, rather frighteningly uncivilized towns he had encountered on his journey through Yorkshire. It was a far cry from what Montford expected to find, considering the returns on the estate.

And it would bloody well never do.

Rylestone Green was *supposed* to be a ruin.

Which made *someone* a liar and a thief.

Without entering the village, he spun around and stalked back to the castle, more disgruntled than ever. From the moment he had received Mr. Lightfoot's letter, he had felt the same way he did when he found a book shelved out of order in his library, or when Coombes lined up his boots with the outer edges facing inward. Except the feeling had been magnified a hundred times over as the days wore on and Stevenage remained silent, no doubt because of Miss Honeywell's machinations. With the added stress of his upcoming nuptials and the bedamned restlessness that had lately plagued him, Montford had grown, in short, hysterical. It was the only explanation he had for undertaking a journey he would have never considered otherwise.

And now that he was here, now that he'd seen Rylestone's prosperity, he was more certain than ever that the Honeywells had been cheating him for years. He had no idea what to do to fix things. This was not a situation easily resolved by changing the order of his boots or reshelving a book in its proper location.

How, he wondered, did one reshelve a family?

Well, at least one thing was clear to him. Until he got a straight answer out of Miss Honeywell, he was not going to get anywhere. She held the key to this muddle. If only she were not so . . . so insufferable. Insolent. Flip. If only just the mere sight of her didn't make him want to howl in outrage.

He'd have more luck capturing the moon and hauling it to earth than having a rational conversation with Miss Honeywell. But the angrier he got and the more hopeless it all seemed, the more he wanted to do just that—not necessarily have a rational conversation with the woman. *That* would never happen. But he *did* want to defeat her. Not very noble of him, but there it was.

By the time he returned to the castle, the only thing he knew for certain was that he was *not* going to allow Miss Honeywell to hoodwink him.

How to do that was another matter entirely.

As it seemed, she was determined to avoid his company—no doubt in order to hatch some nefarious scheme against him—he supposed he was going to have to avoid her avoidance.

In other words, he was going to have to attach himself to her hip.

He shuddered in revulsion. Or at least he attempted revulsion. Otherwise he would have to acknowledge to himself that his shudder had another cause, which had also inspired a tightening of his loins and an image of bounteous breasts to flash behind his eyelids. He had never been impressed by women's bosoms before. Bosoms were bovine. Bosoms were coarse, so very plebeian. Why could he not get Miss Honeywell's out of his mind?

He shook his head and tried to breathe deeply as he entered the castle keep.

Follow her, he told himself. *Plague her. But do not touch her again. And do* not, *for Christ's sake, look below her neck.*

It had been too long since he had given up his last mistress and asked for Araminta's hand, and that must be the source of his problem with Miss Honeywell. He needed a woman.

His spirits fell as he realized how little a chance there was of *that* in the near future. He supposed that the next woman he bedded would be his wife.

An arctic breeze crept up his spine at the thought of Araminta, and he welcomed it, for as he watched Miss Honeywell descend from the stairwell in the front hall, he felt no return of his former unruly feelings regarding her bosom, even though it bounced with each little hopping step she took.

From the speed with which she moved, she was still obviously trying to evade him. But he stood at the bottom, effectively cutting off her escape route. She came to a halt a few steps above. She held a bonnet and a pair of gloves in her hand as if prepared to dash outside once more. Her face was pinkened with exertion, and her eyes flashed with vexation.

Her ire pleased him. He was glad to know his company piqued her as much as hers did him.

"Miss Honeywell. On your way out?"

She studied him with suspicion. "Yes, I was on my way out."

"In that case, I should like a look at the books while you're conducting your business."

A flicker of exasperation crossed her features. "Of course, Your Grace. We have an excellent library."

"The estate books, madam."

He did not think he imagined the way she paled at his statement. Oh, the little strumpet definitely had something to hide.

"I do not think that will be necessary—" she said.

"Oh, but I do, Miss Honeywell."

"There is nothing to interest you in that quarter—"

"Oh, I doubt that."

She moved across the front hall and peered outside. Her expression changed from hunted to devious. He followed her glance. A curricle had pulled up the front drive.

"Besides which," Miss Honeywell said, "I don't think it's any of your business."

"How do you figure that?"

She threw him a look over her shoulder that was pure smug victory. "Because my brother has arrived."

Chapter Seven

In Which Miss Honeywell Attempts to Dig a Hole to China

MONTFORD WATCHED at a distance of a few paces as Miss Honeywell and her sister Alice greeted the new arrival. The young man was mop-haired and handsome in a pleasant, vapid sort of way, his eyes large and brown and earnest. He was clearly related to the Honeywells, as evidenced by his red hair, freckles, and snub nose. Montford was quite sure, however, he was not their brother. Not only because his solicitors had verified that Aloysius was heirless years ago, but also because of the way the young man was currently staring at both Miss Honeywells, like a besotted mooncalf.

Montford snorted.

"Astrid!" cried the man, bounding toward Miss Honeywell, embracing her impulsively. "It's been ever such a torture to . . ." He blushed when he noticed Alice standing off to the side, also furiously blushing.

"Alice!" cried the moonfaced fool, jumping back from Miss Honeywell and trotting over to Alice. He looked ready to embrace her, thought better of it, and took her hand instead, kissing the top of it awkwardly.

Alice's face turned from pink to crimson. So did the visitor's. "Hello, Alice," he mumbled.

Montford rolled his eyes. It seemed this gentleman was in love with both Honeywell sisters. The poor sod.

"Hello, Wes—" Alice began.

"*W-An*thony. Hello, *Anthony*," interrupted Miss Honeywell, moving quickly to separate the two. "We're ever so glad you're home."

As Montford had expected, the gentleman's face creased in confusion. He looked from Astrid to Alice, then back to Astrid, blinked, then noticed Montford loitering a few paces away. Eyes lighting up in comprehension, he started forward, arm extended. "Very nice to meet you, er, Anthony—" the man began. Poor, poor sod. Astrid jerked on his arm in a panic, and he stumbled backward. "Astrid, what in the blue blazes—" he hissed.

"*Anthony*, you silly peahen," Astrid laughed. "You know very well who you are."

"Anthony" glanced at Alice, who just shrugged.

"You've arrived just in time, for look who has come to call. May I introduce His Grace, the Duke of Montford?" Astrid continued breezily.

"Anthony's" jaw dropped to the ground. Or it would have if it had not been hinged to his head. He drew himself up and gazed at Montford with eyes the size of dinner plates.

"Your Grace, may I present my *brother*, Mr. Anthony Honeywell." Astrid elbowed Anthony in the ribs.

Anthony struggled for several moments to say something, but nothing came out. At last, he seemed to find some measure of self-control, for he finally managed to bow quite correctly and murmur, "Your Grace."

"Mr. *Honeywell*," Montford ground out.

"I am . . . shocked," "Anthony" blubbered.

"Not so much as I," Montford murmured dryly. "I was *not* expecting you."

"Oh, well . . . erm, I came over straightaway from Mother's—*egad*, Astrid!" "Anthony" cried, rubbing the spot where Miss Honeywell had just thwacked him with an elbow. "What are you about? And why do you keep calling me . . ."

"You must be starving after your long journey. And *parched*," Astrid cut in smoothly, pulling the confused young man toward the castle entrance.

"Not really, I . . ."

"Let's go inside, and you can tell us all about your trip."

At that, "Anthony" brightened considerably, clearly on even ground once more. "Yes, my trip." He turned to Montford with an anxious expression as he was pulled along. The poor fellow stood absolutely no chance.

Montford tipped his hat at the man and turned to Alice, who was staring wide-eyed at her sister's back. She turned to Montford with a worried frown.

They both cleared their throats and looked toward the curricle.

"*Hardly* a practical vehicle for a long journey," he drawled.

Alice squeaked out a response through her terror.

Montford sighed. "Don't worry, Miss Alice. I'm sure your sister can explain everything to us in due course. But let's give the two of them a minute." He paused with what he thought was an appropriate measure of drama. "To get their stories straight."

She stared at him in surprise. "You're not going to . . . I mean, Wes . . . er, Anthony . . ."

"Oh, I wouldn't *dream* of stopping your sister from digging herself a hole. Where would be the fun in that?" he said drily, repeating

Astrid's own words from earlier. He offered Alice his arm, and she took it hesitatingly.

And as they strode together inside, Montford realized that he had spoken the truth to Alice. He was, as demented as it seemed, starting to be immensely entertained by Miss Honeywell's scheming. He was, in fact, having fun. More fun than he'd had in years.

And on the heels of that realization followed a healthy dose of apprehension.

Good God, *fun*. The last thing he needed.

⊷ ⊷⊱≢⊰ ⊶

"WHAT DO you mean I am to pretend to be your brother?" Sir Wesley hissed as Astrid pulled him toward the parlor and whispered instructions in his ear. "You don't have a brother."

"Which is precisely why you are pretending," Astrid explained through clenched teeth. Her cousin had never been the quickest study, but really. Did she have to spell out every word to him?

"But Astrid, I can't lie to the Duke of Montford," Wesley whispered.

"It is not a lie. *You've* never actually said you're my brother."

Wesley looked unconvinced and very confused. "Well, that's because I'm not, am I?"

Oh, for the love of . . . "Wesley, I *need* you to do this."

Wesley's brow creased with annoyance. "Look here, old girl, I don't want to get mixed up in this . . . this whatever it is you're trying to accomplish . . . what *are* you trying to accomplish?"

"I am trying to save Rylestone Hall. For heaven's sake, Wesley, do try to keep up. The duke has come here because he knows about Father. He thinks Rylestone Hall belongs to him now . . ."

"Doesn't it?"

She waved this away. "Details."

Wesley sighed. "But I've told you in the past you don't need to worry about trying to stay here when you can come to the Grange. Mother—"

"Would have a fit of vapors."

"She'll get over it." Wesley grabbed her hand, an earnest expression falling over his face, reminding Astrid of a startled kitten. "You know what I want, Astrid, and that is for you to be . . ."

Astrid shook her hand free and forestalled Wesley from an outright declaration. Another proposal of marriage was the last thing she needed. "And you know what I want, Wesley. I think I have been clear on that. I want Rylestone Hall. It is my home, and Alice's home. I'll not let the Duke of Montford take it from us just because of some two-hundred-year-old piece of parchment."

Wesley gave her a pitying stare. "What *happened* to you, Astrid?"

She stiffened. "What are you talking about?" she demanded.

"I remember a time when you dreamed of a different sort of life. You never wanted to run the estate. You never even wanted to stay here. You couldn't wait to leave Rylestone."

Astrid turned away from Wesley and stared out the window to hide her expression from her cousin. She was shaken by Wesley's words, had not thought her cousin capable of such cutting insight. Yes, she *had* once dreamed of something very different. Travel. Adventure. Romance. Silly dreams of a silly girl.

But then her mother died in childbirth, and her father went . . . well, *crazy*, and there was nothing for it but to take up the reins. Ardyce had been two years old and Antonia had been newly born, and Aunt Emily had threatened to take them both from Rylestone Hall to give them a "proper upbringing." Astrid had been all of fourteen, but she had fought her aunt and won. Her family had stayed together, and after a time the estate began to prosper. She couldn't imagine how her life could have turned out any differently.

Oh, who was she fooling? Of *course* she could imagine. But only that.

She would not change what she had now for all the travel and adventure and romance in the world. And she would not give up Rylestone Hall without a serious fight.

"That was a long time ago," she murmured.

Wesley touched her shoulder. "Not so very."

She moved away from his hand. "You don't know what you're talking about."

"I know that trying to keep this estate afloat single-handedly is too much for you."

She stuck her hands on her hips and glared at him. "You think me incapable."

"No, of course not. Good gad, Astrid, you have a way of twisting a body's words. What I mean is it is not the life you chose. It is not the life you were meant to live."

She laughed humorlessly. "And you think *you* are the one to give me what I need?" she asked bitterly.

Wesley remained silent for so long that Astrid finally turned to him. He was staring at her with a stricken expression, and she felt immediately guilty for her harsh tone.

"I don't know if I am anymore," Wesley said in a quiet voice. "But you need something. Someone. Before you wake up and find yourself . . ."

He trailed off, unwilling to complete his thought, his cheeks flooding with color.

At least one of them had a filter.

Though Astrid knew precisely what he would have said.

Before you wake up and find yourself alone.

Which was ridiculous, because she had Ardyce and Antonia and Alice. And Aunt Anabel, who would not be around for much longer, granted, but who loved her. She had Hiram and his family and Flora, and Charlie and Mick and even Sir Wesley himself. She had countless people who loved her and depended upon her.

How could she ever be alone?

The duke chose that moment to step into the room with Alice on his arm. Astrid moved away from Wesley's side and tried to compose her face, though her emotions were in turmoil. When she turned back to the others, the duke was studying her questioningly, wryly. After a moment, he turned his attention to Wesley, who cleared his throat several times and avoided making eye contact with anyone.

Astrid could read nothing on the duke's impassive features but the mildest of interest in the new arrival. As if Astrid had not just thrown an obstacle of monumental proportions in his path. There was no way the duke believed her, but he was not calling her bluff.

Which was interesting.

And worrying.

Astrid had a devious mind, and knowing what she herself was capable of made her fear that others were equally cunning and unscrupulous. But while she generally held the male mind in low esteem, she was not inclined to underestimate the one belonging to her current opponent. If she was plotting against *him*, chances were good that he was also plotting against *her*.

Astrid felt rather like the fox at the hunt, which meant that the duke was definitely the pack of hounds dogging her heels. But for the life of her she couldn't think of a single prevarication to throw him off the scent at the moment. Wesley had upset her with his unexpected wisdom, just like Hiram had done earlier in the morning.

What was *wrong* with everyone? Did they *want* her to fail? Did they *want* her and her family to lose their birthright?

The silence in the room stretched until it was so taut Astrid feared Wesley was going to blurt out the truth. He was definitely beginning to squirm under the duke's steady gaze.

"So, Mr. *Honeywell*," the duke finally said abruptly, startling everyone in the room. "Why don't you tell us about your trip."

Wesley's shoulders visibly relaxed. "Ah, yes. My . . . er, trip."

"I'll send for tea," Alice said, darting from the room, as if escaping from a trap.

The duke indicated a chair for Astrid, and, after a bit of hesitation, she sat down on the edge of it, feeling distinctly nervous.

Wesley settled across from her after the duke claimed one of the high-backed, throne-like Jacobean chairs Aunt Anabel favored. He crossed his leg over his knee and propped his chin on his hand, arching a brow, as if waiting for the action to continue, a king at his leisure.

"Steam engines," Wesley finally blurted after an interminably long and awkward interval.

Astrid tried very hard not to roll her eyes. *Here we go*, she thought with grim satisfaction. Montford wouldn't know what hit him after Wesley started in on his favorite subject.

The duke's brow caved downward in puzzlement. "I beg your pardon."

"The purpose of my trip. I'm interested in steam."

"How . . . fascinating," the duke said in a tone that betrayed how very *un*-fascinating he thought it was.

Wesley leaned toward the duke confidentially. "Don't tell my moth—" Wesley blanched and gave Astrid a look of alarm. "That is, I would rather not the world know where I've been. It's rather a sensitive matter. Not very many people understand or appreciate my interest in steam."

Few people understood or appreciated Wesley's tinkerings *full stop*. He was constantly building strange contraptions and making things explode. The roof over the conservatory at the Grange had had to be replaced last year because of one of Wesley's "scientific" experiments gone awry.

"You see, I've been up north on the coast because I heard of a man who was working on an engine powered by steam. Can you imagine it, Your Grace? A horseless carriage? Faster than a team of twenty."

The duke grimaced. "I shall try very hard not to," he murmured.

Wesley apparently missed the duke's sarcasm, because he continued brightly: "Some have gone so far as to suggest fitting out ships at sea with steam engines, but I don't know if I agree on the physics of such an idea."

"Sounds outlandish," the duke agreed.

"One day the world's going to be powered by steam, mark my words," Wesley said, riding high on his soapbox. "It is why I am investing in it."

Her heart sank. "Oh no, Wes . . . I mean Anthony. Do you *really* think that wise?"

Wesley looked annoyed by her superior tone, but she didn't care. Someone had to be the voice of reason. He was always plunging what little funds he had into ridiculous schemes like this. Steam engines indeed.

"Of course," Wesley huffed.

"But have you seen an actual engine that works?" she pressed.

Wesley paused, his expression falling. "Well, no, but some have come terribly close. The problem is combustion, you see."

No, she didn't see.

Astrid sighed and sank back into her chair as Wesley began to explain in detail the inner mechanics of steam-powered locomotion. He wasn't usually quite so voluble, but the duke's presence had made him nervous and disinclined to pause for breath, lest the duke question him regarding his identity.

Thankfully, they were all saved from dying of utter boredom when a loud thunk, followed by a howl, sounded outside the window.

The duke looked pained and squeezed the bridge of his nose with his fingers. "What now, I wonder," she heard him mutter.

A moment later, Flora appeared at the door, gracing them with a very agitated bow. She avoided looking at the duke as she said, "Miss Astrid, I think you might want to come out in the yard with me."

She followed behind Flora down the corridor, through the servant's entrance, and down into the stable yard. Wesley, Alice, and the duke trailed behind.

Petunia was loose once more and in high dudgeon, squealing and running about the yard with Ant and Art trailing behind, laughing and chanting in Greek. The object of Petunia's pursuit appeared to be a stick insect covered in mud, squealing in much the same manner as the pig.

It was Coombes.

At last the beleaguered valet managed to hoist himself upon a barrel and shoo the pig with his hands.

She laughed and hazarded a look back at the duke. She was surprised to find a hint of a smile curling the corners of his lips. It quickly disappeared when he discovered her staring at him. He cleared his throat and resumed his usual stern expression. "Coombes, what is going on here?" he bellowed.

"That . . . that *beast* . . . those . . . those . . . *heathen* children . . . !" Coombes spluttered, pointing in the direction of the pig and the girls, who were disappearing around the stables into the garden. "I'll not stand for it, Your Grace. This is . . . this is beyond the pale," Coombes continued. "I demand that we return to London immediately."

The duke's jaw twitched worryingly. "*You* demand?"

Coombes paled beneath the mud staining his cheeks, his courage waning. Then he seemed to recover a bit of nerve, taking a deep breath and puffing out his chest. "I . . . I'll not remain another moment in this . . . this *pit*."

"I would hardly call Rylestone Hall a pit, sirrah," Astrid retorted.

"You're right. It's a madhouse," Coombes intoned. He stepped off the barrel, lost his balance on the way down, and slipped into the mud. He flailed about for several seconds, then finally regained his feet. His dignity now completely in shreds, he faced his employer with a furious expression. "I'm returning to London, Your Grace."

"Wonderful. The mail coach departs this afternoon in the village," Astrid replied breezily.

The duke stepped toward Coombes, who took a step backward when he saw the icy look on his employer's face. "If you leave, Coombes, I shall be most displeased," the duke warned.

Petunia chose that moment to reenter the yard. Squealing at the top of his lungs, he lunged straight for Coombes, who yelped and climbed back upon the barrel.

"I don't care," Coombes cried over his shoulder. "Nothing could make me stay another moment in this Bedlam."

"Coombes, I'll have your head if you leave me here," the duke cried, raising a fist, a hint of panic seeping through the cracks of his icy displeasure.

Coombes mumbled something that sounded distinctly like "I don't give a rat's arse," as he attempted to pull his leg out of the way of Petunia's snout.

Then the barrel toppled over, sending Coombes sprawling once more. He scrambled to his feet and began running toward the kitchens, Petunia on his heels.

The duke made as if to follow his valet, stopped at the edge of a mud slick, and cursed.

Astrid giggled behind her hand until the duke spun around and glowered at her. She broke off and tried to glower back. "Your valet is all that is sensible. You should return with him, you know. How will you ever survive without him?"

"You'd like that, wouldn't you?" he muttered. His glance moved from her and pinned Wesley in its sight. Her cousin froze like a startled deer. "You. *Mr. Honeywell.* I suggest you attempt to bring your family under control. A man who allows his females to run riot is a disgrace to his sex."

"Now see here—" Wesley began.

"I did not come here to be mowed down by pigs and bluestockings," the duke said, flashing a significant glance in Astrid's direction. "I want to see the books to this damnable pile. I want straight answers to my questions. If these blessed events occur, I shall reconsider razing this pile of stones and everyone in it."

"Now *see here*—" Wesley attempted again.

The duke growled at Wesley and stalked toward the castle without another word. Horrid, horrid man.

Wesley followed him with his eyes, then turned back to Astrid and Alice, his brow furrowed. "I say, he's rather upset, isn't he?"

"I think he was born that way," Astrid said.

"Raze Rylestone," Wesley said speculatively. "Do you think he's serious?"

"I think he's never anything *but* serious."

"Well, that will never do." He stared up at the north tower, which was looking suspiciously drunk. "Don't think the Hall could survive a razing. Mebbe you should just show him the books."

Astrid and Alice exchanged panicked glances. "Absolutely not," they said in unison.

"Look here," Wesley said petulantly, "what's wrong with you? How do you expect to keep this up? The longer this goes on, the worse things are going to get. Where are the books? And what are you two hiding?"

"Nothing. You're not trying to bring us under control, are you?" Astrid countered.

Wesley snorted. "Someone needs to." Seeing he would get nothing from Astrid, he turned on Alice. "You've always been a steady sort, Alice. A real brick. You must see it shall be impossible to fob off on Montford. Where are the books?"

Alice's face flooded with color around the moment Wesley called her a brick. Then the color intensified until her face was scarlet, and not with pleasure. She was livid.

Astrid took an involuntary step backward. She had never seen her mild-natured sister look so . . . terrifying. So very like . . . well, *herself* in a temper. But she hardly blamed Alice. If a man she loved had called *her* a brick, she'd have put her fist through his mouth.

"I don't know where the books are, *Sir Wesley*," Alice said in a too-calm voice.

Astrid wanted to cheer her sister.

Wesley studied Alice's countenance in mounting puzzlement. "Alice," he began placatingly. "Be a good girl—"

Alice snapped, stomping her boot in the earth and clenching her fists. "Don't Alice me in that condescending tone. And don't ever call me a b-b-brick again. Idiot man. Idiot, blind man! I don't know where the books are, and even if I did, I'd not tell you. You're no better than the duke, thinking you know what's best, trying to manage us. Well, I'll tell you something, Sir Wesley Benwick. We don't need managing. You and Montford will *manage* us right out of our home. Astrid's right. All men are m-morons!"

With another stomp of her foot and a toss of her chin, Alice strode back toward the castle.

Wesley stared after her, eyes wide.

"What did I do?" he murmured. "What did I say? Gads, Astrid, what's gotten into *her*?"

Astrid sighed and patted Wesley's arm. "Oh, Wesley, you really are an idiot."

⊷⊶ ⊰⊹⊱ ⊷⊶

AN HOUR later, Astrid and Alice turned over the last stack of hay in the loft above the stables to no avail.

"It's gone," Alice cried, pulling straw from her hair. Her face was still flushed from her sharp exchange with Wesley, her pale blue eyes glistening with pent-up emotion. She hadn't talked or met Astrid's eyes since the encounter, other than to mumble out the location of the estate book. Astrid had thought it best to commandeer the book in case Alice compromised its whereabouts. But it seemed she was too late, for the book was missing. They'd turned over the entire stable from top to floor without coming across it.

Alice's hands were trembling and her chin quivered, sure signs she was a breath or two away from tears. Astrid had never seen Alice so worked up. Wesley's arrival and dunderheaded behavior seemed to have pushed her into near-hysteria. But Astrid did not have time to deal with a hysterical sister. She felt near tears herself, and, as was becoming usual, angry. At the duke. At Wesley. At herself, for being so stupid as to entrust the book to scatterbrained Alice.

"How can it be gone?" Astrid cried, falling back onto the hay. "Are you quite sure you hid it here?"

Alice turned away from Astrid and busied herself with sorting through a box of old horse tack. "I'm certain."

Astrid blew the stray hair out of her eyes and rubbed her temples. "This can't end well. Devil take it, Alice, are you very certain? Because you do have a tendency to forget—"

"*Quite certain,*" Alice bit out, her voice breaking at the end. She threw down an old brush with uncharacteristic violence, and her shoulders began to shake.

Astrid stared at her sister's back, at a loss for words. Of course she knew very well what the problem was. Wesley. He had picked a most inopportune time to visit. And he couldn't see his own nose for his face when it came to Alice. Neither could Alice, it seemed.

But the last thing she needed right now was to sort out her sister's wounded feelings. She tsked impatiently. "You know, he isn't worth all of this emotional upheaval," Astrid remarked, which only made Alice's shoulders shake harder. "You said yourself he's an idiot. I don't know why you insist on being infatuated with him."

"I'm not infatuated with him," Alice sniffed. "I don't know what you're talking about."

"*Wes-ley*. You're infatuated with him and have been since you were both in nappies. Although why, I don't know. He's a widgeon."

"He's *not* a widgeon."

"He is. He's not good enough for you," Astrid retorted. She began picking out the straw from Alice's coiffure, hoping to put a short end to this conversation and get on to the business at hand. "Look at you, darling, you're the most beautiful girl in three counties. Everyone agrees. You could have your pick of eligible young men."

Alice stiffened and threw Astrid's arm away. She stalked across the hayloft and rounded on Astrid, tears soaking her face, a mix of incredulity and fury contorting her normally placid features. "Do I really have my pick, Astrid?" Alice said venomously.

Astrid crossed her arms in a defensive posture, completely caught off balance by her sister's display of temper. "Of course you do."

"How old am I?"

"What does that have to do—"

"How *old* am I?" Alice repeated impatiently.

"Twenty or so."

"*Three* and twenty."

"And?"

"And? *And?* Heaven on earth, Astrid, sometimes I think you are as dunderheaded as Aunt Anabel! Three and twenty is on the shelf."

"*I'm* twenty-six," she mumbled, a bit miffed.

"Precisely my point. Do you know any gentlewoman my age or yours who is not married?"

"There is Katrina Evans—"

"Besides Katrina Evans!" Alice bit off, clenching her fists. Katrina Evans was the daughter of a baronet in the next county, whose nose was roughly double the size of the entire British Isles and had a wart on it the size of Yorkshire. "I am three and twenty and have received not one offer of marriage. Not one."

"We aren't exactly at the center of the world. Gentlemen are low on the ground—"

"There are plenty of respectable men about. Even Miss Bourke has had at least three offers, one from a baronet."

"Miss Evans's brother, might I remind you, who inherited the family nose."

"*Not* the point," Alice said through her teeth.

Astrid held her ground. "I should hardly think you interested in anyone who has the bad judgment to court Miss Bourke. You are miles above her in every regard."

"In what way, precisely?"

Astrid was incredulous. Did she really need to explain why Miss Bourke, a first-rate bully with blonde curls, was loathsome? "She has the brain of a peahen and the character of a snake, to begin with."

"Mayhap, but she has the fortune and respectability to make her character very pleasing indeed."

Astrid gasped. "What exactly are you saying, Alice? We may not be rich, but we are ten times above the likes of Miss Bourke in breeding and station. Our mother was an earl's daughter."

"Sometimes I think you must live on another planet," Alice burst out, a fresh round of tears falling. "It doesn't matter what our mother was, and it's not as if her family even deigns to acknowledge us, aside from horrid Aunt Emily. We have only the barest of footholds above being considered *in trade*."

"And what's wrong with being in trade? The way the upper classes in this country cultivate idleness is absurd. As if honest labor is a sin."

"You see? You have all these . . . convictions, and while I'm not sure they're wrong, neither are they helpful, because all of your convictions are not going to change *how the world really is*."

Astrid stared at Alice, stunned. They were treading into deep waters now, waters Astrid had no idea Alice even knew how to navigate. Like

Hiram had done this morning, and Wesley this afternoon, Alice was bringing up a whole host of unpleasant considerations that Astrid did not want to face.

"Excuse me," Astrid said rather peevishly, "for having *opinions*. Sorry for using my *brain*."

"You miss the point, as usual," Alice sighed, looking resigned.

"What is the point?"

"Unlike you, I don't want to end up an old maid. I want to be married, to have a family of my own. To get out of this madhouse. And Mr. Coombes was right. This *is* a madhouse."

Astrid was hurt by Alice's words. Hurt and completely taken off guard. She had had no idea Alice felt this way about Rylestone. Alice was understandably angry with her for being the object of Wesley's pursuit. Though Astrid did nothing to encourage Wesley's suit, a fact that Alice knew quite well, it was only human for Alice to feel some jealousy toward her.

Yet Astrid wondered if Alice's resentment ran deeper, if somehow Astrid had failed her sister in a more fundamental way. It was one of Astrid's deepest fears. She'd been trying for the past decade to make all of her family members happy, and she thought she had been doing a decent job of it, at least where Alice was concerned. But apparently she'd been wrong.

"I had no idea you felt this way," Astrid murmured.

She reached out to her sister, but again Alice dodged her hand. "No, Astrid," Alice cried, moving toward the ladder. "I'm twenty-three years old and have had no offers, and do you want to know why? Because of you. No respectable men dare approach me because they think my sister is a . . . a hoyden. A shocking, forward, proselytizing hoyden."

"Alice!"

"What do you expect people to think of you? Running the estate? Speaking at the tenant meetings? Filling the workers' heads with Father's nonsense?"

"Adam Smith and Thomas Jefferson happen to agree with Father's nonsense," Astrid cut in. *I thought my sister did, too.*

"You show no one the slightest deference, attend church infrequently, argue with the vicar. You curse in company, converse with the farmhands, and *wear trousers.*"

"I never wear trousers in public!" she interjected. "Only around the castle. And in the garden."

Alice gave her a doubtful look. "You ride about the county *astride.*"

"Sidesaddle is dangerous."

"It is when you tear off hell-for-leather like you're riding into battle. Which you do all the time."

"I wear a perfectly respectable habit."

Alice snorted. "Which comes up past your ankles."

"What is so shocking about ankles? I'll never understand it."

"Nor I, but that is *just the way things are.* Respectable ladies don't ride astride. Respectable ladies don't bare their ankles. Respectable ladies do not run breweries."

"What would you have had me do? Let our family starve?" Astrid burst out. "Someone had to run the estate when father cracked. Someone had to take care of you and the girls. Who else was going to do it? Aunt Anabel?"

Alice blanched at Astrid's harsh tone. "You make me sound like an ungrateful wretch."

"Perhaps that is because you are! I have done everything for this family, and you chastise me for it."

"No! I am merely pointing out that your manner of doing things for this family is so very . . . *blatant.* Do you really need to wear trousers to save the estate? Really, Astrid."

"I wear trousers because they are comfortable and practical, and I ride astride because it is also eminently practical. All of these petty rules and codes restricting the behavior for ladies are designed solely to subjugate our sex."

Alice rolled her eyes. "Of course they are, but flaunting those rules is not going to earn you any friends. Or a husband."

"I don't want a husband."

"But I do! And what of Antonia and Ardyce? What's to become of them when they're grown? Your conduct reflects on all of us. It's a wonder we're still received as it is."

"I had no idea the opinions of small-minded gentry were so important to you," she huffed.

Alice groaned in frustration. "You just don't understand, Astrid. You never think beyond this pile of stones. Whether you like it or not, the opinions of other people matter. You'll discover this soon enough when we're tossed out of here."

"Don't talk like that."

"What? It's true. The duke has the right. And the way you've treated him thus far does nothing to help our cause. We'll be lucky if he doesn't put us all in the workhouse." Alice began down the ladder and paused. "You know you'd solve all of our problems if you'd just accept Wesley's proposal."

"Are you insane? Me? Marry Wesley? You are actually suggesting *I* marry Wesley?" Astrid blustered.

"Why not? He wants to save you from yourself, you know." Alice's tone was deeply bitter.

"I don't need saving. I am the one trying to save the lot of you!" Astrid cried.

"How can you do it when you won't accept the truth? Rylestone doesn't belong to us anymore."

Alice started down the ladder. When she reached the bottom, she looked back up at Astrid, who stood staring down at her sister, dumbfounded and heartsick.

"I suggest you find the book and give it to the duke," she said in the bossy sort of voice Astrid usually used.

"*You're* the one who lost it," Astrid retorted.

"It's probably for the best, since I suspect *you* would have burned it."

"When did you become so . . . so . . ."

"Practical? Reasonable?"

"Cynical."

"I've always been like this, Astrid. You were just too busy to notice."

"I never knew you hated me this much," Astrid murmured.

Alice just shook her head and walked away, as if to say that Astrid was just never going to understand.

Chapter Eight

In Which the Duke Visits the Library

ASTRID STOOD on a ladder in her father's library, thumbing through the titles on the shelves and sniffling. She blamed her watering eyes and running nose on the fine layer of dust covering the books and woodwork, not her argument with Alice earlier in the hayloft.

Her eyes pricked with tears, and she paused in her search to wipe her face inelegantly with the back of her sleeve.

She did not mean it, she tried to convince herself. Alice was just upset over Wesley, and she'd taken her anger out on her. But these assurances landed rather hollowly in her gut, for she knew deep down that Alice had meant every word.

Alice was ashamed of her, and had been for years. Somehow Astrid had failed to notice. She thought she knew her sister, but it seemed she didn't know her at all.

Was Alice right, then? Had she been so caught up in the estate she had been blind to her sister's true feelings? Had she ever really *seen* Alice at all? She *thought* she had. She had taken care of Alice and her younger sisters ever since their mother's death. Astrid had never begrudged Alice her beauty and grace. In fact, Astrid had celebrated her sister's looks, foregoing new dresses herself so that Alice could be outfitted with a wardrobe that could make her beauty stand out. Alice was the prize of the Honeywells, and in Astrid's opinion far too good for any of the young gentlemen who had come sniffing at her heels. In her heart, Astrid held out hopes of a fabulous match for Alice.

Not that she personally put any great stock in the married state. But it had been obvious to her that that was what Alice had wished for from a very young age. With that in mind, Astrid had even begun to set aside a pound here, a pound there, for Alice's dowry. It wasn't much, but at least it would be something when the time came.

But it never would, it seemed, since Astrid suspected the only man her sister wanted was never going to propose. When Alice began mooning over Sir Wesley, Astrid had hoped their cousin—unworthy though he might be of the perfect Alice—would return her sister's affections, but that had not happened. Wesley seemed perfectly oblivious to Alice's attachment, and instead seemed determined to court Astrid.

How preposterous was that?

She would never, ever, understand the workings of the male mind. She couldn't swallow the notion that Wesley found her the least bit desirable. Alice's assertion that Wesley wanted to save her from herself seemed more likely. Which was just like a man. Even an immensely stupid man like Wesley.

She didn't need saving. She didn't need rescuing, especially at the hands of her bumbling cousin.

Astrid pulled a book from the shelf at random. It wasn't the estate ledgers. It was in fact a rather boring tract of sermons that likely hadn't been opened in years, judging from the thick layer of dust coating its spine. She couldn't read the words on the page through the haze of moisture in her eyes, but she suspected there was a reason the book was on the top shelf, far corner.

Honeywells generally avoided religious tracts.

She snapped the book closed and shoved it back into the corner. Dust flew off its spine, tickling her nose.

She sneezed. Loudly.

Then she sneezed again.

Evidence that her tears were caused by the dust, *not* her emotions.

"Excuse you," came a voice behind her.

She spun around and spied the duke leaning lazily against the doorframe, his arms crossed, one leg propped up against the jamb. He studied her with his inscrutable silver eyes, one eyebrow arched in cynical appraisal.

She lost her balance and flew forward, grasping the edge of the ladder. She managed to right herself—barely—and scowled at him.

"Looking for something?" he drawled.

She sneezed again, then wiped her nose with her sleeve.

He cringed ever so slightly and pushed himself off the door. He glanced around the room at the jumble of books and papers, and a furrow wedged itself into his forehead. He turned his attention back to her, looking faintly accusing, as if to say, *How do you live in such squalor?*

She turned back to the shelf and began to pull books at random from the shelves, ignoring him. Or at least attempting to. She was aware of his every movement at her back as he prowled about the room, scanning the rows of books, lifting and sorting as he went. She was *definitely* aware of him when he reached the ladder. She looked down at the top of his head as he studied the shelf in front of him.

For an ogre, he really did have splendid hair. Thick and wavy, despite his attempts to tame it into submission, and as luxuriously colored as the burled wood shelves filling the room. She had the urge to reach down and run her fingers through those fiercely styled chestnut locks, for she suspected they would look even better freed from their pomade's stranglehold.

As if he felt her glance, he looked upward, catching her in his intense silver gaze.

She turned back to the shelf, scolding herself.

Fool, fool! Thinking about her archenemy's hair at such a time!

What was *wrong* with her?

"You're still here," she ground out, gripping the sides of the ladder until her knuckles turned white. "Was there something you wanted?"

"You," he said.

She gasped and glanced down involuntarily at him once more.

His eyes went wide, and for a moment something resembling panic floated across those silvery depths. "That is, I wanted to *speak* with you, Miss Honeywell," he went on quickly.

"Oh," she murmured. That was *not* disappointment curdling her stomach. "Well, what is it?" she continued, returning her attention back to the shelves.

"Am I to talk to you while you remain ten feet up in the air?"

"I am busy. Looking for something."

"The estate books?"

She snorted. "Of course not."

"No, that would be too much to hope for. Is it your copy of *Le Chevalier d'Amour*?"

She froze. Then she began to splutter as a furious blush rose on her cheeks. She was glad she was ten feet in the air so that he could not see. "Certainly *not*. What nonsense. Poetry? Good God, Montford. Do I *look* the sort to enjoy scandalous verse?" The lie sat very heavily on her tongue.

"Then you are at least acquainted with the title."

"Well, yes. Who is not? But to suggest that I would read such *poppycock* . . ." She had no words to complete her sentence, so she just snorted disdainfully again.

"You do not approve, then?" he asked in a deceptively lazy voice. "I would not have pegged you for a prude."

"Oh! Oh!" she exhaled, her fury rising at his nettling.

"*Someone* in your household enjoys Mr. Essex. I found a copy of *Le Chevalier* tucked between Sir Thomas More." He began to study his fingernails. "Shockingly inappropriate, wouldn't you agree? I thought for certain it must be *your* doing. But perhaps I am wrong. Perhaps Miss Alice? You must have a talk with your sister, Miss Honeywell. It is one thing to read scandalous verse, quite another to disguise it behind lofty pretension. Thomas More indeed."

She could almost hear her temper snap in violent response to his goad. "Pretension? Ha! You are one to call *me* pretentious! And I'll have you know that I have read Utopia *several* times. Thrice, to be exact. And in case you are operating under some false delusions regarding my intelligence, I can inform you I *quite* understood every word of it."

She broke off in chagrin, realizing she had just as good as admitted the Essex was hers. His eyes flashed in triumph.

"Thrice?" he replied doubtfully.

"You do not believe me?"

"I don't believe a word that passes from your lips. And I cannot imagine how it is humanly possible to read that twaddle three times without wanting to pull one's hair out."

She wanted to pull *someone's* hair out. "Twaddle? You think More is t*waddle*?"

"He's a dead bore. Tried reading it at school and fell asleep."

"Well, *you* would, wouldn't you? What need have you of broadening your mind with revolutionary ideas? I'm sure you are *quite* pleased with the status quo."

"I *am* Montford," he said, as if that explained everything. But his mouth curved at the edges mockingly as he said the words, as if he weren't so satisfied with his place in the world as he would have her believe.

She attempted to harden her heart against him, but it just simply wouldn't turn entirely to stone. A small, stubborn pocket of pity and something else she didn't want to examine too closely remained pulsing in the center of the brick in her chest. Why he inspired this conflict of emotions inside of her she would never understand. He was a beast. With nice hair, granted. But a beast nonetheless.

Exasperated with herself and with him, she muttered a few well-needed curses as she descended the ladder.

"Miss Honeywell?" His voice sounded dangerously close to her person.

She froze near the bottom and looked through the slats of the ladder. Montford stood on the other side, at eye level with her now, only inches separating their faces. His omnipotent eyes scanned her face, and the furrow in his brow deepened. "You've been crying."

She blew the hair out of her face. "Absolutely not. The dust in here has made my eyes water."

"You *are* covered in dust," he agreed. Before she could react, one of his index fingers touched her cheek and trailed its way down her face to her jaw, his eyes following its movements.

His touch affected her like an electrical storm. And she couldn't move. She knew she should finish climbing down the ladder and get as far from the duke as possible, but she couldn't make her legs work, and her hands seemed determined to grip the ladder, as if afraid of doing anything to make the duke's finger cease its movement across her face.

"You're filthy, Miss Honeywell," he said in a soft voice that belied the accusation of his words. His eyes darkened. "You're *freckled*."

He was insulting her, which would never do, but she could not seem to find her voice.

His finger arrived at her chin and stopped.

She forgot how to breathe.

Then he began to lean toward her, and she began to lean toward him, feeling precisely the way she felt after one too many sips of Honeywell Ale. And she realized somewhere in the midst of all of their mutual leaning that he was going to kiss her. Or *she* was going to kiss *him*.

Hell and damnation. They were going to *kiss each other*.

Heat flashed through her veins and pooled low in her belly, shocking her. She had never been kissed. Opportunities had presented themselves in the past, and she had adroitly avoided every one of them. None of the men who had tried to kiss her had ever made *her* want to kiss them. She'd never felt the slightest stirrings of passion. Perhaps mild curiosity, but nothing to make her actually want to satisfy that curiosity. But now, staring at Montford's lips—full, rather sensuous lips when they weren't pinched with their usual disapproval—she felt positively ravenous.

She licked her lips nervously, and something ticked in his jaw, his own mouth parting in surprise, as if she had dealt him a blow.

Gads, she wanted this. She wanted *him* in that moment more than she had ever wanted anything. His lips on hers. Her hands in that marvelous hair. More than just his finger touching her jaw.

How was this possible? she wondered. This was Montford, the villain she had loathed for years, her greatest adversary. Why, then, did he have to be so handsome? He didn't *look* like a villain at all at the moment, what with those parted lips and those intense gray eyes.

Her innards practically quivered in anticipation.

Then her left foot chose to slip from its perch, and her ribs hit the slat in the ladder, knocking her back to her senses.

She jerked from him, anticipation replaced by blind panic. "What are you *doing*?" she hissed.

"What am I . . . ? What are *you* doing?" he retorted, jumping away from her and hitting the shelf behind him. His shoulder dislodged a book, and it tumbled down his body, its heavy spine thudding against his toes. He grunted in pain and hobbled out from under the ladder.

She finished descending and backed across the room, not taking her eyes from him, her heart thudding wildly.

He growled in annoyance and bent down to retrieve the fallen tome. He scanned its spine, then turned to put it back on the shelf. His brow furrowed in vexation as he did so. "Your shelves are completely out of order," he clipped out, tapping the spines of the books in front of him with enough force to bend them. "Donne next to Swift next to . . ." He let out a pained sigh. "*Anonymous*. Really, it is insupportable. How can you find anything in this chaos?"

He pulled out one book, and then another and another, and Astrid realized he intended to try to order the shelves.

She rushed forward, their near-kiss on the ladder a distant memory in the face of his latest outrage, and tugged one of the books from his hand.

"There is an order," she protested, stuffing the book back on the shelf.

"D next to S. I don't see how."

"They're both British."

"They're from different centuries."

"They're both poets."

"Gulliver's Travels is not poetry," he ground out between clenched teeth. He waved one of the books in front of her face. "And this one is anonymous." He turned the front cover to the title page and squinted down with disgust. "And a novel. *Pride and Prejudice: By the Author of Sense and Sensibility*. A *ladies'* novel. No doubt written by a woman."

"What's that supposed to mean?"

He held up the book between the tips of his fingers as if it were soiled. "There is only one thing worse than an anonymous novel writer. An anonymous *female* novel writer."

She snatched the book from his hand and barely resisted the urge to cosh him with it. "You are a cretin."

He clenched his hands at his sides and watched her reshelve the book with something resembling pain in his eyes.

"You really can't bear it, can you?" she asked, turning back to him, crossing her arms over her chest.

"Hmm?" he mumbled, staring bleakly at the shelves.

"The disorder. The chaos. Donne next to Swift. It is really upsetting your delicate sensibilities."

"*You* are upsetting my delicate sensi . . . Oh, devil take it, what am I saying?" He swung away from her. He raised his hand to rake his fingers through his hair, then checked himself, muttered an oath, and let his arm drop to his side. He flexed his fingers against his hip as if attempting to contain himself. "Miss Honeywell."

"You keep saying my name, but never get around to stating your business."

"You keep distracting me."

"Oh, good. Exactly part of my master plan."

He swung around to her, suspicion crowding his features. "Is it?"

She laughed. "You think I have a master plan?"

"Don't you? Some devious scheme laid out that ends with me roasting on a spit?"

"You give me much credit."

"Do you not think you deserve it, since you profess to be so clever?"

"I have never professed—"

"'In case you are operating under some false delusions regarding my intelligence,'" he said, pitching his voice to imitate hers, but making it sound quite pedantic and smug—she did not sound like *that*, did she?—"'I can inform you I have read Utopia *thrice* . . .'"

She ended his little recitation by picking up a book and hurling it at his chest.

It hit him squarely in the cravat and dropped to his toes.

He broke off and glared at her incredulously. "If I were not a gentleman, Miss Honeywell, I'd take you over my knees and thrash you."

"I believe you are fond of making such threats. I heard the same one only this morning as you stared at my breasts."

"I did no such—"

"*Please.* It would be ungentlemanly of you to become a liar as well as an ogler."

"An *ogler.*" His hands clenched his cravat, ruining the folds entirely, and his face began to grow increasingly red. "That's not even a word."

"It should be."

"I think I *am* going to strangle you."

"I'd like to see you try."

He stepped forward as if intent on just that, and she backed away, suddenly realizing that he was quite serious and quite capable of following through with his threat. She had pushed him too far.

But then his boot caught on the rather large book she had thrown at him, and he tripped, landing on his hands and knees with a grunt of pain. She caught her breath, and when she was sure he was not terribly injured, judging from the flurry of oaths that flew from his mouth, she began to laugh.

He sat back on his haunches, startled and furious. He sent her a scathing look and pushed his fallen hair out of his eyes.

Her laughter trailed off. Just as she suspected, his hair did look much better when disheveled. So much better that the annoying ache began pounding away in her stomach once again.

He raised his fist in her direction. "You'll not laugh at me when I get my hands on you, you little—" He broke off and reached under his backside, pulling out the book she had thrown at him earlier. He studied the cover, began to toss it aside to continue his rant, then paused and brought it back up to his eyes.

"Oh, hell and the devil," she muttered, her veins filling with ice. The estate ledgers! Of all the books in the entire castle, she had to go and throw the one she least wanted him to find right into his clutches.

Well, at his chest.

But still, it was in his clutches now, and he was thumbing through the contents with a smug look dawning across his face.

He held the book up over his head and waved it tauntingly. A victorious grin animated his lips, revealing a set of absurdly white, wolfish teeth. "What have we here, Miss Honeywell?"

She groaned, her heart seizing in her chest. She could not let him see the accounts. She should have burned the book yesterday. What had she been thinking, entrusting it to Alice? If he discovered her creative bookkeeping, he was going to thrash her for sure. Or throw her in Newgate.

Hell. Bloody triple hell! What was she to do now?

There was only one solution that presented itself.

Without hesitation, she launched herself forward, trying to grab the book from his hand. His eyes widened at her onslaught, and he jerked the book backward, attempting to rise to his feet before she could reach him.

He managed to get to his knees when she grabbed for the book again, her legs knocking against his shoulder. He muttered a curse into her skirts as she tumbled over his head, knocking them both flat against the carpet. The book flew from his hands, skidding across the floor, and she began to crawl toward it, digging her right knee into some part of his anatomy—hopefully his brainbox—that caused him to bellow a four-letter oath so inelegantly foul—beginning with f, ending with k—even *she* didn't use it. She was straining out her hand to retrieve the book when she felt something hard clamp around her ankle and pull her back. Her arms failed beneath her, sending her stomach smashing against the floor, taking the very breath from her lungs.

She glanced behind her and saw the duke holding her foot and attempting to crawl around her. She kicked out with her other foot, landing her boot heel squarely against his shoulder.

He gasped in pain and released her. She started forward once more, but so did he. They both grasped the book at the same time, she tugging one way, he the other. He had an unfair advantage, being several stone heavier than she was and padded with muscle, so she felt rather like a sparrow attempting to pull a worm from the beak of an eagle. She had no choice but to level the odds and bring her knee back into the equation. It shot out, catching him in the ribs, and he fell back with a groan. Refusing to relinquish the book, she fell on top of him.

Her forehead knocked against his chin so violently that she saw stars behind her eyes. She gasped in pain, and so did he.

"Umph!"

"Ouch!"

She shifted her weight on top of him, and he gasped again, his grip on the book loosening just enough so that she snatched it free of him and rolled to one side, clutching it with both hands, her chest heaving with exertion.

He sat up next to her, panting, his hair at sixes and sevens, his cravat dangling loosely from his shirtfront, his jacket torn open and missing several buttons. If looks could kill, she'd be a pillar of salt. "You devil's spawn!" he breathed. "Do you really think you are going to win?"

She hugged the book against her chest tightly and jutted her chin defiantly.

"I could crush you, you know," he intoned.

"Haven't done a very good job so far," she sniffed.

His jaw dropped incredulously, and he made a move as if to attack her.

Astrid reacted on instinct. Nothing about their struggle had been in the least dignified, but she held out hope that at least some bounds of propriety could not be crossed even at this late juncture—though there was nothing proper in what she was about to do. But desperate times called for desperate measures, and she'd never been so desperate as this. Montford was sure to send her to gaol if he saw what she'd done.

She sat up quickly, lifted her skirts, and shoved the book into her drawers.

The duke froze.

He stared at her as if he'd been hit by a load of bricks. Or every book in the library. At once.

At length, he seemed to find his voice. "You didn't just . . ." It wavered on the last word.

She laid her hands over her lap protectively. "Oh, I did." She arched her brow challengingly because she couldn't help herself.

His jaw snapped shut, his lips thinned to a hard line, and his eyes narrowed.

Her heart jumped in terror at the clear look of intent written on his cold features.

He moved forward.

She promptly moved backward. A bookshelf stopped her progress abruptly. She clutched her stomach protectively, her pulse now racing furiously. "You wouldn't . . ."

He arched one of his perfect brows in fair imitation of her. "Wouldn't I?" he practically growled, prowling toward her on all fours like some predatory beast stalking its prey.

She kicked out her leg, but he caught her ankle in a hard grip and continued forward. He didn't stop until he was straddling her and pinning in the sides of her head with both of his arms. His face hovered inches from her own. He was breathing as heavily as she was, his face flushed.

She hadn't until this moment realized how massive he was. He seemed to fill all the space around her and all of her senses with his imposing presence. His scent—clean male, sandalwood—invaded her nostrils, and his heat crept into her bones. And though no part of her touched him, other than the sides of her legs entrapped by his knees, she could feel his strength. He was no featherweight beneath his fashionable wardrobe. No fake padding filled out *his* figure.

She had the absurd desire to reach up to those broad shoulders and run her hands over his jacket, feel the ridges of the body beneath. She knew he would be hard and chiseled and . . .

She let out a hysterical laugh. He was practically holding her hostage, and she was thinking about his *shoulders*.

Better, she thought grimly, than to think about what he intended to do, which she still couldn't quite believe. The idea of him reaching up her skirts made her body twinge, her pulse race, and her skin break out into a cold sweat of pure . . .

Anticipation?

That blow to the forehead must have disordered her mind.

"You cannot be serious," she breathed. "You will not . . . do what I think you are going to do . . ."

He expelled a laugh every bit as hysterical as hers had been. A fine sheen of sweat covered his forehead, and his eyes went opaque. "If you didn't want me to reach up your skirts, Miss Honeywell, you should not have put the book there."

"You are a gentleman, sirrah, and I am a lady."

He barked out another laugh. "When in the last two days have you behaved like a lady, Miss Honeywell? Chasing a pig in trousers? Cursing like a Seven Dials pickpocket? Brawling with me like some common . . . common . . ." He trailed off in his harangue, astonishment and annoyance replacing his ire. "Miss Honeywell, don't you dare cry."

"I'm not crying," she sniffled, tears streaming down the sides of her face. She turned her head away from him and squeezed her eyes together. His words hit very close to Alice's own earlier imprecations. She hated herself for dissolving into tears, but she could not help it. She was a lady, she *was*!

No, she wasn't. Alice was quite right. And so was Montford. She was a cursing, brawling, common strumpet. And she couldn't help it. It was the way she was, the way she had to be to keep this family together. If she didn't fight for the Honeywells, who else would? Aunt Anabel?

"You're crying, which is entirely unfair," he growled.

"Go ahead, take the bloody book," she said, going limp underneath him.

"Oh no, you're going to give it to me."

"Never. Take the book. Just like you'll take everything else."

He sighed and rested his forehead on her fallen hair. The scent or touch of it seemed to rouse him to his senses, because he immediately jerked his head back up. "I didn't think you a female who would use tears and guilt to have her way."

"Have my way? Do you think I want you to reach up my skirts and—" She broke off, her face flooding with heat, her tears drying abruptly. He stared down at her in that slack-jawed way he had developed since beginning their wrestling match, and if she wasn't mistaken, a faint hint of color rose over the bridge of his nose.

"No, of course, that's not what I meant. You think you can get away with this act of yours, play upon my sympathies," he murmured.

"I'm well aware that you possess none of those."

He groaned in frustration. "What is so damned vital about that book that you would shove it down your drawers?"

"Just get it over with," she challenged. "I dare you."

"You dare me, do you? You little terror. I should. I should just do it," he said, his words more certain than the querulous, bemused tone he'd used to say them. His chest heaved with exertion as he hovered over her, clearly torn.

Awareness flooded her once more. He was so close, so warm, so pleasant-smelling, she could drown in him and be lost forever.

She tossed her head, trying to shake out her mutinous thoughts, and squirmed beneath him. This was a mistake, for he caught her by the wrists and pinned her hands above her head with effortless ease. He held her in place with one hand and lowered his other.

"You aren't . . ."

"You leave me no choice, Miss Honeywell," he said in a strangled voice.

His hand touched an ankle, gripped the edge of her skirts. She squeezed her eyes shut. This couldn't be happening.

"Montford," she warned, trying to recover her senses. "Montford . . . Oh!"

His fingers skimmed past her stocking, which had fallen down around her boot, then up her leg. She felt his fingers touch the hem of her pantaloons gathered at her knee, and they just stopped there, hovering.

She dared to crack one eye open. Why had he stopped? What was he doing?

His head was bent into his chest, and his eyes were closed tighter than hers. He seemed to be in some sort of physical pain, judging from the anguished expression on his face.

Neither of them breathed for several seconds

Then his hand began to move, gliding past her knee, his fingers trailing paths of exquisite fire up her thighs. His touch was slow, languorous, caressing. Scorching. Her breath hitched in her throat. Good heavens, she was on fire.

She must have made some sort of noise, for his eyes flew open. He stared down at her with eyes that smoldered as much as his fingers. Agony gripped his features, and something else that made her heart thud against her breastbone, half in fear, half in triumph.

He desired her.

And God help her, she desired him.

Somehow, his other hand slipped down her body and up her other leg. She felt two sets of fingers running up her thighs, drifting over her hips, caressing and squeezing her flesh with a greedy impatience that left her breathless.

His body lowered onto hers, the hard, heavy length of him pinning her to the floor. His hands roamed up and down her legs, and a groan escaped from the back of his throat, reverberating through her entire body.

She raised a hand to his face without realizing what she was doing, felt the smooth-shaven flesh of his cheek, the tangle of hair falling over his temple. It was as soft as silk. "Montford," she whispered.

He rested his forehead against her own, his lips a mere hair's breadth from her own. His breath was hot and frantic against her skin. "Why are you not screaming?" he whispered. "Do you have no sense? Do you think I'll stop?"

She hadn't considered such weighty questions. She hadn't considered anything at all since around the time his hand had touched her leg.

"You impudent little baggage. Shoving a book up your skirts . . ." He made a strangled sound. "As if that would *deter* me! You have no idea what I want to do to you right now."

He ground his hips into her own, and there was no mistaking the hard ridge of his desire jutting into her tender flesh despite the layers of fabric between them. She knew enough of the barnyard to know what *that* meant. But she had not known it would feel so stunningly wonderful.

She moaned and shut her eyes.

He bit out a curse. The movement of his hands abruptly stopped, and he sat back, leaving her feeling oddly bereft on several counts. For one, her mutinous body had not wanted him to leave. For another, he now held the book in his hands.

She didn't know which made her angrier.

He clutched the book to his chest like she had done earlier and sat back with a thud on his behind. He looked as if he had been through a mill, cravat askew, hair flying every which way, jacket and breeches crumpled beyond compare. His chest heaved and his face was flushed. His eyes surveyed her as he would survey some rare species of poisoned flora. He swallowed several times without speaking.

Then he seemed to come out of his trance. He looked down at his book, looked up at her, looked down, then up again, and that smug grin she was really coming to hate broke across his lips.

Astrid, who had been too stunned to do anything other than lie there, her skirts lifted nearly to her knees, her head too dizzy to hold up after his furtive caresses and hungry words, was knocked back to her senses when she saw that gloating smile on his lips.

She bolted upright, humiliation and shame flooding her in one giant wave. He had clearly tried to seduce her in order to win back the book. And it had worked. So well she had forgotten about the book somewhere in the middle of all the touching and panting.

What a prize idiot she was! To have believed he wanted her! To have let him touch her! Despite what anyone accused her of, she was not some common tart, to be groped and pawed by this overbred oaf. Why, she hadn't even been kissed in her life.

He hadn't even kissed her during the proceedings of the last quarter hour.

Not that she had wanted him to.

Oh, whom was she fooling? Of *course* she had wanted him to. Which was precisely the problem. She had wanted him to kiss her since that business on the ladder. And she had definitely wanted him to do more than kiss her when he had her pinned beneath him. Which he had done. He had molested her. Thoroughly.

How dare he!

"How dare you!" she cried, launching herself at him.

She managed to get a handful of his hair in her fist and yank it, and he managed to do the same to her hair, still holding on to the book.

"Ouch, you beast!"

"You minx!"

"Ogler!"

"Strumpet!"

They were in the midst of a hair-pulling contest, when a voice in the doorway caught their attention.

"Your Grace!"

They froze and turned toward the door. It was Montford's driver, the burly Liverpudlian, and behind him hovered a very pale-looking Roddy. Both of their eyes were as wide as the doorway.

She and the duke simultaneously jumped to their feet, released each other's hair, and then moved as far away from each other as the room allowed. Montford tugged on his jacket and smoothed back his disordered coiffure, squaring his shoulders.

As if *that* would recover his lost dignity.

He cleared his throat. "What is it, Newcomb?"

"Er . . . We can come back later if you're . . . engaged," the man said, deadpan, but with mischief twinkling deep in his eyes.

"I was . . . just concluding my . . . business with Miss Honeywell," Montford answered, tucking the book into his lapel.

She snorted and tossed back her hair.

Newcomb's eyes turned in her direction speculatively, then back at his master. He shrugged, as he had the day before, as if the matter were none of his concern.

"Miss Honeywell!" Roddy cried as she stalked toward the door. "Are you—"

"Quite all right, thank you very much, Roddy," she rushed to say. "The duke was so gracious as to pull a large—"

"Insect!" the duke cut in, looking panicked by whatever it was she had been about to say. "Out of her hair. There was an insect in her hair. A poisonous one. With fangs."

Roddy and Newcomb narrowed their eyes simultaneously but said nothing to contradict the duke's utter nonsense.

"You heard him. A poisonous insect with . . . fangs. I believe it is a new species. Too bad he coshed it with his boot." She shot him a seething glance.

He glared back. "Yes. Too bad."

She twitched her skirts into place and started from the room.

"Miss Honeywell," the duke called.

She looked over her shoulder.

He patted his jacket, where the book jutted haphazardly from an inner pocket. "We'll continue our discussion later."

"Discussion? Is that what we are calling it? Very well, until *later*. I look forward to it," she growled.

"Do you indeed, Miss Honeywell?"

The other occupants of the room swung their heads in unison between the two of them, as if following a tennis ball lobbed across the court.

"I do. Indeed."

"Indeed."

"*Indeed*," she ground out, and stalked from the room before he could have the last word.

Chapter Nine

In Which Yet Another Calamity Strikes Rylestone Hall

"DEVIL TAKE it, I shall refuse to go if you insist upon this indecency," Sir Wesley hissed, grabbing the saddle and jerking it off Astrid's mare. He staggered under the weight of it and handed it off to a stable boy, then ordered the sidesaddle mounted in its place.

Astrid clutched her riding crop until her knuckles were white and thought about swatting Wesley's backside with it. "Don't think you're going without me," she ground out.

Wesley was incredulous. "Gads, Astrid, do you think I *want* to be alone with him? Sinister look in his eye, that one. No, you're coming with me. But I'll be demmed if you ride astride."

"You're terribly tiresome when you're being an old stick," Astrid muttered.

Wesley looked mightily offended. "I'm being sensible. Not only of your reputation, but your family's. Montford already thinks very ill of you, I reckon. No need to tear about the countryside astride as if you were . . ."

"Boadicea?"

Wesley nodded, scratched his scalp. "Yes, rather. Or was it Lady Godiva?"

"Both used their mounts in a shocking manner. I rather think I am in good company."

"If you were a Hun," Wesley retorted.

Astrid heaved an exaggerated sigh as Princess Buttercup was fitted with the dreaded sidesaddle. "Fine. You win. But if I fall and break my neck, it is on your head, Wesley Benwick," she warned, poking him in the ribs with her crop.

Wesley looked satisfied with her acquiescence and stepped out of range of her whip to greet the duke, who strode into the stables, tugging on his riding gloves impatiently. His top boots gleamed in the sun, his hat uncreased and spotless. He wore a coat of bottle-green wool, cut to emphasize every hard plane of his shoulders and arms, and a pair of dun-colored breeches that fit his long, powerful legs like a second skin. The only evidence of his valet's defection was a certain air of neglect about the folds of his cravat. Astrid took satisfaction in this imperfection and could only wish the rest of his rigidly regimented toilette suffered the same fate as it had the two days previous.

The duke stopped when he noticed her standing next to Wesley, and a muscle worked in his jaw. A sign he found her company as unwelcome as she did his. But he didn't seem surprised to see her there, even though he had not invited her to join him and Wesley on their tour of the estate this morning. There was no chance Astrid was going to allow Wesley to go unaccompanied on such an expedition, as she could imagine all sorts of blunders her cousin would fall into if left alone with Montford.

It was clearly Montford's intention to see that this happened. Or at least to goad her past all measure. She knew *he* knew perfectly well that Wesley hadn't the first clue about the estate. When he had asked

Wesley—or "Anthony Honeywell"—to ride out with him to reconnoiter Rylestone, he'd done so at breakfast in her presence, never taking his intense gaze off of her. Wesley had spluttered, hedged, then finally assented to the trip because he could do no less. Astrid had shoved her eggs about her plate and refused to meet the duke's daring glance. It was the first time she'd seen him since the Incident In The Library of the day before, and every time she so much as glimpsed him out of the corner of her eye, she remembered his hands upon her and the heat and smell and strength of him, and she wanted to die of mortification.

Horrid man—he may have been a duke, but he was no gentleman despite his fine clothes.

She recognized his command to be shown the estate for what it was: a gauntlet thrown down at her feet. Instead of exposing Wesley for a fraud, the duke seemed determined to play some sort of game with them all. She was not going to let him win, even if she had no bloody clue what the game was anymore. He had the book now. He must've seen how she had cheated him, so there was no need to drag things out with a tour. He was bent on torturing everyone. Even, it seemed, himself, by remaining a further day at Rylestone. Whatever he was planning to do to them, she wished he would just get on with it.

And some absurd part of her wished she could convince him that her management of the estate had not been folly. She wished to make him understand and—dare she hope—appreciate her methods. Rylestone Green was prosperous, its people fat and satisfied, and it was because of her reforms.

He would be a fool to interfere, in her humble opinion.

"Miss Honeywell. What a surprise to see you here," the duke murmured, sounding not a whit surprised. "Riding into town?"

"Stuff," she sniffed. "You know very well I am accompanying you."

He arched a brow. "Are you indeed?"

"Indeed." She winced, recollecting similar words spoken last afternoon.

The duke scanned her from top to toe in an impertinent manner, then dismissed her from notice as Mick presented him with his mount, Cyril, Astrid's roan gelding and the prize of the Honeywell stables. Astrid had felt very peculiar about allowing the duke to ride her baby, but she couldn't very well put him on Twinkle, the old piebald dray who pulled their cart, even though she would have loved to do just that.

The duke scanned the horse in much the same way he had scanned her. She gritted her teeth as he stroked the roan's nose with his long gloved fingers.

"Fine bit of horseflesh, what?" Wesley babbled nervously.

The duke nodded noncommittally. "I expect he'll do."

"Name's Cyril," Wesley continued.

The duke abruptly stepped away from the horse. "I beg your pardon?"

"His name is Cyril."

The duke looked pained and muttered something under his breath. Apparently, he did not approve.

Could nothing please this man?

"What's wrong with Cyril?" Astrid demanded, striding forward and petting the roan's head soothingly, as if to assuage his hurt feelings.

"I beg your pardon?" he repeated.

"It's a fine name."

He blinked at her several times. "You *like* the name, Miss Honeywell?" he asked as if he couldn't quite believe his ears.

"Of course I do. I named him myself." She shot him a glare over Cyril's head. "I shouldn't have told you that, for now you are sure to loathe it."

"No, I . . ." The duke faltered and searched her face earnestly. "I've never encountered someone who actually *liked* the name Cyril."

"Well, I do. I happen to like it very much," she said.

"*I'm* not terribly fond of it," Wesley chimed in. "One of them names like Nigel or Reginald that makes you wonder what their parents were thinking."

Astrid glared at her cousin's attempt to defect to the duke's side. The duke, surprisingly, glared at Wesley as well.

"Piffle," she declared. "Cyril's the name of kings and saints. In Greek, it's the word for lord and master. It's a good, strong name. Like Cyril here. Doubtless you have thirty-seven stables full of *fine* horses, Your Grace, but that doesn't mean Cyril isn't as good as any of them."

She caught the duke's glance as she finished her lecture and was completely knocked off balance by what she found. The tense, austere planes of his face had softened, his mouth had gone slack, and his eyes glowed bright with bemusement and something that looked very much like longing.

Her body responded to his expression, a wash of heat spreading from her core into her extremities. She felt her face flame.

As if roused from a daydream, the duke's brow furrowed with suspicion. "You're not grousing me, are you?"

His words were as effective as a dousing of cold water. She stiffened and scowled at him. "Grousing about what?"

"The name. Cyril."

"Why ever would I?" She didn't wait for a response. She turned and stalked toward Princess Buttercup. "Are we going out, or are we to stay here all day discussing word etymologies?"

She scrambled onto the mounting block and plopped down upon her seat. Buttercup started forward nervously, and she nearly slid off the opposite side, unused to the precarious slope of the saddle.

She heard a smothered laugh and turned to Wesley to give him an earful. But Wesley was leading his black gelding into the stable yard. She swung her attention toward the duke and found that he was the one responsible for the laugh.

He was actually *smirking* at her.

"Like to see *you* try to ride sidesaddle," she muttered, prodding Buttercup forward.

The duke mounted Cyril effortlessly and soon caught up to her outside. "All ladies of quality ride sidesaddle as if born to it," he said, leaning toward her confidentially.

"You are doubtless insulting me, but I don't care," she said, squirming on her seat.

"You don't? Whyever not?" He sounded mildly curious and entirely pompous, and just looking at him made her want to smack him across the cheek with her whip.

"Because I take satisfaction in knowing I could outrace you any day," she asserted.

"What makes you so sure of that?" Now he sounded amused, which made her even angrier.

"Call it intuition," she bit out.

"I think it more a case of hubris. You couldn't match me."

"Is that what you think?"

"It is a fact, madam."

She snorted. "A fact, is it? How interesting. So you would say unequivocally that you could precede me from here to the brewery."

He considered the stretch of lane before them. "Quarter mile up the lane, good road, decent cattle, yes. I daresay I could."

"Care to wager on it?"

His eyes swung from the lane to her face, startled by her question. "I beg your pardon?"

She pointed her crop at his face. "You say that a lot, you know. You heard what I said. Care to make a wager?"

Wesley, who had thus far remained silent, trailing behind Astrid to attract as little notice as possible, spurred his mount to come abreast of them. He looked nervously from one to the other. "Now, Astrid," he began, sounding condescending and fearful at once, "surely you're jesting . . ."

"I am not. I wager I can outrace His Grace."

Wesley turned to the duke pleadingly. "Your Grace, you understand, of course, that she's not serious."

The duke gifted Wesley with his driest look. "Ah, Mr. Honeywell, but she is."

"I am," she seconded, reining in her horse and fixing a challenging eye on the duke.

Montford stopped Cyril and turned to her, forcing Wesley to do the same. He studied her with an intensity that made her want to squirm.

Now that the challenge was issued, she wished she could take it back. He had goaded her into it, and though she was confident of her ability to beat him astride, she *was* on a damned sidesaddle. And the way he handled Cyril gave her pause. The normally high-spirited gelding followed the duke's direction with uncommon meekness. Montford was clearly a strong rider.

He must have seen some chink in her bravado, for his mouth curled up into a half smile. "What are your terms?" he asked.

Wesley guffawed loudly. "Your Grace! Astrid! You cannot be serious."

"Oh, I am," Astrid ground out, her heart sinking in her chest.

"So am I. Quite serious. Terms, madam."

"We shall race from that stand of beech trees over there to the brewery. Wes—*Anthony* shall ride down first and mark off the finish. He shall judge the winner."

"I shall?"

"You shall. Go on, *Brother*. We'll give you five minutes."

Wesley looked from her to the duke and back again with growing incredulity. "Astrid. Be reasonable!"

She groaned. "I hate it when you use that tone with me."

"I suggest you do as she says," the duke drawled. "She is determined to be bested by me."

"*Astrid!*"

Astrid reached forward and swatted her crop at Wesley. He just managed to avoid being thwacked. After one last-ditch effort at changing her mind, he took off down the lane, throwing anxious looks over his shoulder as he went.

Astrid bit her bottom lip and watched her cousin go reluctantly to his task.

She was an idiot. An impulsive, reckless idiot, who had once more, in the space of ten minutes in his company, allowed the duke to prod her into some foolish endeavor. She had vowed to try to be more demure after Alice's set-down, but that had not lasted above a half hour. She'd allowed a peer of the realm reach up her skirts after all.

"Shall I give you a handicap, madam?" the duke drawled when they were alone.

She needed more than a handicap. She needed a miracle. She'd be lucky to keep her seat for the duration of the race. But she snorted derisively at his offer. She'd rather eat glass than let him see how tentative she was. "*You'll* need the handicap, Montford," she said with utmost pomposity.

Montford looked amused in that remote, patronizing way of his that made her gnash her teeth. She'd rather he lost his temper, as he had done yesterday. She wanted to bait him, not amuse him.

"We haven't discussed the wager," he continued, studying the course, allowing Cyril to dance forward a little. "Perhaps we should make it . . . interesting."

She didn't like the sound of that, but she seized upon the idea as she might have done to the hull of a sinking ship. "Yes. How right you are. When I win—"

"*When* you win?" he snorted.

"*When* I win, you return to London and leave me to manage Rylestone as I see fit."

He shot her an exasperated look. "You are like a dog with a bone, Miss Honeywell."

"I shall take that as a compliment."

"Don't know why you should, as it wasn't," he muttered.

"So do you accept my wager?"

He sighed and turned his attention back down the lane. "Do you think that's what is best, Miss Honeywell? For me to leave here and for things to continue as they were?"

She was taken aback by his sudden gravity. "We were managing quite well before you came."

"Were you indeed?" he murmured in a doubtful tone.

Astrid bristled. "This is hardly the time or place for such a monumental discussion. However, now that you brought it up, I'd have to say that yes, Rylestone Green is flourishing. I admit the management is a tad . . ."

"Irregular?" he suggested drily. "Unlawful?"

She would *not* pick a fight with him. "Irregular. But the system works."

"For everyone, it seems, but you. And me, but I suppose I, the property owner, am irrelevant in your utopian vision."

"I have no idea what you're talking about."

He twisted in his saddle and gestured with his crop back toward the castle. "The towers, madam. They're crooked!" he cried, as if that explained everything. "You haven't the funds to fix them because you insist on pouring them back into the estate and giving the tenants outrageous salaries. I have deciphered the books, madam, and am onto you. The castle is rotting, and you can't support a proper staff. God knows how you have managed to keep these mounts. I suspect your field hands live better than you do."

"We muddle through just fine, thank you," she said, sticking her nose in the air.

"Muddle through. Bloody Jacobin nonsense is what it is. And look how well that turned out for the French."

"This is not France, sir."

He just rolled his eyes and fastened that intense gaze on her once more.

"What of your family? Do they agree that you were muddling through just fine?"

If he had a cudgel in his hands and applied it to her gut, he couldn't have landed a more direct hit. "My family is none of your business," she bit out.

"Maybe not. But it is clear *they* are far from happy."

"Happy! What right have you to speak of my family's happiness?" she exploded. "What would you *know* of happiness, anyway? You wouldn't know what happiness was if it hit you on the head and called you by name."

His expression hardened a little more with every word she spoke. Then when she was done, he was silent a long time, staring away from her into the distance, his eyes remote and cold. "You are doubtless right," he said at last in a brittle tone that made something dislodge in her heart and stick in her throat.

Was that guilt she felt? "Oh, for the love of . . ." she groaned. "Are we going to race or not?"

He looked at her then, and the stiff set of his jaw eased a little. "I haven't changed *my* mind."

"So you accept my wager?"

His eyes narrowed suspiciously. "I can't believe I am agreeing to this nonsense. But yes, I accept your wager, since I am going to win anyway."

"Oh, are you now?"

"Of course. And since your stake is quite high, I suppose mine shall have to match it. What shall it be, I wonder?"

Astrid had not thought this far into her scheme, and her palms immediately began to sweat. Oh, hell! What deviltry was he going to ask for? She shouldn't have made the wager at all.

Stupid, stupid girl!

He could win and make her give up everything.

Which he was doubtless going to do anyway.

But still.

Still . . .

Who was she fooling? Not the duke. Certainly not herself, not any longer.

Astrid had not felt so hopeless as she did in that moment, and she had no one to blame for it but herself. She had talked herself into this untenable position, dug her own grave. Now there was nothing for it but to lie down in it and watch Montford shovel dirt over her.

She tilted her chin upward at a defiant angle and clutched her reins, preparing for the worst.

"I think when I win, I should like to have Cyril as a prize," he said.

She gaped at him, totally thrown by his wager. "You want my horse?"

"I do."

It could have been a whole lot worse. She told herself this, but somehow it didn't make it easier to stomach. She loved Cyril as much as Princess Buttercup. She'd been present at both of their foalings and had helped train them. She almost wished he had wanted something to do with the estate. At least then she'd have a clear idea of what to expect from him.

But her horse! "Why would you want him?"

"It should amuse me to have him. And I think it would make you very angry to know that I did. And that, madam, should make me *quite happy.*"

She continued to gape. "You are truly awful, Montford."

He smiled cynically. "You bring out the worst in me, Miss Honeywell. Shall we get this over with?"

"By all means!"

They brought up their mounts to the line of beech trees. He allowed her to count down, which she did, with growing anticipation and dread. Perhaps she would win, she thought when she called out "Five!" At four, she thought perhaps the best she could hope for was to not break her neck. When she arrived at three, the troubling image of herself lying in a ditch with a broken neck put her former theory in doubt. But when she called out two, she imagined Montford's form lying broken in a ditch in her stead, which raised her spirits immensely. Finally, at one, she imagined the look on Montford's face in the event of her victory, and she vowed then and there to give the race her all.

She spurred Princess Buttercup forward with all the enthusiasm she could muster.

She realized after about three seconds that Montford had not followed. She risked a glance over her shoulder and saw him lounging in his saddle. He lifted his hat brim in acknowledgement of her concern and slowly whipped Cyril into a gallop.

Astrid turned back to the road and spurred on Buttercup even harder, a sound that was half scream, half oath escaping her throat. He'd held back on purpose, giving her a handicap she hadn't asked for. Just to prove a point.

The point being that he was the most odious, contemptible man she'd ever met.

Well, damn his eyes, she'd take his bloody handicap, and she'd win the bloody race, and she'd have no qualms about insisting upon her prize.

Montford out of her life forever.

Though he'd done a fine job of taking the wind out of her sails. Victory in such a manner was no victory at all, in her opinion, and he knew this. He'd held back precisely because he knew it would drive her insane.

And just when she thought she couldn't get any angrier, she heard Montford coming up on her heels. She tried to press Princess Buttercup into a longer leg, but the mare was having none of it.

Out of the corner of her eye, she saw Montford and Cyril drawing abreast, and she heard Montford's cynical laughter floating to her ears over the din of horse hooves and autumn wind. The quarter mile was quickly covered, and already she could see around the bend in the road to the brewery, where Wesley waited along the edge of the lane with a couple of curious field hands. Montford soon pulled ahead of her, sitting Cyril as if he was hardly working for it at all, which infuriated her even more.

She was going to lose.

Montford and Cyril sprinted ahead so that not one, not two, but three lengths separated them. And there was not a chance in hell she could make up the distance. She would have done anything in that moment to be spared from the smug look of victory Montford was sure to bestow upon her.

Or at least she *thought* she would have done anything, or wished him a thousand ill turns, until she actually got her wish.

The noise came from the left, somewhere from the dense stretch of ancient forest that composed the northern reaches of Rylestone. Astrid reined in Buttercup immediately, sensing danger, the race forgotten. Having been raised among hunters, she recognized the sharp tattoo of a rifle splitting the air. She followed the sound and saw through the foliage the rise of smoke from the blast about fifty paces deep in the wood. She saw the flash of a green hunting coat, the gleam of the gun, and a figure retreating into the shadows.

Then her attention was pulled away to the result of the gunshot, still echoing around them. She wasn't sure who was hit: Montford or Cyril. It was difficult to tell whether Montford jerked on the reins or Cyril lost his footing, but whatever the cause, both horse and rider went careening off the lane to the right, down the side of a small embankment. Cyril whinnied in agony, and Montford was ominously silent as they tumbled together down the slope out of sight.

Then everything went quiet, the sound of the gunshot fading.

Astrid's heart stopped.

Then she heard someone screaming in terror. She thought at first it was Montford or Wesley or one of the field workers who were heading toward the direction of the duke. But then she realized she was the one who was screaming.

She came to her senses long enough to urge Buttercup into a sprint.

She reached the top of the embankment the same time as Wesley and jumped to the ground, praying that she found some life below them.

She saw Cyril on his side, something black and wet coating his neck. He was as still as death, and Astrid's eyes pricked with tears at the sight.

"No, no!"

She raced down the hill toward the horse, and that was when she caught sight of Montford, who had been thrown from the roan at least fifteen feet, lying limply on his back in a stand of elderberry bushes, his jacket torn open, his shirt and cravat stained blood-red.

Astrid's legs nearly gave way beneath her as she turned away from Cyril and rushed to Montford's side. She knelt beside him and peered down at his face, afraid to touch him.

He was the color of old ashes, and there was a cut above his temple from his landing. But she wasn't worried about that so much as the blood on his chest.

Oh God, he's been shot! she thought bleakly.

He looked dead. And when she finally plucked up the courage to touch him, she lifted his wrist, and it fell down to the ground like a limp noodle.

Her heart cried out in despair. He couldn't die. He was a horrible man, she hated him, but she did not truly want him to die.

"Montford! You idiot, you can't die," she hissed, touching his face, wiping away the blood. He felt very cold. She bent her head toward his lips and felt a faint, weak breath against her cheek.

Her heart sighed in relief. He wasn't dead.

Yet.

"Montford! Come on, Montford, wake up." She patted his cheek, then shook his shoulders, and when she got no response, she began to take off his cravat and unbutton his waistcoat, searching for the wound. She felt his shoulders, his chest, for a point of entry. There was a great deal of blood on him, but she couldn't determine where it was coming from.

"Bloody fop. Wearing more clothes than I am," she mumbled between sobs.

She folded back his clothes to his thin cotton lawn shirt, also soaked in blood, and began unbuttoning it as well. Her fingers trembled from fear and something else not entirely commendable. She refused to acknowledge any desire to see his naked flesh in such a time of crisis, but she would have had to be inhuman not to appreciate the fine, hard swell of male torso beneath her fingers.

Really, did he have to be attractive even while he was dying?

Then a hand shot out, imprisoning her wrist in a hard grip. She shrieked.

"Finishing me off, are you?" drawled a voice.

Montford sat up, pushing her away, scowling. His face had regained some of its color. He looked disoriented and very, very disgruntled. He released her wrist and began to climb to his feet. This took some concentration on his part, but he refused her aid.

She stood up and put her hands on her hips with some exasperation. "Montford, you're injured."

He touched his temple as if it pained him and shook his head. "I'm fine."

"No, you're not!" she cried. "You've been shot!" She pointed toward his torso.

He looked astounded by this pronouncement and began to pat his body. Then he glanced down, which was clearly a mistake. His face lost all of its color again when he saw the blood, and his eyes rolled back in his head. He fell back to the ground in a dead faint.

MONTFORD CAME back to his senses to find Miss Honeywell's head spinning around him. Her corkscrew hair was sticking out at odd angles from her cap, and her mismatched eyes were gleaming with tears. At first her head was above him, then below him, then to the right, and then the left. Dust smudged her nose, and streaks of blood covered one cheek. He nearly fainted again at the sight.

She is injured, he thought with alarm.

Then he remembered everything. The sound of the rifle. Cyril faltering beneath him. A long, seemingly endless flight through the air. Then darkness. And blood. Buckets of blood covering him.

He squeezed his eyes shut as other memories came to him. Painful memories he'd thought long-since buried, of another time and place when blood had covered him. His blood, his parents' blood, running around him like a river. For ages it had been on him, sweetly acrid, metallic, drying so that it was black and his clothes were stiff with it. He remembered reaching out to a woman—his mother—trying to wipe the blood from her eyes, which had stared up at him without seeing him. He'd tried to make her wake up, even though he wondered how she could sleep with her eyes open like that. But she hadn't awakened, even when he had cried for her to do so. He'd cried and cried, and she'd done nothing but look at him with those strange eyes.

There had been days and days of those eyes, and the blood, and the stink of death.

Montford forced his eyes open again, forced the nightmare back down, but it went unwillingly, clawing at the recesses of his mind like a rabid beast refusing to be put in its cage.

He was going to be sick.

Miss Honeywell put a hand to his cheek. It was warm and gentle and infinitely comforting. His nausea subsided.

"Montford," she murmured.

With great effort, he sat up. Her hand fell away, though some part of him wished it had remained. He took a shuddering breath and attempted to take stock of his injuries. He felt bruised and shaken, but he wasn't shot. "I'm uninjured," he managed.

Relief flooded her face, and she sat back on her heels, wiping her cheeks with her sleeve.

"Good gads, man," came a voice over their heads. He raised his glance to Sir Wesley/Mr. Honeywell, who was staring at him in alarm. "Are you all right?"

"I'm fine."

"But the blood, man, the blood!" the gentleman exclaimed, indicating his shirtfront, his features puckering with apprehension.

Montford cringed and refused to look down. "I don't think it's mine."

Miss Honeywell's face contorted with renewed anguish, and she climbed to her feet. "Cyril!"

She ran toward the fallen horse, over which two laborers stood, shaking their heads grimly.

Montford staggered to his feet and followed after her. It was clear the gelding was done for. His neck was snapped at an odd angle, and no air worked in his massive chest. A dark patch of blood stained his side and pooled onto the grass beneath his lifeless body. Montford schooled himself not to swoon at the sight.

Miss Honeywell threw herself over the horse, sobbing violently. He turned away. He must have looked unsteady on his feet, for Sir Wesley clutched him under the elbow. Montford did not pull away. There was too much blood, and his head was still spinning.

"Damned shame. Damned bloody shame," Sir Wesley muttered. "A foul business."

A man appeared at the top of the ridge. He was large, dressed in tweed, with a pipe sticking out the corner of his mouth. He bit out several colorful oaths as he saw the carnage before him, and lumbered down the hill. The large man pulled the pipe out of his scowling mouth, a harsh furrow slashing between his bushy brows. "Wot's happened here?" he demanded in a thick Scottish burr.

"Foul business, Mr. McConnell," Sir Wesley babbled. Montford gritted his teeth. Sir Wesley was no help.

The Scot turned his attention to Montford. He took his measure in one swift, intelligent glance, and nodded. "Duke," he said, without an ounce of deference.

Not that Montford cared at the moment. "Someone shot at me. As you can see, his aim claimed my mount instead."

The Scot's lips thinned to a harsh line. "Aye. An' what makes ye so sure it were ye an' not the poor beastie the bullet was intending to hit?"

Montford was all astonishment and affront. Or as much as he could be under the circumstances. "Oh, I don't know. Common sense. Intuition? It hardly signifies, however, as the result was doubtless the same either way. 'Twas only blind luck that saved me from breaking my neck," Montford said in as calm a voice as he could manage.

The Scot looked unconvinced, but Montford decided not to argue with the man.

Miss Honeywell's sobs broke into his consciousness once more, and his heart twisted painfully in his chest. He hated the sound of her despair, hated his own weakness that prevented him from offering her some comfort—even though in the back of his mind he could almost believe that she had something to do with this business. If she wasn't so distraught over the gelding, leading him to reason with what little wits he had left that she would never do anything to endanger the animal, he wouldn't have put it past her to arrange his assassination.

He turned his head and glimpsed her kneeling by the horse, cradling his head in her lap, her shoulders trembling, and his heart flipped over again.

No, he could not believe she'd arranged this.

But someone had.

He turned back to Sir Wesley and Mr. McConnell and tried to manage an authoritative scowl. "Should one of you aid the lady?"

Sir Wesley looked startled and bounded forward. "Yes, yes of course."

Mr. McConnell held Sir Wesley back by the arm. "She'll be wantin' her sister. Why doan ye take yerself back to the castle and prepare Alice?"

Sir Wesley looked confused but agreeable to this plan.

Mr. McConnell went to Miss Honeywell's side and knelt down. Montford heard her sob, "Oh, Hiram!" then pitch herself into the Scotsman's embrace.

"I'll ride back to the castle, then," Sir Wesley said, climbing the hill. He hesitated and turned to Montford. "Shall you come?"

Montford was rooted in place. The strangest feeling had come over him when he saw Miss Honeywell fall against the Scotsman's chest. He'd felt physical pain. Anguish. He'd have done anything to exchange places with the man, as ludicrous as that seemed. He remembered her gentle, warm hand on his cheek when she had roused him from his faint.

And yesterday, when she had lain beneath him, so soft, so eager.

"No," he heard himself saying. "I think I'll stay."

Sir Wesley looked surprised, but continued on his way.

Montford stood with the two laborers in uncomfortable silence as Miss Honeywell continued to cry. Mr. McConnell patted her back with one hand and drew his pipe up to his mouth at intervals to take a puff, occasionally glancing down at the gelding and shaking his head in disapproval or offering some stiff word of comfort.

Somehow, Montford found solace that McConnell didn't seem to be besotted with the chit.

Eventually, the man succeeded in coaxing Miss Honeywell to her feet and taking her by the shoulders. "There, there, lass, it ain't like ye to go on so. Pull yerself together, there's a lass."

Miss Honeywell snuffled into a rough handkerchief McConnell produced from his pocket and dabbed at her eyes. "It's just such a . . . a shock, Hiram. Cyril . . . my lovely, lovely Cyril."

Montford's heart once again clenched in his chest. She had loved the horse, and, as unlikely as it seemed, sincerely loved the name.

"Aye, 'tis a great shame. Fine bit of horseflesh he were. Now come away from this place, 'tain't no good to wallow in yer miseries."

Miss Honeywell looked toward the felled horse, and McConnell tucked her under his arm and led her away gently but firmly. "Come on, lass. Dunna look back at such horrors."

Miss Honeywell expelled a shaky breath and allowed herself to be guided up the slope. Montford followed in their wake. McConnell barked out orders at the laborers to fetch a cart, and the two men departed in the direction of the brewery. Then he led Miss Honeywell in the direction of her mount, which had wandered across the lane, prancing nervously about, as if sensing trouble in the air.

McConnell seized the mare's reins and soothed her in the same gruff manner he'd soothed Miss Honeywell.

Montford turned his attention back to Miss Honeywell. She'd stopped crying, but her eyes were puffy, her skin mottled from her tears. She blew her nose into the handkerchief in a very unladylike manner and squared her shoulders. She could not meet his eye. Montford reached out to pat her shoulder or perhaps touch her hand, something to comfort her, but he let it drop to his side.

What was he thinking?

McConnell guided the mare in their direction, but Miss Honeywell could not look at the creature either, as if the sight of it was too painful.

"I suggest ye take Princess back to the stables, let us take care of the . . ." McConnell coughed into his hand.

"Corpse," Miss Honeywell provided in a remarkably even tone.

McConnell nodded.

Miss Honeywell made a vague gesture of acquiescence, but made no move to grab the reins McConnell offered her. Montford grabbed them instead.

"I . . . I saw something," Miss Honeywell said.

McConnell's eyes flashed with alertness.

"In the wood," she said, pointing into the thick foliage next to them. "The shooter. About fifty paces in. I saw him run into the forest."

"Did ye see who it were, lass?"

She shook her head. "No. He was tall. He wore a dark green coat."

Montford exchanged grim looks with McConnell. "It seems someone wished to do me harm," he said. "I cannot believe this was an accident."

"Aye, ye've the right of it," McConnell acknowledged.

"Who, I wonder, would wish me dead?"

McConnell removed the pipe from his mouth and fixed Montford with a steady, slightly wry expression. "I reckon nigh on everyone in the county, Yer Grace."

"That certainly narrows it down," he muttered.

"No one would dare," Miss Honeywell insisted. "No one from the estate, surely. Murdering you would hardly be in their best interest. The authorities would think that I . . . I had something to do with it, and then the estate would be seized . . ." She turned to him, wide-eyed. "You don't think I would do such a thing!"

"The thought had crossed my mind," he allowed.

She looked indignant. McConnell looked fairly murderous.

"Of course I don't think you arranged this," he finished. "But someone did. Do you have any idea who might have done this?"

McConnell and Miss Honeywell looked at each other, and some mutual idea seemed to pass between them, rousing Montford's suspicions. But they shook their heads and stared at the ground.

"You two suspect someone," Montford insisted.

McConnell fixed him with a hard look that said he would be answering no more questions. "The pair of ye've had a fright. And ye, Yer Grace, be out of sorts from yer fall. Go on back to the castle an' repair yerselves. I'll see to what's left and go into the forest for a look 'round. Whoe'er did the deed is come and gone by now, but I'll see what can be done."

After he'd made sense of the Scot's brogue, Montford started to protest, but the pain in his head left him dizzy, and the smell of blood left him weak. He decided to heed the man's advice. "You'll come and report to me when you've completed your work," Montford said.

McConnell's eyes narrowed at the implicit command. "Aye, Yer Grace."

"Good." He turned to Miss Honeywell. "Shall I help you up?"

"I think I'll walk. I have no desire to ride at the moment."

"Neither do I," he said wryly.

McConnell left them, and they started down the lane. He held the mare's reins and leaned his right arm against her shoulders as he walked, not yet trusting his own legs.

They were silent for a very long time, Miss Honeywell trudging at his side, her face downcast so he could not read her expression. He cleared his throat and searched for the right words. "I am very sorry this happened. Please believe I did everything I could to turn Cyril."

She made some noise at his side, and he feared she was crying again. Dear God.

But when he looked at her, he saw she was smiling bleakly. "You cannot blame yourself. I cannot even blame you. Besides, I think he would have died either way."

"Foul business," he muttered, then cringed when he realized he was mimicking Sir Wesley's insipidity.

"I would not want you dead. I may wish you to the devil, but it is supposed to be metaphorical," she assured him.

"Likewise."

"I had nothing to do with this," she insisted in a defensive voice. "I hope you believe me."

He stopped walking, which made her stop as well.

"Miss Honeywell, I do believe you."

She looked at her boots. "Thank you." Then she looked up at his face searchingly. "You *are* terribly banged up."

"I feel banged up."

She reached out and dabbed at his temple with her handkerchief. He leaned against the mare and let her gentle touch soothe his aching head. At length, she pulled away and presented him with the evidence of his wound, which soaked through the linen handkerchief.

He averted his glance and tried not to swoon. "Thank you, Miss Honeywell," he said tersely, resuming his stride.

"You're welcome," she said equally tersely, no doubt baffled by his abruptness.

They walked on in strained silence.

"Just trying to help," she muttered after several minutes of obvious stewing.

"I said thank you, Miss Honeywell," he repeated through his teeth.

He heard her sniffle next to him and barely suppressed a groan.

Surely she wasn't crying.

But when he turned to her, he found her face wet with tears, her nose bright red. Instead of annoyance, he felt sympathy well inside of his untried heart—sympathy and something else that made him want to reach out to her and squeeze her in his arms. He wanted to kiss her nose, even if it was horribly red and dripping. He wanted to do a thousand inappropriate things to her, even while she was in this dreadful state. It was utterly inconceivable.

He had hit his head very hard.

"I'm not usually a watering pot," she insisted, wiping her cheeks with her sleeve, since the other one was ruined with his blood. "I've not cried . . . oh, in years and years. Not since my mum . . ."

He offered her his handkerchief, which had somehow survived the recent carnage, and she took it gratefully, blowing her nose into the costly lace.

He would not want *that* back.

He searched around to find something comforting to say to her, but he found nothing. Then a crazy thought struck him, and he blurted it out before he could stop himself, even though it could not in any conceivable way be considered consolatory. "My name is Cyril."

She stopped blowing her nose and looked up at him, startled. She lowered the handkerchief. "What?"

He sighed and rubbed his sore neck. What the blazes was he doing? "My name. My given name, that is. It's Cyril."

She looked at him as if he were a lunatic. "Oh."

"But no one calls me that."

"Really?"

"I hate it. Hate all my names. People just call me by my title."

Now she looked faintly amused, which was irritating. He was going for gratitude, or a show of understanding on her part, not amusement. But he supposed it was better than tears. He expelled a breath and resumed walking. "Just forget it."

"Cyril."

"Don't call me that. I told you because of your roan, and I don't know why, but I thought it would help."

He felt a hand covering his own, stopping him. He looked down and saw Miss Honeywell's dirty, snotty fingers covering his palm, and for a moment he could not breathe from the wall of heat that bombarded him. He dared to look at her and saw she was staring up at him, her eyes glossy with unshed tears, a tremulous smile hovering on her rosy lips.

His heart stopped beating.

"Thank you, Montford. It did help."

There was the gratitude he was aiming for. But beneath that gratitude and those shining tears lurked a layer of mischief that made him quite apprehensive. As if she knew precisely the value of the weapon he had given her in his weakness. Namely his given name, and the fact that he hated it.

She *would* use these facts against him, the strumpet.

But for the moment, he was safe.

No, not safe, because he was drowning in her eyes. Drowning in *her*, bit by bit. She touched his hand—his hand!—and he wanted to sink into her flesh, wrap himself in her limbs, kiss away her tears.

"Miss Honeywell," he began. "I think I hit my head harder than I thought."

"I think so too. You are looking quite odd."

And thus they resumed their walk back to the castle.

Chapter Ten

*In Which the Curse of the Black Crinoline
Casts a Pall Over Rylestone Hall*

ASTRID WAS concerned by the duke's strange manner in the lane. Although he appeared to be uninjured by the tumble he'd taken, he had a nasty cut above one eye that continued to bleed despite her attempts to stanch it, and he kept looking at her in a peculiar manner that made her alternate from hot to cold and back again.

Then he'd begun babbling about his name. Or names. He seemed to have a lot, and he didn't seem to like any of them. Except for his title.

As Astrid couldn't imagine him as a Cyril, she had to agree with him. He was Montford. Less a real person than a title.

Though at the moment, he was looking all too human, covered in blood and rumpled beyond repair, his face pale and his eyes slightly discombobulated. She felt sorry for him, and a little apprehensive about his brainbox. It had taken quite a coshing. The last thing she needed at this juncture was a concussed duke staggering about and attempting to be nice to her.

Which was what he had been attempting when he'd told her his name. Cyril. He'd been trying to make her feel better in his own lame way. And she was surprised to find that he had succeeded. She did feel better after his admission. Not because he had told her his name, but rather because he had been so sheepish about it. He clearly thought his name was ridiculous, and he had regretted telling her almost immediately. She had found it endearing.

Poor fellow. It *was* a rather ridiculous name.

She was fully prepared to throw it back in his face at some point, but at the moment, she was in sympathy with him. He'd been amazingly understanding about the whole shooting incident, and she didn't want to push her luck. Besides which, she was embarrassed to have displayed such grief in his presence. He'd seen her cry not once, not twice, but thrice in the space of two days, and he probably thought she was a ninnyhammer.

But she had good cause on all three occasions. Just thinking about her poor Cyril, lying broken and bleeding in that ditch, made her tear up.

Who could have done such a thing?

She was not lying when she had told the duke none of her people would have shot him. But she had her enemies. And everyone knew that if anything happened to Montford while he was visiting, she would be blamed.

There was only one person she could think of who had it in him to arrange such a dastardly plot. But how could Mr. Lightfoot even know of the duke's surprise visit? And how could murdering the duke further that man's own designs? He didn't want her swinging from a hangman's noose, did he?

No, she thought grimly. He wanted her under her thumb or worse.

They reached the stables and handed Princess Buttercup off to Mick. When she related the news of Cyril's fate, Mick's face went pale, and he crossed himself. He was a Roman Catholic, and quite religious, and Cyril had been his special charge.

They had made it across the yard and into the gardens, when a flurry of black crinoline caught her eye through the hedgerows.

Astrid reacted on instinct, knowing exactly what was attached to the crinoline. She tugged Montford's arm toward a row of rosebushes.

"Where are we going?" he demanded.

"Shhh!" she said, crouching down, signaling for him to do the same.

He was having none of it, and stood above her, hands on his hips. "Miss Honeywell, what is going on?" he intoned.

"I am attempting to save your neck," she muttered.

But it was too late. They were discovered.

A tall, robust woman appeared at the entrance to their hiding place, dressed in an elaborately ruched and gusseted black crinoline gown a decade out of fashion. Her neck was encircled in an ornate gold necklace set with rubies, and her gray hair was topped by a silk turban. She was handsome and middle-aged, with dark blue eyes that were never anything but vexed.

They were very vexed now.

In her considerable wake followed Alice, who was looking distraught, and a young woman dressed to the nines in pink silk taffeta with a dizzying array of bows and flounces. Astrid thought uncharitably that the gown was a very unbecoming color and made her cousin Davina's pale skin look sallow. The profusion of bows and flounces were just downright absurd and did nothing to ease the girl's haughty, pinched features. Davina was only slightly less dreadful than Lady Emily.

She knew exactly why this pair had deigned to call on them, and the reason was standing stiffly at her side. Astrid sighed and rose to her feet to greet her aunt Emily and cousin Davina, but before a word could escape her lips, her aunt began to talk. And talk.

"Astrid! What in heaven's name are you doing, skulking about the roses? You look a disgrace. As usual. Stand up straight, gel." Aunt Emily lifted her lorgnette and peered at Astrid and Montford with a mighty frown. "My son has just informed me that you've been *racing* in the lanes again. Disgraceful, disgraceful. And that some ill had befallen you. But you seem to be in one piece." She didn't look relieved at this discovery. In fact, she looked extremely disappointed. "Racing like a common ruffian! If your mother were alive . . . and now to find you thusly, crouching in the gardens with this . . . this . . . *swain* . . ." She indicated the duke with a dismissive cut of her bejeweled hand. "It is just like you to have no regard for your reputation." She paused, raised her lorgnette again, and peered at the duke's shirtfront. "Good God, is that blood?"

"It is—" Astrid began.

Aunt Emily raised her hand dramatically to her brow. "This is beyond the pale. Cavorting in the roses with this . . . this *person* in such a state. And with a duke under your roof. Have you no sense of propriety? What must he think of us all? I swear, you shall be the death of me." She fixed the duke with a look of icy contempt. "Now off with you, young man, and repair yourself. I shall overlook this . . . *contretemps* this time, since I am sure it is not your fault she has led you to such a pass."

"Madam," the duke began in a chilling tone that could not bode well.

"Dare you speak to me, sirrah!" Aunt Emily gasped, all astonishment at his audacity, as she seemed to be under the impression the duke was a servant.

Astrid could feel the duke turning to stone at her side.

She exchanged looks with Alice, who had clasped her hand over her mouth to hide her smile. This was not going to be pleasant for her aunt, and Astrid planned on enjoying every minute of it. She stepped aside a few paces to allow herself a better view of the proceedings.

Even rumpled and bloody, the duke was a sight to behold in his ire. His silver eyes glinted with fire, his perfect features set in stone. "Dare *you* speak to me, madam?" he said in a deceptively cool voice. "May I have your name?"

"Of all the—" her aunt spluttered.

"Your name, madam," the duke interrupted. He turned to Astrid. "Miss Honeywell, who is this person?"

Astrid hated to enter such an amusing scene, but it appeared she had no choice. "This is my aunt, Lady Emily Benwick, and her daughter, Miss Davina." She indicated the vision in pink scowling in her direction. She turned to her aunt. "Aunt, may I present His Grace, the Duke of Montford."

Aunt Emily's face went white beneath her paint. Her haughty features screwed up first in disbelief, then with alarm when the truth finally hit her. Her lorgnette fell out of her hands and hit the earth. Miss Davina had a similar reaction, but not being in possession of her mother's backbone, she swayed on her feet and looked seconds away from a full-fledged swoon.

Alice coughed into her hand. Astrid didn't bother to hide her smile of satisfaction.

Aunt Emily recovered herself and proceeded to grace His Grace with a curtsy that would have rivaled any at court. She tugged on her daughter's arm, and Miss Davina was forced to do the same. The hems of their gowns, Astrid thought uncharitably, would be quite ruined in the mud.

"Your Grace, it is an honor. Indeed . . ."

Montford looked at Astrid and rolled his eyes.

It was apparent Aunt Emily and Davina weren't going to rise without a direct order. But it was equally apparent that Montford was not going to give one.

So they remained squatting low to the earth, with Montford glowering above them. Astrid had not witnessed such a pleasing spectacle since Montford had fallen in the mud two days before, and she didn't feel the least bit of pity for her relatives. They were horrible people, and she was quite happy to see them grovel.

"Miss Honeywell," the duke intoned. "It appears you have callers. Don't let me detain you."

He gave her a stiff bow and strode off, leaving Astrid and Alice to pull their relations out of the ground.

⊶— ⊨✦⊨ —⊷

"YOU COULD have had the sense, gel, to tell me who that man was before you let me make such a dreadful *faux pas*," Aunt Emily said to her, applying the smelling salts to her daughter's nose.

Astrid and Alice had managed to help the baroness and her daughter to their feet and lead them into the parlor, where Miss Davina promptly fainted, quite elegantly, against the divan. Astrid wanted to tell her cousin that the duke was no longer present to witness such a charming display of feminine sensibility, but she bit her tongue and ordered tea to be brought around while her aunt attempted to revive her daughter.

"But I suppose that would be too much to ask of you," Aunt Emily continued, scowling at her niece. "No doubt you enjoyed seeing me humiliated."

I reveled in it, she wanted to retort, but she held her tongue and attempted to look contrite.

"It is surely a reasonable mistake to have made," Alice interjected, ever the peacemaker between the two women. "He was covered in blood and looked a fright."

"Indeed." Aunt Emily inclined her head, somewhat mollified.

"I believe it was the duke who took a tumble today," Alice continued. She looked at Astrid with some concern. "He is uninjured?"

"Yes, but Cyril was not so lucky. He's dead."

"Cyril? Who is Cyril?" demanded the baroness.

Astrid sighed and clenched her fists in her lap. "The horse His Grace was riding."

"I'm so sorry, Astrid," Alice cried.

Astrid nodded and looked at her hands, willing her mind away from the afternoon's tragic turn. She could not think of her horse right now, or she would cry in front of her aunt, something she'd vowed never to do.

"It was the *duke* who was racing you in the lanes?" Aunt Emily cut in. "What folly have you led the poor man into, gel? I should have known you'd have no respect for his station. Racing indeed! Lucky for you it was only his mount who suffered the consequences of your impetuous display."

Astrid gritted her teeth. She found anger an amazing remedy for her sorrows.

Aunt Emily had fallen out of patience with her daughter, who still refused to be roused. She shook her by the shoulder. "Pull yourself together, Davina, and sit up. There's no one here to appreciate your theatrics."

Davina sat up and arranged her skirts fussily. She stared daggers at Astrid through narrowed eyes. Astrid, quite used to her cousin's petty jealousies, arched an eyebrow.

"It was a good thing I learned from my staff of the duke's arrival," Aunt Emily continued, after Flora had come in with the tea. Flora rolled her eyes behind the baroness's back as she departed, which raised Astrid's spirits considerably. "Someone must be here to show His Grace that not everyone in the county is without manners or sense."

"I am sure that is what you meant to show him in the garden," Astrid could not help but mutter.

"What did you say, gel? Speak up. Don't mumble like a half-wit."

"I said, it was very kind of you, Aunt, to think of such a thing," she lied.

The door to the parlor cracked open, and Astrid saw Aunt Anabel poke her head into the room. When she spied their callers, however, she shut the door without entering.

Astrid couldn't blame her.

Aunt Emily waved away Alice and began to pour the tea for them all, not bothering to ask how they liked it. In Aunt Emily's world, everyone liked their tea precisely how Aunt Emily said they liked it. Sugarless, and swimming in cream.

"You will invite me and Davina to dinner tonight," Aunt Emily said some minutes later. It was an order, not a suggestion.

Astrid gripped her teacup until she was certain it would shatter. "I had not thought to host a formal dinner tonight, Aunt," she ground out.

"Nonsense. Of course you will. And I have taken it upon myself to invite the vicar. To round out the numbers."

"How kind of you, Aunt Emily," Alice said with a remarkable dearth of sarcasm. "You have thought of everything."

"You shall instruct your kitchens to prepare game hen for the main course. I shall send Monsieur Roualt over later to oversee the preparations. I'll not have the Duke of Montford believe that we are incapable of decent cuisine in Yorkshire," Aunt Emily continued.

"We wouldn't want that," Astrid murmured.

"And you shall sit the duke next to my Davina," Aunt Emily intoned, patting her daughter's hand. "She's had a Season and knows just the sort of conversation to please His Grace."

Davina bowed her head demurely, though her face looked smug.

Astrid felt a surge of rage toward her aunt and cousin. She knew exactly what they were up to. It couldn't have been clearer had they shouted it from the rooftops. Aunt Emily meant to put Davina into the duke's path. As if her cousin stood a chance of garnering that man's regard! Why, he couldn't be expected to locate Davina's face amid all of those ruffles. And as for her brain, her cousin didn't have one.

Well, she did have a brain, but it was reserved solely for formulating snide remarks.

The duke would never countenance such a blatant attempt at matchmaking. Would he?

The thought of Montford in thrall to Davina was utterly inconceivable, but nevertheless, Astrid's heart shriveled just contemplating it.

She didn't like the duke, she reminded herself as she sipped her tea. She loathed him, so what should she mind if her aunt and cousin importuned him? Why indeed? It would be infinitely amusing to see how he reacted to Davina over one of Monsieur Roualt's creations.

Infinitely. Amusing.

And even if he were taken in by Davina's simpering, dull-witted conversation, she would not be in the least bothered. In fact, it would be no less than he deserved for falling for such a twit. "I think, Aunt, that that is a wonderful idea," she said at last.

Aunt Emily and Davina both looked surprised by her agreement.

Davina even had sense enough to look a little suspicious as well, leading Astrid to speculate that the girl was not as empty-headed as she appeared.

Astrid smiled graciously and set down her cup. She rose. "You will need to go back to the Grange to prepare for the night," she said.

Aunt Emily and Davina, who had not finished half of their tea, rose as well. "Of course," Aunt Emily said.

"We shall not keep you then."

It was a dismissal.

Aunt Emily frowned, but said nothing, probably thinking it wise to leave while she apparently had the upper hand.

"Until tonight, Aunt, Davina," Astrid said, still smiling stiffly.

"Yes, well, we *should* be going anyway," Aunt Emily said, wanting the last word.

Astrid and Alice escorted their relations outside to their waiting barouche and waved them off. Astrid's smile immediately faded when the barouche was out of sight.

"Well, *that* was interesting," Alice said. "Did you see the look on her face when she figured out who the duke was?"

"It was a moment I shall treasure for the rest of my days."

"You were devilishly clever in getting rid of them," Alice continued.

"I have my uses. Now if you'll excuse me, Alice, I think I'll change."

Alice placed a hand on her arm, looking concerned. "Are you all right?"

Astrid could not forget Alice's harsh words from the day before. She winced from her sister's concern. "I shall be fine. I always am," she said, pulling her arm away.

"Astrid," Alice started, looking contrite.

"We have much to do," Astrid said, evading another argument. Or a round of apologies. "You heard our lady aunt. We cannot allow the duke to believe that all of Yorkshire is without manners or sense."

"Are you actually going to go through with this dinner party?"

"What choice do I have? And maybe Aunt Emily can succeed in scaring away the duke. God knows I have tried and failed."

"Aunt Emily won't, but Davina might."

"Yes. Let's hope one of her bows strangles the duke over the soup course."

Alice giggled, and they went inside on each other's arms in awkward silence.

Things were not repaired between her and her sister, but Astrid hadn't the strength to undertake such an endeavor, nor the desire. She had not forgiven Alice her harsh words, though they were probably well deserved. She would sort things out later, she assured herself, as she mounted the stairs alone to her room, waving off Alice's offer to help her out of her habit.

She wanted to be alone. It was not yet noon, but the day was already shaping up to be ten times worse than the day before. Poor Cyril.

When she reached her room, she locked the door and threw herself across the bed.

She cried herself to sleep.

Chapter Eleven

In Which Alliances Are Made and Villains Are Revealed

THE SCOTSMAN found Montford in the castle's library, reordering one of the shelves in alphabetical order. Montford had managed to gather as many volumes of poetry as he could find strewn about the room, and he had carved out a space on one of the shelves to accommodate the collection. He decided to file them by author, like his own library. Most would have thought his occupation quite beneath his station and not a little peculiar, but Montford found the work soothing. There was nothing like putting something in its proper place to calm his frayed nerves.

And his nerves were very frayed at the moment.

Mr. McConnell must have stood behind him watching for several minutes, for he had to clear his throat before Montford noticed he was no longer alone. He turned around and attempted to hide the latest volume of Essex smut behind his back.

Mr. McConnell looked puzzled by his action, and pulled the pipe out of his mouth. "Duke."

"Mr. McConnell."

He set down the book and motioned for McConnell to have a seat. The Scot took him up on his suggestion and eased himself into a chair gingerly, sighing in relief as he did so. He looked quite worn out.

"Did you find anything in the wood?"

"Aye. Shell casing, bit of powder. It were a rifle what killed the poor creature."

"No sign of the perpetrator?"

"The perpe-*what*?"

"The shooter," Montford clarified through clenched teeth.

"Nay."

Montford waited for an elaboration, but none came. McConnell, it seemed, didn't mince words.

"And you've no idea who might have done it, Mr. McConnell?"

Something flashed in the man's eyes, but he shook his head.

Montford crossed his arms and gave the Scot his best ducal glare. "You've some idea, do you not?"

"Nay."

"Shall we call in the constable? Maybe he would have a different opinion on the matter. Someone tried to kill me, McConnell. It is a hanging offense, need I remind you?"

McConnell puffed on his pipe and looked quite unconcerned by Montford's threat. "I'm the constable 'round these parts, Your Grace."

"*That's* hardly reassuring."

McConnell looked at Montford as if he'd have no problem wiping the floor with his face, duke or not. Montford believed the man could probably succeed. Montford was a large man, well over six feet, but next to McConnell, he felt rather petite. The Scot had the shoulders of an ox. "I'm the constable, and the estate manager, as a matter o' fact. I've known Miss Astrid since she were a wee bairn, an' if you think I'll help ye to put her in danger of a neck stretching, you've got another thing think comin'," McConnell said, punctuating his speech with a jab of his pipe.

"You think Miss Honeywell had something to do with this?" Montford asked, incredulous.

Mr. McConnell looked alarmed. "Nay, nay. I dunna think so. But *ye* do."

"I most certainly do not. Miss Honeywell is many things, but she is no murderer."

Mr. McConnell looked taken aback. "Oh. Well then."

"Yes, *well then*. I don't think Miss Honeywell is behind it, but she does inspire a certain amount of . . . devotion in her followers. Perhaps one of them decided to do me in."

"No one what works under me or her," Mr. McConnell said, affronted by the very notion.

Montford sighed, feeling as if he were pushing a boulder up a very steep hill. "The shot did not come from the heavens, Mr. McConnell. I don't think I have yet done anything so villainous that the gods would wish to smite me from on high."

McConnell's eyes narrowed. "Ye ain't be one of them papists, are ye?"

Good God, where had *that* come from? "I am not a Roman Catholic," he found himself saying. He was not exactly intimidated by McConnell, but he was treading very carefully.

"Twaddle about gods and smiting. Sounds papist to me."

"I would point out that papists are monotheistic."

Mr. McConnell looked as if Montford had spoken in Greek. Montford sighed. He supposed he had. "I am *not* a papist," he repeated.

"What are ye, then, C of E?"

"What business is . . . I suppose I am."

"Ye *suppose*? What? Ye dunna ken what alter ye worship at?"

"I do not attend chapel—"

McConnell jerked to his feet, and the pipe nearly fell out of his mouth. The movement was so sudden that Montford involuntarily leaned back, just in case McConnell decided to swing his large ham hock of an arm in the direction of his face. "It's worse, then. Ye be one of them nonbelievers."

Montford bristled. Brawn aside, this was simply too much. "Mr. McConnell, it is none of your concern what altar I worship at."

"It is when ye bring yer fast, unholy ways into this house."

"You shall remember who you are addressing, Mr. McConnell."

Mr. McConnell didn't look inclined to do so.

Montford wondered if *anyone* within a thirty-mile radius had any regard for his title besides himself. Montford couldn't very well throw the constable at the man for his insolence, since Mr. McConnell *was* the constable. But he had had lesser men horsewhipped for such cheek.

No, he hadn't. But he'd considered it on occasion.

He was considering it now, but he had a sneaking suspicion McConnell would turn the horsewhip on *him*.

He decided to try a different tack. Mollification. It went against his nature, but he'd found himself mollifying several times during the space of the last forty-eight hours, to some effect.

"Mr. McConnell, I was raised in the church, and I do attend on occasion." Weddings (reluctantly), and funerals (reluctantly, unless he had disliked the deceased). "But I'll not lie to you"—yes, he would—"and tell you I am religious, because I'm not. I'm indifferent."

Mr. McConnell considered Montford's statement and did not find it entirely lacking.

"Dunna ken if it's worse or no. Dunna ken if I believe ye. Ye've a good deal o' anger in ye—"

"*I* have anger!" he burst out. "You're the one who was yelling at me!"

"I weren't yellin'," Mr. McConnell said, sticking his pipe back in his mouth and daring Montford to contradict him.

Montford clutched his head, which was a mistake, because he hit the bandage over his right temple. He winced and tried to rein in his temper. "Mr. McConnell," he said evenly. "May we get back to the matter at hand?"

"Certainly, Yer Grace. What were the matter at hand again?"

"For the love of . . . is there something in the water here that makes everyone talk in circles?"

McConnell grinned and puffed on his pipe.

"What do you suggest we do about this shooting?"

Mr. McConnell scratched his neck. "Dunno. Not much to be done. 'Twould solve everyone's problem if ye were to depart."

"Would it indeed?"

"Solve *yer* problem, at least," he muttered into his pipe.

"I'll not construe that as a threat. I want the shooter found and crucified. I do not care to be shot at, Mr. McConnell."

"Course not."

"There shall be a thorough investigation."

"Aye, there will be an accountin'," McConnell said grimly, "dinna worry about that. Cyril was a goer, an' he didna deserve such an end. I'll catch the piker what done him in an' string 'im up by his bollocks for fashing poor Miss Astrid."

McConnell was certainly getting into the spirit of things. Montford cleared his throat, thankful he was not on the receiving end of McConnell's Old Testament justice. "Well, then, since I see you're on the job, I'll leave you to it. I'm departing for London tomorrow, and you can send word there if you find our man."

McConnell nodded, as if he'd expected this. "Scared ye off, did she?"

"What?"

"Miss Astrid. Scared ye off. Reckon ye'll hightail it back to Lunnon an' send some stuffed shirts down in yer stead to finish her off."

"I don't know what you mean."

McConnell crossed his beefy arms over his chest and studied Montford for a long, tense moment. "I'm gonna speak my mind to ye, Yer Grace, an' yer gonna listen. Ken?"

Montford blinked. As if the man hadn't already. "Please, by all means, Mr. McConnell. Proceed."

"I dunna care what a piece of paper says, this is the Honeywells' place, an' 'twould be criminal to toss them out like yesterday's dishwater."

"I am not going to toss them out," he gritted out.

"Nay?" McConnell said, looking surprised.

"Nay. You people have the mistaken idea I am some sort of ogre. It is plain to see I cannot merely ask the Honeywells to vacate the premises."

McConnell's stern expression faded as if it never was. He beamed at Montford as if they were now old friends. "Well, then, I dinna know ye had such sense, lad. I mean, Yer Grace."

Montford rolled his eyes. "No need to start groveling *now*, Mr. McConnell. Sit down, if you please, and do something with your pipe before I yank it out of your mouth and shove it down your throat."

McConnell laughed and did as Montford ordered. "I'm beginning to like ye, lad."

"How lovely," he said dryly.

"Despite ye bein Indifferent."

Montford ground his teeth together and forced himself back to the main point of this interview. "I am not going to kick them out, but to my mind, there are some issues that need to be addressed. I own this property, in case anyone has forgotten, and I cannot in good conscience let it continue to be run at the behest of Miss Honeywell."

Surprisingly, McConnell did not protest.

"I am willing to let the Honeywells remain at Rylestone Hall, but the management shall have to change."

At this, McConnell opened his mouth to say something, but Montford raised his hand. "I don't want to replace you, Mr. McConnell. If you are indeed the estate manager-cum-constable, then I have to congratulate you on running the estate so well, despite Miss Honeywell's interference."

"She weren't an interference. A couple of odd notions here and there, but nothing to do real harm."

"Besides cheating me?"

McConnell looked chagrined. "She dinna do anything foolish, did she? She likes to fancy herself a bit of a Robin Hood, spread the wealth around to those more . . . ah, deservin' than yerself."

"*No one* is more deserving than myself."

"Of course not," McConnell averred drily. "Yer not to be sending her to gaol for a bit of cookin' of the books?"

"McConnell, she threw the books in a vat of grease and fried them. But I'll not send her to gaol. Good God, who would protect the other inmates?"

"Or the guards," McConnell added in a fond tone. "She's a canny one, that."

"She's a menace. A hoyden. A danger to herself and others."

McConnell's smile dimmed. "Dunna go too far, Your Grace. She's a good lass, and has tried her best with what God provided her."

"Be that as it may, she needs to be reined in."

McConnell sat back in his seat and surveyed Montford. "Aye. An' are ye the man to do that?"

At some point, around the time Miss Honeywell was brought up, the conversation had become unhinged. He was not quite sure what McConnell was asking, but the way he asked it was implicating. It was the kind of question a father might ask when attempting to intimidate his daughter's suitor.

Montford was alarmed at the idea that McConnell seemed to hold that he was interested in Miss Honeywell. *In that way.*

Which he most certainly wasn't—notwithstanding their encounter of the day before in this very same room. His eyes wandered over to the ladder, where he had nearly kissed her, then the spot on the floor where he had run his hands up her legs and . . .

Couples had been married for less than that. He would have been *obliged* to marry her, had she been a London lady. Thank hell she wasn't. And thank hell no one had seen them together, for even if she was not precisely genteel, he didn't see how he could have wriggled out of an engagement and kept his honor as a gentleman.

But marriage to Miss Astrid Honeywell? *Her?*

Montford tugged on his cravat. It was suddenly very warm in the library. Stifling, in fact. "I am not . . . that is . . . we are not . . ."

McConnell arched his brow and looked satisfied by Montford's incoherence, as if he had expected no less.

"Mr. McConnell," he continued when he had collected his wits, "I am not interested in Miss Honeywell."

McConnell looked surprised by this statement. "Ne'er implied ye were."

"Did you not?"

"No, I didna." McConnell paused, studied Montford in a hawkish way that made him want to squirm. "But 'twould look verra odd for ye to allow four females to remain here under a roof not their own. Not to mention how verra difficult it would be to keep Miss Astrid out of yer affairs."

"I see. And what would you have me do?"

McConnell smiled, as if he had finally coaxed the exact question from Montford's lips he had wanted to hear all night. He leaned forward and replaced the pipe in his mouth. "I'll tell ye what ye can do, and it will get ye free and clear of the Honeywell lasses for good."

That was precisely the sort of thing Montford had wanted to hear. He leaned forward, prepared to take in all the advice the Scot could give him. "I'm all ears, Mr. McConnell."

CONTRARY TO what the Duke of Montford might surmise regarding her reading habits, Miss Honeywell did not care for gothic novels. She liked academic tomes and, yes, scandalous verse. She read the occasional light novel of manners, but she found gothic novels incredibly ridiculous. Miss Alice Honeywell, however, devoured gothic novels like boxes of chocolates, often in one sitting, and always to excess. She reveled in the same overblown sentiments and absurd, lurid plots that her sister declared "piffle" and "a waste of typeset." She knew all the conventions, could anticipate plot twists and entire speeches from out of the characters' mouths. She often skimmed ahead to read the titillating parts, and discreetly dog-eared the pages upon which these parts were written in order to reread them at a later date. Which she did. Often.

She knew the hero from the first trite word out of his mouth, and she could spot a villain even before he entered the scene from some poorly veiled foreshadowing on the author's part—usually something to do with shifting shadows, or thunder rumbling in the distance. And the villains in her favorite novels were usually afflicted with the following maladies: a) a case of unrequited love for the heroine, b) insanity, or c) some combination of both. Alice tended to like these brooding, lost souls better than the heroes and often wished they would succeed in their dastardly schemes.

The villain in question, who was, alas, not the fictional "Mad Pasha" from Alice's latest book, and who was currently sitting behind an oversized mahogany desk in a cavernous office some fifty miles north of Rylestone Green, was not cast in shadows, nor did thunder rumble in the distance to alert onlookers to his malevolence. Nor would Alice have liked this particular villain, as he possessed none of the romantic allure—brooding eyes, raven's wing hair, broad shoulders, et cetera—common in the ones from her stories. But he did suffer from the afflictions subscribed to his kind: he wanted a woman he couldn't have, *and* he was slightly barmy in his brainbox.

Many of his cohorts suspected the former, as they'd watched him pursue the county hoyden for years, but they subscribed his occasionally obsessive behaviors to uncommon strength of purpose. It was why Samuel Lightfoot was such a success, some said, because of his devotion to his work and his willingness to call a spade a spade.

No one under his employ, even the henchmen he occasionally called upon to do his dirty work, suspected that he worked twenty-hour days or shouted imprecations at them or anyone in his proximity because he was cracked in the head. They just thought he was a bit of an arse.

But a successful, rich arse who kept them employed.

So they minded their manners, even if he didn't, and continued about their business.

One of Mr. Lightfoot's henchmen currently stood at the foot of the mahogany desk. He was tall and strapping and wore a long green hunting coat. He was newly hired and greatly concerned for his future at Dunkirk Brewing Company, as evidenced by the state of the hat mashed between his hands.

Mr. Lightfoot was still sitting behind his desk, which might have been a good sign, but he had remained silent long after his new employee had finished his tale, which didn't bode well. Mr. Lightfoot's silences never remained silences for long. Nothing could be heard in the room but the ticking of an ornate clock over the hearth and the sound of Mr. Lightfoot's breathing.

The henchman had the very bad idea to break the uncomfortable silence with his apologies. "I'm surely sorry, sir. Didna mean to actually hit 'im. But like I said, the demmed scope must have been off. I aimed over his head, just like you told me to—"

"Cease. Speaking. Worm," Mr. Lightfoot growled, rising to his feet.

Mr. Lightfoot was a good deal shorter than him and a bit paunchy, as if he enjoyed a pint or two of his recipe of an evening. The henchman was certain he could take Mr. Lightfoot in a fair fight. But he suspected he'd never see a fair fight with Mr. Lightfoot. He didn't trust the gleam in the man's dark eyes. So he backed up a step or two and watched out for knives or any other flying objects.

"You tell me you nearly succeeded in killing the Duke of bloody Montford," Mr. Lightfoot said quite pleasantly.

"He took a tumble, an' the horse was done for, but he ain't dead," the henchman assured him. He'd loitered about the castle for a while until the young popinjay, Sir Wesley, had come and told the story about the duke's spill, before riding up to inform his new employer of the proceedings. "His Majesty's hale and hearty and no doubt dustin' up a storm at the castle."

"Then I wonder why you feel the need to apologize," Mr. Lightfoot said evenly, "when you succeeded in doing the job I assigned. Nothing I hate more than apologies for doing your job, Mr. Weeks."

Mr. Weeks crimped his hat brim together end to end and stared at the brewer in surprise. He'd not thought of it in that way. All he could think when he saw the duke tumble down the embankment was that he was a dead man. He'd nearly wet himself imagining the noose tightening around his neck. A body did not shoot dukes.

Mr. Lightfoot began pacing at the foot of his desk, deep in thought.

"This is better than I could have planned. A shot overhead, she might not have taken seriously. But this, *this* is hard to overlook. No, it's better this way. Good work, Mr. Weeks."

Mr. Weeks was confused and a bit apprehensive over this commendation, but he allowed himself to breathe a sigh of relief that he was off the hook. "Thank ye, sir."

"Now, tomorrow I shall attend the harvest festival in Rylestone Green to assess whether Miss Honeywell has changed her mind regarding my suit," Mr. Lightfoot continued.

"Will she be knowing you had something to do with the shooting?"

"I suspect she'll have an inkling. If not, I shall suggest it to her on the morrow and warn her that the next time you shall not miss, should she continue to be difficult."

"Right." The henchman's brow furrowed. "I mean, we ain't actually going to kill His Grace?"

Mr. Lightfoot looked annoyed. "Of course not, you fool. It's a bluff."

"Oh." He scratched the back of his neck, then his backside, trying to wrap his mind around Mr. Lightfoot's elaborate scheme. It didn't make a bit of sense to him, but then again, he'd never been terribly clever at puzzles.

Mr. Lightfoot stopped pacing and crossed his arms over his girth. "And if she doesn't prove amenable, we'll move on to our next plan. She'll have no choice but to wed me then."

"Right," Mr. Weeks said, clearing his throat, full of doubts now. He'd known Miss Astrid for years and years, and it was hard to imagine her wed to anyone, especially Mr. Lightfoot. But as Mr. Lightfoot assured him, she needed a husband. Mr. Weeks couldn't agree more. Someone needed to take the wench in hand, for all she was a generous manager. She was a woman and ought to know her place. Mr. Lightfoot, of all the men in the county, seemed quite up to the job. Yet Mr. Weeks wondered, not for the first time, whether his new employer would be kind. He didn't like the idea of handing Miss Astrid over to a villain.

"Remember," Mr. Lightfoot said in a conciliatory voice, seeing his henchman's doubts. "We're doing this for her own good. She'll be rich and well-treated by me."

"Right," Mr. Weeks said, not feeling very assured. "For her own good."

"And don't forget your own family, Mr. Weeks. Four wee ones and another on the way. When the duke tosses you out, you'll find no better work than with my company."

"Right," he said, more firmly now, and feeling quite assured he was doing the right thing in light of this reminder.

"Good man. That will be all."

Charlie Weeks nodded, put his crumpled hat back into place, and left his new employer, resolved to the work ahead, whether he liked it or not.

Mr. Lightfoot returned to sit behind his desk and considered what he had just learned. Miss Honeywell wouldn't dare refuse him now, he thought grimly. He opened a desk drawer and pulled out a bottle of single malt he kept for special occasions and poured himself a hefty dose into a tumbler. He sat back and sipped the amber liquid, feeling quite satisfied with himself.

Miss Honeywell would be his wife in a matter of days, one way or another. He almost hoped she would refuse him tomorrow, just so he would have the pleasure of seeing the look on her face when he had her trussed and gagged and on her way to Gretna Green the day after that. He loved a woman with a bit of fight in her. And oh, how she would fight him!

Mr. Lightfoot chuckled into his whiskey, aroused by the mere thought of that strumpet writhing beneath him. He could hardly wait for his wedding night.

He chuckled again and toasted himself. "Who's to say I have to wait?" he muttered. He'd have her long before they reached Scotland. Just to show her who her lord and master was. That proud bitch had toyed with him for too long, and it was about time she got what was coming to her.

As he finished his drink and poured himself another, the sun began to set outside, casting the room into strange shadows. And just in case the heavens had not made their point, the clear skies began to darken and the sound of thunder rolled in the distance.

Miss Alice Honeywell would have known exactly what these signs portended. Indeed, they would have given even the recently departed Mr. Weeks, possessed of a wife and four and a half babes, significant cause for concern.

Chapter Twelve

In Which Miss Honeywell Hosts a Dinner Party

ASTRID DECIDED to wear her best frock to the evening's entertainments not out of any misplaced notions of pleasing her aunt, but rather because she was not going to give the old bag the satisfaction of calling her out for not dressing for the occasion.

The occasion being the chance for Aunt Emily and Davina to lick the duke's boot heels.

Furthermore, she did not want her aunt to think she could not play the part of a genteel hostess when she put her mind to it. She was going to be the perfect lady tonight. Contrary to what Aunt Emily might think, Astrid was not raised in a barn.

In a brewery, maybe, but not a barn.

And if she wished to look her best partly because she knew Davina was going to look *her* best, then that was her feminine prerogative. Not that she had anything to worry about. Davina would doubtless show up in some awful bowed concoction that Aunt Emily had chosen for the poor, vicious creature.

And not that Astrid cared what certain persons of the male persuasion might think, either. That was *not* why she was wearing her best dress.

Astrid's best dress was a simple round gown made of striped green silk taffeta. One of Alice's castoffs that had been hemmed at the ankles and let out at the bust. It was not in the first height of fashion, but neither was it too dated. It had capped sleeves and a bit of fichu peeking out of the bodice. The color and cut suited Astrid, and together with her mother's pearls and a pair of Alice's gloves, she looked quite elegant indeed. Flora had even managed to tame the riot of her hair into some semblance of order on top of her head, only a few sprigs escaping their pins and curling over her neck.

She would never be a beauty like Alice, what with her unfortunate eyes. And hair and freckles and height. But she had never aspired to beauty.

And in the candlelight, no one could remark upon her eyes anyway.

Alice accompanied her downstairs, and they greeted their aunt and cousins at the door, followed by the vicar, who nearly fell over himself in his haste to kiss Astrid's hand and stutter out his greeting. "M-may I say, Miss H-H-Honeywell, w-what an h-h-honor it is to be invited to d-d-dinner tonight. Simply an h-honor, and a d-d-delight. Y-you look smashing. Oh, dear, can I say that?"

The vicar was a stutterer. It made Sunday mornings a true test of Christian fortitude.

"Of course you may, Mr. Fawkes. It was my intent to look smashing," she said, as she led the party into the drawing room.

Aunt Anabel, who was dozing by the fire, perked up a bit and lifted her cane. When she saw Lady Emily, her eyes widened in alarm, and she promptly fell back into a suspiciously deep sleep.

Lady Emily arranged herself in the biggest chair in the room. She made Davina sit on the settee next to her and would not allow Mr.

Robert Benwick, Wesley's insufferable younger brother, to take the spot next to his sister. Robert muttered something under his breath and crossed to the decanter. He swallowed his first port of the evening in one gulp.

Astrid sat next to Davina, just to make her aunt scowl. She knew her aunt was attempting to manage things so Montford would have to take up the seat when he arrived, and though she didn't like the duke, she liked giving her aunt any sort of satisfaction even less.

She smiled unpleasantly at her aunt and turned to her cousin. She only just refrained from shielding her eyeballs against the glare cast off Davina's gown. It was hideous, just as she had expected, done up in some sort of color that hovered between green and purple, and embellished quite liberally with bows. Bows on her shoulders, bows on her bosom. Bows encircling her waist and hem.

"How lovely you look tonight, Davina," she said. "Is that a new gown?"

Davina smoothed her hands over one of the bows. "It is. I had it made in London. It's all the rage."

Astrid was once again thankful she had never had the honor of visiting the city. "That color is very . . . unique."

"Puce is quite fashionable this Season. Not that *you* would know."

"Of course not. You are so very lucky to be so fashionable. That gown is quite . . . singular. Only you could wear something so . . . utterly one of a kind."

Davina's eyes narrowed, as if she suspected she was being insulted in some way—which she was—but was uncertain quite how.

"So where is he?" Aunt Emily demanded.

"Where is who, Aunt?"

"You know very well."

The gentlemen fled *en masse* to the sideboard at Aunt Emily's tone.

"You mean His Grace. I do not know what could be keeping him. Shall I check the garderobes?" she retorted breezily.

Aunt Emily glared at her.

She smiled back. "He is no doubt wishing to make a grand entrance. You know how dukes are."

Davina sighed dreamily next to her, as if she *wished* she knew how dukes were.

After a few minutes with no sign of the duke, Aunt Emily began to fidget. "He's lost. You should really keep a proper butler, Astrid. His Grace is not used to having to enter a room unannounced. Nor am I," she added.

At that moment, the door pushed open, and Montford strode into the room, groomed and polished to a high gloss. He wore an evening suit and waistcoat of unrelieved black, his cravat of snowy white linen spilling gracefully over his collar and pinned with a large black opal. Save for the small cut above his right eye, he looked even more imposing than he had the first time Astrid had seen him.

Everyone rose to their feet simultaneously and dropped into low bows and curtsies. Even Astrid found herself following her aunt's lead.

As she rose to her full height, she found the duke's dry gaze settled on her.

Then he came to her side and did the most surprising thing. He took her hand in his own and kissed her fingertips. "Miss Honeywell, you look a vision."

She did not blush. She was too startled to do that. "Thank you, Your Grace. So do you."

He arched his brow as if to say touché, and turned toward the other ladies.

Aunt Emily simpered—actually simpered!—under Montford's scrutiny. "Your Grace, how nice of you to join us at our little family gathering. We were not properly introduced before . . ."

"You are Lady Emily. I remember from the gardens," he said, giving her a perfunctory bow.

Aunt Emily looked chagrined.

The duke turned to Davina and did a double take when he saw her gown. "You must be Miss Davina Benwick," he said unenthusiastically. He bowed shortly again, then strode to Alice's side and took up her hand. He kissed it as well. "You look stunning, Miss Alice. An absolute picture."

"Th-thank you, Your Grace," Alice said haltingly. She threw Astrid a veiled look of satisfaction.

Aunt Emily's face was red from the obvious snub. Davina looked as if she wanted to hide behind her bows. For once, Astrid was immensely pleased with Montford's behavior.

"Montford," Sir Wesley called from the sideboard. "Care for a tipple?"

"No, thank you, Mr. Honeywell. I rarely indulge," he said, moving over to Aunt Anabel.

All the guests, who had not been informed of his recent adoption, looked puzzled by Montford's address to Sir Wesley. Sir Wesley flushed and busied himself with pouring his port.

Unaware of the ripple he'd caused—or perhaps very aware, Astrid couldn't be sure which—the duke reached Aunt Anabel's side. The old woman roused herself long enough to recognize her attacker and waved her cane in his direction. "Young man, if you make love to *my* hand, I'll thwack you with my cane. Now, make yourself useful and fetch me a sherry."

Aunt Emily groaned.

"It would be my pleasure," he said smoothly, changing his direction and walking toward the decanter. He fetched a sherry from a visibly nervous Sir Wesley and returned to Aunt Anabel's side. After handing her the glass, he took the seat beside her.

Having recovered from the duke's initial slight, Aunt Emily resumed her seat with stiff dignity. She shot Astrid a quelling look, as if it were somehow her fault the duke preferred Aunt Anabel's company to Davina's.

Finally before they could grow any more uncomfortable—except for the duke, who was looking quite satisfied with himself, and Aunt Anabel, who wouldn't care if she was sitting next to the devil himself—Flora came in and announced dinner.

The duke offered Aunt Emily his arm, since she was the highest-ranking female, and Aunt Emily took it with less enthusiasm than she had displayed earlier in orchestrating this party. She had been caught off guard by the duke's formidable intractability and was doubtless reconfiguring her campaign. The rest followed behind in awkward silence, Astrid on the arm of Robert, who clutched his port in his other hand and muttered something about missing another engagement for "this bloody farce."

When they were all seated, Aunt Emily glanced first at her daughter, looking satisfied by her placement next to the duke. When she saw Alice, however, on the duke's left, her eyes narrowed. They narrowed even further at the two empty settings near the end.

"You have laid the table for too many, Astrid."

Astrid smiled. "No, I haven't. I told Antonia and Ardyce they could join us. It is so rare you join us at Rylestone Hall that they wanted to be in attendance. They are so *fond* of you, Aunt."

Aunt Emily clutched the side of the table and shut her eyes in silent prayer.

On cue, the two children in question appeared at the door, looking deceptively innocent in their dresses. They bobbed curtsies to their aunt and the duke and made their way to their seats. Everyone seemed relieved when they were seated without incident.

The first course came out, a *pot-au-feu*, as her aunt called it. Astrid called it soup, but not the sort of soup they normally enjoyed at the Hall. It was green, brothy, and very French.

"I have loaned my French chef, Monsieur Roualt, to my cousins, Your Grace," Lady Emily began when the course was laid out, seeing that Davina was having no luck starting a conversation with her partner.

"How kind of you," the duke murmured.

Astrid saw Lady Emily surreptitiously nudge her daughter under the table. Davina jumped and cleared her throat. "Do you have a French chef, Your Grace?"

The duke, who was in the middle of his first taste of soup, paused and lowered his spoon. He turned to Davina. "I do."

"He must be an excellent chef. Has he any particular specialties?"

"Ham sandwiches and meat pies," he said flatly.

Astrid nearly blew her soup out of her nose.

"Oh!" Davina said, startled. "How . . . er, unusual in a French chef. I had the pleasure of attending many elegant tables when I was in London these past months."

"My daughter made her debut last Season," Lady Emily explained.

The duke returned to his soup.

"I am surprised we did not cross paths at the Devonshire ball last month," Lady Emily continued to name-drop, undeterred.

"I was not in attendance. I see very little of the Season," he said shortly.

Davina looked crestfallen.

"His Grace is active in Lords, my dear. He hasn't the time for balls," Wesley chimed in helpfully.

"No, I simply do not like balls. Or routs. Or parties in general," the duke said. "I find society terribly dull."

Davina looked gutted.

Astrid smiled into her *pot-au-feu*.

Lady Emily stared at the duke through pursed lips, immensely displeased by his contrariness.

The vicar, seated across from the duke, found courage enough to break the tense silence that had descended over the party. He leaned forward into his soup bowl. "Such an h-honor, Y-your Grace. It really is serendipitous, q-quite serendipitous indeed, for I was just remarking to m-m-my Lady Emily how p-p-pleasant it is to h-have someone of y-y-y-your exalted station in our little h-hamlet. As you are our landlord, m-m-m-may I welcome you at church services tomorrow m-m-myself?"

The duke set aside his spoon and smiled mildly at the vicar. "Thank you, no. I don't attend services as a general rule."

Astrid exchanged knowing glances with Alice. This just kept getting better and better.

Mr. Fawkes blinked behind his spectacles. "Oh, oh, that is . . ."

"I am indifferent on matters of religion," the duke announced to the table, as if daring anyone to contradict him.

"I-i-indifferent? Why, h-how . . ." Mr. Fawkes blanched at the duke's dour expression. "H-how *interesting*."

"Surely, Your Grace, that is not so," Aunt Emily said after a moment from the head of the table with a little laugh of disbelief.

The duke, having resumed holding his spoon, set it down once more and turned toward Lady Emily. "What isn't so?" he asked evenly.

"Why, your being indifferent. Surely you jest."

"I rarely jest." He turned to Astrid. "Miss Honeywell, am I the jesting sort?"

She smiled at him. "You are the least amusing man of my acquaintance."

He nodded as if receiving a compliment and took up his spoon.

Aunt Emily continued to watch the duke with a mixture of awe for his station and disgust for his lack of faith. Despite being the most uncharitable person of Astrid's acquaintance, Aunt Emily was a devout church attendee.

Aunt Emily laughed. "But how could someone of your station be indifferent? What sort of public example do you set? And with all that you have been blessed with . . ."

The duke's stare intensified, and Astrid was enough acquainted with him to know he was growing very agitated. "I? Blessed?" He laughed without humor. "But surely, madam, you do not consider material wealth to be a sign of God's grace? Christ was scripted as a pauper, was he not, vicar?"

"I, er, scripted? That is . . ." Mr. Fawkes stuttered, looking severely uncomfortable at the turn of conversation.

"He was reported to have walked about the desert in sandals and rags. No doubt he begged in the streets. If, in fact, he existed," the duke continued.

Lady Emily gasped and covered her mouth with her napkin.

"He was very p-p-poor, granted . . ." Mr. Fawkes looked as if he might weep.

"There you have it," the duke intoned. "Good Christians eschew vulgar displays of wealth. Thank heavens I am not a good Christian, or I would be in serious trouble. I have so very much wealth, you see." He smiled coldly. "Although I am never vulgar."

"Unless talking of your great estate," Astrid cut in, "or nonconformism at the dinner table."

His smile deepened. "You are so very astute, Miss Honeywell." He turned to Aunt Emily. "Is she not astute, my lady?"

Aunt Emily glared at Astrid, as if the duke's intractability were her fault.

"What a serious discussion to be having," Sir Wesley said next to her. "I avow I haven't heard the like since Cambridge. Everyone at Cambridge is an atheist. It is the fashion these days."

"*I* ain't an atheist," muttered Robert, who ignored his soup and was well into his third glass of port.

"I should hope not," Aunt Emily huffed. She gave one final look at the duke, then sat back against her chair with a huff.

Astrid was immensely grateful to the duke for having rendered her aunt speechless.

He took up his spoon to finally begin his course—he had only managed one or two sips since it was set in front of him—but he set the spoon aside once more after tasting it. "It's cold," he declared, pushing away his bowl.

The courses passed amid a trickle of conversation. The vicar and Sir Wesley attempted to stir up safe subjects for discussion, but the duke usually managed to stall these discussions with some non sequitur or other. Around the fifth course, Lady Emily and Davina had both given up on garnering the duke's notice after a short exchange over the color of Davina's gown, in which the duke had stated that he had curtains of that exact shade in his London retiring room.

At this pronouncement, Davina's face turned puce.

Astrid was immensely entertained by the duke's manner. He might be her adversary in general, but tonight she thought he made a fine ally. His contempt for her aunt was quite in line with her own feelings. She was rather jealous of him for handling Lady Emily so well. Astrid was not free to be as honest in her feelings toward her aunt as he was.

She found herself silently applauding the duke as he deftly mowed down every attempt at polite conversation thrown his way. He was quite a master at the indirect insult.

She tended to insult in a very direct manner.

Seeing him interact with her relations, she finally saw how very formidable he could be. In three counties that she knew of, no one dared to cross Aunt Emily. Though only a baroness, she was the daughter of a very powerful earl and never let anyone forget it. But she was no match for Montford. He couldn't give a jot what Lady Emily thought of him, as his manner made abundantly clear. He knew—and Lady Emily knew—that he was so far above her and everyone else at the table he might as well have been sitting on a cloud staring down at them all. In all of England, he was said to wield even more clout than the Prince Regent himself.

It must be very useful to be Montford, having most everyone, even the likes of Lady Emily, currying his favor. And it must be most vexing to encounter people like Astrid herself, who didn't give a toss about his rank. No wonder his trip to Rylestone had undone him so, as no one deferred to him.

Still, he had his own peculiarities. She'd never seen someone so particular about his toilette, and she'd seen Aunt Anabel's snuffbox collection and suspected he was behind its rearrangement. And with every course that came out, she watched him arrange his food on the plate so that none of the items touched—no small feat. He even made the servant drizzle the sauce for the game hen, normally poured over the bird, into a puddle on one side of his dish.

He must have sensed her scrutiny, because he turned to her, looking rather defensive, as if he knew precisely how odd his plate looked. "Is there something amiss, Miss Honeywell?"

She tore her gaze away from his plate and cut into her hen, which was swimming in sauce. She took a lusty bite and smiled at him. He frowned disapprovingly but watched as she devoured the rest of her bird, as if fascinated by it.

The downside to having the duke deflect her aunt was that Lady Emily turned her attention to Astrid and proceeded to vent all of her frustrations by pointing out everything that was wrong with Astrid, Astrid's sisters, Astrid's behavior, the castle, the estate, and anything untoward that could be laid at Astrid's feet.

Astrid nodded at intervals and pushed the food around on her plate, having lost her appetite as soon as her aunt started in. She was quite used to such litanies and knew it was best not to try and defend herself. *That* never ended well with her aunt. She did not think anyone would appreciate a screaming contest over dessert, and she had promised herself to be on her best behavior for Alice's sake. The dinner was already dismal enough anyway.

Once, she caught the duke staring at her, and it was as if she could read his thoughts behind his droll expression. *What*, he seemed to say, *are you not going to fight back?*

By the pudding, Aunt Emily arrived at the subject of Astrid's riding habits, which was a particularly sore one given today's events.

"I heard it from Mrs. Regina Thurgood, who heard it from Mrs. Bourke, that certain of my cousins have been seen riding through Rylestone *astride*," Aunt Emily said with severe disapproval.

At the end of this announcement, one of the servants—very loyal to Astrid—plopped Aunt Emily's portion of syllabub—dyed an improbable red color—in front of her with a thud. The gelatinous substance leaned toward the lady's bosom, nearly touching it, then wobbled in the opposite direction, as if distancing itself from an unpleasant association.

"Indeed, ma'am?" Astrid said smoothly. "And did Mrs. Bourke see this cousin of yours with or without the use of her spectacles?" Not that it mattered. Mrs. Bourke was blind as a bat even with her spectacles.

Aunt Emily narrowed her gaze. "Irresponsible behavior like that reflects poorly upon the whole family. How am I to explain to my friends and the many people who look to me for guidance the reason for such behavior? I call you eccentric and remind them of my dear sister's premature death. But how am I to continue to defend you, Niece, when you persist in such misguided acts? It is a good thing we have so little truly good society in the district, or your reputation would most surely be unsalvageable."

"Yet I thought you said just this afternoon how blessed we were with a surplus of truly good society in the district," Astrid replied sweetly.

"Don't presume to tell me what I have said. I said nothing of the sort."

"Then we have no good society in the district?"

"Don't be difficult, Astrid."

Astrid stabbed her spoon into her dessert and watched it slither in half.

"If your mother were alive . . ."

Astrid rolled her eyes.

". . . she'd never let you go tearing across the countryside in such a manner."

"Ah, but she's not."

"Driven to an early grave by *that man*."

Astrid stiffened at the allusion.

"My father, god rest his soul, was right to cut her off when she defied his dictates and married so very beneath her station," Aunt Emily murmured.

That does it, Astrid thought grimly, letting her spoon clatter rudely against her plate. It was one thing for Lady Emily to malign her, but to malign her parents was quite another. Aunt Emily had gone beyond all bounds of propriety by airing the family's dirty laundry over dinner anyway, and so Astrid felt not the least bothered by loosening her tongue and answering her aunt in kind.

"My father was a gentleman, and of a family far older than the Earl of Carlisle," she retorted.

Someone choked across the table at the mention of the earl. Astrid looked up and saw the duke coughing into his napkin, a look of astonishment plainly writ upon his face.

She dismissed him—*what was his problem?*—and turned back to her aunt.

"'Twas only after the Restoration that the earldom was even created. I believe the first earl was a favorite haberdasher to the king."

Lady Emily turned as red as her dessert.

Astrid turned to the duke and smiled. "Charles II was fond of hats."

He raised an eyebrow. "Ah, indeed."

"Do not insult your ancestors, gel."

"As your family has chosen not to acknowledge us—excepting, of course, for you, Aunt—I don't very well see how they are *my* ancestors. And is it an insult merely to recount history?"

"Insolence. Forwardness. It is no wonder you shall never find a husband."

"But I don't want a husband, Aunt."

"Nonsense. Everyone wants a husband."

"*I* don't," Robert murmured at her side.

Astrid burst out laughing. It was either that or scream.

Aunt Emily glared at her youngest son, then glared at Astrid. "And what of your sisters? What's to become of them?"

Alice sank in her seat.

"That is a good question, my lady," the duke cut in drolly. "What indeed is to become of the Misses Honeywell?"

Lady Emily inclined her head toward the duke in gracious acknowledgment.

"It is a shame, madam," continued the duke, "that these poor orphaned creatures had no sympathetic relations willing to do their *Christian duty* and see them properly settled. The granddaughters of so esteemed a peer as the Earl of Carlisle should have taken their place in society, do you not think?"

Lady Emily's eyes narrowed as she realized the duke's subtle criticism.

Astrid's eyes narrowed as well. Just what was Montford about now?

The duke, who had not deigned to touch his syllabub, sat back in his chair and settled a glacial gaze on Lady Emily. "Tell me, Lady Emily, when Miss Honeywell and her sister came of age, should they not have been brought out? Isn't that what one does with females of a certain breeding? I profess myself most ignorant in such matters, as I have no family of my own."

"In most cases, that would be the course of things," Aunt Emily replied carefully.

"You were perhaps not in a position to offer such assistance?"

Lady Emily pursed her lips.

Aunt Anabel, who had fallen into a doze in her dessert, brought her head up. Her wig was noticeably embellished with a dollop of syllabub. "I told *her*, put the gels up on the auction block, see if there's any takers. Sure to be some young buck who'd come up to scratch for our Alice. When I was a young thing, gadding about Versailles, I seen the queen herself, but she hadn't a patch on our Alice's beauty. I told *her*"—this was punctuated by a shake of her wig in Aunt Emily's direction—"one Season, down in our capital, for each of my girls, as she well had the blunt for it."

Alice blushed and sank even lower in her seat. Lady Emily looked as if she wanted to do the same.

"Thank you, Miss Honeywell," the duke said. "You have been most enlightening, as usual."

Aunt Anabel nodded, and so did her wig. She drifted off once more.

"Since Rylestone Hall has come into my possession, so, it seems, do the Misses Honeywell," the duke continued.

"What?" Astrid burst out.

"What?" cried Aunt Emily.

"I am your cousin, Miss Honeywell, or shall we have another recounting of history?" he said grimly. "My great-great-great-aunt wed your great-great-grandfather, or something of that sort, is this not so? That makes you quite possibly my nearest relation. Aside, of course, from my odious second cousin Rupert, who seems to think he's my heir. But that's neither here nor there. We're talking about you and your future."

"Are we?" she ground out.

The duke smiled mildly. "It is clear you and your sisters have been sadly neglected. With no other relations *willing* to do their duty by you, it falls onto my shoulders to see that you take your place in society. Mr. McConnell was most eager to point this out to me earlier tonight."

"Hiram!" Astrid half rose from her seat.

"He seems to think it would behoove all parties involved if you were to be given a Season."

"A Season?" Astrid cried, incredulous.

"A Season!" Aunt Emily and Davina burst out, equally incredulous.

Alice looked dumbfounded, and Sir Wesley and the vicar looked as if they might burst into tears. Only Sir Robert, Aunt Anabel, Ant, and Art seemed entirely immune to the pronouncement.

The duke's smile was brittle. His eyes glinted with self-congratulation. "As I have no sisters or cousins to chaperone you, I have taken it upon myself to write to a good friend of mine, the Countess of Brinderley, and ask that she accommodate you during your stay in London. She is quite the best *ton*, and shall find you husbands."

"Husbands!" Astrid cried.

"The Countess of Brinderley!" Aunt Emily and Davina cried.

The duke turned toward the pair. "Do you know the countess?"

"We have . . . heard of her," Aunt Emily said in a choked voice.

"Then you shall agree there is no better patroness in London."

"Indeed." Lady Emily looked as if she might choke on her jealousy.

The duke turned his attention to Sir Wesley, whose head kept snapping between Astrid, the duke, and Alice in confusion. "And you, *Mr. Honeywell*, have you any objections to turning your *sisters* over into my keeping? You must be as anxious to see them off your hands as I am."

Wesley sputtered his response.

"Mr. Honeywell? Sisters?" Lady Emily barked. "Benwick, why is he calling you Mr. Honeywell? What deviltry is going on here?"

"I . . . I couldn't say, Moth—Lady Emily—er, Mother. That is . . . I *can* say, with all honesty, that I've quite lost the thread of the proceedings," Wesley finished resignedly.

"Of course you have," the duke said indulgently. He turned to Lady Emily. "Thank you, madam, for providing me with such a detailed accounting of your niece's wayward behavior. I was undecided, before I sat down at this table, whether to pursue my course of action. But you have made it so abundantly clear how dire the situation is. I thank you for making up my mind."

"Yes, well . . ." Lady Emily trailed off, clearly defeated.

He threw down his napkin and rose.

Everyone at the table was obliged to do the same, except for Aunt Anabel, who was still asleep in her pudding. "Commend me to your chef, madam. Now that it is all settled, I think I shall have that glass of port, *Mr. Honeywell.*"

"Certainly," Wesley blustered.

Lady Emily knew when she had been dismissed. With a sniff, she turned and walked stiffly out of the dining room, followed by Davina. Alice trailed behind reluctantly, throwing a despairing glance at Astrid.

Astrid remained where she was, eyes locked with the duke. He seemed as determined as she not to break the stare.

His lips slowly lifted at the edges. He was well pleased with himself, having managed to simultaneously slay two dragons this evening. He had routed Aunt Emily, but he had trampled Astrid in the process.

She did not feel at all guilty when she took a spoonful of her syllabub and flicked it across the table at him. It landed with a plop against his cravat.

His smile only deepened as the viscous substance slithered down his waistcoat.

She hadn't needed Ant and Art after all. She turned to her younger siblings, who were looking quite confused at having to leave their puddings—which they had combined together to form a bulbous-looking figure of a man—and bid them to accompany her to the drawing room.

They left Aunt Anabel to her own fate.

⊷ ⚎ ⊶

AN HOUR later, Astrid found herself blessedly alone in the drawing room. She poured herself a sherry and sat back in her seat. She found no enjoyment in the liquor, only a slight easing of tension in her muscles after a very trying day.

Aunt Emily had left the castle in high dudgeon after dinner, Davina huffing along at her side, the vicar stuttering apologies at everyone, as if *he* had ruined the evening. Astrid had been spared having to endure sitting with them in the drawing room, which was a small mercy, but she knew that one day her aunt would make her pay for tonight's insults. It was not a comforting thought.

However, at present, her lady aunt was the least of her problems. The duke had been quite serious over dinner, of that she hadn't a doubt, yet she still couldn't quite believe her ears. A Season!

She would have rather gone to gaol.

What the devil could he mean by sponsoring a Season for them?

Well, perhaps in Alice's case it was welcome news. It was what Alice had always wanted, acquiring a little Town Bronze, as they called it. As the duke had implied, Lady Emily had been too hateful and greedy to ever give them a come-out. Astrid had never minded for herself, but she had always thought it had not been well done of her aunt to slight Alice when she had come of age. Astrid knew that this was partly on account of Alice's beauty, of which her aunt and cousin were jealous. Davina showed to disadvantage next to her cousin.

Anyone showed to disadvantage next to Alice.

Astrid was not against the idea of sending Alice to London, if it was what her sister wanted. But as for herself, it was out of the question. She was six and twenty. She was unattractive, sharp-tongued, and firmly set against matrimony. If the duke thought he was going to make her leave Rylestone, he had quite another thing coming. He'd have to physically subdue her. Which meant he'd have to catch her first, hog-tie her for transport to London, and put a gun to her head before she'd agree to step foot in a London drawing room.

She was not going to do it, and it was as simple as that.

But as she sipped her sherry, tentacles of dread worked up her spine. No amount of alcohol was going to banish them, for the fact of the matter was the duke held all of the cards, and he knew it. There were other ways of hog-tying a person other than with rope. There were subtler means of exerting his will. He could snap his fingers and have the whole Yorkshire constabulary—minus Hiram, of course—descend upon Rylestone to arrest her, for one.

She sighed and leaned her head wearily against the chair back.

She'd known it was always going to end in defeat. She only wished she'd had just a little more time.

"Astrid! There you are! I've been looking everywhere for you. We must talk!"

Astrid lifted her head and wearily surveyed the intruder. Sir Wesley, flushed, rumpled, and agitated. Astrid barely contained a groan.

"Was His Grace serious about taking you and Alice to London?" he demanded.

"It seems so."

Wesley looked astonished, vexed. "When were you going to tell me?"

"I did not know there was anything to tell until tonight."

Astrid rose and went to refill her empty glass. Two sherries were bordering on indecent, but she felt she required extra fortification.

Wesley paced in front of her, pulling at his hair. "But this is ridiculous! Utterly mad!"

"Isn't it?" she asked between deep gulps.

"You have no need for a Season, nor Alice."

Astrid grunted her agreement and decided to top off her glass one more time before returning to her seat.

"If the duke wants you wed so much, then we'll just have to push up the date of our nuptials."

Astrid choked on her drink so badly it went up and out of her nose. She glanced at Wesley in shock. "Excuse me?"

"Our wedding," he said as if she were daft. "We'll just have to do it sooner rather than later."

"Wesley, I never agreed to marry you."

Wesley brushed aside this fact with a wave of his hand. "Of course you're going to marry me, Astrid. We've been practically betrothed since the cradle."

"I was unaware of this betrothal."

Wesley looked at her beseechingly. He grabbed her hand. "Come now, we've always known we would wed. I never pressed it before in the past because I knew you weren't ready, and there was my mother . . ."

"Wesley . . ."

"But now the duke has come and threatened such an . . . absurd . . . proposition as to send you to London, I can see no solution but our marriage. It is logical, and it is prudent."

Astrid could see neither logic nor prudence in the plan. She loved her cousin, but she would not marry him. No one would benefit from such an arrangement.

And there was no way on God's green earth she was going to have Aunt Emily for a mother-in-law. She'd rather . . .

She'd rather have a Season in London than that.

So there *was* something worse than the duke's proposition, after all.

"Wesley, I'm not marrying you."

"Nonsense," he said, taking the glass from her hands and setting it on a table. Then he caught her off guard by putting his hands on her waist and pulling her near.

"What do you think you're doing?"

"I'm going to kiss you," he said as if speaking to a child. "Then we'll see about your answer."

"I was unaware you had proposed."

Wesley scowled. "Come on, Astrid. You'll see I'm right in a moment."

"I am not going to . . . oh, stuff!" she managed just before his lips clamped onto hers.

His lips were warm, soft, and wet. She could taste the sweetness of his port and pudding on them. The sensation of his lips covering hers was not unpleasant, but neither was it particularly remarkable. Astrid had read a lot of poetry. She knew what physical raptures kisses were said to be capable of producing, but she felt none of that. Either every poet since Homer had been guilty of gross misrepresentation, or Wesley was simply not capable of provoking such a response in her.

And after a while, the kiss became a shade uncomfortable, as if she were kissing her brother or Aunt Anabel. Or a fish.

She pushed against his chest, ending the kiss.

He ceased without a fight and stared down at her, as if puzzled by something. He did not look as if he had enjoyed the kiss either and was at a loss to explain why.

She could explain why very easily.

They were not suited.

"That didn't work," Wesley said, dumbfounded.

She rolled her eyes and started to give him a dissertation as to why, when a voice interrupted them across the room.

"I thought kissing one's brother was illegal."

Astrid's heart skidded to a halt. Wesley blushed to the roots of his hair. They jumped away from each other and faced their intruder.

Astrid cleared her throat and met a pair of livid silver eyes.

He was angry?

How very interesting.

She regained her composure and smiled sourly at him. "Montford."

Chapter Thirteen

In Which the Duke's Holiday Steams Up

MONTFORD HAD had many successes that evening. He had put a self-satisfied, mean-spirited baroness in her place; he had managed not to swoon when the impossibly red syllabub was placed in front of him, reminding him of a clot of congealed blood; he had blasphemed not once but twice against the Christian God—once, he thought smugly, at the dinner table!—*and* he'd rendered Miss Honeywell speechless.

The latter was by far the sweetest.

But his one failure was costly. He had failed to conquer his inexplicable lust for Miss Honeywell. Indeed, when he had first seen her in the drawing room this evening, scrubbed up, trussed, and pinned into the first attractive article of clothing he had seen her wear, her hair piled into a halfway fashionable coiffure, her graceful neck adorned with a simple strand of pearls, he had lost his head.

He had not meant to kiss her hand. But he had thought he'd burst for sure if he didn't touch her.

And afterward, to save face, he'd had to kiss Alice's hand, too. He would have done the same to the Lady Emily and her daughter, if he could have stomached it.

Miss Honeywell was not pretty. Next to Alice, she didn't stand a chance. No woman did. But even next to Alice, she was hard to ignore. The hair was unsightly. The eyes were monstrous. The freckles outrageous. She was too plump. And she exuded from every cell of her being a restless, ungovernable spirit that seemed to him physically palpable, pulsing in the air surrounding her. Did no one else feel it? Did no one else understand what a horrible power she wielded?

Lady Emily, perhaps, did, and she did her best to break Miss Honeywell's spirit with every word she spoke. Montford could hardly blame Lady Emily for committing the unpardonable sin of openly criticizing her relative at the dinner table. Miss Honeywell had the effect of turning one inside out.

Montford himself burned to defeat her.

All through dinner he'd wanted to reach across the table with his knife and saw off the three little corkscrews of fiery hair that had escaped their pins. He wanted to yank the uneven puff of fichu out from her bodice, whose asymmetry made his palms sweat. He wanted to gouge out one of her eyes with his soup spoon and replace it with one that matched. But the problem was he didn't know which one to keep: the one the color of ripe autumn wheat, or the one the color of the heavens.

And when she'd flung syllabub on him, he'd gone as hard as a rock.

It was not to be borne.

Even two uncustomary after-dinner snifters of port had not calmed him down one iota.

He was glad he was leaving on the morrow.

Yet he had to face Miss Honeywell at least once more before he could retreat to his room and hide until dawn. And he was determined to be the victor in their last confrontation. He would inform her of his plans for her and her family, and she would be made to see that she had no choice but to comply.

He had the upper hand.

Or at least he thought he did, until he entered the drawing room and observed Miss Honeywell locked in a passionate kiss with her cousin/brother. His vision clouded, his head thrummed, and his heart gave out for several astonished moments.

He struggled to regain his composure, but three days of torture and two glasses of port took their toll.

He was out of his mind with blind rage.

He'd thrash Sir Wesley. He'd thrash *her*.

He'd . . . he'd . . .

He'd pull himself together if it killed him. "I thought kissing one's brother was illegal."

The two guilty parties jumped apart and faced him with alarm.

Sir Wesley looked as if he might cry.

Miss Honeywell was red-faced and defiant.

"Your Grace! I know what this might seem—" Sir Wesley blurted.

"Please, don't let me interrupt such a lovely family moment."

"You already have," Miss Honeywell retorted. Another corkscrew sprang from its pins, making his pulse jump.

"Your Grace, you misunderstand. I am not—"

He held up a hand to stop Sir Wesley. "You are not her brother. Yes. I know, Sir Wesley. What kind of imbecile do you take me for?"

"Shall I answer that?" Miss Honeywell muttered.

He gave her a deadly smile.

She glared at him and clenched her fists. "Wesley, I think you had better leave. His *Excellency* and I have much to discuss."

Wesley glanced uneasily between them and decided to cut his losses. He fled the room.

Montford waited for her to break first. His diligence was rewarded, for at length she turned from him and stalked to a table, where she retrieved a glass of sherry and drank its contents in one gulp. "Well?" she bit out as she refilled her glass.

"Shall you explain yourself?"

Her eyes cast daggers at him over her glass. "I don't know what you mean."

"Let me make myself clearer. Do you make it a habit of kissing every man who crosses your path?"

Her color heightened. "Don't be absurd."

"I should warn you now that such fast behavior shall not be tolerated in London."

She laughed. "If that is the case, perhaps I should stay here."

"No. It is quite decided. You are going to London with your sisters."

She set her glass aside and closed her eyes. Several clicks of silence ensued. He was uneasy what lay on the other side. He felt the air was electrically charged, and the next words out of her mouth would incinerate both of them.

He was almost disappointed when she merely sighed with resignation. "Tell me what you have decided."

It was the voice of defeat. He should have felt victorious. All he felt was deflated.

And he hated her for making him *feel* at all. "You have cheated me," he began.

"If that is how you must see it," she muttered.

"You have cheated me," he began anew, telling himself to stay calm, "and you have committed fraud. But rather than profiting from it, you have invested it back into the estate in some misguided effort to restructure the social order."

She snorted.

"I could throw you in gaol for what you've done," he continued.

"Then do so. Get it over with."

"Miss Honeywell, I am not a bloody monster."

"Are you not?"

He ignored her and clutched his hands behind his back so he wouldn't be tempted to strangle her. "When I determined to travel here, I admit I was ready to hang the lot of you. And you have made it very, very hard not to make me want to follow through with it. Never in my life have I been treated so infamously. However, I am not unreasonable. I can understand why you have done what you have done, and the situation is not at all unsalvageable. Clearly, I cannot make you give up Rylestone Hall—"

She glanced up at him, clearly taken aback. Her eyes were wide with shock and something that looked like hope.

He looked away. "Of course it is your family's home, and it has been so for centuries, no matter what the contract says."

"Your Grace!" she breathed, the relief in her voice unmistakable.

"However," he said quickly, "by law it is mine. By extension, all who live under it are mine as well."

Her relief vanished abruptly. Fury replaced it. "I am not your property!"

"You are four unmarried women in a very precarious position. Clearly, things cannot continue as they are. You cannot continue to run this estate, for one. Mr. McConnell shall assume full responsibility from now on. And he shall take his orders from me."

"Has my management been so terrible? Tell me!"

"No, it has not," he answered honestly. "But it is unlawful. And unseemly. You are an unmarried female with no legal right to administer my lands."

"Perhaps not. But I am better at what I do than ten men."

"I will not argue with you on this point. You can't win."

She groaned and ran her hands through her hair in frustration, pulling half of it from its pins. "How unfair it is that simply because I wasn't born a man everything can be taken!"

She stared at him in abject misery, and he felt a pinprick of guilt. "Not everything. Upon your contracting a decent marriage, Rylestone Hall and a good portion of its acreage shall be settled upon you, as well as an income. For your sisters, I shall provide dowries for each of them as well."

"You mean, our husbands shall be rewarded for taking us off your hands. Rylestone Hall won't belong to me. It will belong to my husband."

"I cannot change English law."

"You bloody well can! You're *Montford*! You're more powerful than the Prince Regent." She turned away from him, her shoulders visibly shaking. "And I suppose I have no choice in the matter. You have damning evidence against me that you're more than willing to blackmail me with."

She was entirely correct. It was precisely what he was doing. But once again, she had sucked all of his enjoyment out of his victory over her. "I think I am being more than generous, under the circumstances. Most females would die for a Season."

"I am not most females. I have no wish to be auctioned off like a damned brood mare!"

"I think it a bit more civilized than that," he said, wincing at the lie. She was quite right. The social whirl in London was little better than an auction block for families to trade their daughters and sisters to the highest bidder. He himself had just bought one of them for his duchess.

She turned back to him, her rage as palpable as the fire burning in the hearth next to him. "You think you have concocted a fine plan, don't you? Throwing a bit of your blunt around, packing us off to the marriage mart, and ridding yourself of a most unsavory complication to your perfect little life. But did you ever consider that it won't work? You expect me to land a fribble of a husband? Me? Your Grace, look at me!"

She spread her arms wide, causing her gown to stretch tight across her breasts. He forced himself not to squirm and to keep his eyes trained on her face. He could not breathe from the weight of his lust.

"I am six and twenty years old. I am not pretty by any stretch of the imagination. I cannot hold my tongue, and you yourself think I am a common strumpet. I do not think how you can expect me to find a husband."

"I'm sure you can browbeat someone into it," he said before he could stop himself. "And you come with a castle."

She burst into hysterical laughter. "A crooked castle. Yes, that does sweeten the pot. I'm sure many men would marry a castle—and take me in the bargain."

They stared hard at each other.

"I'm to be grateful for your condescension, I suppose," she said after a moment, her head cocked to one side, studying him intently.

He shrugged. "I do not care for pretense. You are free to loathe me."

A shadow of a smile flitted over her lips. "How very generous you are." She paused. "However, I have no need to go to London shopping for a husband. I have had three offers for my hand already. I shall simply marry one of them and have done with it."

Something inside of him withered. It was one thing to imagine Miss Honeywell in the far distant future in a far distant city barreling her way through society gentlemen, and quite another to be faced with an immediate prospect. He did not like this at all, and it must have shown on his face, because she turned away from him with a satisfied smile and began to shuffle around the contents of one of the tables he had rearranged earlier, placing everything at sixes and sevens.

"You have had *three* offers?" he demanded.

"It is unlikely, isn't it?" she said softly, moving a small dish to the edge of the table.

His pulse thundered in his veins. No, it wasn't unlikely, he realized. For all of Alice's beauty, half the village was in love with her unsightly sister.

"Mr. Lightfoot has asked twice—"

"Mr. Lightfoot!" he bellowed.

"And Wesley has asked, oh, three times. So, including the vicar's proposal, I suppose that technically makes six times I have been asked to leg-shackle myself to a fool." She sighed. "Since I doubt I shall find any better in London, I suppose I shall make do with what I have. Though

Mr. Lightfoot is out of the question, as I think he's a blackguard as well as a fool. No, it shall be either the vicar or my cousin."

She tapped her bottom lip, as if considering her options.

He stepped toward her, quite against all of his reason. "The vicar or Sir Wesley. You can't be serious." He had a sudden, queasy feeling in his stomach. "Was that what happened earlier? Did that idiot propose to you?"

"Of course. Why else do you think he was kissing me?"

His breath hitched as he came close enough to smell her—sharp, vibrant lavender, the whisper of something else beneath the perfume, earthy and female and distinctly her own. She faced him squarely, setting her chin at a defiant angle. Her mismatched eyes were full of rage and contempt, but her expression was serenely mocking, as if she knew precisely how she affected him. *Did* she know? Did she know how she plagued him? She was so hideously wrong, yet he burned to possess her.

"Did you accept?" His voice sounded like gravel.

She curled her lips into a smile that was almost feral. "He was trying to convince me when you interrupted."

"Would he have succeeded, I wonder? Are his kisses enough to overcome your aversion to his mother?"

Her smile dimmed. Her eyes shifted away from his ever so slightly.

"They were not, then," he murmured, reading her expression, triumphant in the knowledge that the popinjay had not moved her.

"As I said, we were interrupted." She paused, and her eyes snapped back to his. "And it was a kiss. Singular. And as it was my first, I have no basis for comparison. But I am sure it was quite satisfactory."

He felt as if he had run a mile. He could not draw a decent breath. She had stunned him. "Your first kiss," he repeated in a strange voice.

She held his gaze. "You do not believe me. But I expected that, of course. I know what you think of me."

She must have seen something in his face that she did not like, for she made to move away from him. But he could not let her go.

His hands were on her shoulders instantly, then around her forearms, and he was pulling her toward him. She resisted, of course, raising her hands to his chest as if to shove away from him, but he wrapped his arms around her, crushing her in his embrace. She was warm and soft in all of the right places.

He was intoxicated, maddened by the touch of her. He spread his hands over the small of her back, feeling the ridges of her spine beneath the satin gown, the swell of her backside. He wanted to move his hands lower and cup that delicious softness, but he refrained. She was trembling, and her eyes had become uncertain, her expression as skittish as a wild animal who'd been cornered. He remembered that look from when he had touched her in the library so inappropriately, and now he knew what it was.

She was innocent.

"I believe you," he murmured. And he did. He'd thought her a strumpet, but she wasn't.

Desire electrified every molecule of his body. He wanted her even more than before, and he was ashamed and confused because of it. He was *not* a despoiler of virgins. He did *not* lust after innocents.

Except that he did. He wanted to consume her.

And he felt a primitive rage that Sir Wesley had touched her first. It was one kiss, but it was her first, and it had been lost to him forever.

Mine, an inner voice shouted inside of him. *Mine, mine, mine!*

"What are you doing?" she asked in a shaky voice, pushing against his chest.

He took in a deep breath and expelled it slowly. "Providing a basis for comparison."

Her brow furrowed. A sprig of hair fell over her forehead. His control—such as it was—slipped a little bit more, and he raised his hands to her head, smoothing back her impossible hair. His fingers tangled in it, and the remaining pins popped out, pinging against the parquet floor. He watched her hair spill over her shoulders, down her back, in a chaotic miscellany of spirals and corkscrews. The fire burning in the grate next to them seemed colorless next to the unnatural mass, alive with an inner light. It was out of order, and any attempt to smooth it was fruitless. The curls just sprang back to life once his fingers left them. It was a war he could never win.

With great effort, his hands fell back to her shoulders. He dug his fingers into her tender flesh, anchoring himself to her, his knees weak.

"Did he hold you like this?" he whispered.

She shook her head, staring up at him with apprehension and something else not unwilling that heated his blood.

"No? But I thought I saw it was so." He adjusted his embrace so that his arms encircled her waist, the whisper of silk against satin. "Like this?"

"Close," she murmured.

He lowered his head—what was he doing?—and brushed his lips over hers. She tasted of sherry. Her lips were soft, full. They affected him like opium. He drew back before he lost his mind.

"Like that?" he said huskily.

"'Twas . . . 'twas longer. Deeper," she whispered. Then she licked her lips with her tongue.

Hell. Hell. *Hell!* That did it.

He kissed her again without restraint, squeezing her against him, his mouth hard and punishing. She cried out and attempted to move away once more, but he followed her with his body and raised his hand to the nape of her neck, so that he could hold her in place. He kissed her and kissed her until all the fight went from her, and she clung to him as desperately as he clung to her. When his tongue demanded entrance, her lips parted eagerly, welcoming him inside. She was hot and wet and sweet, her mouth to him the embodiment of all the sin and temptation and gluttony he'd always spurned but secretly craved. He thrust into her in a parody of what he wished to do with another part of his anatomy, which had long since grown rigid and impatient with need.

When she began to kiss him back, learning quickly under his tutelage, her tongue tangling with his, her teeth nipping his bottom lip, teasing him, enticing him, he lost the last vestige of his sanity.

He moaned against her sweet mouth and clutched one of her breasts in his hand. It was full and soft, and its peak tightened underneath his palm.

They stumbled across the room. He hit something hard with his backside, and something crashed to the floor. Oblivious to everything but her, he spun her around and lifted her onto the desktop he had hit, never breaking their kiss. He moved between her legs, enveloped by her heat and softness, and stuck his hand down the front of her dress clumsily, like a green lad. He could not stop himself. He had to know what she felt like.

He groaned. She was soft as silk, heavy and ripe in his hand, her nipple rigid with desire. She made some sound in the back of her throat and arched into him, filling his hand even more completely with her flesh.

It was almost too much. He nearly came right then, just from the feel of her breast, so full, fuller than he'd ever known before. He pressed himself against the juncture of her thighs, reveling in her soft heat, the feel of her hands on him, feather light, searching his torso, his shoulders.

He wanted to see her, not just feel her. He couldn't think past his need. He withdrew his hand and began to fumble with the buttons on the back of her gown. He tore his mouth from hers and concentrated on his shaking fingers.

He cursed. He could not make them work. A button popped off, and then another, and then in his clumsiness the fabric tore.

He cursed again.

Then he made the mistake of glancing at her face. She was dazed from kisses, her lips swollen, her eyes glistening. She stared at him strangely, as if she'd never quite seen him before. She was afraid and a little repelled by the intensity of their passion, but she was aroused as much as he. He knew that if he succeeded in getting her dress off of her, he would take her, and she would let him. She was powerless to stop the force of her own instinct, much less his.

They were like animals.

His stomach soured with self-disgust.

God, he was like a bloody beast in the field. She made him less than what he was, and so twisted with primeval urges his brain turned to marmalade. He hated this loss of reason, this disconcerting vibrancy of emotion she engendered. It had no place in the carefully ordered citadel he'd so painstakingly erected out of the mire of his childhood. She was excess and disorder and unfathomably dangerous to the foundations of his very identity. She demanded of him something beyond the physical— her spirit called out to his like a siren's song, and if he let himself too near it, he would be destroyed. Rutting with her on a desktop would satisfy an immediate need, but he knew instinctively his thirst for her would not be quenched. It would grow worse.

He could not do this.

Yet even with all of these distressing thoughts running through his head, he still couldn't keep his hands off her, he couldn't keep his body from trying its best to take its animal satisfaction, whether he liked it or not.

He tried her buttons again. His fingers still would not work.

"Montford."

His name, whispered against his ear, finally succeeded where his will had failed.

His hands fell away, and he stepped back, out of the circle of her skirts and the heat of her body. It was like stepping out of an enchantment. He was still painfully aroused, and he was glad of the shadows filling the room, hiding his loss of control.

She seemed to come back to herself as well. Her eyes focused, her body tensed. She glanced down at her ruined bodice, then up at him, one hand raised to her lips, the other covering the tear at her bosom. Her face heated with shame.

He turned away, tried to draw breath into his lungs. "I shall leave at first light."

"Yes."

He hesitated. "The countess shall be here within the week. If you decide your . . . suitors here do not . . . suit, you will accompany her to London. I shall have my solicitor convey the terms of our arrangement in writing and provide what funds you shall need for London. You can contact me through him. I do not think it necessary for us to meet again, Miss Honeywell."

She didn't answer.

He did not run out of the room. He couldn't with the damned pole between his legs. But he wished he could. He wished he could run all the way back to London and forget Miss Astrid Honeywell had ever existed.

⊷ ⊶⊰⊱⊷ ⊶

THOMAS NEWCOMB was one of the few of the duke's servants who actually liked his employer, one of the fewer still who was not afraid of him. Newcomb was an ex-boxer who could well take care of himself, if it came to falling out of the duke's favor. However, Newcomb knew that this was highly unlikely for two reasons: a) the duke rather liked him, and b) the duke was, beneath his cold, remote exterior, a bit soft in the heart. Newcomb's own position attested to this.

After a precipitous end to his boxing career, he'd fallen on hard times and into bad company. The duke had caught him out in a swindle at Tattersall's, where Newcomb had been successfully selling rum goods to the young bucks. Instead of giving him over to the constable, the duke had offered him a job. He said he'd liked Newcomb's eye for horseflesh, but Newcomb knew the duke need not have done what he did. Most of his class would have had Newcomb drawn and quartered or transported to some tropical colony. The duke had seen something in Thomas Newcomb that not even Thomas Newcomb, who had given up on himself long before, had seen at the time.

The duke had saved him.

It was high time he returned the favor.

It had been clear to Newcomb for a long time that the duke was slightly . . . er, off. Those of His Grace's station called him "aloof" and "eccentric," but as far as Newcomb could tell, those were fancy words for "unhappy" and "cracked." For all of the duke's power and money, Newcomb didn't envy the man. The duke conducted his life as if walking a very thin tightrope above a very deep chasm. Newcomb had never encountered such a stuffed-shirted, self-flagellating, thoroughly miserable geezer in all of his years.

Newcomb's opinion of his employer happened to coincide with Viscount Marlowe's own assessment: what the duke needed was a good roll in the hay. And Newcomb, whose take on the married state was rather different than the viscount's (Newcomb had recently wed Nora, the love of his life), went a step further in his opinions. The duke needed a wife.

Not that frosty ice princess the duke had contracted to make his duchess. But a real woman, one who'd give the duke a merry chase and knock some life back into him. The duke was a well-made, well-set-up bloke, and he was every bit as red-blooded as the next fellow. He just needed the right bit of skirt to make the duke realize he wasn't made out of granite.

This was an opinion Newcomb had harbored for years. He'd watched and waited for the duke to finally meet his match, but he'd watched and waited in vain. Until now. Newcomb had known the moment he'd seen the duke look at Miss Honeywell that first day, when His Grace had been on his arse in the mud. His certainty had been reinforced when he'd come across them pulling out each other's hair in the library, their clothes suspiciously disordered.

Miss Honeywell had succeeded where every other female in the kingdom had failed. She'd undone the duke. She'd reduced him to a bundle of frayed nerves. He was like a puddle at her feet, and the poor man didn't even realize it.

Newcomb was thrilled. In his opinion, Miss Honeywell was the best thing that had ever happened to the duke.

But when the duke appeared at his door in the servants' wing of the castle late in the evening, Newcomb knew that the course of true love was not running as smoothly as he had hoped. The duke never came to his room, and the duke never looked so discomposed as he did now. His fine evening clothes were wrinkled, his cravat stained with something red, and his eyes were anything but calm. He looked . . . torn, distraught, and, to be perfectly frank, a bit frightened.

Newcomb knew immediately Miss Honeywell was the cause.

"First light," was all the duke said. "I want to be off at first light."

Newcomb agreed and, ignoring all social conventions, offered the duke some of his whiskey, since the poor bloke looked as if he needed it. The duke refused the offer and left him abruptly. Newcomb watched him walk down the hallway in the wrong direction, reach the end, curse, and turn around. He wisely shut his door before the duke reached it again, in case the duke saw his broad grin.

Newcomb waited another half hour before he left his room for the stables, his decision made. It was not an easy one, for he had no wish to prolong his stay in Yorkshire. He was anxious for his wife Nora's sharp tongue and soft embrace. The sooner he was back in London, the sooner he could get on with the business of procreation. He wanted a daughter. Nora wanted a son. Hopefully they would one day have several of each. And he could not bloody well start on such lofty endeavors with over a hundred miles separating the appropriate body parts.

For another, Newcomb took pride in his position as head of the Montford stables. He saw to it Montford had the best horseflesh in London and the latest models of equipage as befitting his station, even though His Grace, owing to his peculiar aversion to moving conveyances, rarely deigned to travel in them. And Newcomb was quite fond of the new town coach he himself had purchased a month ago. She was a dashing machine, her brass fittings shined to a high polish by his own hand, the ducal crest boldly emblazoned on her doors. Newcomb had the same abiding affection for the coach that captains had for their ships. He'd even named the bloody thing after his own wife. He would take no pleasure—indeed, he would be acutely pained—in what he was about to do.

When he reached the stables and set aside his lantern, he found a heavy sledgehammer in the tool room and approached his pride and joy, grim-faced but resolved.

He was doing this for the duke's own good, he told himself as he lifted the sledgehammer over his head.

One day in the distant future, the duke would thank him, he told himself as the sledgehammer descended against the front axle.

He didn't stop until the axle was shattered beyond repair.

Chapter Fourteen

In Which the Duke's Holiday is Extended

MONTFORD DID not sleep at all that night, acutely aware that two doors down from him a certain female lurked, cutting up his peace. He tossed and turned and was unable to think of anything but what had happened between them in the drawing room. He could still taste her in his mouth, though he had scrubbed it raw. He could still smell her on him, though he had bathed and changed. He could still feel the weight of her breast in his hand and the warmth of her body pressed against him. And every time he recalled the sounds she had made deep in her throat as he kissed her, he broke out into a cold sweat.

His arousal would not subside. It was there, tormenting him underneath his sheets, mocking him. He thought about relieving himself, but that thought filled him with shame and rage. He wouldn't give himself the satisfaction—he wouldn't give *her* the satisfaction. He'd not pleasured himself since he was a green lad. He wasn't about to stoop so low as to behave like a randy adolescent merely because some impertinent chit had got into his blood.

He'd take a mistress as soon as he arrived back in London. Araminta Carlisle bedamned—his future duchess was not going to satisfy this black craving. No, he'd find some buxom widow or courtesan and take care of this little problem of his.

A redhead, he decided. With generous breasts. He'd not had one of those, and he was certain it was the novelty that had him so drawn to this particular female.

Yes, that was it.

But this solution offered no solace to his aching body. It didn't want some random woman. It wanted one woman. One completely unsuitable, frightful-looking woman who angered him with her very existence.

He hated her.

He hated this place and cursed himself for ever stepping out of his London palace.

He fell into an exhausted stupor around dawn, when he was supposed to be hightailing it back to London. By the time he dragged himself out of bed, it was well past midmorning and approaching the noon hour. He felt as if he'd been run over by a mail coach.

His only consolation as he crept downstairs was that his erection had subsided out of sheer exhaustion, and that the castle seemed to be empty. He could not face any of the Honeywell clan—he could not face *her* again. He'd likely lose his mind.

Newcomb was waiting for him down by the stables. His coachman's face was grim, and he could not quite meet his master's eyes. This was unusual in his normally frank, no-nonsense servant. Montford felt his first prick of apprehension.

"'Tis some bad news I have for you, sir," Newcomb said, leading him into the stables.

Montford froze in his boots when Newcomb indicated the carriage and the unmistakable crack in its axle. "What the bloody hell?"

Newcomb thrust his hands in his pockets and rocked on his heels. "Must've happened on the trip up, only it didn't give way 'til recently. Didn't notice it 'til this morning myself."

Montford was dumbstruck. He turned to his coachman in disbelief. "Didn't notice it? You, Newcomb? I find it hard to believe."

Newcomb furrowed his brow. He looked affronted that his skill at his job had been maligned, and just the slightest bit . . . guilty?

But surely not.

Surely Montford's nerves were so shattered by the past three days he was merely seeing things that weren't there. Newcomb was a high stickler when it came to his job. He'd never purposely sabotage his precious carriage.

But someone had. The idea that this was the result of an accident on the journey north seemed flimsy.

Someone did not want him to leave Yorkshire.

An absurd idea. Everyone, including himself, wanted the Duke of Montford on the King's Highway back to London. That was made perfectly clear the day before when he'd nearly been assassinated.

Unless whoever had shot at him yesterday had done this for some nefarious reason as yet understood.

Which made no sense whatsoever.

He pinched himself to make sure he wasn't having a bad dream. "This looks deliberate," he said.

Newcomb's brows shot up in surprise. "You think someone did this on purpose?" He snorted in disbelief.

"It's a little convenient, don't you think? And you yourself said you hadn't noticed anything wrong until this morning."

Newcomb shook his head determinedly. "It was a hairline fracture that didn't snap loose for some time. I remember myself that bit of rough stretch we had outside Hebden. Must've happened then."

Newcomb seemed bloody sure of his theory. So sure of himself, in fact, that Montford was increasingly suspicious. He narrowed his eyes on his driver. "I suppose this shall take some time to fix."

Newcomb nodded and trained his eyes on the carriage. "A week at least."

Montford's heart sank. "A week! Damnation! I'll not stay here another week! I'm leaving today. Saddle up one of the grays."

Newcomb looked alarmed. "They're carriage horses, not saddle bred. You'll not be riding one of them back to London, Your Grace."

"Then I'll buy a horse in the village."

Newcomb shook his head vehemently. "It's Sunday. No place open."

"They'll open for me," Montford muttered.

"Don't think so, Your Grace. It's the festival today."

Montford growled and clenched his hands. Oh, yes, the bloody festival. *That* was where everybody was.

"Begging your pardon, Your Grace, but you look a bit green about the gills," Newcomb said with some concern and a whiff of amusement.

"This is a damned nightmare!" Montford roared, pointing at the broken carriage. "How am I supposed to stand another day in this god-forsaken place?"

"Reckon you'll survive," Newcomb muttered.

Montford glared hard at his driver. Newcomb shrugged and stared at the ceiling.

Why did Montford have the feeling Newcomb knew more than he was telling?

"Damn and blast!" he exploded, turning on his heel and stalking outside. "I'm going to the village. I'm going to find a damned mount and get the hell out of this damned bloody backwater today if it damn well kills me!"

Newcomb fell into step beside him. "Let's hope it won't come to that, sir," he said, too cheerily for Montford's liking.

THE SKY was clear, the air crisp, but not uncomfortably chilly for October, the fall foliage vibrantly hued and at its peak, a pleasing, picturesque backdrop for today's revelries. Sunday was usually a day of reverence, but not when the annual harvest festival arrived. Only the highest sticklers—few and far between in Rylestone, thank God—eschewed the festivities.

The vicar himself was not among this pious vanguard, however. His sermons on the day of the festival were always the liveliest and most stutter-free sermons he delivered all year. And under the pretense of shepherding his flock, he joined in the day's events with enthusiasm every year, and every year this enthusiasm culminated in a noticeably wobbly retreat to the vicarage, often aided by one or two favored parishioners.

Farmers and businessmen from all around the district had driven into the village in the early morning hours to set up their stalls, where all manner of food and sundries could be bought. Honeywell Ale, donated to the festival, flowed freely from the personal tankards of Rylestone's citizenry, both men and women.

Owing to the carnival atmosphere, the normal laws governing conduct between men and women were loosened, leading to many public embraces and more than a few kisses stolen behind the paltry cover of a tree or building. Many marriages were hastily contracted in the weeks that followed the harvest festival, many more babies in the village born nine months to the day afterward. It was somewhat of a badge of honor to bear a festival baby.

Spirits were high, as they always were, and only one or two troublemakers cast a temporary pall over an otherwise merry day. There were not many bad seeds in Rylestone Green.

And the worst seed of all had thankfully departed for London.

Astrid was relieved that when she went back to the castle *he* would no longer be there. She truly was.

But she was in no mood to celebrate. In fact, she felt rather depressed.

Not to mention rather . . . distracted. Her mind kept drifting back to The Encounter, as she had dubbed it in her mind, and every time it did, her body became all tingly, her stomach fluttered, and her cheeks burned. Had he kissed her? She didn't even know what to call what the duke had done to her mouth. It had been obscene. It had been meltingly wonderful. He'd awoken parts of her body—parts of her soul— she'd not known existed.

She would never forgive him for making her feel so . . . so . . .

Ruined.

He had stuck his hand down her bodice, and she had let him. She had craved his touch, and she had wanted more, even as her mind protested. If he hadn't been unable to unbutton her gown, if he hadn't broken their kiss and come to his senses, she didn't know if she would have had the wherewithal to stop him. He'd turned her wits to mush, her body into a raging inferno.

Why? Why had he done it? To humiliate her? To punish her with some primitive display of male dominance?

She would never know, and it did not matter. She'd never see him again. Or if she did, she would make sure she was not alone with him. They seemed to bring out the worst in each other.

And, she reminded herself bitterly, she'd be married by then.

All three of her prospective grooms were at the festival. She'd seen Mr. Lightfoot lurking in the crowd and had promptly hidden herself behind a stall to avoid him. She would not be marrying *him*, that was for certain. As for her cousin—well, that too was out of the question.

Which left the vicar.

She studied Mr. Fawkes from the other side of the green as he attempted to order a meat pie from one of the vendors. As Mr. Fawkes was no good with his m's or his p's, the vendor had plucked up a pie, wrapped it in paper, handed it over, taken his money, and given him change, before he could finish his request.

Astrid liked the vicar. Astrid liked the fact that she would have no problem wrapping him around her little finger. But she could not marry the poor man. It would just be cruel.

She sighed. London it would be.

Alice seemed amenable to the scheme, which wasn't surprising. Sir Wesley was never going to get around to noticing her, and if she couldn't have him, then a Season away from him sounded like music to her ears. It was Wesley's loss if he was an idiot, and Alice had always wanted a Season. To her mind, the duke had been more than generous. He had given them everything they'd ever wanted. Dowries, the Hall, the chance to catch a husband in London. She hadn't seen why Astrid was so upset, as this was what Astrid had ostensibly been working so hard to provide for her sisters to begin with.

But to Astrid's mind, the duke had taken away everything. He had reduced her to what she had worked so hard to deny: an unmarried, dependent, powerless female. Now Astrid knew how Napoleon must have felt when he was exiled to Elba. Sick to his stomach and bristling with indignation.

Well, she'd find a way to escape, just like Napoleon had. She'd go to bloody London and find some poor doddering old thing to shackle herself to. The older the better. He'd likely die during the wedding reception, and she would own the castle and lands outright as a widow. The duke couldn't do anything about it if she married an octogenarian who'd kick off within a few months.

Bastard.

And she was not giving up her managerial duties quite yet. Tomorrow was one of her favorite days of the year, when all of the brewery's employees rode out in different directions to deliver the seasonal supply of ale to cities and towns across the country. She was not going to give up her customary spot on the cart to Hawes, come hell or high water.

She determined to make this clear as she crossed through the crowd to reach Charlie Weeks's side. He was talking to Hiram in front of a keg, the two men deep into a pint of ale. Charlie blanched when he saw her approach, which doubtless meant that news had already spread of her fall from the throne.

She sniffed in Hiram's direction as he doffed his hat to her. "I'm not talking to you, turncoat," she said stiffly.

"Well, now, ain't that a surprise," Hiram answered wryly.

She turned to Charlie and pointed her finger at his chest. "Don't think I'm not coming to Hawes with you tomorrow, Charlie Weeks." She swung her finger at Hiram. "And don't think you can stop me. I'm going, and you can all hang if you don't like it."

Hiram held up his hands in mock surrender. "Easy, lass, easy. I weren't gonna stop ye, for cryin' oot loud."

"Well, good!" she sniffed. "Because I'm going." She turned back to Charlie. "First light?"

Charlie, still rather pale, nodded. "As always, Miss Astrid. I have the cart made up and ready to go already."

"Fine." Astrid crossed her arms and settled her glare on Hiram.

Charlie, sensing the discord in the air, made his excuses and left them.

Hiram cocked an eyebrow and pulled his pipe out of his pocket. "Ach, dunna look at me like that, lass. I done wot best for the lot of ye."

"How is that, I wonder?"

"Himself were beyond fair, all considering. Yer sisters are well set, an' ye won't be caught in yer aunt's web of hatefulness. He be givin' ye the castle, an' that's more'n we ever thought ye'd see."

"If I *marry*, Hiram."

"Aye, an' wot so wrong with tha', pray tell? It's aboot time yer settled in an' had a passel of wee bairns."

"I thought you knew me better, Hiram."

Hiram's brow furrowed. "Wot, ye doan want bairns? Ye doan want a family of yer own? Or a man to warm yer bed?"

Astrid was stung by his harsh tone and didn't know how to answer him. Did she want a family of her own? How would she know, since she had enough trouble dealing with the one she already had? "I've never thought about it. I've been too busy."

"Well, now yer not. Now ye have time to think on it. Now ye have the privilege of figurin' out what ye want. Not what yer sisters want, or the workers want, or yer auntie wants, but what *ye* want."

Her shoulders relaxed. "I'd never thought of it like that, I suppose . . ." she began cautiously.

"Well, mebbe ye should. I'm sure ye'll be thinking a lot in Lunnon. It's a whole nother world there ye've yet to see."

"I won't like it," she said stubbornly.

He puffed on his pipe and shrugged his shoulders. "We'll see, woan we?"

With a harrumph, she stalked off. A few paces later, she stopped and turned back. "You're a traitor, Hiram McConnell. And I'll never forgive you."

"Mayhap. Mayhap not," he said, grinning broadly and saluting her with both his tankard and his pipe.

She harrumphed again and turned to continue her dramatic leave-taking, nearly colliding with an innocent bystander who had the audacity to crowd her path. She looked up to apologize—or snarl—at the person in question. Instead she bit back an oath.

It was Sir Wesley, staring down at her with clear concern. "There you are, Astrid. We must talk."

She rolled her eyes and waved away the arm he'd extended. She turned and stalked in another direction, but he fell into step beside her.

"I wanted to apologize about last night. I don't know what came over me," he said.

"I believe I can say the same," she muttered, thinking not of Wesley but of a silver-eyed scoundrel who'd ruined her life—and her lips. They were still quite tender from his abuse. The thought filled her with a shameful heat.

"I just thought it was the right thing to do," Wesley continued, kicking a pebble with his boot. "It seemed the only thing . . . but it wasn't right, was it?"

She stopped at the distress in his voice, taking pity on her cousin. She turned to him and decided to do everyone a favor and set him straight. God knew someone needed to do so.

He stopped too and stared down sheepishly at his boots. "I just wanted to help. I've always just wanted to help. You know I like you, Astrid. I like all of you . . . better than my own family." He admitted this last bit without the slightest twinge of guilt.

"I imagine you do, Wesley, but I can't marry you."

He grimaced.

"For one, we do not suit. I would run roughshod over you, and you know it. And I have no patience for your . . . hobbies. Steam engines? In boats? Really, Wesley. No, I love you, but as a dear friend. Just as you love me. As a dear friend."

He scratched his head. "Suppose you're right."

"And for another, I hate your mother."

He didn't look the least surprised.

"She's horrible, and I hate her, and I'm not one bit ashamed to admit it."

"She ain't so fond of you either."

"And for another," she continued, taking a deep breath, and hoping she was doing the right thing, "Alice would never forgive me."

His head snapped up. His brow creased in confusion. "What?"

"I said, Alice would never forgive me. She'd likely stab me in my sleep if I married you."

He looked affronted and hurt. "Why'd she want to do a thing like that? I ain't so bad she'd not think me good enough for your husband."

Astrid sighed wearily. "Wesley, you really are an idiot. She'd kill me because she's in love with you, you dolt."

Wesley's eyes grew wide. His jaw attempted to drop off his face. "What?"

"Alice is in love with you. She's been in love with you since she was—oh, about four years old, and you threw your pudding over her head in the nursery."

Wesley's face turned scarlet. "You can't mean it . . . really . . . *Alice*? In love with me?"

"And you're in love with her. Which was why you dumped your pudding on her in the first place."

"Alice? Alice? No, it ain't possible. She can't . . . I mean, I never dreamed she'd . . . But I thought I'd . . . And I'm not . . ."

Astrid wanted to take him by the shoulders and shake him into a complete thought.

He seemed to gather his wits enough to give her a level stare. "I never thought she'd give me the time of day, Astrid. I never thought I was good enough for someone like her." It took several beats for him to realize what he'd implied about Astrid, and the color in his face deepened until it was nearly purple. "Not that you aren't every bit as—"

Astrid snorted to silence his dimwitted apology. "I know what you mean. Alice is . . . Alice."

"Alice is . . . she's an *angel*. She can't love me!" he insisted.

They both turned to study the object of their conversation, who was currently conversing with several earnest-faced young men. Alice was looking particularly lovely in her sky-blue day gown and rust-colored pelisse, her cheeks rosy from the nip in the air. She laughed, and the sound of it carried over in the wind like a birdsong.

Wesley sighed at Astrid's side.

"Nonsense, Wesley, if I say she loves you, she loves you. You're an idiot for not noticing. And she's an idiot for not making her affection clear to you, though God knows it's quite clear to everyone else in the district!"

Wesley didn't seem to hear her any longer, his attention settled firmly on Alice. "God, Astrid, how can I even speak to her now!" he moaned, looking miserable and full of longing.

Astrid's spate of benevolence was over. Now she was feeling distinctly irritated. What had she done? "You'd best figure out how soon before she's out of hearing range. I understand London is quite some distance from Rylestone."

He looked sick. "London! But she can't go to London . . ."

"You might tell her that," Astrid suggested, pushing him in the direction of her sister.

He stumbled forward as if he'd forgotten how to walk.

Really, this was ridiculous. She took him by the arm and tugged him toward Alice. He went quite reluctantly for someone so violently in love.

"Look who I've found," Astrid said, brushing aside the young men crowding Alice. "Wesley's been looking everywhere for you. I believe he wants to say something."

Wesley's mouth worked, but no sound came out.

Astrid decided her job was at an end. She glared at her sister, with whom she was still quite angry, and said, "You may thank me later. I think."

Alice was confused, but Astrid did not wait around to clarify her statements. She stalked off. She was doing quite a bit of stalking today. And as the clock in the chapel tower finally tolled out the noon hour, she thought it was high time she enjoyed a bit of the free ale on tap. Even ladies were permitted a sip or two on festival days.

Astrid planned on sneaking several pints.

She was surreptitiously filling a mug to the brim from a tap located at a discreet distance from prying eyes, glad for a few moments alone, when she heard someone approach from behind. She looked over her shoulder and cursed under her breath.

Lightfoot. Looking particularly oily and toadish, his dark eyes filled with a strange light, and his face—unpleasant to begin with—painted with an unmistakable leer. She looked involuntarily to her right and left and cursed again. She certainly didn't want to be alone *now*, with Mr. Lightfoot, but she was. And she felt . . . uncomfortable. She'd never liked him, never liked the way he looked at her. It made her shiver, and not in a good way.

"Miss Honeywell, how lovely to see you."

She inclined her head and attempted to move past him. He didn't exactly trap her where she was, but he made it impossible to get around him without some part of her touching him. And she most certainly did *not* want to touch him.

"I have heard you've had a houseguest," he said conversationally.

"The duke has been and gone. He'll not be here today, if you were hinting to be introduced."

Something unpleasant flashed across his eyes, but he smiled at her, revealing a set of small, uneven teeth that reminded her of Petunia's. "I have also heard that he has . . . come to some understanding with you regarding the estate."

"That, I'm sure, is none of your concern."

"But I *am* most concerned. I am *always* concerned for you, my dear. For instance, I was most concerned when I heard about the duke's little . . . accident yesterday. If he had been injured, then I . . . and I hate to be unpleasantly blunt . . . I feared that you might be implicated."

Astrid stiffened and clutched her mug before her, certain that her wild suspicion the day before had not been so wild after all.

"It would be terribly inconvenient for you if something were to happen to the Duke of Montford."

"Nothing *happened*. Nothing is going to happen, as he's left for London."

"The road can be so dangerous this time of year. Brigands every-where, storing up for the winter."

Astrid did not tremble. She would not give this toad the satisfaction of betraying such an emotion. But she was afraid. Very afraid. And she was afraid of no one, not even Montford. Unless he was kissing her, of course.

But she wouldn't think of *that* right now. She needed to focus on making an escape from her current companion. Before, Lightfoot had been an annoyance, but now he was something else entirely. She'd never trusted him. She'd never trusted that strange light in his eyes. "You did it," she stated, meeting his glance steadily.

He smiled. "Did what?" He sounded innocent, too innocent, and she knew in that moment beyond a doubt he'd arranged for the shoot-ing. Rage consumed her. "You killed my horse."

"That was truly an accident. I'm sure the shooter only meant to make a point."

"What, do you think, was the point?"

"Oh, I don't know," he said, shrugging insouciantly. "Perhaps that there are consequences to leading certain gentlemen on. That, perhaps, it would behoove a certain lady to reconsider an offer that was made not once, but twice."

She laughed, though she felt like crying. "Do you know, that is the second attempt to blackmail me in as many days? It would be amusing, if it were not so pathetic."

She shoved past him, not caring if he touched her, just that she had to escape him. But he caught her by the arm. Ale splashed all over her sleeve. "You'll reconsider, Miss Honeywell," he snarled in her ear. His breath smelled like old boots. Her stomach churned.

She yanked her arm away from him. "I'll not reconsider, you odi-ous man. Kill the bloody duke. He's no friend of mine."

He grabbed for her again, but she sped forward, out of his reach, her heart pounding with fear and rage.

"You'll be mine, one way or another," she heard him call behind her.

She gritted her teeth and lengthened her stride. She didn't slow until the general throng once more surrounded her. She needed to find Hiram. She had to tell him about Lightfoot, though there was precious little to be done. He'd not exactly confessed, and there was little proof of his involvement.

She felt a pang of worry. Was the duke truly in danger? Would he be accosted on the road by one of Lightfoot's agents? Surely not. Surely Lightfoot would not be so foolish!

But he would. He was . . . well, insane. He must be, to be going to such lengths to marry her. Her!

She had to warn the duke. She had to find Hiram. She had to do *something*.

Astrid pushed her way through the crowd, which was thrumming with excitement and heading toward the start of the much-anticipated foot-and-ale race. Many of the contestants were already there and doing odd stretching exercises to limber up their legs. The young men of the village and surrounding district saw the foot-and-ale race, instituted a century ago by one of Astrid's more harebrained ancestors, as a rite of passage. The race covered a two-mile circuit around the village and its surrounding environs, with booths holding pints of ale set up at intervals along the way. The young men ran barefoot over the course as fast as they could, and they were required to guzzle down a pint at each of the stations before continuing on.

Many started the race. Only a handful crossed the finish line, and only one or two managed to do so still standing. The first one of these was declared the victor, crowned king for a day, and allowed to claim for himself a queen by kissing her in front of the entire assemblage. The king rarely made it to this point in the proceedings until much later, as sprinting for two miles and drinking eight pints at the same time did not mix well.

It was quite the most ridiculous spectacle Astrid had ever seen.

Astrid began to notice that not all were moving toward the course. In fact, a good portion of the throng was milling about at the edge of the green, casting curious glances toward something out of Astrid's line of vision, and whispering behind their hands.

She spied Aunt Anabel adjusting her wig at the corner of this crowd, and decided she'd go assist her before the thing leapt off her head and ran away. When she reached her aunt's side and completed her task, she felt an odd tingling on the back of her neck, a heightened awareness, as if she felt someone's eyes watching her. She looked around and wished she hadn't, for now she saw what everyone was making such a fuss about. Or rather, *whom*.

Montford. Damnation!

What was he doing here?

And looking like an alien species in his expensive, fussy clothes amid the rustic woolens of most of the villagers. There was no mistaking who he was or the effect he had on the crowd. If an elephant had been planted next to him covered in pink paint, *he* would without a doubt be considered the greater curiosity.

He seemed oblivious to the scrutiny, however, his eyes locked in on her, like a bird of prey's on a field mouse.

Her heart leapt up into her throat, then thudded to her feet and stayed there, an aching, miserable mound.

What the bloody blue blazes was *Montford* doing here? He was supposed to be on the road back to London, being attacked by highwaymen.

Alice came up beside her with a worried expression. She tugged on Astrid's arm to get her attention. "What did you do to Wesley?" Alice demanded.

Astrid tore her attention from the duke. "What?"

"He's acting very peculiar. I think he might be ill or something. He can't seem to speak."

And that was a bad thing? Astrid wanted to retort. Clearly Wesley had yet to work up his courage to speak to Alice.

Alice frowned. "*And* he's entering the footrace. Perhaps he's had too much ale."

Astrid could imagine why Wesley was entering the race—to make Alice his queen. But that was if he won, which was unlikely. Gentlemen did not participate in the race, not just because it was considered *de trop*. It was an issue of pride, as gentlemen had no wish to be bested by the common lads who made their living through physical labor. Gentlemen were not generally a hearty lot.

Lady Emily would discover her son's disgraceful behavior, and Astrid wished she could be a fly on the wall when *that* happened. But she didn't have time to deal with Wesley. She had a mission to complete . . .

A mission she had totally forgotten. What was she on her way to do? Montford's appearance had knocked it clear out of her head.

Alice was similarly distracted from her train of thought by something she saw over Astrid's shoulder. Astrid didn't need to see Alice's round eyes and slack mouth to know what had caught her attention. Astrid's arms broke out into gooseflesh. She could *feel* the duke drawing near.

"What's he doing here?" Alice whispered.

Astrid shrugged and raised the mug to her mouth. She drank the entire pint in one gulp for fortification. She choked at the end, and someone thumped her on the back. It was Roddy, grinning and already a bit wobbly. "All right?"

She shook her head. Then Roddy saw the duke and gave her a commiserating look. "Oh bloody hell. He doesn't look pleased," he muttered and turned to flee.

"Don't you dare run away from me, Stevenage!" boomed the duke.

Roddy blanched in defeat and spun back around, dropping the duke a remarkably steady bow.

Astrid glanced around and saw that everyone in the vicinity was attempting some sort of bow or curtsy, to varying degrees of success. Now that word had spread—like a bloody wildfire—that the duke would not be chopping off anyone's head, he was no longer *persona non grata*. In fact, it looked as if Rylestone's denizens were more than happy to start currying his favor.

Astrid's blood boiled.

He ignored everyone around him and addressed his former man-of-affairs. "I need a mount," he said.

"A . . . mount? A horse?" Roddy was clearly in no state to deal with the duke's problem.

"Yes, a horse, you idiot."

"Why do you need a horse, Your Grace?" Sir Wesley asked, coming up to join them, avoiding Alice's eyes.

"So I can leave," the duke said with impatience.

Wesley looked baffled. "What about your coach? Fine piece of equipment."

"It's broken."

"Broken? Oh dear, that *is* a problem." Wesley's brow bunched up. "Rode my high-stepper over here, so can't help you there. Got plenty of good stock back at the Grange if you want one of 'em."

"Fine," the duke bit off. "Shall we go?"

Wesley was taken aback. "You mean now? Can't leave *now*. The Grange's a good hour away, and the race is about to start."

The duke looked irritated. "Race?"

"The foot-and-ale race."

"The foot and what?"

"Foot-and-ale," Wesley said slowly. He explained what the race entailed, to the duke's growing incredulity.

"What nonsense," he said with utter disdain.

"It ain't," Wesley protested. He puffed out his chest. "I'm running this year, and I mean to win it and claim my kiss." At this last vow, Wesley's face turned scarlet as he glanced in Astrid and Alice's direction.

The duke's expression grew thunderous. "You expect me to wait until you run barefoot and drunk around the village so that you might make a spectacle of your cousins and yourself? I think you must forget who I am, Sir Wesley," the duke growled.

Wesley looked mortified. He glanced to Astrid for support.

"Surely you cannot deny Sir Wesley a chance to win his lady love, Your Grace," she said with a forced smile. "To win the foot-and-ale race is a great honor."

"I don't give a damn," he snarled.

From Wesley's abashed look, the duke was going to have his way, and this was not something Astrid was willing to allow on principle alone. Montford could wait an hour for Wesley to run his silly race. Astrid certainly had no desire for Montford to stay another minute, much less another hour. But if anything could be done to inconvenience him further, then Astrid was all in favor of *that*.

"Not many gentlemen have the courage to enter the foot-and-ale race, Your Grace. Sir Wesley has bravely entered the fray. To pull out now, after he has already given notice, would make him lose face. You would not have him dishonor himself, would you?" she asked sweetly.

He settled his attention on her—or on the space right next to her head, as he couldn't seem to meet her eye. "He could only be dishonored if he were competing against others of his own class," he said stiffly.

Bastard.

Astrid gasped in a horrified way that was not entirely an act. "Why, you utter snob! It is just this kind of feudal thinking that drove the French to chop off their rulers' heads."

"Oh, dear," Roddy repeated, smelling trouble and backing away.

She glanced around her and noticed that everyone—even Alice—had taken a few steps back from the two of them. A crowd of curious onlookers had formed around them, but at a safe distance, as if everyone sensed the electricity in the air. Only Aunt Anabel, who was dotty anyway, remained at Astrid's side, nodding her head as if she'd fallen asleep standing up.

Montford stood before her, fists on his hips, his face hewn from granite, his silver eyes nearly translucent with rage.

She gave him her mildest smile. "Do you know, I have often thought that the reason gentlemen refuse to engage in a fair fight with a member of the lower orders has more to do with fear than pomposity," she continued conversationally.

His expression hardened even more. "Oh?"

"Yes. It wouldn't do for a gentleman . . . oh, say an aristocrat of your similar station . . . to be bested by a mere field hand in a . . . oh, say, a footrace. How can one rule when one is shown to be weaker than his subjects?"

"Weaker," he repeated.

"Yes. Soft. Effete. *Vestigial.*"

"Vestigial?" His voice was soft, but every syllable was spoken with knife-edged precision.

"As in, no longer necessary to the body as a whole, like one's appendix. But in this case, it is the body politic, and the atrophied organ is the aristocracy—"

"Some would call your statements seditious, Miss Honeywell."

"I would have thought *all*, not just some. But I only meant to point out the general difference in physical strength between the upper orders and the common man. The higher one is born, it seems, the less one is required to . . . well, *move*. Have you found this to be true, Your Grace?"

He was quiet for a long time. At last, he spoke in an undertone. "You think I can't see what you're doing? You're trying to goad me into running this blasted race."

She feigned affront. "I would *never* do such a thing. I was only suggesting that Sir Wesley is a very *brave* gentleman, to risk losing to a mere field hand. *Few* gentlemen would have the nerve to put themselves in such a position. You should let him race."

"You think I can't win this ridiculous race," he insisted.

"I never suggested anything of the sort." She smiled at him.

"You think I can't even *finish* this race."

"Absolutely not." It was an ambiguous statement at best.

He stared and stared at her until something seemed to explode inside of him, and then he turned on his heel abruptly and began striding across the green, catching Wesley by the arm and pulling him along.

"Wh . . . what's happening?" Wesley asked.

"We're going to race," the duke practically roared.

Astrid stared at the duke's retreating back, dumbstruck, as did the rest of the crowd who had overheard his declaration. Then a rumble of anxious chatter swelled louder as the news spread, and the crowd began to follow the two noblemen down toward the start of the racecourse.

She honestly hadn't meant to provoke the duke this far. But things, as usual, had gotten out of hand quicker than she could have anticipated, once her tongue got the best of her.

Someone really must pass a law forbidding herself and the Duke of Montford from coming within a hundred miles of each other. They made fools out of each other. In this case, however, Montford alone would be the fool.

A duke running in the foot-and-ale race? Stranger things might have happened in Rylestone, but not in Astrid's lifetime.

Once her initial shock faded, her heart lifted in anticipation of his defeat, for surely he would lose. She doubted if Montford had ever run anywhere in his life, and she knew for a fact that he was quite abstemious in his drinking habits. Combining the two seldom-enjoyed activities could only end in a rather splendidly ignoble thrashing at the hands—or rather, feet—of Rylestone's farm boys.

Or at least that was what she hoped.

She hurried to catch up with the rest of the crowd.

Only when she reached the starting line did three worrying thoughts intrude. Number one: what if—and surely she was merely being paranoid—what if Montford actually won? Number two: if number one happened, would Montford choose a queen? Which brought her to number three: if number two happened, would he choose her?

Would he kiss her again? That was her concern. Would he kiss her again, in public? Or . . . Oh God! She'd just thought of something even worse. What if he should kiss someone else?

And then she thought of something even worse than that. Why did she *care* if he kissed someone else?

Astrid was so caught up in these pressing worries that she totally forgot about Mr. Lightfoot and that gentleman's poorly veiled threats until much, much later.

By then, of course, it was too late.

Chapter Fifteen

In Which the Duke Enters His Second Race of the Week

THE WAGERS started flying as soon as word spread that the Duke of Montford, Rylestone's erstwhile landlord, was going to run in the foot-and-ale race. The assembly was buzzing with excitement, gossiping about Miss Honeywell's challenge, and calling out bets as the contestants gathered at the edge of the green, giving a wide berth to their liege, who was staring at the starting line, looking as if he'd like to murder them all.

Or one in particular, and everyone knew who that was.

It was on account of Miss Honeywell calling Himself a vestigious organ, the butcher said to the milliner, who had not been close enough to hear the already legendary conversation. As far as the butcher could figure, being called vestigious was a terrible insult, and Himself had no choice but to defend his Honor. Miss Honeywell, answered the milliner over his pint, may have overstepped her bounds this time, as one just didn't go around calling a man's organs vestigious, especially if the organs were belonging to a duke.

The butcher agreed with this assessment and eyed the duke appraisingly as the duke began to take off his jacket and loosen his cravat. Himself was a well-set-up fellow, beneath all of the fluff he wore, and the butcher liked the look of his long legs. The butcher also figured that Miss Honeywell had made the duke's blood boil so hot—as she tended to do to most men—that the fellow would carry himself through the race on steam power alone. He promptly laid out a sovereign on the duke. The milliner, who enjoyed quite a lot of business from the Honeywell girls, remembered where his loyalties lay (and the exact shade of Alice Honeywell's eyes) and bet a sovereign against the interloper.

Transactions of this sort were made throughout the crowd, and it was noted even the vicar had thrown down a few shillings on the duke—for the poor box should he win, he assured everyone. And while the men bet on the outcome, the women speculated on what the duke would do afterward if he won. Furious primping and preening began in every unmarried female under the age of one hundred, excluding, of course, the Misses Honeywell.

Although, one observer, who shall remain nameless, but who had a vested concern for Miss Honeywell's person, and who was lurking at the back of the crowd in a particularly ominous manner, noted that Miss Honeywell tucked back her hair not once, not twice, but thrice, behind her ears, an act of vanity heretofore unrecorded, and never took her eyes from the Duke of Montford as he stripped down to his waistcoat. These were troubling signs to the observer, who began to wish the duke had indeed tumbled to his death along with his mount on the previous day.

Unaware of the upheaval he had caused in the surrounding crowd and the enemy he'd made, Montford glared at the small group of young men who loitered around him, looking severely uncomfortable in his presence. Sir Wesley was half bent over, trying to pull off his stockings, blushing furiously. A few of the other fellows were stretching out their legs and contorting their bodies in a fashion that looked extremely painful to Montford's eyes.

What the devil had he done?

He didn't dare turn to find Miss Honeywell. He feared that just seeing her again would drive him to do something even more outrageous. Although what could be more outrageous than what he was about to do?

Nothing.

If any of his acquaintances back in London ever heard that he participated in a drunken footrace, he would be laughed out of the House of Lords. Or locked in Bedlam on suspicion of insanity.

Sherbrook and Marlowe, of course, would think it hilarious. If they believed it at all. They thought him the King of Stuffed Shirts, after all.

As did Miss Honeywell, apparently, last evening notwithstanding.

Last evening . . .

His blood simmered. He reached down to tug off his boots. They were tall Hessians and did not disconnect so easily. He needed to sit down to take them off himself, and that was something he wasn't about to do. The ground was rather damp.

He stared down the racecourse, and his heart sank. He was going to be running barefoot in grass and mud for two miles? He was going to be more than *damp* by the end of it.

Sir Wesley, seeing his predicament, came to his aid and offered his services as valet. The baronet was as incompetent in this as he was in everything else and ended up straddled over Montford's outstretched leg, his backside thrust in Montford's face as he pulled off the first boot. It finally slid off with surprising ease, causing Sir Wesley to stumble forward and Montford to stumble backward.

Montford tried his best to ignore the ripple of amusement that ran through the crowd. Sir Wesley returned to remove the second boot, but Montford waved him off and tugged the bloody thing off himself, anger giving him the extra force required. His stockinged feet squelched in the damp ground, and he cringed.

After several murmured oaths, he managed to tear off his stockings and toss them aside. He glanced down, his legs bared from his knees to his toes, and muttered another oath. He glanced up at his opponents, who were staring at him as if he had a tail.

"You will not let me win," he snarled at them. "I'll not bloody well have this turn into any more of a farce than it is already."

Some of his opponents looked affronted he'd even suggested it. Some looked scared witless. Others nodded to him with newfound respect. A few of the brave ones suggested he do a bit of limbering up so as not to cramp. They demonstrated how, and Montford watched these contortions in a daze of incredulity.

He did *not* take their advice.

He moved stiffly to the starting line with the others and saw Stevenage, also equally barefoot, fall into place near his side. He gave Montford an uneasy salute and began to hop in place in some sort of attempt to loosen up. Stevenage didn't seem to need it, as he looked, in Montford's opinion, as loose as three sailors after a night out at the public house.

Then Miss Honeywell appeared out of the throng and approached the start. She climbed an upturned barrel, took a stick wrapped with a red banner from the hands of a villager, and held it above her head.

"What the bloody hell . . ." he muttered.

"A Honeywell always starts the race," Sir Wesley informed him. "It's tradition."

Montford groaned and watched as she lowered the stick. The crowd went wild. The contestants started to sprint down the course. Stevenage tripped after only a few strides, picked himself up, and carried on, a dark stain on his rump. Sir Wesley loped off, looking like a giant flightless bird, his elbows pumping at his sides.

For a moment, all Montford could do was watch the spectacle before him, a knot in his stomach. He could not seriously follow all of these morons!

Then he made the mistake of looking up at Miss Honeywell on the barrel with her red flag. She was smirking down at him from on high. It was as clear to him as if she had shouted for all to hear that she didn't think he stood a chance in hell of winning.

Which would never do.

He glanced down the course at Sir Wesley, who was leading the pack, and he saw red. The thought of that idiot winning was insupportable. Montford had seen the way Sir Wesley had glanced in Miss Honeywell's direction earlier, and he knew just what that idiot intended to do once he crossed the finish line first.

Montford would be damned if he had to witness Sir Wesley kiss Miss Honeywell again. He would be damned if any of those idiots planted their lips on her. In fact, if any idiot were to be kissing Miss Honeywell, that idiot would be Montford and Montford alone.

Not that he was going to kiss her again! Not that he *wanted* to . . .

"Damnation!" he muttered as he found his legs carrying him down the course at lightning speed.

He'd caught up to the rest of the pack after the first hundred yards. After the second hundred yards, the crowd's cheers had dwindled to a distant roar in his ears, and his feet were beginning to feel the pain of the rocks, twigs, and other debris they encountered. He passed a few of the stragglers, and then a few more, though his accomplishment—such as it was—was rather diminished by the fact that these stragglers were the paunchy ones, or the short ones, or the ones—like Stevenage—who'd already had too much to drink.

At the quarter-mile marker, he encountered the first "station," where a tankard full of ale was placed in his hands. He observed the other men around him guzzling their drinks in between gasping for their breath, and he cursed—or tried to. He was so winded he couldn't seem to form a word.

After a brief hesitation, he turned back his tankard and began to drink the first pint of Honeywell Ale he'd ever had. It was fizzy and rather bitter, and he wondered not for the first time why people liked the swill. But reflection was something he could not afford. Speed seemed to be the key to this farce, so he drank down the ale in two gulps, tossed aside the tankard like the other men, and continued to run.

The ale sloshed about in his stomach, and a stitch started to form in his side, but he observed no other effect on his body, so he pushed through the discomfort. He let his fury carry him to the second marker, where he tossed back his second tankard, threw it aside, and continued to run across a footbridge spanning the Ryle and onto a knotty, muddy path through a field of grazing sheep. He had to dodge several of these creatures and nearly succeeded in twisting his ankle in a giant mudhole.

By the next quarter-mile marker, his feet were numb, his lower body was caked in filth, his knees ached, his lungs burned, and his head was beginning to feel distinctly muddled. As he took his third tankard, he saw one lad doubled over by a nearby tree, losing the contents of his stomach, and another stretched by the side of the path, staring dazedly up at the sky. He hesitated, wondering what in the hell he was doing once more, but then he noticed Sir Wesley throwing down his tankard and taking off down the path, looking none the worse for the wear.

Montford upended the tankard and gulped down the entire pint, wiped his mouth with the back of his hand, and took off once more.

He was a good thirty paces on when he realized he still held his tankard. He tossed it in some shrubbery and quickened his pace. He found himself in the middle of the pack, huffing along with the two field hands who'd assisted him in the ditch yesterday. They nodded in his direction, and he nodded back, keeping his sights on the baronet's gangly form ahead near the lead position. He gritted his teeth and picked up his pace.

He reached the fourth marker behind Sir Wesley, but ahead of the two field hands, and downed his pint, ale dripping down his lawn shirt, along with splattered mud and sweat. When he started to run again, he could no longer feel any pain in his feet or knees, and the stitch in his side seemed miraculously disappeared. He was pulling ahead of the majority of runners, aside from the pocket ahead of him that included Sir Wesley. He was encouraged.

They began up a small incline, then down the other side and around, back in the direction of the Ryle. Everyone around him was stumbling and sliding along the route, and he felt like laughing at their clumsiness, until he realized that he too was stumbling and sliding. He hadn't even noticed.

The fifth marker was at the edge of another footbridge leading over the Ryle, back toward the village, but by the time he reached it, he didn't really notice the river or the village up ahead. All he noticed was a tankard being placed in his hands. Gasping for air—why was he so out of breath?—he stared down into the ale, wondering what he was supposed to do with it.

Oh, yes. He was supposed to drink it!

Which he did with great enthusiasm. He was suddenly very thirsty, and the brew was beginning to taste incredibly good. Honeywell Ale was not so bad after all. In fact, he decided, he rather liked it. No wonder Marlowe and Sherbrook swore by the stuff.

He glanced around him to share this revelation with someone, but the only person he saw was a red-faced young man leaning against a tree, relieving himself.

Montford felt a corresponding pressure below the belt and thought hazily that the lad had the right idea. He moved over toward the tree and began to unbutton the placket in the front of his breeches, but then he noticed another lad running by him.

Where was *he* off to in such a hurry? he wondered.

Oh yes, the race!

He decided his business with the tree could wait and started to run after the lad who had passed him by. He soon caught up with him, weaved around him, narrowly avoiding a tree—where had *that* come from?—and continued down the path.

He glanced up at the sky as he ran and saw that it was a wonderful, vibrant blue, the exact shade of one of Miss Honeywell's eyes. The comparison made him giggle. Or try to giggle. He was too winded to manage anything but a little wheeze, and the sound amused him even more. He was still staring up at the sky when one of his feet caught underneath something hard—a tree root, he imagined—and he went flying through the air. He landed with a thud in a patch of tall grass, the contents of his belly lurching up his throat, his hands clutching at the earth. He rolled over, wheezed again, and shot back to his feet. He began running again, but then he saw the runner he had just passed coming in his direction at a dangerous speed.

Now why was the lad running at him?

The lad pointed ahead of him in an urgent manner. "This way, gov," the lad rasped as he passed him.

Montford turned around, not really understanding what had happened until he reached the sixth marker.

He'd been going the wrong way.

"I got turned around," he said to the lad in amazement.

The lad, who could not speak by then, just nodded, and took up his tankard, swaying back and forth.

Montford was doing much the same. He drank deeply of his ale, sputtered at the end, and lurched onward.

He passed several more bodies strewn about the pathway, some groaning, some retching, and some unconscious. He had the sense that he was looking for someone in particular, but he couldn't quite remember who it was, so he continued on his way as quickly as he could in the hopes his memory would be restored.

Soon he came to an open stretch with some brick buildings swaying in the distance. He decided they warranted further investigation, so he hurried his pace, occasionally picking himself off the ground, but otherwise having a fine time.

An exhilarating time.

In fact, Montford could not remember any time in his life he'd ever felt so . . . wonderful. So free. He couldn't feel the entire lower portion of his body, and his head felt as if it were floating about ten feet in the air. He'd forgotten why he was running in the first place, but he was certainly glad he was. It was a fabulous mode of exercise, he decided. He'd have to do it more often. He'd introduce the practice when he got back home—wherever *that* was. He'd start a rage.

Running. Sprinting. Leaping through the air, over puddles and tree roots and bodies.

Wait. He'd just jumped over a body. Not a dead one, he hoped. He tried to glance back, but this motion threw off his balance, sending him sprawling in the mud.

He hauled himself up and stumbled onward.

He rounded a bend in the path and nearly collided with another person.

"So sorry—"

"Pardon me—"

He righted his balance and trotted onward, looking to his side. The person he'd nearly collided with bobbed in and out of his line of vision. The fellow was nearly his height, he thought, and lanky, with a shock of reddish hair.

It was Sir Wesley, weaving along, his face cherry-red, and his tongue lolling out of his mouth. He glanced over at him, his eyes bugged out, and his mouth curled in a wobbly grin. He raised his hand and tried to doff his hat, even though he wasn't wearing one. "Mont—ford! Haloo, old—chap. Fancy—us—last—ones—standing—" Wesley broke off as he swayed to the left, then the right, nearly running into Montford.

Montford didn't know what the hell Wesley was babbling on about. But he knew it was important not to let the idiot out of his sight. Or better yet, to put the idiot behind him.

He concentrated on making his legs work, even though he couldn't feel them, and he gritted his teeth, his good mood vanishing with each puff of air Sir Wesley expelled next to him.

Really, did the man have to breathe so hard?

But why were they running in the first place? And what was that fellow doing up ahead with the cups?

He reached the man's side, and the man thrust a large cup in his hand, and then one in Sir Wesley's. Sir Wesley started to drink his, so Montford did the same, having no idea what it was, but not liking how it felt going down. When he finished it, he started to run on, but the man stopped him and shoved another cup in his face.

"What-the-bloody-hell—" This exclamation came out as one word, one syllable.

"Two this time 'round, Yer Excellency. Last leg," the man explained, grinning broadly.

Montford glared at the man and drank the beverage in his hand. It didn't taste like water to him. It didn't *feel* like water going down his throat, burning his insides.

Wesley choked on his last sip, looking a little green beneath his red face.

Montford threw down his cup and swayed on his feet. Now that he wasn't moving, the world seemed to be turning around him.

The man who had dispensed the drink gestured to his right. "Well, go on, gov, go on!"

Wesley stumbled forward, righted himself, and stumbled on. Montford did the same. They rounded another curve in the path, and then suddenly stretched before him was a sea of people making the most god-awful racket he'd ever heard.

Wesley, some paces ahead, waved him onward. "Well—come on, old man—*hic*—not—*hic*—gonna let—you win."

"Winwhat?" he belched.

"Th'race—*hic*—wanna—*hic*—kiss—*hic*—Miss A—Miss A—" Wesley gave up on his speech and puffed out a breath, taking off at an unsteady lope toward the ocean of screaming people.

Montford wasn't sure he wanted to go in that direction—what *were* they carrying on about?—but instinct told him he couldn't let Wesley go without him, so he lunged forward. Then forward again, one foot in front of the other, or as near as he could manage. He was having the devil of a time even making out his feet.

He was engulfed on all sides by screaming plebs, waving banners and all sorts of strange objects in his direction. They surged around him like driftwood on a sea, and he tried to block them out. They made him feel—strange—in his stomach. As if he were going to cast up an entire sea himself.

He did not feel so good.

He heard an odd sound to his left. Sir Wesley had curled up on all fours and seemed to be hacking at the ground with his head.

Montford spun away and tried to focus on something. He stumbled forward, and when he felt something thwack him across the backside—he wasn't *that* numb—he lengthened his stride, which may or may not have been a mistake, for he was suddenly falling against several bodies. They pushed him upright and shoved him forward.

Something loomed a few feet in front of him. A blue line, floating above the ground. What on God's green earth was that? And how was it floating? He reached it, stopped, and extended his arm to touch it. Several attempts later, his finger at last connected with it. He poked it, and it stretched back.

A ribbon. A blue ribbon. What was it doing here?

He felt someone shove his shoulder, and he stumbled through the ribbon, snapping it with the weight of his body.

Well, that was a shame, to ruin a perfectly good ribbon.

The crowd, which he had forgotten, erupted into a cacophony of catcalls, laughter, applause, and whistles. He tried to gather up the ribbon, but he was mobbed by people who insisted on slapping him on the back or shaking his limp hands, congratulating him for something.

He looked at one well-wisher, a man with beady black eyes and a balding pate, who was shaking his hand and smiling at him in a way that reminded Montford of a cat just before it pounced on a mouse.

"What the devil are you shaking my hand for?" he demanded, or tried to demand. The words didn't sound quite right.

"You've won, Your Grace," the man explained.

"Won? What've I won?"

"The race."

He vaguely remembered now.

"Ah yes. Race."

Then he tumbled forward.

⊷ ⊷

ASTRID WATCHED with a mixture of horror and amusement as the Duke of Montford, mud-splattered, red-faced, and entirely perplexed, poked his finger at the finish line ribbon, as if it were some new species of animal, and swayed forward and backward on wobbly looking legs. Then someone pushed him through the finish line—he was the clear winner, as Sir Wesley was sprawled out in the grass some twenty paces back and no one else had yet to appear around the last bend of the course—and he swiveled about, trying to save the ribbon from the mud.

The crowd went wild. Even those who had wagered against the duke seemed well pleased with the result. Who could not be? A peer of the realm was standing barefoot and drunk, wet with sweat and ale and mud, looking about as regal as a stable boy after sneaking gin from his master. Astrid's nerves jangled when she saw Mr. Lightfoot among the throng shaking Montford's rather droopy hand, and she finally remembered that odious man's horrid threats against her and the duke.

She started forward. She had to warn Montford. But the crowd was thick. She could not get by.

Montford seemed unconcerned by Mr. Lightfoot, and Astrid realized he was in no condition to digest her admonitions. In fact, the duke attempted to say something, laughed, and fell on top of Mr. Lightfoot, nearly bringing them both to the ground.

The crowd caught them at the last moment and hauled them back to their feet.

Then the chanting began.

"Kiss! Kiss! Kiss!"

At first it was a few of the more mischievous young boys, but it soon spread to the older men, then the women as well.

Even the vicar had joined in. The chanting grew louder, more insistent.

Astrid's heart sank. She did not try to get to the duke's side any longer. She was frozen in place.

But she was close enough to hear him slur out, "WhaddayameanI-havedakisssommone?"

As this was explained to him repeatedly, Astrid began to move backward. Then forward. She couldn't decide where she wanted to be any longer.

But it was apparent where every other female wanted to be. They were clawing their way to the front of the crowd, anxious to draw the duke's eye.

Astrid could see that this was not going to be an easy task. The duke seemed to have trouble focusing his eyes at all. He shut one, then opened it and shut the other. He tried squinting through one, then the other, then both.

Astrid frowned. She couldn't imagine any female in her right mind wanting to kiss him at the moment. His face was splotched in red, he was covered in sweat and breathing heavily, and he couldn't seem to stand on his own.

She certainly didn't want to kiss him. He looked . . .

Drunk. Frightful.

He grinned stupidly at no one in particular.

Her breath caught in her throat. She'd never seen him grin like that, with such genuine glee. It made him look all of five years old and entirely . . . delicious.

Astrid's heart thudded against her ribs.

Oh, dear.

He swayed on his feet, turning in a half circle as if looking for something in the crowd, and his gaze fell on her. He stopped. His grin faded, and his head bobbed up and down. He squinted at her and raised one of his arms. He extended his finger and pointed at her.

Well, not *at* her. Somewhere in her vicinity.

"You," he said.

A collective groan of disappointment ran through all the females present. All eyes turned in her direction.

She looked around her, hoping he was not really pointing at her—*dreading* he was not really pointing at her—but the only other female in a good ten paces was Aunt Anabel, who was looking extremely amused by the spectacle.

Montford lurched forward, past Mr. Lightfoot, who stared at his back with narrowed eyes. The crowd parted, letting him stumble to his destination. He kept his arm extended, and every now and then he would hiccup and sway to the right or left.

Astrid braced herself for the inevitable. What could she do? This was tradition. The winner of the race got to kiss the female of his choice, and if Montford chose her, then tradition demanded she accept her fate. She *had* to kiss him, there was no other choice. She had no wish to do so—in fact, she detested the very notion—but she would be the last person to break a custom her own family had begun.

She would take no pleasure in it.

None at all.

Her breathing ceased all together. Her cheeks burned. Anticipation bubbled up inside of her stomach.

Montford loomed above her for a second, and then he staggered to the left, lost sight of her altogether, and fell atop Aunt Anabel. He pinned the aged woman to the earth, knocking off her wig, and planted his lips on the side of her mouth.

Aunt Anabel screamed, raised her cane above them, and brought it down across Montford's back. He howled in pain and rolled onto the grass, his hand tangling in Aunt Anabel's wig. He jerked back and tried to shake the wig off of his hand. This took several tries. Meanwhile, Aunt Anabel had climbed to her feet and continued to batter him with her cane.

Astrid managed to pull her aunt away, and someone helped the duke to his feet. The crowd was ecstatic. Many were hunched over, laughing too hard to stand straight. A couple was crying with their mirth. It was without a doubt the most memorable festival Rylestone had seen in generations.

Astrid had to grudgingly agree. She was not at all disappointed, of course, that the duke had been too drunk to kiss her, and had, in fact, mistaken her aunt for her. If indeed there had been a mistake at all. Surely he had not *meant* to kiss Aunt Anabel?

No, she was *not* disappointed, she told herself as she watched several burly men heave Montford onto their shoulders and dance away with him into the crowd. Montford wore an expression of bemusement and surprisingly good cheer. He did not know where he was being taken—to the nearest keg—nor did he seem to care.

Not disappointed at all.

She turned and caught Mr. Lightfoot's eye, and a cold chill crept up her spine. He smiled at her, but it was the most menacing smile she'd ever seen.

She turned away. She'd deal with him later.

She glanced in the direction of Sir Wesley and saw that Alice had him well in hand, then bent over to pick up Aunt Anabel's wig, which now resembled a dead poodle. She fluffed it out and set it on top of her aunt's faded red hair.

Aunt Anabel was flushed and very perplexed. "I do believe I've been molested, my dear," she said. "Who *was* that oafish fellow?"

"The Duke of Montford."

"What? A duke? Where?" Aunt Anabel spun about, trying to find a duke in the crowd.

She had no success.

Chapter Sixteen

In Which the Duke Serenades His Ladylove

THE DUKE of Montford cleared his throat, leaned into Sir Wesley's embrace as they stumbled down the lane, and began his eleventh recitation of the evening:

"*There was a young fellow from Kent,*" he began in a stage whisper that was more accurately a near shout.

"*Whose anatomy was very bent—*"

Roddy burst into giggles behind them, along with Flora. So did Montford. It took him several moments to compose himself so he could continue.

"*When he thrust to go in, / He got stuck on her shin, / Back home to his wife he was sent.*"

It took several moments for Wesley to comprehend what had been said, and when he did, his face turned scarlet, and he sniggered with laughter against his tattered sleeve.

"Oh, my!" Alice murmured next to Astrid. She was also noticeably wobbly on her feet, and kept glancing in Wesley's direction in a coy manner that had the poor man so flummoxed he could not meet her eyes. He *definitely* could not meet Alice's eyes after this last delightful obscenity. "That's the worst one he's done yet!"

Astrid could only nod, her ears burning. She had no words to describe the past half hour's journey from the village back toward the castle. They had been among the last to leave the festival. Wesley and Montford had to be picked up off the ground by Newcomb, who now trailed behind them with Roddy and Flora. All three of these stragglers looked as soused as Sir Wesley and Montford.

In fact, Astrid could safely say that she was the only one of their little company who was marginally sober. Even Alice, it seemed, had had considerably more. She had to prop her sister up. She'd been glad when Hiram, traitor that he was, had offered to let Antonia and Ardyce stay with his girls tonight, as she didn't think she could have put up with wrangling two more children back to the castle. She already had five on her hands as it was.

Someone had managed to replace the gentlemen's discarded clothing, with little success. At least they had been shoved back into their boots. Their cravats were in tatters, and Wesley's fine gray wool jacket was split up the back. They'd lost their hats entirely, and Montford's cravat pin was sticking through a hole in his lapel as if it were a carnation, not a giant ruby.

She was surprised he'd managed to hold on to that precious commodity. She'd seen it fall into the dirt, and the duke trod upon it at least half a dozen times since he'd won the bloody footrace.

She was equally surprised to learn that Montford, apparently, was a poet. Since they'd begun the long journey home—the longest journey of her life—he'd recited at least ten of the crudest, most idiotic little bits of rhyming nonsense she'd ever heard.

She'd struggled not to laugh.

Everyone else was. Wesley was in hysterics on Montford's arm. Montford was in hysterics as well. They had their heads together as they lurched down the lane, giggling like little boys.

It seemed Montford and Wesley were now bosom friends. He whispered another verse into Wesley's ear, this time too softly for the others to hear—though Astrid managed to catch a couple of very naughty words—and Wesley stopped in his tracks and gaped at Montford.

Then he doubled over, clutching his middle, laughing like a lunatic. "You're a devil, old boy," Wesley declared, "a devil."

Montford looked very pleased with himself.

Astrid found herself secretly wishing to know what he had said, even as she sniffed disdainfully as she passed them by.

Where had Montford learned all of these dreadful poems? She would have never dreamed he had it in him to be so . . . scandalously silly.

"Tell us another," Wesley begged as they approached the back garden.

Montford gazed unsteadily toward the castle, craning his head left and right as if trying to puzzle something out. "Nuther?" he mumbled.

"One more, old fellow."

"Yes, one more!" Alice seconded enthusiastically. Somehow she managed to disconnect from Astrid's arm and attach herself to Wesley's free one. Wesley glanced down at her with a startled expression that soon relaxed into something resembling a smile.

The duke thought about it for a moment, tugging on one side of his head, then swung his gaze in Astrid's direction.

She caught her breath but managed to scowl at him. "I think we've heard quite enough."

"Have I offended your delicate sensibilities?" he asked her. Or at least that is what she thought he might have asked her. He was slurring his consonants and massacring his vowels.

She harrumphed and crossed her arms over her chest. "You are behaving like an imbecile. All of you."

Alice and Wesley ignored her and pestered the duke to give them another rhyme.

Never taking his eyes off of her, he began.

"There was a young lady whose eyes, / Were unique as to color and size, / When she opened them wide, / People all turned aside, / And started away in surprise."

Wesley began to snicker. Alice laughed uneasily. Astrid felt her heart sink to her shoes. She would not let him upset her, she vowed to herself, even as her breath became shorter and shorter, and the garden became blurry. She was not tearing up. She was merely suffering from the roses blooming next to her.

Wesley finally realized he shouldn't be laughing, as no one else was. "Hey, that ain't dirty. Is it?"

"No, it isn't. It's just stupid," Astrid retorted.

"Oh, I don't think that was very nice, Montford," Alice said quietly.

"What wasn't very nice?" Wesley asked, lost.

Alice started to explain it to him, but Astrid had had quite enough. She abandoned them to their fates and stalked into the hedgerows. She'd enter through the back of the house and avoid other human beings for the rest of the night.

She'd just reached the edge of her vegetable garden when she felt the hand on her sleeve. She knew who it was by the scent of him—ale, sweat, mud, and whatever musk he exuded that made him smell wonderful despite those other things. She attempted to jerk her arm away. He held on tenaciously. She stumbled against the wall of the garden. He stumbled with her, into her, a wall of heat against her back.

She shoved him away and attempted to sidestep him. He caught her shoulders and turned her around to face him. Now the wall of heat was against her front. The cold garden wall was against her back. His cravat pin was at eye level. It swam before her eyes. "Let go of me."

"Hold on, now, wanted to 'pologize," he managed to get out.

"I don't want your damned apologies. Get out of my way."

"Th'poem. It wasn't meant to hurt."

She latched on to her anger, which was great at getting rid of her hurt. "Of course it was meant to hurt."

"No . . . I don't know why I said it. Just came out. Can't seem to help myself 'round you, Astrid."

She froze. He'd used her first name. He'd never used her first name before.

But it meant nothing. Just like the rhyme. Just like his kiss the night before.

She sank against the wall. "You're supposed to be gone. Why aren't you gone?"

He just stared down at her face, his brow furrowed, his jaw clenched.

"Can't seem to help myself," he repeated. "Astrid."

He raised a hand to her cheek. She courageously batted it away. "Don't call me that. Let me by."

She attempted to push him away, but he only swayed back a little, then swayed forward, mashing her backside onto the wall's cold ledge.

"*Astrid*," he said again.

"You're drunk."

He nodded. "Very. Very drunk." He paused. "I never get drunk. D'ya know it feels good? Say my name."

"What?" she cried, pushing against his chest.

He grinned down at her. "Say my name. Y'know the one."

"You are ridiculous."

"C'mon, Astrid. Say m'name."

She rolled her eyes. "Cyril."

His grin broadened. He closed his eyes as if she'd sung an aria.

"Quite the most ridiculous, stupid, idiotic name in the world," she continued.

"I know," he moaned. Then he opened his eyes and squinted down at her. "I like it when y'say it. I like your eyes, too. Th'don't match, y'know."

"Yes, I know."

"Like your hair, too. It's red."

He stated this fact as if it were of national importance.

"Yes, I know," she said, irritated and disarmed and uncommonly aware of the heat and strength of him mashed against her.

He squinted down at her, as if trying to solve an equation in his head. "You're wrong, Astrid."

She bristled. "About what?"

"No," he said, looking annoyed. "*You're* wrong. *You.*"

She snorted. He was making absolutely no sense, but her pulse was racing, her palms were sweating, and her legs felt like jelly.

"*Astrid.*"

That was it. She'd had enough. She shoved at his chest. "For heaven's sake, just let me go."

"Can't," he said, his head swaying toward her.

"I swear, if you don't—" His mouth covered her own, forestalling further speech. She turned into a puddle in an instant. His lips were warm, smooth, gentle, and he tasted of Honeywell Ale. He stank of it, in fact, but she didn't mind. He clutched her shoulders, pressing against her, his mouth working softly against hers, coaxing her lips apart, tasting, licking, nipping.

"Astrid," he murmured against her lips. He brought the back of his hand against her cheek and caressed it tenderly. "Astrid," he repeated, as if he couldn't help but repeat her name endlessly, even as he kissed her endlessly. It was nothing like last night. She felt a similar heat rise up inside of her, but the white heat that had burned so out of control the night before was refracted, like light through a prism, distilled and sweetened by his gentle touch, the near reverence of his mouth as it tasted her. Sampled her. Reveled in her.

Now, *this* was a kiss—or, rather, kisses—for his mouth would pull away, murmur her name, and then come back for more. And more.

Then his kisses moved lower, down her throat, over her collarbone, each contact of his lips to her flesh leaving a burning wake. A million butterflies began fluttering about in her stomach. She wrapped her arms around his neck, drawing his head nearer, craving him, burning for him.

He arrived at the edge of her bosom and buried his head there. Her pulse leapt as she waited for what he would do next. But he didn't move for the longest time, his full weight pressing her against the wall. His arms fell from her shoulders, and he sighed into her bosom. The garden around them was quiet, still. All she could hear was the steady sound of his breathing and her pulse thundering in her ears.

After a minute or so passed, she grew uncomfortable and a little cold, her inner heat fading.

What was he doing down there?

A sound ripped from the back of his throat. It took her a moment to comprehend what it was. When she did, she went completely cold.

A snore.

The cad! The utter cad! He'd kissed her senseless, then buried his head in her breasts and *fallen asleep!*

"Oh, you . . . you beast!" she cried, shoving him away from her.

He didn't wake up. He just slowly crumpled to the ground like a folding accordion and continued to snore with his cheek mashed up against the garden wall.

She stared down at him in incredulity. She kicked his shins and stepped over his body, storming toward the castle.

She hoped he froze to death.

⊷ ⊷ ⊷

NEWCOMB WAS congratulating himself on a job well done as he, Stevenage, and Flora spied on their employers from behind a clump of shrubbery. Flora sighed wistfully as the duke kissed Miss Honeywell, as if it was the sweetest thing she'd ever seen.

Newcomb didn't know about *that*. But he felt quite justified in his ploy to linger in Rylestone.

Who'd have thought the master could be such good company after a few pints? Well, more than a *few*. Himself had had enough to pickle the insides of ten soldiers, Newcomb reckoned. Not that Newcomb had had a doubt in his mind but that his master could hold his own against the heartiest of the Yorkshire bumpkins. Newcomb had won five quid on the race. He would have had ten, but His Grace had been too off his face to kiss the right chit.

The duke didn't seem to have trouble finding Miss Honeywell's lips now—a feat Newcomb would have appreciated several hours before.

"If he tries it on with her," Stevenage muttered at his side, "I'm not standing for it."

Oh, Newcomb was sure the duke was going to try it on with Miss Honeywell, or at least attempt to. The kissing changed course. Montford bent over until his head was stuck in the vicinity of Miss Honeywell's chest.

"Why, that *dog*!" Stevenage huffed, rising up and attempting to intercede.

Newcomb pulled him back down.

Flora giggled into her hands.

"What's he doing?" Stevenage whispered some moments later when the duke had made no further advance. His Grace just kind of listed there, smashing Miss Honeywell against the wall, his arms hanging limply at his sides.

Then they all heard the unmistakable sound of snoring.

Miss Honeywell let the duke crumple to the ground—not that Newcomb blamed her—kicked him in the shins, and ran away in distress.

Newcomb slapped his forehead and muttered an oath. The bloody oaf had fallen asleep in the middle of a seduction.

Not well done at all.

They stepped out of the shrubbery and approached the slumbering duke. Newcomb nudged his shoulder with his boot. He didn't stir.

"He's bloody well knocked out," he concluded. He himself had been more conscious after ten rounds in the boxing ring.

"What're we gonna do now?" Stevenage murmured. "He just cocked things up royally with Miss Astrid."

"Aye, but she were liking it well enough 'til then," Flora said with amusement.

Newcomb scratched his head. Only one thing was still clear to him. He couldn't let the duke leave until he fell in love with Miss Honeywell.

"He'll be in the devil of a temper tomorrow, and all afire to leave," Newcomb said.

"Well, we can't let him," Stevenage declared.

Newcomb and Stevenage had come to a mutual understanding down at the festival after witnessing the argument between the duke and Miss Honeywell, as well as its unlikely result.

The duke had clearly met his Waterloo, and it was about damned time.

Now they only needed the duke to realize he had already lost the war.

That meant more time in Miss Honeywell's company.

"Well," he said, bending over to heave Montford up, "we can't leave him here. Grab his legs, Roddy."

Roddy hunkered down and grabbed Montford's ankles. "Where're we taking him?"

Newcomb braced Montford's torso against his chest. "Heard Miss Honeywell was off to Hawes tomorrow. 'Twould be a shame to let her go alone, don't you think?"

Stevenage sniggered so hard he nearly dropped Montford's legs.

Flora shook her head and helped Stevenage with one of His Grace's ankles. Her eyes danced with merriment, and her spectacular bosom jiggled with exertion as she helped haul the Duke of Montford to his fate. Newcomb could see why Stevenage had elected to remain in Rylestone. "Oh, this is terrible naughty, ain't it?" she whispered without the slightest trace of remorse.

"Remember, we're doing it *for their own good*," Newcomb said solemnly.

They found Montford a bed for the night, but it wasn't in the castle, and soon it wouldn't even be in Rylestone.

Chapter Seventeen

Meanwhile, Back in London . . .

AT THE precise hour Montford fell across Aunt Anabel, dislodging her wig, Lady Katherine, Marchioness of Manwaring, was encountering her own bit of mayhem several hundred miles away in London. She discreetly pulled her skirt hem out of the way of three pairs of tiny feet as Lady Victoria, aged five, was pursued by her twin cousins, the Ladies Beatrice and Laura, aged six, in a lively game of tag in the formal drawing room of the Earl of Brinderley's London residence.

Katherine winced when the game terminated in a loud crash. One of the earl's prize Chinese vases was shattered.

So was the Countess of Brinderley's patience with her eldest child and nieces. A harried nurse was summoned, and the children were packed off to the nursery, a course of action Katherine would have prescribed fifteen minutes before when the matching vase had suffered a similar fate at the other end of the room.

But the countess was an indulgent (i.e., inconsistent) mother, and let her children run riot, especially when their cousins visited. The countess's nieces were famously unmanageable, and Elaine professed herself unequipped to discipline them. Such a task was, she claimed, more exhausting than simply letting them run amok.

That point was debatable, as the countess was looking quite exhausted at the moment, reclining on the divan, fanning her flushed face. Katherine suppressed the urge to roll her eyes. Elaine had been possessed of a theatrical streak ever since they were girls together at school.

If Katherine had children, *she* would not have raised them in such a haphazard manner.

But she hadn't any children and never would.

The pain of this fact was always significantly lessened after a visit to the countess's home. Her children were a cautionary tale.

Elaine sighed again and munched on her biscuit. "I'm quite put out with Marlowe, fobbing the twins on me while he's off in Cornwall with you-know-who doing god-knows-what."

Katherine could only guess what the latter euphemism was meant to include—no doubt drinking, carousing, and cavorting with loose women, the viscount's usual regimen when he repaired to the country—which, incidentally, was the same regimen he employed in the city. The *you-know-who* was easier to pinpoint. Mr. Sherbrook, the viscount's bosom friend, was always referred to by such a code in her presence. Owing to the estrangement between her husband and his nephew, it was considered *de trop* to speak Sherbrook's name to her face. As if it would somehow offend her sensibilities, which it would most certainly not. Mr. Sherbrook *himself* offended her, not his name.

Elaine, quite recovered now that the children were packed off, sat up with alacrity and refilled her teacup. "Now, tell me how fares your upcoming event at Saint George's?"

Katherine had been wondering how long it would take Elaine to mention her sister's wedding. "My sister and mother assure me every-thing is going famously."

The wedding was sure to be the social event of the year, if not the decade. *Everyone*, her mother had told her in that disapproving, slightly anxious tone she used whenever she addressed her eldest daughter, was well pleased with how things had turned out.

Everyone but Araminta. But Katherine knew her parents well enough not to confront them about this small hitch to their grand schemes. Her own marriage was proof of how well such opposition worked upon her father. No, a subtler game must be played in her sister's case, if she was to escape this marriage and marry her Mr. Morton.

Katherine held no romantic notions of true love between Araminta and Mr. Morton. And she didn't think Mr. Morton, a younger son who fancied himself a poet, was the better man. In fact, she didn't like her sister's choice of mate any better than she did their parents' choice. Katherine was determined to help her sister for one reason only, and that was to vex her father. Not very noble or kind of her, but there it was.

She hated her father.

He hated everyone.

And this time, Lord Carlisle could not punish *her* for thwarting his will, as she was a married woman.

Katherine smiled into her teacup. She couldn't wait for the day when her father discovered what she had done. "It shall be a wonderful wedding, Elaine. I *do* hope you're well enough to attend."

Elaine's gaze narrowed on Lady Katherine. "You are up to some-thing, aren't you?"

Lady Katherine's smile deepened. "Oh, I'm always up to something, Elaine. It is just most of the time no one notices."

Lady Elaine returned Katherine's smile with a sly grin and pointed her fan in her direction. "Ah, but then I've known you for years and years. Your eyes always give you away. They sparkle when you're scheming."

"I am not scheming," she protested.

"Ah, well, I shall not press you. I suppose I shall simply sit back and discover for myself what all of the twinkling is about."

"I suppose you shall," Katherine murmured into her tea.

At that moment, a servant entered, bearing a letter on a silver salver. He bowed over Elaine's seat. "A letter delivered by courier, my lady."

Elaine was immediately diverted. "Who could be sending a note by courier? Unless it is Marlowe, telling me he cannot come home today. In which case I shall be most annoyed . . ." She stared at the seal, and her eyes widened. "How very, *very* odd, my dear Katie, it's from Montford."

Katherine refilled her tea and ate a biscuit, trying to look discreetly uninterested in the letter, while Elaine ripped the missive open and read the contents, tsking in disbelief now and then at something she'd read.

At length, she lowered the document and gave Katherine a perplexed, considering look. "Did you know His Grace was in Yorkshire?"

"I had heard he'd taken a trip, but I assume he had returned, since the wedding is in a fortnight."

"No, he's in Yorkshire. A place called"—she referenced the letter—"Rylestone Green. Never heard of it. Most irregular."

"Yes, it sounds very irregular."

"He writes to me that he has come into possession of four cousins."

Katherine arched her eyebrow. "Indeed."

"Four *female* cousins. Two of them of marriageable age. He asks me to sponsor them for a Season."

How very interesting.

The countess sighed in exasperation. "I can't figure out what he's thinking. The Season is over. We shall have to wait for next year, unless he means for me to present them during the Little Season. Which shall be impossible to pull off if they need proper wardrobes, which, judging from what he says of these . . . *ahem*, country misses . . . they shall. And then there are bonnets, hats, shoes, and deportment lessons. Can you imagine? Men never think of such details. Besides which, I am in a delicate way and cannot be bothered with such a monumental undertaking," Lady Elaine continued, patting her belly significantly, smiling a secret, smug smile.

"Not again, Elaine. So soon after the last?" The countess was always *enceinte*, which never failed to surprise her acquaintances, who were also acquainted with the introverted earl. Brinderley was more interested in his coin collection than his wife. Except, it seemed, in the bedroom.

"Brinderley wants his heir, and I'm obliged to indulge him," the countess said, looking not at all upset by her duty.

"Well, that is wonderful news."

Elaine's smile faded as she glanced down at the letter. "Four country females from some unknown locale, relatives he didn't even know he had! Goodness me, this is all quite distressing!"

Katherine too was quite astounded, though her outward façade did not reveal this. She didn't know Montford well—no one did—but she was acquainted with him enough to find this behavior a complete about-face. Montford writing to the countess, attempting to fob off four poor relations, was an inconceivable development.

"I fear something horrible has befallen him," the countess murmured, echoing Katherine's own drift of thoughts. "He sounds very unlike himself. And the worst of it is, he expects *me* to drive up to this Riverstone place myself and fetch these girls." Lady Elaine sniffed and tossed aside the letter. "Montford is so used to having his way. But I will not do it, Katie. I cannot. I mean, look at me."

Elaine indicated her person, which looked healthy, plump, and dressed impeccably in the latest fashion, with nary a wrinkle or stain in sight.

Katherine, seeing an opportunity to further her own plans, came heroically to her friend's aid. "Perhaps I could go in your stead. I am soon to become Montford's sister-in-law, after all."

Elaine seized upon this idea with enthusiasm. "Yes! Yes! It's a wonder he didn't ask you to begin with!" Elaine grimaced at the end of this outburst, knowing full well why Montford hadn't written Lady Katherine.

Because of *you-know-who*.

Neither lady mentioned this, however, and Katherine continued, "I can leave at first light, as he has indicated such urgency."

"Yes, yes. First light. Just the thing. His tone is very strange, Katie. I think it best if you fetch him back, too."

"I shall take Araminta with me."

Elaine's eyes widened. "Do you think you should? I mean, of course you should. The wedding and all. But what if . . ."

"What if what?"

Elaine waved away whatever she'd been about to say. "Oh, nothing. Just that his writing was most odd. Do you know, Katie, he used adjectives?" she asked in a low tone.

Lady Katherine failed to see the import of this pronouncement, but clearly it meant something monumental to her friend.

"He never uses adjectives. Here, look," she said, jabbing the letter into Lady Katherine's hands and pointing to a line. "See how he describes the eldest gel."

Lady Katherine read dutifully. "'Forward, argumentative, bluestocking.' Hmm. Do you know, Elaine, but I quite like the sound of this chit."

"You can be sure His Grace doesn't. He never describes things. Something strange is going on up there, mark my word."

"Who are these creatures, I wonder."

"Honeywell is their surname."

Lady Katherine folded up the letter and handed it back to Elaine, careful not to let her surprise show. She knew enough of her family's buried history to know exactly who these Honeywell chits had to be. *Her* distant cousins.

The cousins her father would never have her know existed.

How very, *very* interesting. She was glad she had stopped in for tea.

Yes, a trip to Yorkshire sounded in order. Just the thing, perhaps, to solve all of her problems.

She set aside her tea and rose. "I shall take my leave to prepare for the journey."

Elaine was surprised by her easy agreement to the scheme and rose to see her out. "It is so good of you to take this upon yourself. I do not think the duke would disapprove. Indeed, how could he not approve? His fiancée and sister-in-law should be the ones to take these Honeywell chits in hand, anyway." She pursed her lips. "Besides, it's not as if Manwaring is even in the country. Certainly the duke can't object to your patronage on that particular ground."

Katherine inclined her head. "We shall see."

Elaine furrowed her brow and caught Katherine's hand. "Do be careful, my dear. The roads are dangerous this time of year, and Yorkshire, of all places!"

"Yorkshire? Yorkshire? What's all this talk of Yorkshire?" boomed a voice in the doorway.

Lady Katherine turned toward the owner of that basso profundo and stiffened.

It was Viscount Marlowe. He was rumpled beyond repair with several days' worth of beard growing on his chin. He looked as if he hadn't slept in a week—nor changed his clothes. His cravat was missing, and his waistcoat hung open over the swell of his gut. He appeared to be wearing bedroom slippers.

When he saw her, he looked startled and a little chagrined, and he attempted to tuck in the hem of his shirt into the back of his pants.

Lady Elaine grinned at her brother and rushed over to greet him in the French style. No matter their differences, the viscount was Lady Elaine's favorite sibling. No one else in her family could stand him.

Marlowe feigned disgust at this emotional display and gruffly told his sister to leave off, wiping the kisses from his cheeks. "What's this about Yorkshire?" he repeated. Lady Katherine was shocked he had kept his train of thought. Marlowe wasn't known for his brain.

"Lady Katherine is traveling there tomorrow, my dear, on an errand for me."

"Oh." His brow creased as if struggling with a real thought. Suspicion dawned across his florid features, and his eyes narrowed on Katherine.

Katherine didn't wait for explanations. She moved toward the door. "I must take my leave. I'll see myself out, Elaine. Stay and talk with your brother."

She shut the door behind her and shook her head. The viscount was more than Katherine cared to deal with at the moment. Insufferable, rude, crude. A more unmannerly buffoon she had yet to encounter. Worse, he couldn't hold a serious thought in his head for the time it took him to draw a breath. Though he had seemed serious about wanting to know why she was going to Yorkshire. Doubtless he knew where the duke was and didn't want her or her family to know. The viscount had made it obvious on several occasions how little enthusiasm he had for the match between his best mate and her sister.

If only the viscount knew that they were in complete sympathy on this matter. But she couldn't explain this to him and have all of her own plans ruined.

She thanked the butler for her gloves and bonnet and headed down the long hallway to make her exit, mentally preparing a list for the journey.

A noise down one of the connecting corridors stopped her progress. It was the sound of a child's giggle, followed by the low, easy laughter of a man.

She turned and her breath hitched, as it always did, at the sight of Sebastian Sherbrook. She should have known he would have accompanied the viscount on his errand, since they were notoriously inseparable. He was clad outrageously, as usual, in a robin's-egg-blue silk jacket and yellow waistcoat, his hands nearly hidden by the lace spilling from his sleeves, and his fingers encrusted in jewels. A dozen or so ornate watch fobs crisscrossed his chest. He was currently leaning forward and dangling one of them just out of reach of one of the twins' hands.

He looked ridiculous, but Lady Katherine suspected that he knew this quite well. He dressed to excess because he lived to excess. His cravat was in disarray, and his overlong ebony hair was brushed hastily back from his face, which was shadowed by a beard and dark, cavernous circles under his eyes, giving him a faintly bruised look. If Marlowe looked as if he'd not slept in a week, Mr. Sherbrook looked as if he never slept at all.

Nevertheless, when he noticed her at the opposite end of the corridor and turned those startling, jaded sapphire eyes on her, his smile fading into blank nothingness, Lady Katherine could not breathe. She could not move.

He was the most beautiful creature she had ever seen.

They did not mix socially, obviously, and she could count the number of times on one hand she had actually seen him in company. But she remembered all of those times quite distinctly, remembered every detail of these sightings, for reasons she dared not examine too closely.

She was married to his uncle, and it was no secret that the two men were bitter enemies. She was, by default, then, also Mr. Sherbrook's enemy. And it was clear Mr. Sherbrook felt some personal animosity toward her for her marriage to Manwaring. It was evident now in the way his mouth turned down at the edges and his expression hardened to stone.

She did not like him either. He was even more detestable than Viscount Marlowe and was no doubt the reason the feckless viscount was always in trouble. He led his stupid, fat friend from one outrageous act to another. Sherbrook was a libertine, the worst rakehell in the country, and though admittedly Lord Manwaring had few redeeming qualities himself, it was not hard to figure out why the marquess wanted nothing to do with his nephew.

However, no one could deny that Mr. Sherbrook was a handsome man. More than that: beautiful, as only a woman had a right to be. Clear, olive skin, large, depthless blue eyes, a tall, slender, but powerful figure, and a mouth made for sin. At least that was what her faster acquaintances said about his mouth. All she could determine was that it was large and full and dark red, and when she looked at it she felt quite strange deep in her stomach.

No one had a right to such beauty, especially a rogue like him.

No, she did not like him at all.

They stared at each other without moving or speaking. The tension between them stretched very taut. Neither exchanged even the most cursory of greetings. She gave him her haughtiest expression and arched one eyebrow.

He let his watch fall to his side, and the twin snatched it up and began to tug it, pulling the chain, and him along with it. As if snapped out of a trance, he turned back to his game with the child and allowed her to lead him from the corridor by his watch fob. He said something to the girl, and they both broke down into peals of laughter that sounded very naughty.

Lady Katherine knew when she had been dismissed. She wasted no time in departing the residence. As she settled into her landau and drove toward her empty townhouse, she couldn't decide whether the surprise of encountering him or the surprise of seeing him play with the child as if he were a normal person was the most disconcerting part of their meeting.

Both, she decided.

But she filed away their encounter with all the others, certain details—the fall of his ebony hair, the buckles on his shoes, the single dimple on his right cheek when he smiled at the child, and the dead look in his brilliant eyes—all duly noted.

"WHAT DO you mean," Viscount Marlowe blustered at his sister, "that *she* is going to Yorkshire to rescue the duke? What business of *hers* is the duke?"

"Well said, old man," seconded Sebastian, who had skulked inside the drawing room, only to overhear Elaine's convoluted explanation for Lady Manwaring's upcoming trip to Yorkshire. Sebastian didn't much care what Montford had gotten himself into with these Honeywell chits, but he cared greatly that Lady Ice had taken it upon herself to interfere in Montford's affairs. She'd drag Montford back by his nose and have him leg-shackled to her dreadful sister before the week's end. That was unacceptable.

Egad, just glimpsing Lady Ice in the hallway had been enough to make Sebastian seek out the earl's sideboard forthwith and pour himself a generous snifter of port. She was the second-to-last person on earth Sebastian liked encountering. She left him with a queer pang in his stomach and a horrible taste in his mouth.

He reclined on the most comfortable seat in the drawing room, sipping his port and watching Marlowe and Elaine bicker in an effort to banish the image of Lady Manwaring's face from his mind.

"Montford demanded *I* ride up there forthwith to deal with these Honeywell people. Such an idea is absurd, in my condition," Elaine said, touching her stomach.

Marlowe, thunderous a second before, looked at his sister askance. "You're not—again?"

"I am," Elaine answered.

"Weren't it just a week ago you dropped your last brat?" Marlowe demanded.

"It was two months ago. God, Evvy, keep up, will you?"

"I would, 'cept it's so very hard. Don't see how Brinderley manages it, d'you, Sherbrook?"

"Didn't know he had it in 'im," Sebastian drawled.

"Well, he does manage quite well in . . . that arena. Quite," Elaine said firmly. Then she blushed, realizing what she'd said.

Marlowe blushed as well and looked slightly ill, obviously forming an unwanted visual image of his brother-in-law "managing" with his wife, much like Sebastian was.

Sebastian set aside his snifter. And he thought he'd felt nauseated before.

"Devil take it, what were we talking about?" Marlowe thundered.

"Montford. Yorkshire. Honeywells," Sebastian prompted.

"Oh, yes. Don't know what the blazes is happening up there, but to call upon that woman to intercede on your behalf . . ."

"Come now, Evvy, she is to be Montford's sister, and Araminta, who is accompanying her, his wife."

"Araminta! *She's* going? Bloody hell, Lanie! We are trying to *stop* this wedding from happening, not hasten it. Why not send up a bloody firing squad to finish him off? 'Twould be kinder."

"I will pretend you did not just liken the marriage state with an execution. Nor will I believe you dare insult one of my dearest friends to my face. You know how fond I am of Katie. She is rather . . . aloof, I'll grant you, and can come off as dour and moralistic and—" She broke off when she realized her endorsement of her friend had not come out quite right. "She is *not* a bad person," she insisted after they snorted. "Despite being married to your mortal enemy. Though what *he* has done besides being thoroughly boring and old, I do not know."

Marlowe and Sebastian stared at their shoes and did not provide any enlightenment on this last point.

"Nevertheless, your bosom beau Montford needs a chaperone. Katherine is willing to be that chaperone. What's the hue and cry?"

Marlowe looked to Sherbrook for guidance, but receiving nothing but a shrug, he shrugged as well. "Demmed if I know. Just don't like the smell of this one. What d'ya think, Sherry?"

Sebastian studied his fingernails. "If my lady aunt thinks to run up to Yorkshire to meddle in Montford's affairs, she is free to do so."

Marlowe looked deflated by Sebastian's lack of enthusiasm.

"However," Sebastian continued, locking eyes on his friend over his nails, his lips curling in his sliest smile, "so are we."

It took a moment for this to sink in. When it did, Marlowe laughed gustily and slapped his knee. "For a moment, Sherry, I doubted you. But only for a moment."

Chapter Eighteen

In Which the Duke's Holiday Takes an Unexpected Detour

AT FIRST, he thought he was on a sea voyage, the room around him tilting and heaving like a ship in a squall. He'd been at sea before when he'd been obliged to cross the Channel for the Congress of Vienna. He'd tried to block out the memory of that experience, however, as it had been quite miserable. He'd never found his sea legs. In fact, after returning from Calais a wasted, nervous wreck, he'd vowed to never set foot on a boat again.

So what the devil was he doing on one now?

He tried to raise his head, but this was a serious mistake. Bright sunlight barraged his face through a slit in a wall. His head felt the approximate weight of an anvil, upon which a very well-endowed blacksmith had merrily hammered for days and days.

His berth lurched to one side, and he clutched beneath him for purchase, his hands encountering rough wood planks and a bit of coarse canvas cloth that had a suspiciously foul odor. Then the ship, or whatever he was on, hit a large rock or maybe even a whale, throwing his entire body a few inches in the air. He landed with a thud.

He thought he heard a woman's laughter, but that could have just been the squawking of a gull.

The ship encountered another whale, and he was thrown up in the air again. He crashed back down, every inch of his body in pain, his stomach roiling. His mouth felt like it was stuffed with cotton, and his brain felt smashed. Something thudded against the planks, the vibrations causing his head to throb, then rolled against his side. It was heavy and persistent. He thrashed about with his arms and tried to push it away, but it would not budge. Something was trying to crush him.

He squinted one eye open in an effort to get his bearings. Slowly, by increments, his eye adjusted to the blinding light pouring over him. He had expected to find a ceiling, but instead he was staring at a dingy, tan expanse of canvas hovering a few feet above him. Part of the canvas had become unknotted, revealing a bright patch of gray-blue sky.

He turned his head, which swam dizzily, and faced his attacker. It was a large wooden barrel. It must have been jostled loose from its moorings by the terrible storm. Though how a barrel had landed in his berth, and how it could be storming even though the sky was blue, were mysteries to him.

It hurt to think too hard.

He shut his eye and tried to breathe evenly so as not to be sick. This was impossible, though. It was a matter of when, not if, he'd lose the contents of his stomach. He couldn't very well lose them in his current location, however. He needed to find a chamber pot, or at the very least a bucket. He made himself sit up, his head brushing the canvas above him, his stomach in his throat. On all fours, he made for the slit he'd seen in the canvas, and as he did so, he wondered what had happened to him.

His hands were filthy, and so were his sleeves. The lace at his cuffs was torn and soiled, and the buttons on the wrists of his jacket were missing. Had he been kidnapped by pirates? Was he himself a pirate?

No, no, he was the Duke of Montford. The signet ring glaring up at him from underneath a layer of dried mud reminded him of this.

He fumbled his way to the slit in the awning and threw it back. He expected to be on the deck of a ship, but instead he found himself thrust up against a wooden railing, watching a dusty country road fly by him in reverse. He leaned over and spotted a large wooden wheel spinning and creaking, round and round, in the ruts of the road. He clutched his head with one hand and his guts with the other.

He was on a wagon.

It was even worse than he'd thought. His stomach heaved, and he cast up his accounts all over the wooden wheel.

Several moments later, he sat back against the railing, wiping his mouth with his tattered sleeve, squeezing his eyes shut, and trying to recall what had led him to this horrible fate.

The last thing he could see in his mind's eye was watching Miss Honeywell drop a red flag and smirk at him. After that, everything was a blur. He'd raced in that damned contest. He might have won; he wasn't sure. And he might or might not have been attacked by a white poodle. He'd been very, very, *very* drunk. In fact, he might still be drunk.

And he had been abducted. He would never have voluntarily climbed into a wagon—an even worse conveyance than a well-sprung carriage for someone with his condition—no matter how drunk he was.

His unwarranted mirth died a quick death as his stomach lurched again. He turned over the side and hacked up the vilest concoction of stomach acid, Honeywell Ale, and whatever disgustingly crude food he'd devoured while in his drunken stupor. Whatever it was, it was unrecognizable as it painted the roadside.

Then he heard voices murmuring on the breeze, somewhere at

the front of the wagon. One of the voices was female and familiar. It cut across his throbbing head like the crash of a blacksmith's hammer against iron.

He laughed with grim humor.

Who else had he expected?

He began to crawl forward, hoping he'd have the strength to wring Astrid Honeywell's neck when he found her. At last, he managed to reach the front of the wagon bed and could make out the outlines of Miss Honeywell and a driver on the other side of the awning. The driver was chuckling at something Miss Honeywell was saying, and it took a moment for Montford to make out what it was. When he did, he began to grow extremely worried.

"*. . . young fellow from Kent, / Whose anatomy was quite bent. / When he thrust to go in, / He got stuck on her shin, / Back home to his wife he was sent.*"

"Ach, Miss Astrid!" cried the driver through his laughter. "That was too naughty! You mustn't say such things!"

"I was only quoting. 'Twas not I who said it, but the duke himself. And admit it, you're amused."

"Aye, but I shouldna be."

Montford managed to part the canvas. He peered out at the driver's seat, upon which Miss Honeywell sat with one of her stable hands. She looked bright-eyed and entirely too chipper for his liking, twirling her bonnet around in one of her hands, her corkscrew hair rustling in the breeze. She was wearing a white muslin gown sprigged with orange flowers, and an orange-colored pelisse, which clashed painfully with her hair. He felt like sicking up just looking at her.

He felt like sicking up at the bit of verse she'd just shared with the driver. It was irritatingly familiar. The kind of codswallop Marlowe was fond of belting out when in his cups. Montford had a horrible suspicion Miss Honeywell was not lying when she said she'd been quoting him. He did not remember reciting the limerick, but then again, he did not remember a great deal of the previous day.

"Oh God, oh God," he groaned, clutching his aching head. He must have spoken too loudly, for he heard Miss Honeywell shriek and felt the wagon lurch to a standstill. He wasn't expecting the movement, so he was unable to stop himself from flying forward, out of the wagon bed, and across the driver's seat. His nose became intimately acquainted with Miss Honeywell's boots.

"What are you *doing* here?" Miss Honeywell shrieked somewhere above him, the sound ricocheting through his skull like a gunshot. He groaned and tried to right himself, but he only succeeded in turning his head enough to glimpse Miss Honeywell's face peering down at him from above. She was upside down.

"What am *I* doing here?" he rasped. "I've been abducted, that's what."

Miss Honeywell looked aghast, her cheeks suffused with red, her hair popping out of its pins.

He floundered at her feet for several long, painful seconds, until finally the driver hauled him upright by the shoulders. He managed to put his arse, which had been thrust inelegantly in Miss Honeywell's face for some time, on the seat where it belonged. Though his victory was short-lived. His stomach somersaulted dangerously.

"Abducted?" Miss Honeywell was screeching next to him. "Stuff! How dare you accuse me of . . . abduction!"

He cringed and covered his ears with his hands. "Damnation, woman, don't scream at me!" he whispered.

"I'm not screaming!" she yelled.

He clutched his temple and groaned.

"I did not kidnap you, Montford," she said, moderating her tone slightly. "That's the most ludicrous thing I have ever heard. You are the last person on earth I ever want to see again! You're supposed to be on the road back to London. Or at the very least suffering mightily back at the castle."

"I *am* suffering mightily," he informed her.

"Good. No less than you deserve after the . . . *spectacle* you made of yourself yesterday."

He moaned. He did not want to know what he had done. Snatches of memory here and there were returning to him. The limerick had jarred something loose inside. He seemed to remember having recited quite a lot of them last night.

He eyed Miss Honeywell out of the edges of his fingers. She was facing the road, her arms folded underneath her breasts. She looked quite cross. She wrinkled her nose. "And you stink to high heaven, Montford. You smell like the brewery. And dirty stockings."

"Thank you for that valuable insight. Now, if you shall turn this conveyance around, I should like to return to the castle."

"Not bloody likely."

"What?"

"I said, not bloody likely. The castle's twenty miles back that way," she said, pointing her finger behind them.

"Twenty miles? *Twenty miles?*" he shrieked, then grimaced, as his voice had split open his head anew.

"Mebbe we should, Miss Astrid," the driver interjected, looking worried. "If'n His Grace be wanting to return."

Montford gave the man a gracious nod—or as near to one he could manage in his present state. "Thank you—"

"Nonsense," Miss Honeywell said contemptuously. "We are but ten miles from Hawes. I'll not be put off concluding our business because the duke decided to pass out in our wagon."

"I did not decide to pass out in this . . . I would never choose to pass out in a moving conveyance. Someone put me here!"

"Well, it wasn't me!" Miss Honeywell cried. "Not after the way you behaved last night—" She bit off anything else she had been about to reveal, and her face went from merely being red to something closer to purple.

Montford had a sinking suspicion that he should be remembering something quite important right about now. But his mind was blank. He didn't want to ask, but he had to. "What did I do?"

"You mean you don't remember?" she asked, her eyes popping from her head.

"I don't remember a blasted thing. Except being attacked by a white dog. Was I attacked by a white dog?"

She looked at him as if he'd lost his mind, which was not far from the truth. "You must be thinking of Aunt Anabel's wig. You knocked it off when you kissed her."

Now he was definitely going to be sick. "I . . . what?"

Miss Honeywell beamed at him, seeing his discomfort. "You kissed Aunt Anabel. On the lips. In front of the entire village."

The driver coughed into his hand to muffle his laughter. Montford groaned. "I didn't."

"You did!" she insisted, looking triumphant.

He shook his head in misery and tried to focus. His immediate goal was to avoid being sick all over his boots. He had that under control, as the wagon was momentarily stopped. Of secondary importance was finding his way back to the castle and out of Miss Honeywell's sights forever. She may not have put him in the wagon, but she was to blame nonetheless. He couldn't be near her. She made him do crazy things. Like run in drunken races and kiss old women. Indeed, he was beginning to wonder if London would be far enough away from her.

He wouldn't begin to imagine the sleepless nights ahead when she invaded London. Even if he didn't see her, he would *know* she was there, at the countess's, with her mismatched eyes and goading tongue, plaguing him. As she plagued him now, sitting next to him, holding her nose as if *he* offended *her*.

He couldn't bear the twenty miles back to the castle. Never mind his queasy stomach. The thought of enduring her company was enough to make him want to scream. Which he would have done, had he not suspected that such an act would make his aching head explode.

He didn't think he could even bear ten miles to Hawes. Whatever *that* was. But ten was better than twenty, and perhaps he could purchase a horse there. He needed a horse anyway, which was the reason he'd come to the damned festival in the first place.

"Ten miles. I can do ten miles," he muttered to himself, clutching the seat.

Miss Honeywell snorted. "Do you hear that, Charlie? *His Majesty* can bear our poor company for ten miles. Though how he'll feel about the thirty miles back to Rylestone is another story."

"I'll purchase a horse in Hawes. Not riding back in this," he said, indicating the wagon with a vague pass of his hand. "That's for damned bloody sure."

"Well, good, because we don't desire your company any more than you desire ours." Miss Honeywell sniffed haughtily, then signaled for Charlie to continue, but the driver hesitated.

"Mebbe we *should* turn 'round," Charlie suggested nervously, looking rather pale.

"No!" they both cried simultaneously.

Charlie grimaced, then reluctantly whipped the drays into motion.

Montford gripped the edge of the seat until his knuckles were white, willing his stomach to calm down. But the combination of his motion sickness and his hangover was quite hard to overcome. A few moments later, he could feel his face turning from gray to green. He sprang into motion, clawing his way over Miss Honeywell's lap, crushing her with his body. She fell off her perch, swearing at him and smacking his head. He was too busy scrambling to the railing and leaning over the road to give her much notice. His shoulders heaved, his breath choked, and the most incredible hacking noise issued from his throat as he cast up his accounts.

Charlie pulled up on the reins, and the cart drew to a standstill. Miss Honeywell pulled herself back on her seat, edging closer to Charlie, giving the duke as wide a berth as possible on the narrow perch. When he was through heaving, he slumped exhaustedly against the side rail, his body trembling.

When he glanced up at Miss Honeywell, she was gazing at him

with a mixture of exasperation and concern. "You don't have the plague, do you?" she inquired.

That was it. He could bear it no more. He groaned, pulled himself upright, and then slowly began to climb out of the wagon, every muscle in his body protesting.

Miss Honeywell looked down at him in alarm. "What are you doing?" she demanded.

He lost his footing and fell the rest of the way. He landed with a thud on his backside, dust flying up around him. He heaved himself to his feet. "I'm walking back."

"Don't be ridiculous. It's twenty miles!"

"Don't care. I'd rather walk a hundred miles than spend another second in your presence," he muttered, which was true enough. He didn't add that one more second on that moving wagon was likely to make him cast up his guts.

She put her fists on her hips and glared at him. "You weren't saying that last night," she finally retorted.

What was that supposed to mean? A chill passed down his spine. Oh God, what had he done?

Seeing the look on his face, she gave him a satisfied smirk and reached into one of the baskets behind her. She threw something at him, and it landed against his chest and slid to the ground. He grunted and rubbed the sore spot where it had hit, then bent over and retrieved the object. It was a water skin.

"Wouldn't want you to die along the way of thirst," she explained, settling into her seat.

"How thoughtful of you," he gritted out.

"No, it would just be too easy to let you to die. I want you to feel every step of the twenty miles back to Rylestone."

"Damn you, Astrid Honeywell!" he roared, as the wagon rolled onward and Miss Honeywell and Charlie put their backs to him. He raised his fist at the rear of the wagon. "I hope I never see you again!"

As he turned and began to trudge down the road, he thought he heard her voice drift back to him on the wind. "Same!" it called out, tauntingly.

Five minutes later, when the creaking and groaning of the wagon had all but disappeared in the distance, and his feet were already beginning to ache in his boots, he sat down on the side of the road and stared up at the sky, utterly dumbfounded.

He was alone, on a dusty road, miles from anything resembling civilization, tattered, battered, and reeking of ale and vomit. It was a state of affairs he could not have foreseen in even his wildest nightmares. He'd cry if he had any moisture left in his body to invest in tears.

And he didn't. He'd retched out all of the water in his body.

He stared down at the water skin in his hands and tried to open it. But he couldn't figure out how to manage the top. He didn't know how long it was he sat there, trying to pry apart the blasted thing, but it was long enough to make him lose the last thread of his patience. He threw the water skin down on the dusty road and stomped on it with the heel of his boots.

He stomped and stomped until the water skin was quite dead and water pooled out of a leak in its side, turning the dust underneath his feet into a mud puddle. He wished it had been Astrid Honeywell's head.

He wandered on a few steps, but found his energy quite sapped. He had to sit down. Which he did, on a log a few paces off the road. Maybe his bright idea to walk back to the castle had not been a bright idea after all. Even off of the wagon, he still felt quite ill. What had possessed him to get so drunk? He had behaved like a lunatic, and what was even worse, he had a niggling suspicion that he had enjoyed himself. It was beyond humiliating. It was worrying.

What had Miss Honeywell meant? What had he said to her? What had he done?

He tried to delve into the muddle in his brain, but he could not come up with a single thing, other than some vague recollection of a rhyme about her eyes.

He was still pondering this when a large, black coach, pulled by a team of four large, black stallions, and piloted by a giant man in a black cape wielding a dangerous-looking whip, thundered by him. He could not see inside the carriage, but he thought he spied a pair of glinting, coal-black eyes peering from behind a curtain, sending a chill down his spine. He had no liking for coaches in general, but if ever a one looked like it belonged to Lucifer himself, it was that one.

He rose to his feet and stared at the coach as it tore hell-for-leather to the north like a demon out of hell. What, he wondered in exasperation, could be so interesting up there? Sheep? Hawes, whatever the bloody hell that was? Bloody Scotland?

London is in the opposite direction, he almost called out to the coach.

Just thinking of that fair city (even though it was far from fair and rather stank to high heaven when it rained) was enough to get his legs to move. Every step drew him closer to London, he reminded himself. He could not wait until he was back in his palace, ensconced in his steaming bathing chamber, scrubbed clean of his travels, with the *London Times* financial section in one hand and a bar of soap in the other.

When he got back to London, he was not leaving. Ever. Again.

But then he remembered Araminta. Good God, Araminta! He'd totally forgotten he was supposed to marry the chit in a fortnight! And for their wedding tour—obligatory, unfortunately—they were to go to the ancestral pile in Devonshire.

Montford stumbled to a stop, his mind screaming in outrage.

Like hell he was going to Devonshire. Like hell he was marrying Araminta!

Or was he?

Wasn't that supposed to be a good idea? He couldn't recall. He was lucky he'd even recalled her name.

He clutched his pounding temple. He needed to stop thinking so much.

"Just get back to Rylestone," he murmured. "One foot in front of the other."

That was what he did, for a few more yards. But the screaming in his head seemed to get worse.

It took him several moments to realize the screaming was no longer in his head, however. It seemed to be issuing from somewhere behind him, and it sounded distinctly like Miss Honeywell's voice. He turned around, but he could see nothing but road and trees. Surely it hadn't been Miss Honeywell. She was miles away by now.

He turned back around and trudged onward.

Then the screaming started again. This time it was punctuated by the blast of a gun. There was no mistaking that sound as it rent the countryside like a thunderclap. He clutched his aching head and waited. Nothing came after that but the rustling of the leaves in the wind. Even the birds had been frightened into silence.

Montford didn't breathe. His heart didn't beat. A terrible dread began to unfurl in the pit of his stomach. He'd not imagined her screams. He'd not imagined the gunshot. He'd not imagined the terrible silence that followed.

Montford began to sprint the way he had come, faster than he'd gone at any point during the race on the previous day, though of course he didn't notice. He was too busy praying that he'd find Astrid Honeywell alive and in decent enough condition to wring her neck. He'd never been so frightened in his life, and it was all her fault.

ASTRID USUALLY enjoyed the trip into Hawes, but her heart was not in it this year. She wanted to drive to Hawes, drop off the shipment, and return to the castle to enjoy her final days there before she was carted off to London. Charlie Weeks drove her, as was his custom, but his mood seemed equally low. As the early morning haze burned off and the drays fell into a steady plod along the North Road, they exchanged few words. Charlie was grim-faced, gripping the reins with tense hands. It wasn't until they'd gone nearly two-thirds of the way that he loosened up enough to laugh at the bawdy rhymes she recited. He was in a strange mood, but she couldn't blame him, as his wife was six months pregnant with their fifth child. He was deservedly a little frazzled around the edges.

Poor Charlie seemed to fray apart completely when Montford fell out of the back of the wagon. The cloying reek of stale alcohol and something unimaginably worse had risen off of the duke's person, causing Astrid to cover her nose and draw back. He was wearing the soiled clothes from the previous evening, a tear in his once fine silk jacket running from his shoulder to the middle of his back. One side of his hair was plastered to his head, the other side sticking straight in the air, and every bit of his person was layered in a liberal coating of mud, grass, and other unidentifiable bits of debris.

He was the last person she had expected to see. Clearly Charlie felt the same, for he stared at the interloper as if he were a leper. How Montford had come to be stowed away in the bed of the wagon that she happened to be riding in seemed too coincidental by half, but she hadn't the patience to pursue the whys and wherefores of the situation. Montford had not, either. He'd cast up his accounts, then fell off the wagon and onto the roadside, vowing to walk back to Rylestone.

Far be it from her to stop him. If he would rather walk back twenty miles than "endure her company," then that was his prerogative. She was not hurt at all by his fierce rejection. She was not hurt at all by what had transpired the night before, and what he clearly had forgotten. And she was not about to fill in the gaps in his memory.

But she certainly hoped he remembered kissing Aunt Anabel. And she certainly hoped he was bruised from Aunt Anabel's cane. He deserved to be black-and-blue from head to toe, as far as she was concerned.

And she had *not* thrown him a water flask because she felt sorry for him.

Not at all.

She faced forward and harrumphed loudly as she and Charlie continued their journey. Charlie still seemed to be recovering from the episode, blotting sweat from his forehead with a handkerchief, his hands trembling.

"Don't worry, we're well rid of him. I don't think the twenty miles will kill him. I don't think anything would kill him, short of burning at the stake," she muttered, patting his shoulder.

"We shouldna left 'im like that," Charlie murmured. He hesitated. "Mebbe we should turn back, Miss Astrid."

"Nonsense. We'll be in Hawes in short order. I'll not let *him* ruin our trip."

Charlie pursed his lips, not looking assured in the least.

"What I want to know is how he came to be in the wagon in the first place," Astrid said, to change the subject.

"Dunna know," Charlie said miserably. "Dinna check the bed this morning. Must've climbed in and passed out there last night."

"A very odd coincidence, don't you think?"

Charlie shrugged. "Very odd. Near as jumped out of my boots when he come through the awning."

Astrid held out hope that somehow Montford would beat them back to Rylestone, acquire a mount, and be on his way back to London so that Astrid never had to lay eyes on him again. But that was a slim hope indeed in his current condition. They'd likely intercept him on the return journey. Astrid had half a mind to drive past him without picking him up. But that would prolong his stay in Rylestone, and no one wanted that to happen.

No, until Montford was back in London, she'd not rest easy.

But then she groaned out loud, recalling that very soon she would be in London as well.

"What is it? What's wrong?" Charlie demanded. "Should we turn round? Head home?" He sounded strangely hopeful.

"No, I'm fine. Just thinking about my upcoming trip."

Charlie's face paled. His eyes went wild. "Trip? What trip?" he asked nervously.

She looked at her driver with growing concern. What had gotten into him?

"Calm down, Charlie, for heaven's sake. I was talking about my trip to London."

Charlie still looked flustered. "Lunnon? When're you going to Lunnon?" he squeaked.

"Hopefully never. But probably by week's end. You haven't heard, then?"

"Heard what?" Charlie asked warily.

"The duke's odious plan for us!" she exclaimed.

"The *duke's* plan?" Charlie murmured.

"He's to marry us off. Well, Alice and I, at least. In London. He's to have one of his friends find us some peacocks to leg-shackle."

Charlie looked completely at sea. Astrid sighed deeply and explained the duke's scheme in greater depth and in less colorful prose. For a long time afterward, Charlie was silent, staring straight ahead of him, not meeting her eye.

At last he spoke, in a strange half whisper.

"So lemme get this straight," he said, licking his lips nervously, "Montford's paying for you to fancy yerself up in Lunnon, attend all sorts of ennertainments, and snag yerself any gennleman of yer choosin'."

"Well," she said slowly, "yes, I suppose so."

"Then as a weddin' present, he's givin' you a castle and a fair bit o' blunt to see you set up for life. Then he's settin' up Miss Alice as well, and the young uns, when they're sprouted."

"Yes, though when you put it like that, it sounds . . ."

"Gen'rous?"

She snorted. Montford had not been motivated by generosity. He'd come up with the one plan designed to gall her like no other. But she could hardly explain this to Charlie.

"I suppose it shall not be the end of the world," she allowed, grudgingly. "I have no wish to leave Rylestone for London, and I have no interest in the entertainments of the city. However, if I am to find a suitable husband and secure my dowry, I suppose I'll have to go to London. I'm certainly not marrying Sir Wesley or Mr. Fawkes!"

Charlie looked dumbfounded. "Sir Wesley has asked you . . . and Mr. Fawkes . . . the vicar?"

She nodded. "Of course I turned them down. Though they're a sight better than Mr. Lightfoot." She shuddered. "I'd rather endure Mr. Fawkes's stutter twenty-four hours a day than be tied to Mr. Lightfoot. Do you know, Charlie, I think that man might be insane?"

Charlie looked quite miserable. He looked, in fact, as if he were about to cry. Astrid became quite concerned. "Whatever is the matter, Charlie?"

He swallowed tightly, as if he had a rat stuck in his throat. "Just wished you'd told me. About Lunnon."

"Well, I would have done, but there was the festival yesterday, and so much happening at once."

"Just wish you'd told me," he repeated, shaking his head. "Thought I'd lose my job, I did. Thought we'd all be driven to the workhouse. Thought I had no choice, with my Millie burstin' at the seams again and all of the little uns underfoot. Thought I done what's best for 'em."

She laid a comforting hand over Charlie's arm, growing increasingly troubled by his behavior. He looked as green as Montford had looked before he'd cast up his accounts. "What are you talking about, Charlie? You're worrying me."

He dropped the reins and turned to face her, though he could not meet her eyes. "Oh, Miss Astrid, I think I done a terrible thing. I think yer gonna tear my eyes out, you are."

She grasped his arm. "Charlie . . ."

"I were the one what killed Cyril!" he burst out.

Astrid's heart stopped working. Her hand dropped from Charlie's arm. "No, oh no, Charlie!"

Charlie shook his head miserably. "He said it needed to be done. To shake you up some. I never meant to hurt the poor beast, but the bullet went wrong. Don't know why I let him talk me into it. But he has a way of twistin' a body's thoughts and fillin' it with uncommon fears. He said it were the only way to save you and yer sisters and to keep us all from the workhouse."

"Who are you talking about, Charlie?" she asked, though she already knew what he was going to say.

"Mr. Lightfoot! He said he were gonna marry you and that it was what was best for everyone. I don't know, but it seemed right to me when he said it!"

"Oh, Charlie! He's not right at all! How could you have *listened* to him? How could you have shot at Montford?"

"He offered me a job. Good wages. What were I to do with the threat of the workhouse looming? What were I to do, watch you and yer sisters end up there with me?"

"But I can't marry Mr. Lightfoot. Dear God, Charlie, he's crazy! Insane!"

Charlie's brow creased. "D'ye think so?"

"Charlie, he should be in Bedlam. Surely you have noticed."

Charlie scratched his head. "Thought he were a bit off," he murmured. "Oh, Miss Astrid, I wish I'd known this before! Now it's too late!"

He took up the reins and whipped the drays into as fast a trot as they could manage.

Astrid braced herself against the bench, a chill racing up her spine. "What's going on, Charlie?" she demanded. "Why are we going so fast?"

"Mebbe we can reach Hawes before he's upon us. He'll not be able to take you there," Charlie said, a strange light gleaming in his eyes.

Astrid's stomach bottomed out. "What are you talking about?"

"Mr. Lightfoot. He's comin' to take you off to Gretna Green."

Fear made her body go stiff.

"Such a fool, such a bloody fool," Charlie kept murmuring to himself over and over again, urging the drays faster and faster.

"This can't be happening," Astrid said, more to herself than Charlie, when she heard the unmistakable thundering of hooves coming up behind them. She turned her head enough to see Mr. Lightfoot's imposing black coach barreling down on them, piloted by one of his giant thugs in a black cape. It looked precisely like a scene out of one of Alice's horrid novels.

Oh God, she thought to herself. She was about to become the hapless heroine of her own personal melodrama.

"I didna mean it, I swear I didna mean to kill Cyril," Charlie babbled beside her.

She just stared at him, too stunned to talk, holding on to her seat with every ounce of strength she had. They were going at a reckless pace, and the wagon had no shocks to speak of. Her backside felt every bump, rivet, stone, and branch the wheels encountered. Her pain brought home the fact that what was happening was all too real. Pain in her backside, and pain in her heart for Charlie's betrayal.

How could he have killed Cyril? How could he have turned his back on the years and years of friendship between them? Or had they ever been friends at all? Had Astrid once again failed to see what was so plainly before her? She'd made that mistake with her own sister. It didn't surprise her to know she'd made similar misjudgments.

But to turn her over into Mr. Lightfoot's keeping—that was simply beyond her comprehension. Charlie wasn't the sharpest tool in the shed, but surely he must have had some inkling of the idiocy of such a plan.

"Why, Charlie? Why?"

"Thought I done it for yer own good. Fer my own family's good.

Ach, but I've made a muck of it!" He glanced behind him, and his expression crumbled. "We'll never outrun him."

"Try, for God's sake, try!" she exhorted.

But it was no use. Two aged drays were no match for a team of four. Mr. Lightfoot's black carriage quickly drew abreast of them. She could see Mr. Lightfoot's beady eyes gleaming from the window. Her stomach turned over.

Gretna Green indeed!

The black-caped driver of the coach pulled his team sharply to the right, running the drays off of the road. The coach drew up, pinning the wagon in. Charlie was forced to pull on the reins, bringing the wagon to a complete stop.

He stared at Astrid in terror. "Run," he whispered. "Into the forest."

Astrid rose on unsteady feet and began to climb out of the wagon. It was the first sensible thing Charlie had said in the last quarter hour.

"Not so fast!" boomed a voice from the doorway of the carriage. Astrid glanced up and saw Mr. Lightfoot standing on the runner, brandishing a pistol directly at Astrid's head. She froze. Fear coursed through her veins, and her heart was in her throat, though she still couldn't quite believe this was happening. Everything swam before her, as if happening underwater.

Mr. Lightfoot glanced in Charlie's direction, his black eyes gleaming strangely, a horrible smile curving his lips. "I do believe you were attempting to escape us, Mr. Weeks. How odd, when I thought we had an arrangement."

Charlie blanched, his eyes transfixed on the gun, sweat dripping down his face. "I've changed my mind. Miss Astrid don't wanna go with you," he managed.

Mr. Lightfoot just laughed. "Of course she doesn't, you idiot. That's why we arranged for this little roadside meeting, or don't you remember?" He turned back to Astrid, his smile fading, his eyes growing hard.

"Now come along, my dear. Hop into the carriage like a good gel, and we'll be on our way."

"Never," she replied with rather more bravado than she felt.

Mr. Lightfoot signaled to his black-caped driver, who dismounted from his high perch and approached Astrid. Astrid swallowed. The man was at least two feet taller than she was, and about as wide as a pianoforte. His face was equally grim, with a deep scar running down one side of it, pulling his lips into a permanent frown. Where had Mr. Lightfoot found this man? Hades?

And why was he still carrying the whip? she thought wildly, her heart sinking.

Then she realized it wasn't the whip he was holding, but rope. Astrid tried to climb back into the wagon, but the man seized her from behind. He was terribly strong. She struggled with all the strength she had inside of her, but she might as well have been kicking a mountain, for all the good it did her. He clamped her arms behind her with a single hand. The other one held her off the ground as if she weighed no more than a feather. He began to bind her hands together with the rope.

Astrid stared hopelessly at Charlie, who just watched in growing horror, tears streaming down his face.

"But I don't want to go," Astrid said in a strangely calm voice. She squirmed against the giant until she was facing Mr. Lightfoot. "I don't want to marry you. I don't want you, and I never shall. What good will it do to take me against my will? I'll never stop fighting you."

Mr. Lightfoot grinned in a manner Astrid could only term lascivious. She shivered uncontrollably. "Precisely, my dear. Precisely. It shall be my utmost pleasure to break you. And I *will* break you."

She nearly laughed then, as the giant carried her toward the coach. She had no hope left, no means of escape. She'd never felt so hopeless, so damned sorry for herself in all of her life. Mr. Lightfoot was going to abduct her. Perhaps he was going to marry her or at least attempt it. She wasn't sure about that. But she was a hundred percent sure he meant to rape her. She didn't need to be a genius to figure that one out.

Then some memory tugged at the back of her mind. What was it?

Montford! It couldn't have been but a few minutes since they'd left him behind. Surely if she screamed loud enough he'd hear her. Though it quite escaped her what good he could possibly do. Even if he did hear her and did not ignore her, as he most likely would, given that he hated her, he'd not get there in time to stop her from being taken by the black-guards. And even if by some miracle he *did* manage to sprout wings and fly to the coach in a trice, how could he possibly prevent her abduction?

Would he cast up his accounts all over the villains, rendering them helpless with disgust?

She actually laughed at this thought.

Mr. Lightfoot and Charlie both looked at her askance. Even the giant carrying her paused and glanced down at her as if she'd lost her mind. But she couldn't help herself.

She'd officially become hysterical.

So even though she had no hope in the world of it doing any good, she began to scream as loud as she could for as long as she could. She screamed until her throat hurt, until bubbles of light danced before her eyes.

"Shut up, damn you," Mr. Lightfoot roared, covering his ears. "No one's going to hear you, you little fool!"

She screamed in his face.

"Hurry up, get her inside!" he growled at the giant.

The giant stuffed her through the carriage, but she twisted her body so her legs caught against the door. She screamed, kicking out, attempting to dislodge the villain. She landed a few direct kicks to the giant's chest, but if they affected him at all, he didn't show it. He grabbed up her feet and tied them together with his remaining rope, then shoved her the rest of the way inside the coach. She screamed and screamed until she thought she would pass out.

Then the sound of a gun exploded across her senses. Her breath seized and her heart skidded to a halt as she watched Charlie clutch at his side and tumble down from the wagon and onto the road. He'd been attempting to pull the rifle they carried for highwaymen out from underneath his seat in an effort to save her. Foolish man. But it remained clutched to his side, unused, as he bled onto the ground. Astrid thought she might be sick. Charlie had not deserved to be shot. The poor fool hadn't deserved to be tangled up in any of this.

Mr. Lightfoot stood over Charlie, the pistol in his hand still smoking. He turned away from the man, tucking the pistol into his waistband, and approached the carriage, a dull gleam in his eyes.

Her blood ran cold, and her voice seized in her throat. Mr. Lightfoot pushed her back and climbed into the carriage. He settled himself onto a seat, pulled out a handkerchief, and bound it over her mouth. She inched her way back to the far corner of the coach, struggling against her bonds, staring daggers at her abductor.

Mr. Lightfoot just laughed at her efforts and slammed the coach door shut.

And with it, all hope she had of rescue.

Chapter Nineteen

In Which the Duke Enters His Third Race of the Week

AFTER A half hour's trek up the King's Highway, half-running, half-hopping in an effort to relieve a god-awful cramp that had taken up residence in his left leg, Montford was ready to give up. He had almost managed to convince himself that he had imagined the whole thing—the screams, the gunshot—but just when he'd decide to stop and turn back around, the dread would return, settling in his gut, worse than any nausea or cramp he'd ever known. He didn't understand it or appreciate it, but it would not allow him to turn around, as much as his body wanted to.

"I'm going to kill her," he muttered to himself, in between his pants. "This time, I really am going to kill her."

Though for what, he wasn't quite sure.

God, he almost hoped he found her on the roadside bleeding to death. Then he'd be justified for running down the lane like some bloody lunatic.

Then his gut would clench up again at the very thought. No, he did not want to find her bleeding to death. The mere thought of it was . . . Unbearable.

He'd rather he were insane, he decided. He'd rather he ran all the way to Hawes and discovered her in one gloriously uninjured piece. But just when he decided that that might indeed be the outcome, he rounded a bend in the lane and let out an involuntary cry. The wagon was stopped at an odd angle off to one side of the road, the two drays pacing nervously in their harnesses. A form lay next to the cart, unmoving. It was human, but he could tell from the size and color of the clothes that it wasn't Astrid. It was Charlie.

Relief and concern washed over him in equal parts. He darted in Charlie's direction. Fear, which was only moments before theoretical, now came into sharp, poignant focus. He'd not been imagining things after all.

But as he approached Charlie, he felt his knees begin to go weak, his vision to go dark. The man was bleeding heavily from a wound in his shoulder.

Not now! he cried out inwardly. He couldn't faint now, of all times! But it was no use.

He pitched forward, into the void.

⊷ ⚜ ⊶

SEVERAL SECONDS later—or several hours, he couldn't be quite sure—he came back to consciousness, pushing the dark memories that always surfaced at such inconvenient times back into the recesses of his mind. His eyelids fluttered open. He was staring up at the sky.

Then someone groaned. He rolled over and spotted Charlie crawling in his direction, oozing blood from his shoulder, his face as white as the clouds in the sky.

Montford forced himself to look away from the blood.

Charlie managed to make it a few more inches, and then he collapsed into the dirt. Montford gathered his nerves and went over to assist him, stripping off his jacket and applying it to the wound at the man's shoulder, stanching the blood as best he could.

"What happened?" he demanded. "Where's Astrid?"

Charlie tossed his head from side to side, clenching his jaw, in unbearable pain. "Didna mean for it to go so far," the fellow muttered. "Honest to God, thought I were doing it for her own good."

"What? *What* have you done?" Montford nearly cried.

"It's Lightfoot, sir. He's taken her."

"Taken her? What do you mean, taken her?" Montford cried, the icy tentacles of dread slithering up his spine, into his blood.

"He's come and stole her. Bound for—Gretna Green—to have her—for his—wife—" Charlie managed to grit out.

"Mr. Lightfoot," Montford repeated, trying to wrap his head around their current situation. Mr. Lightfoot was the reason he was in Yorkshire in the first place. He'd yet to meet the man, but he'd gleaned enough to know that he was an ass, and that Astrid had no intention of marrying him.

Which meant, of course—obviously, as Charlie was lying on the road bleeding to death—she'd been taken against her will. Mr. Lightfoot intended to force her into marriage. And the only way Montford could see that happening was if . . .

If the blackguard gave her no other choice.

Montford heaved Charlie up by his good shoulder. He climbed in beside the man and laid him as gently as he could against the footboards. He removed his jacket from the wound and bound Charlie's shoulder tightly with a length of canvas from the wagon bed to stop the worst of the bleeding. Charlie groaned in pain, then seemed to faint.

Montford was unequipped to deal with such drama. He'd never had a man die on him before—aside from his parents, but he wasn't even going to think about *that* right now. He gazed down at Charlie worriedly as he picked up the reins. "Don't die, for pity's sake!" he muttered. "Don't even know how to drive this blasted thing."

He shook the reins as he'd seen Charlie do earlier in the day. The drays just stood there, eating dandelions. "Damnation, move!" he roared in frustration. He jerked on the reins, bringing them down as hard as he could on the animals' rear ends. They jumped forward, then stopped again. He brought down the reins again and again, until the poor creatures were grunting and kicking up a storm down the road.

The wagon lurched along behind them, teetering to the left, and then to the right. Montford had no idea how to control the animals once they got moving. He braced his body against the seat and held on to the reins until his fingernails were digging into his palms. At least the animals seemed to know what they were about, more or less, because he sure as hell didn't.

Charlie moaned weakly when they hit a deep rut, and Montford cursed. His backside was killing him, and his stomach was heaving. It seemed driving the vehicle was no better than being a passenger. He gritted his teeth and willed his nausea aside. He had no time for his delicate constitution. He had a woman to save from a fate worse than death.

He just prayed he wasn't too late already.

The thought of Astrid—Astrid! When had he started thinking of her by her first name?—being mauled by the villain curdled his blood, made his mind go blank with a fear far greater than he'd ever known before.

It seemed an eternity passed before he finally saw a village up ahead. He whipped at the drays to make them pick up the pace. Then, when the wagon began careening down the main street of the village, he began to wonder how he was going to get them to stop. He passed several gape-mouthed rustics navigating the road in their own carts, and a few unlucky pedestrians who just managed to scurry out of the way, shouting curses at him.

The village was bigger than he had imagined, and he hadn't the foggiest idea where he was going. Finally, he spied a sign up ahead advertising an inn called the Barley Mow, and his brain began to work with a half-conceived plan. He attempted to pull back on the reins, half expecting the action to have no effect.

He was wrong. The drays lurched to an abrupt halt, and he nearly flew off his seat and onto their backs.

He cursed again and righted himself on the seat. He stared about him, his heart racing. He was on the edge of the road near a muddy, bustling inn yard. Its denizens had stopped what they were doing to stare up at him in alarm.

He singled out one of their numbers and pointed at him. "You there, fetch me a doctor."

The rustic just gaped up at him.

"I've an injured man," he explained, gesturing toward Charlie. "He needs a doctor, blast you!"

The man dropped the sack he'd been carrying and hurried off.

The yard emptied as Montford descended from his perch. He swayed on his legs and clutched the side of the wagon, cursing his weakness.

A man emerged from inside the inn, dressed in a soiled apron. He studied Montford suspiciously as he approached.

"There is an injured man in that wagon," Montford informed him. "He needs a doctor. And I need a horse. Your fastest horse. And be quick about it, man!"

The innkeeper just squinted at him. "Aye, an' how ye'll be payin' for that?"

Montford gaped at the man. He'd not thought as far as monetary transactions. He'd not thought he'd need to. "I'm the Duke of Montford. You'll be paid."

The man's glance swept from Montford's soiled boots to the top of his hair. Then he burst out into laughter. "A duke? Oh, that's rich, gov. An' I'm the bloody Regent!"

Montford thought about strangling the man, but then he glanced down and cringed. He looked about as ducal as the innkeeper, in his soiled lawn shirt and bloodied breeches.

"I'll not be givin' ye nothing, gov. Not without proper coin," the man stated.

Montford stalked back to the wagon and pulled out his ruined jacket. He pulled his cravat pin out of his lapel and stuck it under the innkeeper's nose.

"Aye, an' wot am I to do with that, gov?" he sneered. "Don't look real to me."

"Bloody hell, you idiot! It's a ruby! It could purchase your inn ten times over."

"That's wot ye'd like me to believe. It's paste."

Montford growled at the man, frozen with impotence.

"Sir," Charlie whispered from the floorboard, "the ale."

Montford groaned. "We've no time for that, Charlie." Good God, the man was at death's door, and all he could think about was ale? What was *wrong* with everyone?

Charlie fainted again.

The innkeeper studied Charlie for a moment, then glanced toward the back of the wagon. "Ale, you say?" The innkeeper crept to the back of the wagon and lifted the awning. He whistled in disbelief. "Why didn't you say you had ale before?"

Montford threw up his hands in defeat. "I don't know. Perhaps because I have a man bleeding to death beside me!"

The innkeeper scowled at him. "I'll take the ale as payment."

Montford would have sighed in relief if he weren't so irritated. "Fine. Take the bloody ale. But I want your fastest horse."

The innkeeper nodded and began to hurry around the side of the building.

"And a pistol," Montford added. The innkeeper stumbled and looked over his shoulder in horror. "Two. Make that two pistols. Loaded."

The innkeeper disappeared without responding, shaking his head.

Montford leaned over the wagon and slapped Charlie's cheek. The man stirred back to consciousness and stared at him through bleary eyes. "You must—hurry, fast as you can—north. Scotland—black coach—"

Montford recalled the giant conveyance that had passed by him earlier, and his heart sank. How would he ever catch up with that?

Just then, the innkeeper appeared around the corner, leading a brown gelding by the reins. Montford investigated the animal briefly and let out a heavy sigh. "Is this the best you can do?" he bit out.

The innkeeper looked offended. "He's a goer, that's for sure."

"He'd better be, for if he turns up lame, I'll come back here and personally run you through," he bit out. The innkeeper paled. "Now, where are the pistols?"

"You're serious?"

"Quite. Serious." Montford paused. "Please," he added. "It's a matter of some urgency."

"Clearly," the innkeeper said, pulling a pair of rusty looking antiques out of his waistband and handing them over.

Montford checked them and shook his head in disgust at their poor quality, but he thrust them into his breeches anyway. He pulled himself up onto the gelding, his tired legs protesting quite vehemently. He looked down at the innkeeper. "Did you see a black coach come through here?"

The innkeeper nodded. "'Bout an hour past. Tearing hell-for-leather northward."

Montford spurred his mount toward the street. He'd gone a few yards when he heard someone yelling behind him. He reined in and turned toward the innkeeper, who stood in the road, gesturing frantically. "What?" he roared, at the end of his tether.

The innkeeper pointed in the opposite direction Montford had been heading. "North's that way, gov."

It was hardly an auspicious start to a heroic rescue.

Chapter Twenty

In Which the Villain Behaves in a Most Dastardly Manner

FOR ALL that it was the worst thing to ever happen to her, being abducted was a bore. Of course she was scared. One would have to be remarkably dull-witted or foolish not to be. But ever since she'd watched Charlie fall from the wagon, bleeding, perhaps already dead, her mind seemed to dislodge from her body, floating somewhere near the carriage ceiling. She knew what was happening, and she knew she was in grave danger—she knew as well with a sort of detached clarity that she had little hope of rescue—yet she felt numb.

She must have been in shock.

Of course, she was not insensible—at least physically speaking. Her hands were tingling from having her wrists bound so tightly. The entire right side of her body, upon which she lay on the floor of the carriage at a supremely awkward angle, felt black-and-blue from having been jostled by the rough road. And she felt a very pressing need to relieve herself—*very* pressing. She'd just finished off an entire flask of water right before she was abducted.

She'd never been so uncomfortable in her whole life.

Nor so bored. One would think that when one was abducted at gunpoint, one might be guaranteed a sustained progression of dramatic events and heart-stopping peril. One would think, at the very least, one's abductor might do one the courtesy of explaining himself more thoroughly, or make a few menacing threats. But all Lightfoot had done was chuckle to himself, poke her with his boot a few times, and then nod off. It was rather anticlimactic.

They'd been traveling for hours, and Lightfoot had snored through most of it. His snoring was the most god-awful sound she'd ever heard. It reminded her of how Montford had sounded when casting up his accounts. It went on and on, as inexorable as the squeal of the carriage wheels turning beneath her. If she'd not been bound up tighter than a Christmas goose, she'd have whacked him over the head.

She was irritated. And bored. And very uncomfortable. She knew that she was not dreaming this because she felt these things, and she knew as well that she probably should be more frightened than she was. But what use was there in that?

Astrid was too practical to spend her time crying herself into a stupor. She needed to conserve her energy to fight Lightfoot—and she planned on putting up quite a fight. She'd never willingly marry him, and if he thought to coerce her into a union by taking her against her will, then he was in for a dreadful surprise.

She was convinced more than ever of Lightfoot's insanity in light of his less than brilliant plan. Would he hold a gun to her head and make her swear her marriage vows? What official, even one of the so-called anvil priests in Gretna Green, would sanction that?

Besides, if it came to that, a choice to marry him or die, she'd choose death. He obviously didn't know her at all if he thought she wouldn't call his bluff. And she knew beyond a doubt she would rather die first than submit to Lightfoot's wickedness. Let him kill her, if he thought that would get him what he wanted.

She thought of those she had left behind and was distantly aware of the crushing pain in her heart. She would not see them again. Yet she knew they would not suffer—they would mourn her and miss her, but they did not need her for their own survival. The past week had taught her that.

Lying bound and helpless in the coach of a madman, she suddenly saw her life with true clarity, and realized her folly. All these years she thought *they* needed her, when the truth was *she* was the one who needed them. She was hanging on to the Hall, the brewery, and her sisters, not because it was in their best interest, but because it was what she wanted. She was so terrified at the idea of change, of relinquishing control over the estate, that she had lost sight of her true goal: doing what was best for her family.

Somewhere along the way, she'd lost sight of herself as well, and she'd blinded herself to truly seeing other people. She had thought she knew so much more than everyone else. She had thought she could control the actions of others, even Montford's. Clearly, her current predicament was a testimony to how wrong she had been. She'd known Lightfoot was a villain and a bit barmy, but she never would have guessed him to be capable of such a scurrilous plot.

This was not how she had expected her life to turn out.

Hours seemed to mount to days, and onward they drove. She was aware of the sun shifting in the sky, from east to west, and of the shadows in the coach lengthening. She tried to change positions. Her right side was completely without feeling, and she no longer had the use of her hands, much good they'd do her pinned at her back anyway. She managed to sit up against the seat. Painful needles pricked down her side as feeling returned to it.

Her need to relieve herself was quite dire now. She could no longer put it off. She kicked out her legs and managed to connect with Lightfoot's boot.

He stirred awake with a snort. He glanced down at her, as if startled to find her there. Then his lips curled into an evil leer. He leaned forward, until his face was inches from her own, and pulled down the handkerchief binding her mouth. She jerked back and tried not to breathe. His breath stank of onions.

"Hello, my dear," he said.

"I need to urinate," she said bluntly.

His brow crinkled, and his leer slipped.

"I said, I need to urinate," she repeated. "It is quite urgent. Unless you wish for me to relieve myself here in the carriage."

He looked disgusted. Clearly he'd not thought about such an inevitability. After a moment's hesitation, he pounded on the roof of the coach and called out to the driver.

They stopped, and Lightfoot stepped from the carriage. She scooted herself toward the door. It was dusk, and a light rain was falling. Lightfoot and the giant henchman stared at her, uncertain how to proceed.

"You shall have to untie my legs," she said calmly.

Lightfoot growled and did as she suggested. She stepped out of the carriage—or rather fell. Her legs did not seem to be working properly after their confinement. Lightfoot seized her under one arm, the giant by the other, and tugged her into the bushes beside the road.

"Shall you untie my hands, or are you to stand over me the entire time?" she demanded.

The two men glanced at each other, at a loss, but then the giant grudgingly untied the ropes at her wrists.

She nearly cried out as the blood rushed back into her hands in a painful surge.

They retreated a few paces.

"Am I expected to go while you watch me?"

Lightfoot's face darkened. "Don't try to run away," he growled.

After a few moments, the men retreated to the road. Satisfied, Astrid hiked up her skirts and squatted.

A short time later, she felt significantly better, at least in one regard. She glanced around her, but she could see nothing but the dimly lit road and dark forest behind her. Nothing was familiar. She judged they were near Cumbria, if not already in that domain. She thought about simply taking off, but they were miles from anywhere, and she could see the giant eyeing her over the bushes. She'd not get far.

Lightfoot returned to her side and hauled her back toward the coach, forestalling any further notions of escape. She was tied up again and shoved into the interior of the coach. This time, she managed to pull herself onto the seat facing Lightfoot as the coach resumed its fast clip down the highway.

Lightfoot stared at her in silence for some time. She faced forward, refusing to look at him.

"Shall we travel through the night, then?" she asked.

"We shall stop soon. Don't worry. We'll have a bed for the night," he said.

A prickling of apprehension went through her. The implication of his words was clear, and it was nothing she had not expected. Yet even so, her pending doom felt significantly more real, now that the words had been spoken. Perhaps he would tie her down, and there would be no hope of fighting him. She had thought at least to be given that much of a chance, but perhaps that had been foolish of her.

She had never expected to be ruined, willing or otherwise. She'd never even thought to marry until this past week, when she had been shown she had no choice. She'd certainly never thought about lying with a man—until the duke had come along and stirred up a whole host of new and unsettling feelings inside of her.

With a strange sense of detachment, as if viewing someone else's life, she thought of that night in the drawing room, when Montford had nearly succeeded in seducing her. She'd been quite willing—at least her body had been. Even her mind had been strangely compelled. She remembered thinking that she didn't want him to stop. Even when he had stopped, she hadn't wanted him to.

Her detachment slipped. Feeling surged through her, hot and urgent, and filled with poignant sorrow. If only he *hadn't* stopped. At least she'd have that memory now. At least she'd have known what it would have been like when there was passion. Even if afterward she had been filled with regret and self-loathing, it wouldn't have mattered.

Now she'd never know. She'd never see the duke again.

For the first time, tears pricked her eyes. And to think Montford was the cause of them! Not her sisters, not even what lay in store for her this night. She would never see Montford again, or touch him, or smell him, or harangue him, and her heart wanted to wither and die. She remembered his last words quite clearly. *I hope I never see you again*, screamed at her back. Well, his wish had certainly come to pass.

She wondered if he'd truly meant it.

Of course he had.

He was probably at Rylestone by now, perhaps even on the road back to London. She held out no false hope that he'd come for her, or even that he'd heard her scream.

When he heard of her fate, he'd probably be relieved, or at least filled with satisfaction. He'd probably think she'd brought this upon herself, that it was nothing less than she deserved for behaving so outrageously.

He'd probably be right.

"Vile coward," she bit out at Lightfoot, her patience with her captivity expired. "Too afraid of what I might do to you without tying me up. You know that if my hands were free, I'd pluck out your eyes and shove them down your throat."

He laughed again, sounding more pleased than worried. He reached for her, and something inside of her snapped. She lashed out with her legs, catching her boot heels in his gut.

He doubled over with pain, then glared at her with glinting coal-black eyes. "You little bitch," he breathed, moving toward her. She kicked him again and caught him on the shin. He howled in pain and brought up his hand to strike her.

She threw herself against the window to avoid the blow, and the coach jolted over something in the road, throwing off his aim. He struck her on the shoulder instead of the face, but it hurt. A lot.

"Pig. You'll have to kill me before I'll marry you," she spat.

Lightfoot too seemed to have lost his patience. He grabbed her by the legs and shoved her back on the seat. She struggled against him as he began to tear at her clothes. Her vision swam, and her head felt as if it were on fire. She turned her face away as he attempted to kiss her, pressing it up against the glass on the window, gasping for air. Then out of the corner of her eye she saw a flicker of movement on the road outside the window. A rider.

A giddy, ridiculous hope rose up inside of her as she watched the rider approach. He was coatless and riding at a furious pace. She could not quite make out his features, but something about the shape of him, the slope of his broad shoulders, was familiar.

She wanted to cry out with joy; she wanted to cry out with terror. It was Montford. She would have known him at a thousand paces. He'd come to rescue her. But her hope was tempered by the very slim chance of his success.

He'd die, the fool.

Astrid turned away from the window. She needed to make this easier for Montford. She spotted a pistol tucked under the opposite seat and kicked out with her foot, knocking it into the farthest corner. But then Lightfoot gripped her by the arms, pulling her beneath him, and jerked her skirts up her legs, intent on his task.

She bit his arm as hard as she could, and he howled in disbelief.

Then a gunshot exploded outside the coach, and Astrid's heart surged with hope. Montford was not such a fool after all, if he'd come armed.

Lightfoot raised himself off of her and peered out the window. He swore under his breath and moved to retrieve his pistol.

Astrid threw herself against Lightfoot, knocking him against the seat. But in the process, she jarred her head against the squabs, sending such an acute pain lancing through her skull that she dropped to her knees. She tried to focus, but saw nothing but shining stars twinkling before her eyes. She was aware of angry shouts beyond the coach window and Lightfoot's furious oaths. The carriage jerked abruptly right, then left, sending Astrid flailing wildly from side to side. She braced her feet against the opposite seat for purchase and tried to shake the stars out of her eyes.

Her vision cleared, and what she saw sent a chill down into the very depths of her soul. Lightfoot had jerked the left window open and was leaning out, cursing profusely and aiming his pistol in the direction of Montford, who was trying frantically to control his horse a few paces off.

Astrid shrieked in terror. The carriage was listing wildly, impairing Lightfoot's attempt to aim the gun. But if he succeeded in his intent, Montford was done for. She gathered what was left of her wits and threw herself forward, hoping she was not too late. But Lightfoot shot his pistol before she could reach him.

Montford's horse bucked in response to the shot, unseating the duke. But he was not thrown entirely. His foot was caught in a stirrup. The horse shot forward, dragging Montford along the dusty road. Astrid cried out in dismay, just as Lightfoot smashed his fist into her cheek, sending her into a gray void of unconsciousness once more.

Chapter Twenty-One

*In Which the Hero Mounts a Daring Rescue
Along the North Road*

MONTFORD MANAGED to pull his recalcitrant horse alongside the coach long enough to wave his pistol at the driver. He was a huge beast of a man, with a scarred face and not a hint of fear in his dark eyes. He snarled and whipped his team into a sprint.

Words were useless. He'd not convince the man to pull over. So he did the only thing that had any chance of succeeding. He pulled the trigger.

His shot was not entirely successful. The bullet caught the man in the shoulder, throwing him off his perch and causing him to drop one of the reins. The coach horses, startled by the gunshot, jerked forward and veered off course. But the man must have been made out of iron, for he soon shook off his injury and picked up the fallen rein, pulling the horses back on course.

Montford was not so lucky. His own mount was more than startled from the shot. It whinnied in terror and began to jump wildly beneath him, jerking abruptly to the right, nearly colliding with the coach. Montford cursed and attempted to bring the creature back to its senses. It was all he could do to keep his seat.

Then the window of the coach shot open, and a dark, balding man, purple-faced with fury, leaned out, shouting abuse at him and leveling a gun at his head. Montford tried to reach for his second pistol, still stuck in the saddle behind him, but his mount was too out of control to let him. He cursed and attempted to pull his mount back, out of line of the man's aim. But the horse was determined to keep pace with the coach, instinct pulling it along with the team of four. The damned beast was going to get him shot.

The man at the window pulled the trigger, the explosion so close Montford could feel the acrid, burnt gun smoke choking his lungs. He flinched and braced for the impact of the bullet with his flesh. But the bullet went whizzing over his head, his hair parting in its wake. A fraction of an inch, he feared, and he would have had a bullet in his brain-box. He could barely believe his luck.

But his relief was short-lived. His mount was now beyond control. It bucked so violently that Montford was thrown from his seat. For the second time in as many days, he went flying through the air, then smashed to the road on his back. The impact took the breath from his lungs and jarred every bone in his body. He couldn't breathe, could barely focus his vision. He knew nothing but the dust of the road, the ache of his bones, and the searing, burning sensation of his body being dragged over sharp stones. He was still moving, and it took him several moments to realize why. His left foot was still caught in the stirrup, and the horse was galloping onward, pulling him along.

Adrenaline coursed through his veins, powering his battered body, as some part of him recognized that he was fighting for his life. He had to get loose, unless he wanted to be dragged to his death. He clawed at the road, twisting on his stomach, feeling every rock and rut scrape the length of his body, but he pushed aside the pain. Nothing mattered except getting loose and saving Astrid.

He kicked out with his foot until at last—by chance or the grace of God—it fell free of its prison. He skidded forward a few more feet by sheer momentum, and then finally stopped moving. He lay sprawled for a moment, his face in the dirt, every bone, muscle, and tendon he possessed in agony, and his hands and arms scraped raw from the road.

He realized he'd not breathed since he'd been thrown. Black motes danced in front of his eyes, presaging oblivion. He rolled onto his back and schooled his lungs to work, trying to bury his pain enough to focus on his next move.

Which was to sit up. All of his muscles were in revolt, and his hands burned. He didn't dare look at them, knowing they would be bloody and mangled. His vision spinning, he looked down the road. He saw his mount prancing nervously fifty yards ahead, throwing its head from side to side and neighing in distress.

Bloody useless creature! he wanted to shout. But he couldn't find his voice. It was hard enough to breathe, much less form words.

He turned his attention to the coach. It raced down the lane at a dangerous pace, careening erratically from left to right. Whatever the state of its driver, however, it didn't seem in any danger of stopping.

Something inside of him withered. The coach would get away, and with it, any hope of Astrid's rescue.

He rose to his feet and attempted to walk, but his legs felt disconnected from his body, his left ankle throbbing. He dropped to his knees and watched helplessly as the coach moved farther and farther from him. He'd been so close. He'd even heard her screaming inside the coach. The pain and terror in her voice had been palpable. He could hear her voice even now, reverberating through his mind, filling him with renewed fury and a sense of helplessness.

His heart clenched in his breast, and a strange moisture filled his eyes.

He'd failed her. He'd never see her again—at least, not as she had been. He'd known her so briefly, yet it felt as if it had been forever. He could not recall what he'd been before he'd met her. She'd changed something inside of him, jarred something loose. She'd made him feel. Rage. Confusion. Doubt. A thousand ugly emotions.

But for all of her faults, she did not deserve this. No one deserved this.

Montford let out a ragged moan of frustration, defeat, and sorrow. How could he have failed?

Then something caught his eye up ahead. The coach lurched to one side, and the door sprang open. He saw Astrid standing on the runner one moment, then sailing through the air. He was too far away to see anything but the haze of her fiery hair, the vibrant orange color of her pelisse, a pale face. Whatever she felt—her terror, her urgency, her pain—was hidden from his view, but he could feel it all the same, as if it were his own. She landed in a ditch, tumbling head over heels until at last she came to a stop in a mangled heap of legs and skirts and hair.

The coach continued to roll away, the sound of a man bellowing with rage reaching Montford's ears.

He ignored the screams and clambered to his feet, his stomach hollow and his mouth dry. He felt no relief that she was free of the coach's prison. In fact, he was choked with fury. The foolish creature had jumped from a moving carriage and likely killed herself in the process. He'd throttle her!

Somehow he made his body work, though every fiber of it cried out in protest. He ran, his lungs burning with the effort, his mind sinking by increments into his worst nightmare. He could not but help recall the coaching accident that had killed his parents, the way his mother had lain, in a ditch so very similar to the one he now approached, her body twisted, bloody, and unmoving. He'd been there with her, in the blood, clinging to her corpse, wondering why she would not wake up, not understanding why she would not hold him or comfort him.

He could smell the old terror, the muck, the blood, the decay of death, as if he were still there. The thirty years that had passed since then were stripped away, and he was that four-year-old boy once more, filled with confusion and fear. His eyes burned and clouded over, and an inhuman sound was ripped from his lungs as he fell to his knees beside the orange lump.

She didn't move. He couldn't see her face. He feared that when he did, he would see his mother.

But the hair was not right. His mother had dark hair, like his own, and the hair he glimpsed through his clouded eyes was the color of a bonfire, spiraling and twisting out of control. And his mother would have never worn such a hideous orange coat. No one of his acquaintance would have worn such a garment. Except for one.

"Astrid!" The name was torn out of him. The past and present collided in his mind as he seized the prone figure by the shoulders and pulled her into his arms. She smelled of lavender and sweat and the dirt of the roadside. She smelled wonderful.

He held her tightly against him, not daring to breathe or move. She was warm in his arms and limp. Her head flopped against his shoulder. His heart pounded with fear. Was she dead? He hadn't the courage to discover for himself. All he could do was rock back and forth, trying to master his tumultuous emotions. She couldn't die. Not her, not now, not ever. He didn't think he could bear it.

But then he felt her chest expand and contract underneath his hands and the warm, feeble brush of her breath against his nape.

He shuddered in relief. He could hardly believe he was holding her and that she was alive. He pulled back and dared to look at her.

He did not like what he saw. One of her eyes was swollen and beginning to go black. He brushed back the halo of her wild hair and discovered an ugly red welt on her temple. God knew what the rest of her body had suffered.

A blind rage swept through him. He'd kill Lightfoot. He'd chop him into pieces and feed him to Petunia.

He clutched Astrid tightly against him and lifted his head to stare down the road. The coach was still racing away. Lightfoot was leaning out of the door, shouting at his driver to turn around.

Montford rather hoped that they did so he could exact his revenge. But at the same time, his rational mind knew this would be very difficult under the circumstances. Lightfoot was armed. Montford didn't even have a horse anymore. The damned beast was about as useful as a sack of manure.

He turned his attention back to Astrid. She was coming around, her uninjured eye opening. He noted somewhat hysterically that it was her blue eye. She stared up at him unseeingly for a moment, and then she seemed to realize who he was. Relief—fear—pain—flashed across her swollen face, and her eyes welled with tears, her lips trembled.

"Montford . . ." she rasped.

She sounded as terrible as she looked.

"Fool! Little fool!" he cried, shaking her shoulders. "Throwing yourself from a moving coach! What were you thinking!" He knew it was a stupid thing to say as soon it was out of his mouth, but it was better said than the thousand other half-formed words hovering on his tongue.

She looked at him with disbelief. Then, in a move that shocked him, she let out a laugh. Or a croak. "I'd no other option."

"You could have killed yourself."

"Rather that than remain where I was."

He shook his head, but he couldn't refute her. He raised his hand and cupped her chin. She winced and drew back as if his touch pained her, which it probably did. He wanted to howl.

"You came for me," she said, smiling feebly at him.

"Of course I came for you!" he said with great irritation.

The flurry of movement up the road intruded upon his consciousness. He raised his head and glimpsed the coach turning around in the road, preparing to return in their direction. Damnation, what was he to do now?

Astrid followed his glance and inhaled sharply. He could feel her grow rigid in his arms. "Tell me you have a plan to get us out of this, Montford," she said.

Montford glanced at her battered face, her torn, soiled dress, then down at his own ragged clothes and scraped arms and hands. He raised his eyes and met her wild glance, and saw in it that she knew just as well as he did they were doomed. They had nothing but each other and the rags on their backs. No wonder she was smiling.

He couldn't help himself. He began to laugh.

EVEN THROUGH the fog around her brain, Astrid knew that Montford had become hysterical. He was on his knees in the dirt, shredded, scraped, bloodied, and looking like something that had come out the business end of a sieve. And he was laughing.

Astrid could barely focus her vision, and her head was pounding. Her relief at having escaped the carriage was greatly diminished by her aching body, the renewed threat thundering down upon them, and her mounting irritation at Montford.

But oddly enough, she felt like laughing, too. Their situation was hopeless. He knew it just as much as she did. And it was funny, in an awful sort of way.

Her mouth lifted at the edges of its own accord, but she soon regretted it. The muscles in the left side of her face howled their protest, and her vision went black with pain.

He must have seen her wince, for his laughter ceased, and his face went grim. He glanced down the road, then around them, and she could see the cogs churning in his brain. "Can you run?"

She didn't know. Her doubt must have shown in her eyes, for he gave her a weak, humorless smile. "Me neither," he muttered. He took her by the elbow and hauled her to her feet.

She cried out from the pain in her cramped arms, realizing they were still bound behind her.

His expression darkened with fury. He spun her around and worked at the knots at her wrists. Her hands finally sprang free of their bonds, and she gasped as pinpricks of feeling rushed back into them. She rubbed them together in front of her, her wrists chafed and ringed with ugly black bruises.

She raised her eyes and saw Montford studying her wounds with a thunderous rage gripping his features. "I shall kill them," he said in a strangled voice, emotion thickening his words. "I shall rip them apart."

Some part of her thrilled at his words, and another part of her went cold. He was quite serious. "As much as I would enjoy that, it's neither the time nor the place," she said as evenly as she could.

Montford tore his eyes from her, into the thick forest bordering the road. "Come on," he said gruffly.

He tugged her arm, and together they stumbled into the under-growth. She could hear the coach behind them and the sound of Light-foot's angry voice. The thought of being caught again was enough to make her sore legs work. Her head spun, and she could barely keep from falling over. Only the strength of Montford's grip on her arm kept her from pitching headlong to the forest floor. He pulled her over bushes and logs, ever deeper into the gloom, their pace as slow as it was frantic.

She thought she heard the sound of breaking twigs behind them, but she didn't dare turn around to see if they were being pursued. She concentrated on keeping upright. Her senses swam, the forest little more than a blur of green and brown and shifting shadows, the prickling of brambles and sharp leaves brushing her legs and arms.

Someone shouted behind them—Lightfoot—and her heart nearly leapt out of her chest. Montford's grip tightened around her arm, and he practically dragged her onward, down a sharp incline, over a creek bed. They stumbled up a gully, her knees scraping against stone and fallen limbs, her hands rubbed raw from the bark of trees and the sharp rocks jutting from the loam. On and on they went, until she lost all track of time and place.

They reached a pine forest, the ground covered in a blanket of brown, rotting needles. Their footsteps swished and crunched, breaking the stillness surrounding them, sending birds squawking into the treetops, betraying their every movement.

She risked a glance over her shoulder but could not see any signs of pursuit. Her anxiety eased only fractionally. They were far from being out of danger. And she shouldn't have tried to turn. Her head spun, tilting the world around her on its axis. She stumbled over a tree root, her legs flying out from beneath her.

Montford gripped her tightly and spun around to catch her with his other arm. He held her tightly against his chest. He was hot and damp, his heart thumping erratically against her cheek. He smelled terrible, but she didn't mind.

He set her from him and studied her face, his expression impenetrable. "Can you continue?"

She nodded wearily.

His brow furrowed, his mouth pinched into a grim line. He turned from her and tucked his arm around her waist, half carrying her. She hated being so weak, she hated having to rely on him, but she had no choice. She was too weary and broken to protest.

He lifted her over a fallen tree, tucked her against him, and continued onward.

"I don't suppose you know where you're going," she said.

He snorted. "Of course not. East? We are bound to figure out something eventually."

It was a question more than a statement. She heard the anxiety in his voice. He had no idea what he was doing. She should have been more alarmed than she was. They were lost in a forest in the middle of nowhere, a lunatic pursuing them, and nothing to aid them but their wits. But the farther they went with no sign of being overtaken, the less she worried. She was free of Lightfoot, and that was all that mattered.

Montford had come for her. And they were bound to figure out something, just as he said. She allowed herself to hope and to dream of the life she had thought she had lost forever.

And gradually, those dreams overtook her awareness and sucked her into oblivion.

⚔

MONTFORD WAS not certain how long they had been in the forest. It felt like years. Hours had passed, for the sun was now behind them, their shadows lengthening, the forest steadily dimming. He'd noticed no sign of pursuit and could only hope their trail had been lost. The henchman, at the very least, would be in difficulties with a shot through his arm.

Montford's own ankle was throbbing, along with the rest of his body. He didn't know how he had managed to make it this far, much less haul Astrid alongside of him. She was no pocket Venus, and she was in even worse shape than he, relying upon him to support most of her weight.

He now realized that he was supporting *all* of her weight. Her feet were dragging behind her, her head hanging low. He stopped and tilted her head up. Her eyes were closed, her face drained of color. She had fainted on her feet, and he had not even noticed.

He carried her to the base of a large knotted oak, ignoring his aching limbs, and set her down in the crook of one of its roots. He patted her uninjured cheek in an effort to rouse her.

Very slowly, she came around, her eyes fluttering open—or at least one of them. She tried to sit up, but he urged her back down. The knot on her head was worrying. He'd seen Marlowe sustain a similar injury in a tavern brawl, and it had laid him low for a week.

Montford sat down next to her, pulling her against his side to conserve their warmth. Now they had stopped moving, he was aware of the chill in the air.

He stared up at the darkening sky with a sinking heart. It would be a cold night. Yet another obstacle he had not considered. He'd not slept outside since he'd been a boy and he and Sherbrook had decided to run away to Barbados. They'd left Harrow on foot and spent the night just outside a small village on the border of Kent. They'd given up by the next morning, Sherbrook having lost interest in the idea, and Montford having nearly passed out at the wrinkles in his clothes after a night spent under the stars. He'd not cared for the experience.

His ten-year-old self would have fainted if he saw his present dishabille. But the last thing he needed to start fretting about right now was his toilette. It was amazing how a brush with death—several brushes, at that—put the state of one's cravat in perspective. Now all he wanted was a warm bed, a meal, and Lightfoot's head on a platter.

"We must keep going," Astrid murmured. She tried once more to sit up. He stopped her, putting his arms around her shivering shoulders, drawing her head down to his chest. He could feel her go rigid, then slowly relax in his embrace.

"Rest for a while," he said, cradling her head, running his hands over her knotted hair. He didn't think once about untangling it or taming it into submission. All he could think about was comforting her, giving her his warmth. She was very cold. But he didn't think she should sleep. If she had a concussion, she needed to stay awake. He knew that much.

"Don't sleep, Astrid. You must stay awake."

"I am very tired."

"You are concussed. If you sleep, you might not wake up."

She made no response. He feared she'd lost consciousness again until she spoke. "Do you think we've lost them?"

"I don't know."

She shifted weakly in his arms so that she could look at him. He tried not to focus on her swollen eye and bruised cheek. It was too upsetting. "Thank you for coming for me," she said.

He looked ahead, clenching his jaw.

She must have seen something in his expression, for she stiffened and frowned. "I know what you're thinking, and you're probably right. I deserved this—"

His temper snapped. "Of course you didn't deserve this! How could you think that? And that I would think such a . . . Damnation, none of this is your fault."

She looked surprised, but far from relieved. Her eyes grew damp, and she turned her head, attempting to hide her tears. "I wish I could believe it. But I should have guessed Lightfoot would try something. He's . . . unbalanced."

"That, my dear Miss Honeywell, is the biggest understatement I have ever heard."

She tried to laugh, but shivered instead. He tightened his hold on her shoulders. He felt her tense again, as if she feared his touch. Perhaps she did. After the nightmare she'd suffered, it would be hard to let anyone touch her. It made him sick. Astrid Honeywell was not supposed to be afraid of anyone.

"I'm not going to hurt you," he growled, sounding irritated to his ears, although all he felt was a dark misery.

"I know."

"You're cold. I'm trying to help."

"Yes, I know," she insisted, sounding irritated herself.

"He beat you." God, he didn't want the details, but he needed them.

"Just a little. He never managed . . . well, let's just say he hadn't the time or the *vigor* to do much before you came along."

He sighed in relief.

She brought a hand up to her face and poked at her injuries, wincing. "But it *was* most unpleasant."

"Well," he grumbled, "you look terrible. Your eye's all puffy, and you've a knot on your head the size of an apple."

"Thank you," she bit out tartly. "I am glad to know I look a fright. It makes me feel so much better."

He pulled them to their feet, despite the protest of his body. The day was waning, and night's chill would soon be upon them. "We must find shelter," he said. "Astrid, you must keep moving, for just a little while longer."

She nodded bleakly, and they set off again. He tried to keep the sun behind him so that they moved east. Perhaps it was a mistake, for he saw no end in sight to the forest. But he would rather move in one direction than meander about in circles. He only hoped they encountered some sign of life before nightfall. For all he knew, they could walk straight into the ocean without meeting another living soul, they were that far away from civilization.

After a while, Astrid could no longer hold herself up. He hauled her into his arms and carried her, her added weight making his swollen ankle throb and the muscles in his arms burn. By the time he stumbled into the clearing and saw the small, rotting hovel outlined in the gray-green dusk light, he was so exhausted and hungry and aching he was near to tears. A few actually slid down his face when he realized that he'd found them shelter, poor as it was.

It must have been a hunting cabin long before, or a caretaker's hut, but now it was little more than a ruin, its windows long gone, its roof half torn off, weeds and vines climbing its walls. Inside, the floor was made of dirt and the interior walls were splotched with damp. An odor of mold and old fires hung in the air, and an animal seemed to have built a nest in the fireplace. He could see the night sky through the slats in the roof. It was the most revolting place he'd ever entered.

He blocked out these horrifying details and made straight for the bed. It was little more than a straw-stuffed pallet, and he shuddered to think what lived inside the mattress, or what manner of vermin had pattered across the moth-ridden blankets piled on top.

But it *was* a shelter of sorts. Already the temperature had plummeted, and his teeth were chattering. He'd never been so cold in all his life.

He pulled back the blankets and tucked Astrid's legs inside. She murmured something in her sleep and turned on her side, her fiery hair falling across the tick. She brought her hands up beneath her chin, and his heart wrenched at the sight of the black bruises at her wrists. All of his irritation faded as he watched her sleep, and he vowed he'd never let anyone hurt her again.

He didn't even consider the morality of it as he slid into the bed next to her, wrapping his body around her back, pulling the blankets up over both of them. He was too cold and tired. He never even thought about how lushly rounded her backside felt against his hips, or how he could feel the curve of her breasts where his arm held her. He never even thought about how perfect she felt, nestled against him, or how fiercely grateful he was that she was alive and untouched and in his arms. He never even thought about kissing her.

But he did, almost unconsciously. He kissed the back of her head, his lips brushing against her spiraling, lavender-scented curls, then drifted off into a deep, dreamless sleep.

Chapter Twenty-Two

*In Which the Duke and Miss Honeywell
Valiantly Resist Temptation*

THE SUN returned swiftly, and so did his reason—after a time. He seemed to have just closed his eyes for the night when he blinked them open again and found sunlight pouring in from the slats in the rooftop, gilding Astrid's hair, illuminating the dust motes that danced in the air and the metallic sheen of a fly's wings as it swooped in lazy circles overhead.

For a moment, he didn't know where he was or how he had come to be there. All he knew was that he was wrapped around Astrid Honeywell, using her hair for a pillow, his left arm thrown across her breasts. He was warm—sweltering, in fact—with the weight of the mildewed blankets set across them, and the heat of her body pressed up against his. He was distantly aware of aching muscles and hunger, but only very distantly. He felt too wonderful at the moment to bother with such unimportant details. All he was aware of was the heat and smell and soft, lush feel of a woman in his arms.

The woman. The one he'd wanted with an urgency he'd never known before.

Apparently, he'd gotten what he wanted.

Pity he didn't remember it. Strange, in fact. He'd not thought he'd forget bedding Astrid Honeywell.

Unless he was drunk.

He vaguely remembered having drunk quite a lot in the very recent past. And he knew that she had been somehow to blame.

No matter, he thought blearily. He'd simply have her again, now that he had his wits about him.

He let his hand trail over her hip, up her side, and over the edge of her breast. She was wearing clothes, which was most odd. Nevertheless, he could feel the heat of her body burn into his palm and travel up his arm, down his body, and settle in his groin. She stirred, rubbing her backside up against him, and he was instantly hard. Painfully so. He groaned out loud and ground his hips against her, burying his nose in her hair. The scent of it inflamed him, made him grow even harder. God, he wanted her. He wanted to melt into her luscious warmth.

She shifted against him again and murmured something in her sleep.

But the sound of her voice broke his illusion. Memory surged back in an instant, and the pain of his erection was all but forgotten.

He was on his feet in the blink of an eye, his head spinning, his stomach twisting in self-loathing. He scowled down at the bulge in his breeches, breathing hard, clenching his fists. He glanced around him at the dilapidated hovel, the moss on the walls, and the animal droppings at his feet. His gaze settled on Astrid's sleeping form. The swelling in her eye had subsided, leaving it black-and-blue around the edges. Her cheek was shadowed with bruising, her hair loose, tangled with leaves and twigs. She turned on her back, her arm falling over the place he had occupied. He could see the black ring around her wrist, the dried blood covering the wounds where the rope had chafed her raw.

He choked on the bile that rose in his throat. He was an animal, no better than the beast who had done this to her. How could his body—and his mind—respond so traitorously? And he wanted her still. He was aching with frustrated need. It would not go away. He did not know how long he stood there, watching her, wanting, despite all of his reason, to touch her, to return to the pallet and cover her with his body.

But that would never do. What was he thinking? That he'd rescue her from ruination so that he might ruin her himself?

Sickened by his body's mutiny, he turned from her and stumbled out the door of the shack. He shielded his eyes against the early morning glow and started across the clearing. He needed some distance from her to clear his head and somehow chop off the damned third leg he'd suddenly sprouted. He had few options. Directly ahead, there was forest. To his right, forest. To his left, more forest.

He spun around, chose the first option, and stalked off into the undergrowth.

He half-slid down an embankment and found himself at the edge of a massive riverbed. The water sparkled in the sunlight, lapping lazily over large boulders. He crouched down and ran his fingers through the current. The water was ice-cold.

He, however, was on fire.

He sat down on the bank and tugged off his boots.

He needed a good bath anyway.

⊷⊶ ⋇⊷⊷ ⊷⊷

ASTRID CAME awake to find herself staring at blue sky peeking through a hole in the ceiling. She was cocooned in warm blankets, her face bathed in sunglow. She didn't remember her dreams, but she knew instinctively they had been good. The sense of being held in strong arms, caressed and comforted, still lingered. She had not been afraid.

She was not afraid now, even though she probably should be. Her wounds ached, her body still exhausted despite having slept so deeply.

The terror of the past few days was not easily put aside. But all things considered, she was in a surprisingly good mood.

Because she was safe. And Montford was with her.

Or he had been. She stretched languidly and sat up, glancing around unfamiliar surroundings. She didn't remember coming here, which was probably for the best. The room looked as if it hadn't had an occupant other than animals since the previous century. And they were generally thought poor housekeepers.

She didn't even want to imagine what must have been living in the blankets that now covered her.

She pulled herself up off the pallet and onto her feet. She took stock of her person. She was filthy, of course, and her favorite pelisse was likely destined for the dustbin. Her extremities were sore, and her wrists stung from where the ropes had dug into her flesh. Her face hurt like the devil, but the world was no longer spinning around her.

She was alive, however.

Alive and very hungry. She could not recall the last time she'd had a meal.

She searched the small cabin for signs of food, pulling open cabinets and drawers, surprising a family of mice in one of them. She found nothing edible, of course. Not that she'd expected to. But she did manage to find an old, moth-eaten wool jacket. It was not the sort of thing Montford would normally wear, but maybe he'd appreciate having something more substantial than that grubby old lawn shirt he'd been gallivanting around in since the race.

The day was clear, and the sun was warm, but it was mid-October. She was even growing a bit chilled now that she was no longer under the blankets.

She draped the jacket over her arm and went to the door of the cabin, peering outside. She could see nothing but trees.

A prickle of apprehension went through her. Where was Montford? He had been there not long since, hadn't he? She'd felt him nearby all through the night, even though she'd been deep in sleep. His arms had held her, had been the source of her dreams. Surely she hadn't imagined it all.

She would not panic.

She went outside and called out for him. She waited and received no response. Her apprehension ratcheted up.

He wouldn't have left her. After all the bother he'd gone through to save her, he'd not abandon her now.

Though he *had* seemed rather irritated yesterday. Even when he'd held her so tenderly, she'd sensed the anger in him. He'd not been happy about having been thrust into a situation that he no doubt thought beneath his dignity.

For all she knew, he could have thought his duty to her was dispatched. He had no liking for her and would not want to linger in her company. He'd seen her safely away from Lightfoot, but he'd let her make her way back to Rylestone Hall on her own.

No, no. He was an honorable man.

For the most part.

He would not do such a thing.

Perhaps he'd gone out to relieve himself. Even dukes had to answer the call of nature.

But maybe he'd gotten turned around. There wasn't much in the way of landmarks around them. She began to panic in earnest. No doubt he'd gotten himself mauled by some forest creature or stuck in a bog. Such things happened. More likely, however, was the possibility that he was walking in aimless circles through the dense undergrowth. Montford didn't seem the type to know his way around the countryside.

He'd nearly fainted at the sight of the sheep in Rylestone Green.

Astrid made her way through the forest, calling his name intermittently. She picked her way down a small incline and heard the rush of water up ahead. A stream. She licked her lips involuntarily, thirst overcoming all else. She followed a narrow deer track down to the water's edge and bent down to cup her hands in the swiftly flowing water.

The sound of a splash drew her gaze upward, and she froze, her eyes nearly popping out of her head.

Montford. He was on his back, floating in a deep pool formed by a pair of large rocks. And he was . . .

Naked.

She swallowed once, twice. Her legs lost their footing, and her backside crashed onto the riverbank. She could not have run away, or looked away, for all the tea in China. His close-cropped chestnut hair fanned out from his skull, floating on top of the lapping water, shimmering like sheets of hammered bronze in the sunlight. His long, muscular arms were extended from his sides, gently treading through the water. His naked flesh was the color of spring honey, pale and rich and unblemished. She could see the ridge of his torso, the bands of muscle gathered on his abdomen. Droplets of water shone like tiny diamonds, caught in the small thatch of dark hair that curled at his chest, faded out over his flat stomach, then began again, lower, between the jutting bones of his hips . . . and lower still.

She gasped and blinked and tried to avert her eyes.

He must have heard her, for his head came up and his eyes widened. He paled, and then he blushed to the roots of his hair. He thrashed about in the water, submerging his lower half, for which she was both profoundly grateful and terribly disappointed. He found his footing and stood in the stream, water sluicing down his face, over his torso. He was exposed to her from the waist up, his hands on his hips, his eyes blazing.

"What are you *doing*?" he practically yelped.

She couldn't form words. Her gaze was riveted on his abdomen, her pulse racing. She'd not had a lot of experience with naked men, but she suspected that Montford's body was just about as perfect as they came. He was all lean, hard, chiseled masculinity.

Something strange and frightening and blazing hot burned through her veins and pooled between her legs, taking the breath from her body. Her face was seared by a fierce blush that had nothing to do with embarrassment. For a wild, glorious moment, she considered jumping into the stream and pitching herself into his arms. She wanted to *feel* him, not just look at him.

His eyes widened even more by whatever it was he saw in her face, and he sank a little lower in the water. "For God's sake, go away!" he barked out.

She shook her head to clear it, but that didn't work. With great effort and immense regret, she tore her eyes away from his flesh and stared at the bushes to her left.

"I . . . I'm thirsty," she said lamely. Her voice sounded like gravel.

She heard him splashing about. "Then drink, damn you!" he hissed.

His harsh tone snapped her out of her daze. With shaky hands, she scooped up the stream water and drank, not daring to look up at him. The water was freezing—how did he stand it?—but it did little to assuage the burning heat of her body.

Shame clawed its way through her confused emotions. Shame and anger. She'd not meant to spy on him, but he had no call to be so mean to her. She'd just been thirsty and frightened out of her wits that he was lost. To her utter humiliation, tears burned at the back of her eyes. "I thought you were lost."

More splashing. "Well, I'm not, as you can see."

"Or that you'd left me."

He made no response to this. She risked a glance in his direction. He was staring at her, his hands clenched into fists on top of the water. His face was as rigid as the boulders around him, but his eyes were bright silver and flooded with a thousand emotions, very few of which she recognized.

Then his shoulders sagged. Something softened in his face, and he sighed. He brought a hand up and raked his fingers through his wet hair, causing it to stand on end.

He looked ridiculous. And utterly enticing.

The heat rose inside of her again, knocking her off balance once more. She climbed to her feet and turned away from him. She heard him moving through the water and climbing onto the bank.

"Don't turn around," he said.

"Of course I'm not going to turn around," she said, irritated and confused and itching to do just that.

Clothes rustled, and he grumbled underneath his breath. Something thudded in the soft earth.

"Are you decent?" she asked with impatience.

He snorted. "I'm clothed, if that's what you're asking," he retorted.

She spun around. He was sitting on the riverbank in his trousers and torn lawn shirt, snapping his stockings against his knee. They were stiff with dirt and dried blood. She stared down at his bare feet, and her breath hitched. The soles were covered in a mass of angry, raw gashes and blisters.

Without thinking, she rushed to his side and dropped down beside him, lifting his foot into her lap.

He drew back from her as if stung and glared at her.

"You look like you've been walking on glass, Montford," she scolded.

He tugged on one stocking with a jerk, wincing. "Not glass. Rocks. Twigs. God knows what else."

"Oh, yes, the race."

He jerked on his other stocking and reached for a boot. "Never mind it. It's my own fault. There's nothing to do but endure. How do you feel?"

"Sore. Hungry."

He grunted and tugged on his boot, not meeting her eyes. "Well, you're not puffed up anymore, at least. Just purple."

Her pride was a bit stung. Clearly, he was disgusted by her appearance. She pursed her lips and tried to think of a stinging retort.

He continued before she could. "And I have no clue as to how to feed you. Unless you know how to catch animals with your bare hands. I confess I haven't the skill."

"We could boil your boot. I've heard Hessians are a delicacy in some parts of the country."

He stared at her as if she'd gone mad, then burst into laughter. Great side-splitting guffaws that shook his entire body. He lay back clutching his stomach, tears leaking from the corners of his eyes.

She chuckled, more from the sight of him so out of control than her own joke. When he didn't stop for some time, she grew worried. "It wasn't *that* funny," she chided.

"It is," he insisted. "I'd eat it, too, I'm so damnably hungry. But we don't even have a pot. Or fire. We can't even cook a boot."

Her lips twitched.

"And we're lost. We're likely to eat each other."

"Let's hope it doesn't come to that." She held out the coat she'd found.

He sat up and eyed the article with distaste.

"I thought you might be cold."

He snatched it from her hands and thrust his arms through the sleeves. He attempted to button it, but it was too small for his broad chest. The sleeves didn't reach his wrists, and the whole garment was riddled with holes. He looked like an overstuffed scarecrow.

She laughed as hard as he had, and he glared at her, but without any real malice. "You look ridiculous!"

He picked up his other boot and shoved it up his leg. "At least I'm warm and ridiculous."

"You'd be a lot warmer if you hadn't jumped into a freezing river. What could you have been thinking?"

He stood abruptly, his brow darkening, a curious, almost pained expression flitting across his brow. "You don't want to know." He held out his hand, and without thinking she took it and allowed him to pull her to her feet.

He held on to her hand longer than was strictly necessary and looked as if he were on the verge of speaking.

Then he let her hand drop and started walking down the riverbank.

"Come on, let's try to get out of this jungle," he said.

She laughed and followed him.

By the grace of God, the forest at last gave way to the gentle, undulating pastureland of the dales after a couple of hours walking on their empty stomachs. Sheep and cows dotted the hillsides, grazing and dozing and entirely uninterested in the two strange humans trudging through their midst. The livestock was a promising sign. The appearance of a crude road bordering a crumbling stone wall was even more promising. They stopped upon reaching it, and Montford gazed up and down the road, batting a family of flies away from his eyes. He looked vexed and exhausted—rather how she felt—and not at all relieved.

She wondered how he could bear to walk upon his tender feet. He must have been in considerable pain, but he'd yet to complain. Lesser gentlemen would have long since broken under the strain of their circumstances. She could never say that Montford was faint of heart, or that he hadn't behaved heroically. The rescue had been a bit of a muddle, and she'd had to more or less save herself, but he'd tried. And she wouldn't have been able to escape if he hadn't been there to carry her. He had saved her life. It would be ungenerous of her not to give him his due.

But did she like him?

Yes, she suspected she did, just a little bit. She'd find the devil himself good company after her experience with Lightfoot.

Not that Montford was a devil. Far from it. He was a bit of a prude, really. He'd actually blushed when she'd come across him in the river. He was no doubt the sort to drape fig leaves over statuary to preserve their modesty.

Although when he kissed her . . .

But she would not think of that. It seemed a lifetime ago anyway. He'd never kiss her again, after what had happened. Gentlemen did not kiss women who had been foolish enough to get themselves kidnapped and nigh on compromised.

Or they did, but they never married such women.

Not that she wanted Montford to marry her.

Or kiss her.

She determined which way was south and pointed in that direction, attempting to concentrate on practical matters. "We should go that way."

He scowled at her. "I know which way to go."

No, she definitely did not want to marry a scowling, snappish duke.

His scowl faded when he saw her expression. "I'm just worried. If this road connects with the main highway, we might run into your friend."

She was irritated at herself for not thinking of this. For some reason, she'd forgotten all about Lightfoot.

"Not my friend so much as a lunatic. He's quite mad, you know."

"I think I could guess it."

"He shot Charlie."

"Yes, I know. I found him, and he told me what had happened."

Astrid's heart soared. "He was alive?" she cried.

"Yes. In bad shape, but alive when I left him with a doctor in Hawes."

Astrid sighed in relief, her burden growing lighter. She'd just assumed Charlie had died. She studied Montford out of the corner of her eye to gauge his mood concerning Charlie. Clearly, Charlie had not spoken of his part in this disaster, and Astrid was relieved. She wasn't prepared to send Charlie to gaol, even though he probably deserved it after what he'd done. She had to consider his family. They'd not survive without him.

She stepped onto the road. "We'll just have to hide if we hear someone coming."

"Right," he said, falling into step beside her. They walked for some time without encountering anything more intelligent than a flock of geese crossing the road and a pair of cows napping in the sun.

It was well past noon when Montford made a strange noise—a cross between a laugh and a gasp of disbelief—and suddenly veered off the road and into a stand of trees. He disappeared behind heavy, gnarled branches until all she could hear of him was an occasional rustling of leaves and a snort.

"Montford! What's the matter? Are you ill?"

"No!"

She thought for a minute. "Are you . . . well, you know . . . *going?*"

"No!" A moment later, he reemerged, pulling on the reins of a skittish horse. "I'm procuring our ride home," he said, then eyed the ragged beast with resignation. "Such as it is."

⋯ ❈ ⋯

MONTFORD COULD hardly believe his eyes when he spotted the callow nag that had attempted to drag him to his death the day before casually munching on a patch of grass off of the side of the road. How the horse had arrived in this particular spot, or indeed, how they were to manage the recalcitrant beast to their advantage, seemed beside the point. They had a mount—sort of. All was right with the world.

But then Astrid smiled at him, turned to the horse, and pulled herself onto the saddle.

Astride.

He could not help but stare at the long, well-turned leg at eye level. Only a patch of bare, creamy flesh peeked out the top of her torn stocking, revealing a glimpse of her knee before disappearing beneath the hem of her skirt. But it was one glimpse too many. His stomach bottomed out, and his mouth felt as dry as a desert.

He lifted his eyes, but that did not help. He took in her glorious bonfire hair, spiraling over her shoulders, down her arms, not stopping until well past her waist. Her face might be bruised. And freckled. And her eyes might be mismatched. And her nose no more than an arrogant snub he wanted to reach out and tweak. She might be utterly, completely hideous, but he'd never seen anything more beautiful or dear to his eyes.

He was wrecked.

And in big trouble.

How was he going to keep his hands off her?

He wasn't, because now he was expected to sit behind her on the damned horse.

"I think I'll walk." Though that was the last thing he wanted to do, considering the state of his feet.

"Now that's the most ridiculous thing you've ever said, Cyril, and you've said a lot of ridiculous things."

His lust was somewhat dampened by her words, thank God. "Don't call me that!" he growled, putting his foot in the stirrup and hauling himself onto the saddle, his body sliding into place behind her. He was immediately dazed by the scent of her hair.

"What should I call you then?"

"I am Montford," he growled, reminding her of his station—and himself.

She just sniffed with annoyance.

He snatched up the reins and spurred the horse down the road, trying to ignore the feel of Astrid Honeywell's derriere rammed up against his groin, the feel of her back sliding against his chest, and the way her halo of fiery hair itched his nose.

Chapter Twenty-Three

In Which the Duke and Miss Honeywell Give in to Temptation

IT WAS afternoon before they found themselves on the final stretch back to Rylestone Hall. Owing to their empty pockets, they'd not bothered to stop in Hawes, so their bellies were painfully empty still and their patience with their situation and with each other was running out. She could feel the tension of Montford's body behind her. He didn't like the fact that she was nestled in his arms, relying upon him to keep her upright. But she was too tired and hungry to care about his fragile emotional state, or the inappropriate intimacy of their bodies.

He seemed to care enough for the both of them, anyway.

Good God, one would think she had the plague. It wasn't *her* fault he couldn't seem to keep his hands to himself. As for the fact that she was guilty of lusting after him in return . . . well, that was a moot point. She may have admired the figure he had cut in the stream. She may have even regretted not being thoroughly compromised by Montford while in Lightfoot's clutches. But she was free, and such a wild thought had no place in reality. She had managed to escape Lightfoot without losing her virtue. She was not about to let Montford take it, after all the trouble both of them had gone through to preserve it.

Of course, no one would believe she had not been ruined. She was going to have the devil of a time salvaging her reputation—or what was left of it—when she got home. She had no idea what was being said about her in Rylestone Green, but it couldn't be anything good. She'd been gone for days, and when she turned up in the company of the duke and no one else, the worst was going to be assumed. He'd saved her from Lightfoot, but he'd not be able to save her from wagging tongues.

As if he'd care. He'd abandon her to her fate as soon as they reached the castle. It was not as if he was going to make an honest woman of her. She suspected he'd rather eat nails than marry her. Not only that, but he probably thought she wasn't good enough to be his duchess. The Duchess of Montford would be biddable, overbred, pretentious, and utterly boring. She'd never challenge him or go against his dictates. She'd be a decoration for his station, like a wall sconce or a pretty bit of lace trim about a curtain.

Astrid gagged just imagining it and shifted on the saddle. Her backside had gone numb.

Montford stiffened and drew in his breath, as if she had startled him. "For pity's sake, what are you doing?" he hissed, his arms falling from her sides.

"I'm uncomfortable."

"So am I, but you don't see me shifting about like a . . . a circus act," he said, spitting out stray bits of her hair that had blown into his mouth.

"If you must know," she bit out, squirming about some more, just to annoy him further, "certain parts of my anatomy have gone to sleep."

"I wish I had that problem," he muttered.

She spun her head around to glare at him and nearly lost her balance. His arms came around her again, catching her. "What is that supposed to mean?" she demanded.

His jaw was clenched, and he avoided looking at her. "You don't want to know. Be still, would you?"

She harrumphed and turned back around. But all of that movement had relieved none of her restlessness and caused her to cramp in her right leg. Sighing, she grasped the pommel in front of her for balance and swung her right leg over to join the other in the hopes of ending her agony.

Montford let out a groan and brushed her hair out of his face. She was now riding sidesaddle, halfway facing him. He ground his teeth, looking completely miserable.

"Will you stop it?" he breathed.

"I had a cramp."

She settled her rump more evenly in the saddle so she was no longer sitting on his thighs, but rather between them, her side nestled against his front. He let out a choked sound.

"There. Is that better?"

He looked distraught. "No, it's not better. It's worse, much worse."

"Well, I'm sorry. But you'll just have to get used to it," she said, staring straight ahead in haughty dismissal. "'Tis just a few miles to go."

He said nothing, although she could feel him breathing heavily against her left ear.

The wind gusted again, driving her loose hair back into his face. She gathered it up over her right shoulder and attempted to braid it into a simple plait. She froze when she felt something damp and hot against her neck. She felt it again, right behind her ear, and her hands dropped away, goose bumps traveling up her spine.

"Astrid . . ." It was Montford. Or rather, Montford's mouth, kissing her bare neck, the column of her throat, her ear.

"What are you . . . oh! *Oh!*" She strangled on her words as she felt Montford's tongue trace the outline of her ear, then poke inside it, sending chills down her back and heat into her core. Unconsciously, she arched her neck, exposing more of it to his questing tongue.

"Couldn't . . . bear it . . . another moment . . ." he managed to choke out in between licking her throat.

One of his hands gave up its rein and molded itself against Astrid's breast, and her body reacted as if set on fire. Every point of contact with his body sizzled. He brought his hand from her breast over her hair, to the side of her jaw, turning her head toward him.

She stared up at him in disbelief. This was an unexpected turn of events if there ever was one, but she was quite powerless to stop it. He looked pained and as confused as she was. His breathing was shallow, his eyes glazed, his body tense.

"We are on a horse, Montford," she said stupidly.

He didn't bother to answer. His arm tightened around her, and his mouth closed over hers. He kissed her once, twice, and her body melted against him. She opened her mouth to say something more, but he caught her bottom lip between his teeth, tugging it. His tongue darted inside, tasting her, and he groaned, his hand returning to her breast, squeezing it between his fingers.

She brought her hand to his face and trailed her fingers over his jaw, down the length of his neck, and over the hard muscles of his chest. She'd forgotten her earlier arguments with herself to avoid temptation. She'd forgotten they were on a horse, though it kept walking forward, oblivious to its passengers. Indeed, she was lucky she remembered her name, but that was only because he kept saying it over and over between his kisses.

His hand wandered down her side, over the swell of her hip, then around, to the vee between her legs, clutching her there, making her burn. She gasped and nearly came off the saddle with her hips, her head falling back against his shoulder.

He dropped the other rein, forgetting the horse entirely, and gripped her hand at his chest, bringing it down his front, over the straining muscles of his abdomen, then lower still, to the bulge at the front of his breeches. It was hot and hard and quivering with a life of its own. Astrid's hand jumped away, but he caught it and brought it back to him, pressing against his solid length, urging it down, then up again.

He made a choking sound deep in his throat and put his hot lips against her ear. "Touch me, yes . . . God!" He gasped as she stroked him through his breeches with a trembling hand. She was mesmerized, frightened of the power she felt in him. He moved his hips, thrusting himself more fully into her hand.

She felt his fingers wander up her leg beneath her skirts, over the fabric of her drawers, seeking out her warmth. His fingers found the inside of her thigh, then skirted higher, higher. She cried out as a spark of heat ricocheted through her as he caressed her in a way she'd never imagined possible. Somewhere in the back of her mind, she knew what he was doing was very wrong, but she could not care at the moment. It felt wickedly delicious.

He found a magical spot with his thumb, rubbing it until she was quivering in his arms. She struggled to breathe, drowning in sensation. She was hot all over and restless, a heretofore unfathomable sensation growing between her legs, seeking a release. Then he shifted her somehow, spreading her legs farther, and she had to clutch the threadbare lapels of his jacket with both hands to anchor herself, afraid that if she didn't do so, she'd float away. His head lowered, his mouth seeking out the delicate skin above her bodice, licking her, nipping her flesh between his teeth.

"You feel so good," he murmured. "I want you so much."

He stroked her harder, faster, and the sensation of weightlessness grew, the ache becoming almost unbearable. She strained against his hand, seeking to end the exquisite torture, not knowing how to make it go away.

"Feel me," he urged in a hoarse whisper. "Touch me. Feel how much I want you."

Her hand was shaking, but she lowered it again, felt the rock-hard length of him. She didn't know what to do. All she could manage was to press her hand against him, but it seemed to be enough. He gasped against her throat and thrust himself against her thigh.

She felt a jolt of liquid pleasure burn through her belly. Her vision blurred and her body shuddered as wave after wave of ecstasy shot from her loins to the tips of her fingers and toes. She cried out in wonder.

He clutched her hard and ground his body against her thigh. She felt his hardness swell beneath her hand and a moist warmth seep through the fabric of his breeches. All the furious tension in his body seemed to leave him, a guttural moan ripped from his throat, and he slumped forward, his head buried in the crook of her shoulder, his lungs taking in air with ragged inefficiency.

Astrid felt like the approximate consistency of half-melted butter. He didn't seem to be faring any better, his hand falling away from her, and both his arms dropping to his sides.

She came back to the world slowly, her vision refocusing, her mind reeling.

What had just happened?

She wasn't quite sure, but she had never felt so wonderful, her hunger forgotten, the aches and pains of the last few days completely obliterated. Her body was burning hot, still quivering with the after-shocks of pleasure.

She had a thousand questions to ask him—What had he done? What did it mean?—but she couldn't bring herself to utter a word. Somewhere along the way, her emotions had become engaged in a new and unsettling way. He was no longer simply the heartless duke bent on crushing her to his will, if he'd ever been. He was the quixotic man who couldn't let different foods touch on his plate, and who'd run in a drunken footrace because she'd dared him. The man who was a veritable lexicon of dirty limericks. The man who had nearly killed himself trying to rescue her. The man who kissed her senseless because he couldn't seem to help himself. The man who'd once worn the finest silk, but was now reduced to an ill-fitting, moth-eaten wool jacket that made him look like a scarecrow.

But he was her scarecrow.

And he had the power to hurt her more than anyone else in the world.

Why? How could she be so certain of this? She'd known him barely a week, so it hardly seemed likely that she should be so certain of anything involving Montford. But it had been a very, very, *very* long week.

They shared a physical attraction, yes, but it ran deeper. She'd known handsome men before, but she'd not even think of letting one of them touch her as Montford had done. With him, there was no thought involved. She couldn't *not* let him touch her. Her will demanded her to respond. Even now she craved more of him. He had awakened something inside of her, and it was not going to go away until it was fed again and again. By him. Only him.

She had fallen in love with him.

It was like a blow to the gut, knocking the wind out of her lungs.

What else could this strange disease of hers be, except the irrationality of love? There was certainly nothing easy or joyful at all about being in love. The poets had lied. It was a torture. A complete nightmare. How could she have been so foolish as to fall in love with Montford, of all people?

She was done for. Utterly.

Then she felt Montford's head nudging her neck from behind, and her heart lurched. She knew that eventually she would have to face him, but not now, not yet. And if he thought he was going to . . . again . . .

Had he no self-control?

But then suddenly he wasn't nudging her anymore. He wasn't even behind her. It was as if he'd vanished into thin air.

She heard a faint thud.

The horse continued to lope onward, the reins trailing in the dust of the road. She spun around in the saddle and searched for Montford.

She spied him lying in the lane several yards behind them. He was still, too still. What in the devil had happened now?

She managed to stop the horse and jumped from the saddle. "Montford!" she cried. She fell into the dirt beside him and seized his shoulders.

He let out a yelp of pain, jerked away, and clutched his shoulder where she had grabbed it.

"What happened? Are you all right?"

"I'm fine," he said, propping his weight on his elbows, looking dazed. He finally met her eyes. "I fell asleep," he said helplessly.

She stared at his dust-covered face. He looked like he'd been beaten by a sack of flour.

"I swear, if I fall off a horse one more time," he said, attempting to wipe the grit from his mouth, "I am going to . . . damn it, I don't know what I'm going to do!" He pounded his fists into the dirt of the road like a child in a temper.

"You fell *asleep*?"

"I've had a rough few days."

"You fell asleep after . . . after you . . ." She couldn't even complete that thought, for she had no idea what to even call what had passed between them just moments earlier.

He blushed through the grime on his face, obviously recalling the same thing. "Astrid . . ."

She punched him in his wounded shoulder. Hard.

His mouth quivered, and for a horrible moment she was afraid he was going to burst into tears. But then he did something even worse. He began to laugh, the horrid, wretched creature that he was. His shoulders shook from his mirth, and he lay back on the road, giggling like a schoolgirl.

"It's not funny," she insisted, the corners of her mouth flickering.

"Yes it is," he said, wiping the tears from his eyes.

And because she couldn't help herself, she found herself laughing along with him, laughing so hard tears leaked from her eyes. She was in shock. There was no other explanation for it.

It was a long, long time before either of their wits returned. Her stomach muscles were sore from laughing so hard, her throat scratchy. She wiped the last of her tears away and glanced down at him. He had grown still, staring at her with a pensive expression.

She set herself on guard. The moment now threatened to descend into awkwardness. Or worse: earnestness. She had no intention of mentioning what had passed on top of the horse *ever* again.

She looked down the road to locate the horse. It was in the undergrowth munching grass, as had become its habit when its riders did something foolish, and it threw admonishing glances in their direction in between bites.

"Do you know, I've laughed more in the past two days than I have in years?" he said suddenly.

She turned back to him, flustered. "Nerves."

"That must be it," he murmured, still studying her so gravely. "Astrid, I—"

She cut him off by standing and holding out her hand to help him up. "We're not far now," she urged. "Come on." She didn't want to hear what he might say next. He sat up, glanced down at her palm, then back up at her face. His silvery eyes had gone opaque. A bad sign.

In a flash, he'd seized her hand, tugged her off her feet, and into his arms, kissing her madly.

As was usual when such a thing occurred, she immediately lost all of her resolve and melted into his embrace, twining her hands around his neck and pulling herself closer. He leaned back against the road, cupping her face with his hands as his lips explored her forehead, her cheeks, her nose, even her eyelids. And though he was passionate, he was tender this time, as he had been that night in the garden, which now seemed another lifetime ago. And he did nothing more than simply kiss her, over and over again.

It was more stirring to her spirit than all the other times he had touched her.

Her stupid, mutinous heart didn't stand a chance. She was in love, damn it. And there was no accounting for her taste.

"I could kiss you for an age, Astrid Honeywell," he murmured against her lips.

"I could let you." There. She had admitted it.

She felt the smile curving his lips. His fingers sank into her hair. "Good."

"Not good. We really should stop," she said. It was a halfhearted suggestion.

He did not take it. He seized her mouth with his own, drugging her with its warmth. "Witch," he breathed.

"Idiot man."

He chuckled, turned her head in his hands, and poked his tongue into her ear. She sighed in delight. She liked his tongue precisely where it was.

They were so lost to the world that they did not know they were no longer alone until a throat was cleared.

Astrid raised her head with great reluctance and saw two riders gawking at them. She froze and jumped to her feet.

Montford did the same, seizing her by her arm and thrusting her behind him as if to shield her from attack.

She collected her wits enough to take in the intruders, both of whom were strangers to her but quite remarkable. The one on the left was more than remarkable: he was off-putting. He was the most beautiful man she'd ever seen, slim and dark and slightly foreign-looking, with stunning blue eyes. As if to make a mockery of his beauty, he wore an outrageous pink silk waistcoat, lace spilling out of his collar and sleeves, and a profusion of jewels encrusting his fingers. His eyes were wide, betraying his surprise, but his beautiful face was otherwise unreadable, save for a small, sly smile bending the corners of his lips.

The other man, who was no less intimidating, was dressed like—well, she wasn't quite sure what he was dressed like. He seemed to be wearing his dressing gown. He was not as handsome as his companion—who was?—but he would have been halfway attractive save for the bloat of dissipation that seemed to hover around his chin and stomach. His eyes were dark and presently bugging out of his face. A thin cigarillo dangled between his lips, which were parted in astonishment.

The cigarillo dropped, completely forgotten, to the road. "Monty?" the portly man inquired in a querulous voice.

Montford groaned and looked up at the heavens, as if he wished they would open up and swallow him whole.

⊷ ⚔ ⊶

"WHAT ARE you doing here?" Montford demanded of the two idiots mounted in front of him.

Marlowe couldn't manage another word. He looked too stunned. Sherbrook's eyes danced with amusement between Montford and Astrid. "What are *you* doing?"

"None of your business. And I asked you first," he growled.

Sherbrook tsked and narrowed his clever eyes. "Aren't you going to introduce us?" Sherbrook inquired silkily, smiling at Astrid.

Montford's blood boiled. How dare the rogue smile at her! He tried to tuck Astrid farther behind him, but she shook him off and stepped beside him. "Yes, *Monty*, aren't you going to introduce us?"

"No."

Sherbrook arched an eyebrow and, ignoring Montford's glare, turned back to Astrid. "Sebastian Sherbrook, at your service. And my colleague is the esteemed Viscount Marlowe. You are . . . ?"

"Astrid Honeywell."

"Ah. Honeywell." Sherbrook's gaze settled on Montford, and then he exchanged a knowing glance with Marlowe. "How very nice to meet you, Miss Honeywell. We are Montford's friends, up from London."

"I see."

Marlowe couldn't contain himself any longer. "Good God, Montford, what the devil is going on? Been searching everywhere for you. Out of our minds with worry!"

"I'm sure you were," he said between his teeth.

"Well?" Marlowe prompted.

"Well what?"

"What the devil is going on?"

"None of your—"

Astrid rolled her eyes and stepped in front of him. "I was abducted by a madman. He shot my driver and attempted to carry me off to Gretna Green. Montford came to my assistance. We are now on our way back to Rylestone Hall."

"What?" Marlowe screeched.

"Indeed," Sherbrook replied conversationally. "Sounds perfectly exciting."

"Exciting is not the word I would use," Montford bit out. "And there's a bit more to the tale than that."

"I should say!" Marlowe cried, giving Astrid a significant glance.

Astrid blushed, and so did he. Sherbrook and Marlowe *would* pick the most inopportune time to show up. But then again, they were on a public road, and he should have known better than to loll about in the dirt kissing Astrid Honeywell.

"Now what are you doing here?" he demanded gruffly.

Sherbrook smiled. "Saving your hide. Though perhaps the point is moot. I must say, I am thoroughly confused." He cleared his throat. "We came to warn you. Elaine is knocked up again."

"Sherry, please! Language!" Marlowe breathed, looking pained.

"You came all of this way to tell me that the countess is breeding?" Montford roared.

"Who's breeding?" Astrid demanded.

"M'sister," Marlowe explained.

"Oh, I see," she said, though it was clear that she didn't.

"The long and short of it is, she fobbed off your little request on my dear lady aunt," Sherbrook continued with obvious revulsion, "and *she's* taken it into her head to travel up here. With her sister. They are already at Rylestone Hall, awaiting your return."

It took a moment for the news to sink in. When it did, he felt as if someone had dropped a boulder on his head. He'd forgotten these people existed. And Araminta!

This was icing on the cake of the most disastrous week of his life. "What?" he said stupidly, with a voice that cracked.

Sherbrook's lips thinned with impatience. "Lady Katherine and Lady Araminta. They are at Rylestone Hall," he repeated.

"Who is Lady Katherine?" Astrid demanded. "And who is Lady Araminta?"

Sherbrook opened his mouth to answer, then thought better of it. He stared at Montford with an eyebrow cocked.

Astrid turned to Montford. "Who are they?"

He couldn't look at her. He stared over her head, because he was a coward. "Lady Araminta is my fiancée." They were the hardest words he'd ever spoken.

Astrid was silent for a long time. He finally worked up the courage to look at her face, and he wished he hadn't. She was ashen, and all the light had drained from her mismatched eyes. "Oh," she said, very softly.

"Wedding's in a week. Allegedly," Marlowe added unhelpfully.

"*Thank you*, Marlowe," Montford bit out, never taking his eyes off Astrid's face. He could read nothing in her expression beyond her pale cheeks, her clenched jaw. What was she thinking? Feeling?

And what was *he* feeling?

Nothing. He was utterly numb.

Astrid turned away from him and started walking toward the horse. "Then we should get back. And make ourselves presentable for our *guests*." With stiff dignity, Astrid mounted the horse astride and took off down the road.

He watched her go, his heart shriveling the farther she went from him.

"Well, you might have told her about your bride before mauling her on the road," Marlowe commented drily.

Montford looked up at his two soon-to-be-ex-friends. Sherbrook looked equal parts amused and concerned. Marlowe looked indignant. Apparently he'd taken it upon himself to be offended on Astrid's behalf. When had *that* one developed compassion?

"Looks like you're walking back, old chap," Sherbrook drawled.

Marlowe sniffed. "And it's no less than you deserve. Really, Monty. Don't know what's come over you. But even *I* don't tup a wench in the middle of the King's Highway. It's just bad form."

"I was not tupping her!"

Neither believed him.

"And if you ever speak about her in such terms again, I'll tear out your tongue and stuff it up your arse," he growled.

Marlowe's eyes widened, and he glanced at Sherbrook. They shared a private smirk that made Montford's blood boil and turned their horses to return to Rylestone. Without him.

"Do try to catch up, dear boy," Sherbrook tossed over his shoulder. "And I'd fire your tailor if I were you. You look dreadful."

He stared at their backs until they were lost to sight, then sat down in the road and spent the next few minutes hoping he'd be hit by a runaway carriage.

Chapter Twenty-Four

In Which Rylestone Hall Goes to the Pigs

ASTRID FLUNG the reins of her stolen horse into Mick's hands and strode toward the back entrance of the castle, ignoring the shock on her stable hand's face at the sight of her. She had no time for explanations and no thought for anything except getting to her room without further incident.

She was about two seconds away from bursting into tears.

It was exhaustion, and the emotion of being home at last. It had nothing to do with Montford. Or his two devilish-looking friends. Or two titled ladies besieging the castle.

She nearly did cry when the kitchen door opened and Ant and Art spilled out into the yard, calling out to her, their own little eyes wet with tears. Her heart wrenched as she gathered them in her arms and held them close while they alternately sniffled and demanded to know where she had been all this time. She couldn't explain, and she couldn't let them see her break down, so she stifled her tears and patted their heads. "Don't worry, I'm here now, and I'm not ever leaving you again."

"Ever so much has happened, Astrid," Ant said.

Art nodded solemnly. "The old crow has been here."

"Aunt Emily?" she asked, straightening. This was not good.

Flora came rushing out of the door next, looking relieved to see her, but also completely distraught.

"Where've you got off to?" Flora demanded. "You look a right state. Been worried sick, we have. And where's Charlie and Himself?"

"I'll explain it all later. I hear we have guests."

"That ain't the half of it. Our Roddy is in the drawing room now trying to sort it out."

Roddy? "Where is Alice?"

Flora's expression darkened, and Astrid began to panic in earnest. "Tell you by and by." She looked Astrid up and down, then shook her head. "We better take you upstairs and put you to rights."

Astrid nodded and directed Ant and Art to help the maids carry up some pails of water to her room. She was going to need the entire contents of the well to scrub the muck off of her. Then she followed Flora inside and up the servant's staircase to her room.

Flora began to help peel off her clothes and demanded an accounting from Astrid of her whereabouts the past two days. She provided one in abbreviated form, to Flora's growing horror.

At the end of it, all Flora could say was, "Cor!" her eyes wide, her hands wrenching Astrid's ruined pelisse.

"Indeed," Astrid agreed.

"Oh, Miss Astrid! That bastard didn't do nothing, did he?" Flora cried, clasping her by the hand and studying her face.

"No, he knocked me about a little, but nothing more. Montford came just in time."

"Aye, that's good!" Flora said, her shoulders drooping with relief. "No less than he should've. An' where is Himself?"

"I expect he'll be along shortly," she said stiffly, not wanting to think about the duke's whereabouts at present or ever again. Fiancée indeed!

She wanted to throw her boots across the room, but she restrained herself and merely kicked them under her bed. "And no one had any idea what happened to me?" She was almost disappointed. Of course she didn't want the hue and cry to have been raised. The fewer people who knew about her disappearance the better. But *someone* at least could have shown a little concern.

Flora shook her head and helped Astrid out of her dress, her nose turned up at the state of it. "None, Miss Astrid. By the time we figured out you were nowt comin' home either, we were already in a tither here at the hall."

"What do you mean?"

"It's Miss Alice. Her and that scoundrel cousin of yours ran off together day after the festival, bound for Scotland." Flora paused. "Surprised you didn't meet them on the road."

Astrid had to sit down. Her head hurt. "Repeat what you just said."

Flora took a breath before starting. "Miss Alice and Sir Wesley have made off to Scotland to be married. She left a note and everything. Yer aunt is in a rare mood, been over here barking out orders. She sent poor Mr. McConnell after them, and a good portion of his men. So you see, by the time I noticed you hadn't come back from Hawes with Charlie or the duke, there weren't no one to send out to see what were keeping you. But figgered you were in good hands, what with Charlie and Himself for company. Didn't wager you'd be interfered with by that bastard Lightfoot, though. Pardon my French, Miss Astrid."

Astrid was dumbfounded. Her sister had eloped, the household was in an uproar due to Aunt Emily's hysterics, and *she* had been overlooked entirely. She should have been quite happy. Alice and Wesley had finally come to their senses. She only hoped they made it to Gretna Green before Aunt Emily caught up with them. And Alice's timing had been impeccable. No one had cared where Astrid was in the ensuing chaos.

Alice's elopement was scandalous enough. If anyone got wind of what had happened to *her*, she would be ruined, and so would her sisters.

But still, *no one had cared* enough to worry for her. She felt horribly alone.

A sudden horrifying suspicion occurred to her. "How did you know the duke was with me?"

"Wot yer mean? You just tole me!" Flora cried, her face flushing. She stared down at the dress she held pinched between her fingers, as if loath to touch the filth of it, then went over to the fire and tossed it on top.

"No. You said you didn't worry about me because you knew Charlie and Montford were with me."

Flora tugged out the porcelain hipbath from a closet, then busied herself fetching a length of toweling from an armoire, avoiding Astrid's eyes. "Well, er, I didn't. Just sort of . . . figgered it out."

"Did you?"

Flora spun around, biting her bottom lip. "Oh, Miss Astrid! I confess. It were me and Roddy and Himself's driver wot put Himself in that wagon bed. It were a lark, I swear. And then when you didn't come back, we just assumed it were because you and Himself were"—she cleared her throat—"reachin' an unnerstannin'."

She should have been furious with Flora for such presumption. She almost yelled at her maid, but the door opened, and Ant and Art and two kitchen maids came in and filled the tub with their buckets of water. By the time they departed, Astrid's anger had dissipated, and she just laughed. It was either that or cry, and she was not turning into a watering pot at this critical hour.

Flora looked at her as if she had lost her mind, which she probably had. "Well, no matter your intentions, I am very glad you put the duke in that wagon bed. I'd have had no chance of escaping Lightfoot otherwise."

Flora smiled in understanding, then helped Astrid into the tub.

The water was cool. She'd not had time to bother about heating it. But despite its temperature, it felt wonderful to scrub off the three days' worth of grit and grime from her skin and smell the clean lavender soap as Flora lathered up her hair.

For a few minutes, she wanted to forget the chaos surrounding her and relax. She'd not been on a holiday with Montford after all. But it seemed circumstances at Rylestone were not going to give her a moment's peace. She would have to face those London ladies, though she didn't know how she was going to bear looking at this Araminta person.

All this time, he'd been engaged to marry another woman, and he'd never uttered a word about it. The rogue!

Though he'd made no promises to her, and indeed, she'd wanted no promises from him, she was devastated, and she hated herself for feeling devastated. It made her silly. And weak.

She sighed and leaned her head against the side of the tub.

"You'd best hurry, Miss Astrid. Roddy's downstairs, an' he's his hands full with our Aunt Anabel, who's insisted on having tea with the ladies. She were well into her story about that French sailor of hers when last I checked in."

Astrid groaned. "Not the French sailor!" That story had once made the vicar cry. And Astrid suspected it would shock even the prurient mind of the author of *Le Chevalier d'Amour*. But the damage was done. "Just a few more minutes, Flora. I'm quite exhausted."

"Aye, no doubt you be," Flora said, combing out Astrid's wet hair. "An' I don't mean to pry, but yer sayin' you reached no unnerstannin' with Himself."

Astrid bolted up in the tub and turned to Flora, her face flaming. "Flora!"

Flora shrugged and smiled. "Just thought I'd ask. You didn't . . . er, you know . . . express yer appreciation of Himself going through all that trouble to rescue you?"

"No!" she lied. "How could you think . . ."

"You were quite fond of him afore, in the garden."

"Flora! You were spying on us!"

Flora had the grace to look sheepish for half a second.

"Well, this is just wonderful! No! I have no *understanding* with Montford. Other than a mutual aversion."

Flora pursed her lips, not at all convinced.

"Besides," Astrid said, hauling herself from the tub and grabbing up her toweling, "he's to be married."

"No!" Flora cried.

"Yes. In a week. To one of those fine London ladies downstairs."

"Oh, Miss Astrid!" Flora exclaimed sympathetically.

"And I don't care. Not one bit. The sooner he's out of my life, the better."

And with that, she ordered Flora to her closet to fetch her best dress. Then she thought better of it and pulled open the drawer containing her trousers. She was not going to make this easy on anyone.

⸺✦⸺

WHEN ASTRID entered the drawing room, her resolve faltered. She'd never seen anyone like the two ladies occupying the couch, staring wide-eyed at Aunt Anabel and her wig over the tops of their teacups. When they noticed her, they stood up and stared wide-eyed at her.

Astrid's attention was drawn to the tallest of the pair. She was not as conventionally beautiful as her companion, her aristocratic nose a trifle long, her lips too full, but her idiosyncratic features were arresting, her overlarge eyes, the color of emeralds, breathtaking. Her gossamer hair, scraped back into a simple knot, was paler than her alabaster skin, nearly white. She wore a plain, dove-gray gown, almost stark in its simplicity. It was something a governess could have worn, although the fabric was of the finest watered silk Astrid had ever seen. The woman needed no embellishment, however, to draw the eye. She was quite the tallest woman Astrid had ever seen, easily taller than most men, and on that point alone she commanded one's attention. There was an air of aloofness about her as well, and a cold calculation she wore about her like armor.

The other woman was shorter, fuller of figure, and her hair was a rich honey-blonde, hanging in pretty ringlets about her face. She was almost as lovely as Alice. Her dress was light green satin and tailored in what Astrid could only assume was the latest London fashion, capped-sleeved and high-waisted. Her relation to the other woman was obvious in her eyes. They were also green, but not as sharp or vibrant. The similarities of features ended there, though she held herself with the same stiff dignity.

Astrid's heart sank. They were the two coldest females she had ever encountered.

Aunt Anabel swiveled her head, knocking her wig askance, and smiled broadly at Astrid. "Tea, dear? Look who's come to visit us! I think one of them is a duchess or something."

Roddy, who had been attempting to disappear into his seat, rose, relief painting his face. "Miss Astrid! Oh, thank heaven you're . . . I mean . . . er . . . ." He coughed. "May I introduce you to our visitors?"

"That won't be necessary, thank you, Stevenage," the tall woman said coolly. "I am the Marchioness of Manwaring." She indicated her companion. "This is my sister, Lady Araminta Carlisle."

Astrid regretted her choice of attire as she curtsied awkwardly. So the shorter one was Montford's intended. She was surprised and relieved, though she didn't know why. Lady Araminta was beautiful, just like she'd imagined. But the other lady was the one Astrid had almost immediately assumed Montford would pick. For no reason at all, she would have liked that less. Perhaps because the marchioness seemed to be in possession of a brain.

"You are Astrid Honeywell," the marchioness continued.

"Yes."

They stood in uncomfortable silence for a moment.

"I believe you are our cousin," the marchioness said after a while.

Astrid was stunned. "What?" she asked, most ungraciously.

"Your mother, I believe, was a Carlisle. Our late grandfather's youngest sister. That would make you our second cousin."

"Cousin? What's this about a cousin?" boomed a voice from the doorway.

The marchioness stiffened even more, if that were possible. The two gentlemen from the road stood in the doorway. The portly one in his dressing gown—or was it an Arabian robe?—had his fists on his hips and was staring at the marchioness with great suspicion. The other man—the beautiful peacock—stood slightly behind him. He was also looking at the marchioness, but his expression was inscrutable.

Astrid turned back to the marchioness. The lady was clutching her skirt unconsciously with one hand. She stared not at the speaker, but at the peacock, her expression equally unreadable. The tension in the room was suddenly stretched thin. Astrid did not know the cause, but it was clear to her that her visitors felt a deep antipathy for each other.

Astrid glanced at Roddy, who gave her a helpless shrug and looked as if he wanted to crawl under a rock.

"Haloo!" Aunt Anabel said to the gentleman, breaking the stalemate. "Back for some more, eh? You there, young man." She gestured toward the peacock, then thrust her cane in the direction of the decanter. "If you wouldn't mind pouring me a spot of sherry while you're at it, I'd be most obliged."

The peacock—Mr. Sherbrook—looked amused, bowed elegantly, and sauntered to the sideboard.

Astrid decided to move things along. "My mother was a Carlisle," she told the marchioness. "Her family disowned her when she married my father, however. The relation is quite severed."

The marchioness remembered her and frowned at her coolly. "Nonetheless, we are cousins. We are *un*severing the relationship."

"Indeed," Astrid replied, equally cool. "To what purpose?"

"Yes, to what purpose, *Aunt* Katherine?" the peacock interjected in a drawl, prowling across the room with catlike grace to deliver Aunt Anabel's sherry, his own drink in his other hand. A dangerous smile lurked on the edge of his lips.

The marchioness didn't flinch, though Astrid thought she rather wanted to.

Now Astrid was completely at sea. The marchioness was the peacock's *aunt*? It hardly seemed possible. The lady was his contemporary, if not years younger.

"You are a Carlisle?" she asked Mr. Sherbrook.

He nearly spat out his port in amusement. "Hardly."

"I am married to Mr. Sherbrook's uncle," the marchioness explained, eyeing the peacock with utter disdain. "He is no relation of mine. And my business here has nothing to do with him. Or the viscount."

"The hell it doesn't!" cried the viscount. Apparently, he had no compunction about cursing in front of the ladies. Or sitting in their company while they were yet standing about. He plopped himself into a seat, looking irate. "Pour me one of them, would you, Sherry?"

"Pour it yourself," Mr. Sherbrook murmured sweetly.

The viscount glared at him but made no move to the sideboard.

Astrid didn't know what to do. The marchioness was standing as stiff as a board, unspeaking. Her sister looked acutely uncomfortable next to her. The viscount was fumbling about his pockets and muttering to himself. Mr. Sherbrook was studying the marchioness with cold amusement.

And Aunt Anabel had nodded off into her sherry.

Astrid threw up her hands. She'd had quite enough. "I don't know what is going on here, and I do not wish to know. You may wait here for Montford, since you are here to see him. But I shall not waste my time standing around trying to descry your purpose. Pardon my bad manners, but I am tired. And hungry. And in no mood for company."

The marchioness looked vaguely startled. Lady Araminta looked offended—*good*—and the viscount's jaw dropped.

Mr. Sherbrook chuckled.

Astrid scowled at him. She stalked over to the sideboard, poured a glass of port, and thrust it into the viscount's fingers. He murmured his thanks, staring at her in astonishment.

"Now if you'll excuse me, I have much to attend to—"

The sound of a carriage pulling up the front drive brought her out of her temper. She bolted toward the window and peered out to see Lady Emily descending from her barouche.

"Damnation!" she breathed.

Lady Araminta's breath caught.

Aunt Anabel's head shot up. "What is it, dear? Are the French invading?"

"No. Even worse. It's Aunt Emily."

"Oh, good heavens!" Aunt Anabel murmured, putting her sherry to her painted lips and gulping it down in one go.

"Who's Aunt Emily?" the viscount demanded.

"My aunt!" she cried. She wanted to tear her hair out. Her pulse was racing wildly. She was beginning to hyperventilate. This was very bad indeed. She didn't think she could take any more. She stared around the room full of strangers and spotted Roddy tiptoeing his way toward the door, making his escape. She didn't stop him, although she thought him a traitor for abandoning her to these people.

She felt a hand on her arm. She started and spun around. It was Sherbrook, his beautiful sapphire eyes flickering with concern, though his lips were still quirked with amusement. "You are not looking at all the thing, Miss Honeywell." He thrust a glass into her hands. "Here's a bit of Dutch courage for you."

"Oh, er, thank you," she said lamely. She sipped the drink and nearly gagged. It was straight whiskey.

"You're getting her drunk," the marchioness said with utmost disapproval, gliding over to them and snatching the glass out of Astrid's hands. "Is that your solution to everything?"

"Nearly," Sherbrook replied smoothly, jerking the glass from the marchioness and thrusting it back at Astrid. "And it's a fine solution for her."

The marchioness sniffed. "For *you*, perhaps, not for her." She took back the glass primly.

"I know more about Miss Honeywell's situation than you do," Sherbrook said in a brittle voice. "She needs the drink." He tugged the glass from the marchioness's hand, but the marchioness refused to give it up. Their fingers locked on the glass, and a war of wills ensued.

"This is my cousin, and I'll not have you corrupt her."

"Damnation, woman, I'm not corrupting her. I'm trying to take care of her!" he bit out.

"I'm *sure* you are."

"And I'm *sure* I don't know what you mean."

"Oh, for heaven's sake!" Astrid cried, jerking the glass from the both of them and tossing back the whiskey. It burned fire down her throat.

The drawing room door burst open, and Lady Emily barreled through, her skirts swishing, her furious gaze locking immediately on her prey. She hardly seemed to notice the other occupants of the room.

"Astrid Honeywell, you've a lot of explaining to do. Where have you been? Aiding and abetting your sister's shameful scheme, no doubt! I demand answers, gel. My son shall *not* entangle himself with this dreadful family. How dare Alice lead him into such scandal! How dare you let your sister behave so . . . so disgracefully! And I know you are behind it. Where are they? I demand you produce them."

Mr. Sherbrook stepped between Astrid and her aunt, his expression one of intense disdain. The viscount had risen from his seat to join his friend, looking as if he were spoiling for a fight. It appeared they were coming to Astrid's rescue, as unlikely as that seemed. She wasn't sure if she wanted them to.

Lady Emily blinked between the men, then glanced at the marchioness and her sister. She was noticeably taken aback.

"Madam, I ask you to rethink your manner with Miss Honeywell," Sherbrook said in a silky voice underlaid with iron. "You are causing a most disagreeable scene."

Lady Emily's eyes narrowed with suspicion. "And who are you?"

Mr. Sherbrook grinned and gave her a leg. His smile was an utterly frightening sight to behold. He looked as beautiful and as wicked as Lucifer. "Sebastian Sherbrook, at your service."

Lady Emily's face paled, her lips pursed. It seemed she knew precisely who Mr. Sherbrook was. Astrid wished that she did as well, if only to know the cause of her aunt's discomfiture.

Lady Emily's eyes flashed daggers at Astrid. "What company you keep! Bringing the devil himself into your household! Have you no sense of decency, gel?"

"Here, now," the viscount interjected, his face red with rage. "Who the hell are you to insult my mate? The bloody queen?"

"Last time I checked, we didn't have a queen, old boy," Sherbrook said mildly. "But thanks all the same."

Aunt Emily turned her rage on the marchioness, flicking her quizzing glass to her eye. "And who is *this*? One of these scoundrels' tarts, I reckon. You have brought the worst libertines in all of England under your roof. Sebastian Sherbrook and"—she flicked a contemptuous glance at the viscount—"the wicked Viscount Marlowe! Really, Astrid, you are beyond the pale."

She had gone too far. Mr. Sherbrook's smile was gone, and nothing was left of his easy manner. His beautiful face was thunderous, his body tense. He looked as if he wanted to strike Lady Emily and was only barely restraining himself.

"Apologize!" he roared, towering over her, nostrils flared.

"What?" Aunt Emily breathed, indignant and a little frightened by his threatening manner.

"I said, apologize, madam," he enunciated in an overloud voice. He thrust a hand toward the marchioness. "You have insulted the Marchioness of Manwaring. I demand you apologize to her, before I have you horsewhipped."

Aunt Emily's eyes popped out of her head as she stared at the marchioness.

"The Marchioness of Manwaring!" she breathed, mortified. "Oh dear, I do apologize. I am most sorry for confusing you with . . . er . . ."

"A prostitute," Sherbrook supplied in a deadly voice.

"Yes, er, ever so sorry." And Lady Emily executed an overzealous curtsy.

The marchioness looked down the end of her nose with stiff dignity and did not so much as nod. Her pinkened cheeks betrayed her emotions, but nothing else.

When Lady Emily came back up, her manner had changed completely. She forgot Astrid entirely and focused a brittle smile upon the marchioness. "You are Carlisle's daughter. I am your great-aunt, Lady Emily Benwick."

The marchioness was dismayed. Her lips pursed. She glanced toward her sister, who was still standing by the tea service, looking very unhappy.

"Great-aunt!" the viscount exclaimed. "Egad, it's a bloody family reunion, Sherry, and I'm the only one here who ain't related," he said disgustedly. "Need another drink. Top you off?"

Sherbrook nodded grimly, never taking his blazing eyes off Lady Emily.

"You have caught us at a most inopportune time," Lady Emily continued. "I fear I am dreadfully out of sorts at the moment. Family crisis."

"I gathered," the marchioness said in a dry tone.

"I must speak to my niece alone," she said, making a move to snatch Astrid's arm.

"Hardly necessary," Sherbrook interceded, snatching Astrid's arm back. "You were speaking to her well enough before."

Lady Emily gave him a thunderous look. "Astrid, you shall come with me at once."

"No, she won't," Sherbrook said smoothly.

"Yes, I don't believe she will," the marchioness added.

Lady Emily huffed, grabbed Astrid's arm, and jerked her toward the door. The marchioness reacted swiftly and jerked her back. Astrid felt pulled apart at the seams.

"What the devil is going on?"

The voice came from the doorway. The two ladies tugging her arms froze. Astrid, arms stretched out from her sides, turned her head and saw Montford striding into the room. He'd made some effort to repair himself, having washed and changed into his usual regalia, though his cravat was crooked and he had not shaved the scruff off his face. He was staring directly at her, his eyes scanning her person, his expression a mixture of confusion, irritation, and longing.

Though she might have imagined the latter.

Lady Araminta spoke for the first time. "Good lord, Montford, is that you?" she drawled, incredulous.

He glanced away from Astrid to his fiancée. His brow furrowed. He cleared his throat. So did Araminta.

The marchioness dropped Astrid's arm, and so did her aunt. It was an absurd moment to remember proprieties, but curtsies and bows were exchanged all around. Astrid tried not to look at Araminta's expression, or Montford's, as he came up to his fiancée and raised her lovely gloved hand to his lips, sketching a kiss.

Instead, she took the opportunity and backed up until she was safely shielded by Aunt Anabel's chair, holding on to the top for support. She felt faint and miserable and two clicks away from total collapse.

"Was I interrupting something?" Montford continued, his gaze flickering to Lady Emily, then to Astrid.

The marchioness replied. "This lady seems to have misplaced her son, and she thinks Miss Honeywell has him," she said flatly. Astrid could not tell if she was amused or irritated by the situation. She wished *she* could remain so cool.

Montford looked startled. "What is she talking about, Astrid?" he demanded in an accusatory tone.

Astrid bristled. Really, he had no right to be angry with *her*! Or to use her first name in front of all these people as if he'd the right. He didn't. He never would. "It seems Sir Wesley has absconded with my sister. They have eloped."

Lady Emily pulled out her handkerchief and covered her mouth to stifle her cry of dismay. "For heaven's sake, gel, must you be so blatant?"

Sherbrook and the viscount snorted simultaneously.

"Well, good for her!" Montford stated.

Lady Emily looked thunderstruck.

"And good for that idiot son of yours," he continued, giving Lady Emily his most contemptuous look. "He'll not be sorry for it. Alice Honeywell is one of the finest females I have ever met." He glanced toward his friends Sherbrook and Marlowe as if to impart a revelation. "She's surprisingly lovely."

Sherbrook had recovered his good humor. He smiled in Astrid's direction, as if they shared a joke.

Which they most certainly did not. Astrid had never felt less like joking in her life. What did Montford mean, *surprisingly*? What sort of qualification was that to make?

"He shall most certainly be sorry," Lady Emily continued. "He has married against my wishes, and his *wife* shall not be welcome under my roof. She has betrayed me, after all the kindnesses I have done to her!"

Montford, despite his beard and general dishabille, managed to pull off one of his infamous ducal glowers. "We have already established the reach of your kindnesses, *madam*. And if you are speaking of Benwick Grange's roof, you are mistaken. It is Sir Wesley's roof. I shall be sure to remind him when I see him again. I'll not have that fool installing his wife in the same household as his mother. Alice does not deserve it. Now good day to you."

Lady Emily sniffed with indignation and disbelief. She stared around the room at all the unsmiling faces fixed upon her. She turned to Astrid, her eyes widened with entreaty. "You shall not let this man treat me so insolently!"

Astrid dug her nails into the seat back and smiled bitterly at her aunt. "He does as he pleases, Aunt. He's the Duke of Montford. *I've* no control over him."

Her aunt's eyes narrowed. "That is not what I hear. You've been off with him!" She pointed with her handkerchief in Montford's direction. "Ruining yourself and this family!"

"I thought Alice had done that," she retorted, not daring to look up from her hands. Her pulse had begun to race. What had her aunt heard? How much was she simply improvising to bait her? "I've done nothing wrong."

"Yes, she's done nothing wrong," the marchioness confirmed. "Unless you find my company scandalous? Miss Honeywell has been with us. We have been making a tour of Yorkshire."

Astrid had no idea why the marchioness insisted on interfering, but she was grateful.

Lady Emily looked confused.

So did Aunt Anabel. "No she hasn't," she said, looking at the marchioness as if she were mad. "She's been on holiday with that young man over there. Constantinople, I think."

Sherbrook and the viscount stifled laughter.

Astrid gritted her teeth, not knowing whether to kill her aunt or kiss her. "Thank you, Aunt Anabel. Yes. We've been in Constantinople. Fighting Saracens. We flew there."

"Did you?" Aunt Anabel sounded intrigued.

Astrid couldn't help but laugh in hysteria. "Oh, yes. In a hot air balloon. They're all the rage, you know."

"This is ridiculous!" Lady Emily cried. She jabbed her handkerchief in Aunt Anabel's direction. "She's insane! She belongs in Bedlam!"

"I most certainly do not," Aunt Anabel said haughtily, tossing her head, her wig flapping up and down. "I've more wit than you, Emily. If I say she were in Constantinople, that's where she were. And if she says she were in a balloon, then by damn she were in a balloon. I ain't having you in here spreading vicious gossip about my girls. It's none of your business, and it never were, you interfering old bag!"

"Hear, hear," Sherbrook murmured, toasting Aunt Anabel with his port. The viscount followed suit.

Astrid stared at Aunt Anabel in utter shock as the old woman hefted her cane and swatted it at Lady Emily, nearly catching her in the stomach.

Lady Emily gasped and jumped back. "Well, I never . . . ! Of all the gall . . . !" Lady Emily breathed.

"*I'll* show you gall!" Aunt Anabel muttered, climbing to her feet unsteadily and poking her cane at Lady Emily.

Astrid came to Aunt Anabel's side and took her by the arm to keep her from tumbling. "Thank you, Aunt. You have done enough."

"Not hardly. She's still breathing."

They were all interrupted by the sound of a loud bang in some distant part of the castle, followed by the piercing scream of a woman. Astrid recognized Flora's voice, and her heart caught in her throat. An eerie silence descended.

"What was that?" Aunt Emily finally demanded. "What's happening now?"

"I'm not sure," Astrid murmured.

The banging noise began again, as if someone were shifting furniture around. Then it seemed to grow closer. With it came the patter of feet and the squeal of two children.

Ant and Art.

Oh, hell.

"What is that?" the marchioness asked, returning to her sister's side, taking her hand, as if fortifying themselves for something dreadful.

"Sounds like a cyclone," Sherbrook commented, looking intrigued.

Then Astrid heard another squeal and Flora's scream, this time nearly right outside the door.

Astrid glanced at Montford automatically. Their eyes met. "Petunia," she said.

Montford's brow lifted in surprise, then understanding. He did the sensible thing and moved away from the door.

"Who is Petunia? Is she another sister?" Lady Araminta inquired.

"No. Petunia is a he, not a she. And he's a pig," Montford explained.

"Oh. What has he done?"

"No, he's a pig. A real pig," Montford insisted.

This didn't have time to sink in for Araminta—Astrid thought uncharitably she wasn't the brightest of creatures—before the door was thrown open, and Ant and Art ran into the room shrieking with a mixture of glee and terror, dressed in their makeshift togas. Petunia followed closely behind, grunting in fury, his hooves slipping across the floor, sending his considerable bulk slamming against walls, tables, and chairs, toppling them and anything upon them. *And* he was completely covered in mud. Wet mud. He left giant brown streaks in his wake, upon the fabric of the couch, the Turkish carpet, and the bottom of an ancient wall hanging.

Mayhem ensued. Ant and Art flew over the sofa toward the pianoforte, and Petunia followed, knocking the staid marchioness straight into Sherbrook's arms, their heads slamming together with a painful thwack. Petunia got caught underneath the pianoforte, panicked, and bucked up with his backside, jangling the frame, squealing at the top of his lungs. Then he exited, catching the elegant, dainty leg of the pianoforte with his hoof. The wood fractured, and the pianoforte crashed to the floor, several keys popping off, a discordant, funereal scream of strings reverberating from inside the ruined instrument.

Sherbrook set the marchioness on top of the sofa and moved to do the same to Araminta, who was shrieking in horror.

He was too late. Ant and Art scooted underneath the viscount's glass of port, followed by the pig, who snagged the bottom of the snifter with his snout, sending the glass flying through the air, straight for Araminta. Tawny port splashed over her face and bosom. She had no time to do more than spit a few droplets of port out of her mouth before Petunia had trundled by her, slamming his shoulder against her, knocking her on her arse.

Araminta let out a wail.

Petunia continued his path of destruction straight in Aunt Emily's direction. Aunt Emily had no choice but to flee the room, slamming the door behind her, leaving them all at the pig's mercy.

"Why, that selfish old bag!" the viscount roared. "She's trapped us inside!"

Montford dodged around Ant and Art to reach Araminta's side and haul her to her feet.

"Well, someone do something!" Montford cried, heaving the weeping Araminta onto the couch beside her sister. He turned to Astrid, his silver eyes blazing. "Astrid, do something!"

"What do you expect me to do?" she snapped.

"He's your pig! Your sisters!"

Astrid clenched her hands at her sides, rage coursing through her veins. Petunia continued to circle the room, laying waste to everything he touched. He brought down a table with two vases. He trampled Aunt Anabel's snuffbox collection and overturned a brass bucket full of ashes from the fireplace. He then proceeded to wallow in them.

In the sudden lull, the viscount—the most unlikely candidate for heroics, in Astrid's opinion—sprang into action. He caught first Ant, then Art, by the scruffs of their necks, and hauled them off their feet.

"Caught you, you little brats!"

Ant and Art stared up at their captor, wild-eyed, their amusement turning to deep wariness. The viscount was a frightening enough sight for adult eyes. He carried them toward the door, swung it open with his foot, and deposited them in the hallway.

Petunia, locating his quarry, sprang from the ashes and bolted toward the door. Ant and Art recovered their squealing and ran down the hall.

Astrid cringed when she heard something made of glass shatter in the next room.

"That creature is going to destroy the whole castle," the marchioness remarked in a surprisingly steady voice. She patted her sobbing sister on the back absently. If Astrid wasn't mistaken, a ghost of a smile hovered about the marchioness's lips.

And if Astrid had any sense of humor left, she'd be smiling as well. But she didn't. And she wouldn't.

Astrid raised her eyes to Montford. He stared at her angrily, as if this was all her fault.

She helped Aunt Anabel back to her chair, brushed past the duke, the viscount, and Mr. Sherbrook, and came to the ruins of the pianoforte, which was still reverberating with sound. She drew back her foot and kicked the side of it as hard as she could, so hard she was convinced she'd broken a toe. But it was worth it. She felt much better.

The pianoforte gasped its last, dying breath.

"I say, what did it ever do to you?" Mr. Sherbrook drawled.

Astrid snapped. She spun around and faced the rest of the room, dizzy with rage and exhaustion. Tears leaked out of the corner of her eyes. She couldn't help it. Her attention snapped to Montford, whose anger had faded, an unguarded, tender look taking its place. It was unbearable. "Satisfied?"

He stepped toward her. "Astrid . . ."

"I'm not going to London. I'm not doing a damned thing you say. Show the books to the authorities. Throw me in gaol. I don't care. Just get away from me. All of you."

"You are overwrought—" Montford said.

"Of course I'm overwrought, you idiot!" She picked up a fallen snuffbox and hurled it at him. "Go back to London, marry your . . . your *person* over there." She indicated a stunned and indignant Araminta by jabbing her finger toward the sofa. "I'm sure you are quite suited."

"No they're not," Sherbrook and the viscount interjected simultaneously.

She glared at them, daring them to say another word. They fidgeted under her scrutiny.

"Now, if you'll excuse me," she said, gathering herself up and striding toward the door. "I shall go be *overwrought* in some other location. I would not wish to offend you further."

Once she was clear of the room, she didn't stop running until she was outside.

Chapter Twenty-Five

La Chasse, La Capture, Et La Pompadour

MONTFORD ABANDONED the houseguests to pursue Astrid. He spotted red hair disappearing out the French doors in the parlor. He followed it outside, through the gardens, and into the stable yard. It was coming loose of its pins, flying over her shoulders like a banner in the wind. He could not see her face, but he knew from the way she stalked about in her boy's trousers, splashing through the puddles, her hands clenched at her sides—and the way the servants scurried out of her path, wide-eyed—that she was hopping mad.

So was he. Though if anyone asked him the reason, he couldn't have explained himself. He just knew that he was angry, and it had to do with the pig. And that horrible baroness. And Alice Honeywell and Sir Wesley, for leaving Astrid behind to deal with the consequences of their foolishness. And at himself for caring so much.

And more than ever, he was angry at Astrid, because *she* was angry at *him*. Or hurt. Or whatever it was that had made her so wretched to the Carlisle sisters. He had never made any promises or declarations to her. She had no right to act like such a . . . a . . .

Well, a ninny. A featherbrain along the lines of Araminta. What was *wrong* with her? "Astrid!" he called, tripping over a bucket, splattering mud all over his fresh breeches. Damn.

She didn't even turn. She quickened her stride and disappeared inside the stables. A few seconds later, Mick, Newcomb, and a few other hands scurried outside, glancing behind them as if being chased by the devil.

Newcomb nearly ran into Montford. He pulled his cap from his head and bowed deeply, pulling his companions down with him. "Your Grace! She's toward the back, sir, saddlin' up."

He paused and scowled at the lot of them. "That damnable pig is loose in the castle."

Newcomb grimaced. "Aye, saw Her Majesty's cattle out front."

"Not Lady Emily. Petunia," he growled out. "Now go help them sort it out before it brings the whole place down."

Newcomb and the others complied reluctantly.

Montford strode inside the stable, past his ruined carriage, and past several empty stalls until he came to one with the door opened. He stuck his head inside and saw Astrid heaving a saddle atop her mare, her trousers pulled taut over her rounded backside, her hair flowing down her back like a fiery, swirling river.

A bolt of lust ricocheted through his body, stopping him up short, nearly bringing him to his knees. He gripped the edge of the stall and fought for control, resharpening his anger. "Where do you think you're going?" he demanded roughly.

She pulled the straps through their buckles with jerky motions and caught his eyes over her shoulder. "Anywhere but here." She turned back to her work. "And I expect you and your *friends* to be gone when I return."

"You'll not be rid of me so easily. Besides, the castle is mine."

She spun around on him, trembling with her anger. "Fine. Then stay here. I hope you enjoy sharing it with Petunia."

She began to lead her mare out of the stall, but he stepped in the middle of the door, blocking her way. "You can't just leave. What of your sisters? Damn it, woman. Where are you going to go?"

"Just get out of my way," she retorted, grabbing up her crop leaning against a wall and brandishing it in his direction.

"You wouldn't dare strike me with that," he guffawed with more confidence than he felt.

"Wouldn't I? Get out of my way, or I shall be forced to make you get out of my way."

"But this is ridiculous. Your feelings are piqued—"

"You have no idea what my feelings are," she gritted out.

"You're jealous!" he cried, understanding her at last.

Her lips parted, and her eyes grew wide. "No, I am not!" she answered after an interminable moment.

He couldn't resist a small smile of satisfaction. "Yes, you are. You're jealous of Lady Araminta."

"Jealous! Of that empty-headed block of ice? No indeed."

"You are!"

She raised the crop higher. Her blue eye flashed ice. Her amber eye was filled with fire. "I am not jealous, you fool. I am angry with you for *touching* me, and at myself for letting you. You could have had more honor and told me you were to be married in a week."

"Would it have made any difference?"

She drew back as if he had slapped her. An assent was on the tip of her tongue, but she could not say it. Her face flamed, and she looked away from him. "What sort of question is that to ask?" she said instead.

It was an evasion, and they both knew it. Something resembling victory, but far sweeter and more frightening, blossomed inside of him, warming his bones. He knew with a certainty in that moment that Astrid felt the same unreasonable attraction for him as he did for her.

She would have allowed him to kiss her, to touch her, even if she had known. Would she still?

He should turn around and flee immediately. There was no good in him knowing the answer to that question.

Instead, he stepped farther in the stall. She backed away from him, still holding the crop in front of her in self-defense. He went around to the other side of the horse and began to remove the saddle, though his hands were shaking so much he could barely grip the leather.

"Stop it," she cried. Then she actually *did* use the crop, the minx. She brought it down across his back. He could feel its sting through the fine silk of his jacket, cutting it to shreds and digging into his flesh.

He hissed in his breath at the sting and turned to face her.

She had dropped the crop at her feet. Her hands covered her mouth, and her otherworldly eyes were wide and filled with tears. She backed toward the door.

"I didn't mean to . . ." she stammered, stepping over the threshold.

"Yes, you did," he said, leaving the horse in a state of confusion and following her out of the stall. The blow had startled him and caused him considerable pain. It had also had the rather perverse effect of stoking his lust for her. It was some sort of ugly illness, like a thirst for alcohol or an addiction to cards. He couldn't shake her from his system, and the worse she treated him, the more he craved her.

Good merciful heavens, he was done for. Because deep down he knew this was more than mere lust. When he looked at Astrid Honeywell, he knew he was looking at forever. *His* forever. And it was as frightening as it was wonderful.

"Well, you probably deserved it," she said, regaining a bit of her usual courage.

He grinned at her, which seemed to confound her further. Her brow furrowed, and she bit her bottom lip with her teeth and glanced around for a way out or something with which to defend herself. But the only exit to the stables was behind him.

"Stop looking at me like that," she demanded.

"Like what?" he asked mildly.

"Good God, Montford, I didn't hit you that hard! And you drove me to it. Can't you see I want to be left alone? If you haven't noticed, my life is in shambles. No thanks to you."

"I saved you from a madman."

She gave him a withering look. "I'm unconvinced you're any more sane than Lightfoot!"

"Of course I'm not!" he cried, spreading his arms. "Look what you've done to me! You've driven me insane!"

He stalked toward her, and she dodged behind a workbench littered with tacking. "You have a free will. I did not *force* you to anything. Perhaps you wanted to be ruffled up a bit. God knows you needed it, what with all of your preening and sorting," she said.

"Sorting!"

"Yes! I've seen Aunt Anabel's snuffboxes. And the library. You go mad when anything's not lined up or in order. You *are* mad. And so puffed up on your own importance you're likely to pop. I've never seen a man more in need of a good roll—" She broke off, her face scarlet, and skirted around the corner of the table, away from him.

"In need of what?" he prompted, though he knew precisely what she'd been about to say. "And how would *you* know anything about such things?"

She looked up at him, startled. "You've no idea what I was about to say."

"Oh, I think I do."

She drew herself up haughtily. "Well, that's what Flora says, and the rest of the servants, anyway. And from my own . . . experience, I would venture to say they are correct. Men seem to find . . . a certain measure of . . . *release* in the . . . act."

"Of *rolling*?" he persisted.

"You said you knew what I meant!"

"Oh, I know what you mean. And I think you're probably right." He cut her off before she could run past him, crossing his arms over his chest and spreading his legs wide. He towered over her. "Good thing I'm marrying in a week," he said.

She gave him a murderous look, took up a brush from the table, and hurled it at him. It hit his shoulder and sent him staggering back a few steps.

"Ouch!" he cried, rubbing his injury. "Is it really necessary to keep on doing such things?"

"You provoke me."

"I provoke *you*? Ha!" He came at her, arms extended. He would throttle her. Or kiss her. He hadn't decided which he wanted more.

"Leave me be, you lunatic!" she cried, hopping over a bench, trying to hide behind a stack of hay.

"I can't. Astrid, Araminta never meant anything to me. It was a business arrangement."

She scoffed at him. "Of course! I would expect no less from you! That is what you intended to do with me and my sisters. A business arrangement indeed! How cold you are."

"I am hardly the first to do so."

"Yes, I'm sure it is quite the fashion. And so is Araminta. Go on, off with you!" She threw a wrench at him. He dodged it. "Go back to London! Marry your *fine lady*. I hope you're miserable!"

She picked up a poker and came at him with it.

He laughed in outrage, but in case she was serious—which he didn't quite disbelieve—he backed up until he hit a wall. He yelped as his injured back touched the rough boards. Then she had the audacity to poke him in the stomach.

"Going to run me through, are you?" He couldn't help but grin at her. The situation was so absurd. "Really, Astrid! After all we've been through together," he said wryly.

She narrowed her eyes and pursed her lips. "Don't you dare! And stop smiling at me! What the devil has gotten into you?"

"You. You. *You.* Wretched creature, I don't know what you've done, and I don't like it. Sticking that book down your drawers! Harridan! Witch!"

He stepped forward. She backed away warily, her smile faltering.

"Those ungodly eyes of yours! And those horrible spots! They keep me up at night, wondering if they're everywhere."

"Don't say such things," she cried, her outstretched arm trembling.

He stepped forward again. "And your hair. God, your hair! It's intolerable! I should like to yank it from your head. It makes me crazy."

"Stop! Stop!" she murmured. "Don't come any nearer!"

He stepped forward again. The poker dropped from her hands. She raised her head, eyes wide, as he stopped a length from her, wanting with all of his soul to reach out to her. He lifted his hand and touched his fingers to the end of an errant curl.

Her eyes closed. She swayed on her feet.

He closed the distance between them, driven by some force outside of himself. At the last second, she evaded him and pulled the knot out of his cravat. He choked from the force of her gesture.

Looking well-satisfied, she edged around the bench again. "I'll not be your . . . your . . . plaything."

"I don't want a plaything."

She hefted a pile of hay above her head.

"And what are you going to do with that?" he demanded with a snort.

"This!" And she threw it at him. It bashed him in the head, hay flying everywhere, forcing its way up his nose and in his mouth. He managed to keep his feet, though his head spun. He spat out hay and wiped his nose. It itched abominably.

She made a dash for the entrance. He moved too quickly for her, however, and reached out to grab her. "I've had enough of this!"

She spun in the opposite direction, jumped over the bench, and headed for a ladder. She scrambled up into the hayloft above.

He ran to the bottom. "Come down, Astrid! Stop behaving like a child!"

"What, like *this*?" She began to pick up hay and throw it down at him.

He sneezed and his eyes began to water.

She laughed at him and dumped another load on his head.

He growled at her and started up the ladder while her back was turned to gather more hay. He was nearly to the top when she noticed his approach and took the slats of the ladder in her hands.

"Don't you dare!" he said in alarm, glancing down. He was fifteen feet from solid ground, at least. "Astrid, don't you—"

But it was too late. She'd pushed the ladder from the edge. He clung to the rails as the ladder balanced straight up on its legs. Astrid seemed to finally realize what she'd done. Her eyes widened in horror, and her face drained of color. She reached out for him, but he was too far away.

The ladder teetered for a moment, then began to tilt in the wrong direction.

"Oh God, Montford!" she shrieked. She nearly threw herself over the side in an effort to reach him.

He waved her back, his stomach sinking. "Stay back, or you'll fall!"

"*I'll* fall? Cyril!"

"Don't call me that!" he retorted. He managed to swivel his body around, catching the ledge of the loft with one hand, the wood splintering into his skin. He clung with all of his strength as the ladder tilted farther away. He reached out with his other hand and grasped the ledge as well, then pushed off with his feet, hefting his right arm up on the ledge, digging his fingers around the edge of a slat of wood. His legs dangled in midair as the ladder crashed to the floor below. He watched it land with a shudder.

Astrid dropped to his side and clung to his arm, her eyes filled with tears.

He was furious with her. "Get away from me, or you'll fall, too!"

"No, I'll not let go!"

"You're not strong enough. I'll drop down. If I gauge it right . . ."

She tugged on his arm. "No! It's too far. Come on, swing your leg up. I'll pull you back."

"Damn it, Astrid, let go!"

She shook her head, a stubborn expression passing over her face. He knew that look. A week in her company had taught him that there was no crossing her when such a look took up residence on her face.

"Foolish woman!" he seethed, clawing his way over the edge. She tugged his arm, falling to her backside and digging her heels into the planking. He swung his leg up and heaved his weight forward.

For a moment, he thought he'd failed. He listed precariously on the edge, but she seized his loosened cravat and jerked him forward. She cut off his air supply, but other than that the move was quite effective. He fell forward, right on top of her, knocking the air out of the both of them.

She was all soft, warm curves beneath him, her spiraling hair tickling his face. She smelled of lavender, horses, and hay. Only his near brush with death—or at the very least a good maiming—recalled his floundering senses. He lifted his head and peered over the edge of the loft.

It was a long way to the bottom.

She looked with him, grimacing.

"You nearly killed me!" he breathed. He swatted her hair away unsuccessfully. It floated back as if it couldn't resist torturing him. "Do you really hate me so much?"

Her features softened. The fight went out of her. "No, I don't hate you," she said in a quiet voice. "I want to, mind. I want to hate you." She shifted beneath him and brought her hand up to the side of his face. She squeezed her eyes shut and turned her head away. He watched her heartbeat flicker wildly against the delicate skin of her throat. "It would be so much easier. But I can't."

His own pulse pounded through his veins, but it was no longer on account of the danger he'd been in. He guided her hand down, over his waistcoat, and pressed it to his heart. It was beating frantically against his ribs, struggling to jump free of his body. "For you," he said thickly.

Her eyes opened wide, a mixture of fear and what he was certain was desire crowding her expression.

He could restrain himself no longer. He bent his head down and brushed his mouth over hers.

She sighed and for a moment went limp beneath him. Then in the next instant she sprang away from him, sliding back into the pile of hay behind her, trembling, her breath coming in gasps. Hay tangled through her fallen hair and drifted through the air between them, glinting in the sunlight that drifted in through the slats in the walls.

He had lost his mind to think this was the happiest moment of his life, but it was. He could think of no finer moment in all of his years than the present one, aching, disheveled, and up a hayloft with no way down, in the middle of bloody Yorkshire.

He came up on his knees and pulled off his cravat. Then he tore off his jacket and began on the buttons of his waistcoat. He yanked his arms free of that and fumbled with the ties of his lawn shirt.

Her eyes were as wide as saucers. "What do you think you're doing?"

"Seducing you. What does it look like?"

Her fingers tightened around clumps of hay, her jaw clenched. "Put your clothes back on."

"Make me," he said mildly, flicking the buttons at his sleeves.

"I'm warning you, I'll push you over the edge yet if you don't stop this nonsense."

"You could try."

She looked ready to do him murder. "I'll scream."

"No you won't."

She attempted to push herself farther into the hay, as if she could disappear into it. She shut her eyes, then almost immediately cracked one open to watch him. She couldn't seem to help herself.

He tugged the tails of his lawn shirt free and pulled it over his head. He held it in one hand for a moment, then let it fall away. She gasped. He knelt before her, naked from the waist up. Her eyes flicked over his body, her cheeks darkening with a fierce blush. She licked her lips and tried to speak. No sound came out.

He thought for one awful moment she would reject him, and he would be worse than humiliated. He didn't think he could survive if she did such a thing.

That night in the drawing room, when he had so lost his head and nearly taken her against a desk, he had pulled back out of fear. The power she could wield over him if he succumbed was unfathomable. Something about her—something beyond the physical—pulled at him, demanded its pound of flesh. He could not let her go, and only now he realized why.

She had already taken that part of him he feared, and he'd never have it back from her. He'd never be whole again without her.

No, that wasn't true. He'd never been whole to begin with, which was much, much worse. He'd found something in Astrid Honeywell, of all people on earth, that filled the emptiness inside, the hunger he'd always felt without even knowing it. It was terrifying and exhilarating, and he'd never understand it. He'd never understand *her*.

She raised her quixotic eyes to his own, and they were filled with resignation and something else that made his blood run south.

"This is so unfair," she murmured, and then she launched herself from the pile of hay and threw herself at him. She caught him off guard. She wrapped her arms and legs around him and kissed him of her own accord, clumsily, roughly, and without pretense. She stroked her arms down his aching back, and he cried out, setting her from him.

"Easy, for God's sake."

"Oh, I'll not make this easy for you, Montford," she said against his mouth.

He laughed hysterically. This was much better—and much worse—than he could have envisioned.

She smiled up at him wickedly. "Got more than you bargained for?"

"I never bargain. And I always get what I want."

"So do I," she countered. She tugged his head down and kissed him hard again. She attempted to retreat, but he caught her by the nape of the neck and held her in place. He took his time kissing her this round, exploring her with his tongue, willing her to kiss him back, though she shifted impatiently against him. But he would not be rushed. He wanted to savor every moment, but more than that, he wanted her to savor it as well. He'd *make* her savor it, damn her eyes.

"Montford," she murmured, her mouth opening beneath his, taking him inside. Her iron grip on his shoulders eased. She raised her hands to his face and stroked his cheeks with a tenderness that left him completely at sea.

She clung to him as he pressed her back into the hay, settling his weight between her legs. His hands moved down her body, over the swell of breasts and hips and thighs. She was soft and burning with heat. He buried his nose in her hair and inhaled her scent, drowning in it.

He fumbled with the buttons on her shirt, tore apart the fabric in the end. He stripped away the garment, exposing her naked flesh. He'd seen paintings of luxurious, fertile Renaissance Madonnas before.

Indeed, he collected such masterpieces and displayed them at one or other of his residences. He thought of them as he looked upon Astrid's naked body, and how they paled in comparison to her magnificent voluptuousness. She was creamy white, the freckles fading out at her shoulders, though he spied one or two in unusual places he intended to explore at length. Her stomach was rounded, like the rest of her lush body, and rising and falling with her haggard breath. Her breasts were full and rose-tipped, quivering. They hardened to points under his touch. He hardened as well. He wanted her so much he wasn't sure he could last another second.

He stopped thinking about the history of art at that point. He stopped thinking at all and knew only sensation, the itching need to join himself to this woman, the friction of their skin, the pant of their breaths growing faster, louder with every intake of air. His world was reduced to a pair of lush female breasts, undulating with the nervous rise and fall of her chest. Breasts that had tormented him for what felt like eons.

He lowered his head and took one of those glorious peaks in his mouth. She arched beneath him and moaned. "What are you doing?" she cried.

He didn't answer her absurd question. He cupped her other breast in his hand as he continued to suckle her, squeezing the fullness between his fingers, a groan escaping from deep inside his body. Her skin was salty and lavender-scented, and softer than silk. He wanted to sink into her and never surface again. He shifted his head to the other breast, flicking her nipple with his tongue, and she dug her hands into his hair, pulling him closer.

His hand left her breast and traveled down her stomach, to the fall of her trousers. He jerked the buttons free and slipped a hand inside, feeling the crinkle of hair and the soft, dewy warmth between her legs. She was already aroused. She pushed against his hand urgently, instinctively, nearly unmanning him. He tried to pull back, to do something to rein himself in, but he was adrift in a sea of lust so fierce he feared he would drown. It had *never* been like this before, so unreasonable.

"Oh God, Astrid. Astrid, I am lost," he murmured.

She tugged his hair, but the sting of the gesture did nothing to dampen his ardor. His fingers stroked her, and she arched against him like some feral creature. "For God's sake, Montford . . . please! Please do something! It is unbearable," she hissed. Her hand came down over the front of his breeches, cupping the length of him. "Tell me what to do," she cried.

This got his attention.

Things were moving too fast, he decided in a burst of clarity. He'd not let her drive him to spill himself as he'd done upon that blasted horse. He had some amount of self-respect left. No, he planned to be buried inside of her, with her screaming his name, when he came again.

Sooner, rather than later. He threw her hand away before he exploded and jerked her trousers down her legs. He managed to get one of her feet free before he made the mistake of looking down at her.

Sweet, merciful God in heaven. He was a believer now.

She had red hair. *Everywhere.*

She stared at him urgently, confusedly, seeing the pain in his expression. "What are you doing now?" she asked with a touch of worry in her voice.

He couldn't speak. He groaned, then pushed her legs apart and lowered his head, claiming her with his mouth.

She stiffened underneath him, not understanding, until his tongue tasted her. "Oh, good Lord!" she groaned, melting.

She tasted salty-sweet, her flesh smooth and slick. Her red corkscrew hair, heavy with her scent, tickled his nose and drove him to the brink. He felt her begin to fall apart, her body trembling, her fingers wrenching his hair. He broke away from her with effort, some cruel part of him enjoying tormenting her. And he wanted to see her face. He *needed* to. He came over her body.

She stared at him, wild-eyed, her cheeks pink, and his heart flipped over. "What have you done?" she breathed.

She asked far too many questions.

"Kiss you?" he offered. He brought his lips down upon hers, letting her taste what he had. He kissed her and kissed her until they were both insensible. "I could kiss you. Everywhere."

"So it would seem," she managed.

"You are *red*," he said, sliding his hand back between her thighs, staring down at her in wonder.

"Stop being an idiot!" she cried, burying her head in the crook of his neck, clinging to him. She was mortified, he realized. And he liked it. He liked it even more when she bit his shoulder hard, reached down of her own accord, and undid the buttons of his breeches. She glanced down between their bodies, and it was her turn for her eyes to widen at the sight of his cock. She touched the tip of him tentatively.

He laughed wildly, and then he groaned as her hand closed around him. "Don't," he warned, his voice strangling.

"Why?" she asked with an innocent expression. "Don't you like it?"

"You're going to kill me yet," he gritted out.

"I told you, I'll not make this easy for you," she said.

He captured her hands above her head and lowered himself so they were flesh to flesh. "Stop talking," he commanded, before kissing her senseless once more. His hands ran down her side, molding her flesh, curving over her backside, pulling her up to him, until no air was left between them.

She wrapped her soft, rounded body around him without any instruction, opening herself up to him, like a flower to the sun. She was radiating heat, damp, sweet. His heart thundered, his body shuddered, and his skin broke out in a cold sweat as he guided himself inside of her. He tried to go slow, but she wouldn't let him. She was frightening in her ardor. She rose up to meet him, and he slid all the way inside of her almost by accident.

"Damn it, Astrid," he breathed, clenching his teeth.

He felt her gasp of pain against his throat, and her fingers dug into the flesh of his back as she tried to absorb the shock. He was relieved and ashamed all at once. And so caught up in his lust that nothing else mattered but finishing what he'd started. She was so hot, so tight. It was killing him to remain still.

"Is that it?" she asked, startling him out of his trance.

He raised himself on his elbows and studied her face. The face of a minx. She was smiling gently, relaxing around him, and his heart responded, though he couldn't find words. He shook his head and moved his hips, just a fraction, to test her response. Her smile faded, replaced by a look of startled wonder. "Oh!" He moved again because he couldn't contain himself. "Oh, *Cyril!*"

Really, she was quite merciless. What a time to call him by his given name! It was . . . rather lovely. Horrible, but lovely. And it made him want her even more earnestly, if that were possible. When she began to rise up, meeting his thrusts, he lost all semblance of control. He groaned. She was in all of his senses, pulling him under until he hardly could distinguish where his body ended and hers began. He didn't want to know. He didn't want to stop. He'd never felt this way before, so tangled up in another person, body and spirit. He squeezed her hips, pulling her up to him, and stroked into her frantically, over and over again, frightened at the intensity of his emotions, his body's helpless surrender.

He felt her tip over the edge, her body trembling, her voice crying out against his ear. He thrust harder, longer, feeling so close, and filled with trepidation, the way a climber must feel at the summit of a mountaintop, the atmosphere thin, coherent thought impossible.

She seemed to pull him farther into her, dislodging something that could never be put back. He came in a torrent of white heat and raging emotions. His body convulsed into hers, and he gripped her hips between his fingers so hard he was sure to bruise her. And even though he was quite done, he stayed within her, thrusting upward, chasing the ecstasy that still had his limbs quaking and his blood thrumming. He had never felt so blissfully alive. Nor so terrified.

It was too much.

He wanted more. Even as he slumped against her, exhausted, sweat-soaked, and utterly squeezed dry, he wanted more. And more and more. He would always want more, and he would always want her.

He rolled onto his side and pulled her with him because he could not be parted from her. She had no words left, and she let him hold her, for once doing precisely as he wished. He kissed the top of her head and tried to catch his breath as he formulated a plan to keep her forever.

Mine, mine.

He was going to marry Astrid Honeywell.

The thought was as unsettling—and as spectacularly brilliant—as her eyes.

＊ ▬◆▬ ＊

MOST OF Miss Anabel Honeywell's far-fetched tales were fabricated, though a couple of the more outlandish ones were true. She had, in truth, actually been at the court of Versailles, and had, in truth, actually sailed the seas with a genuine pirate years before the Revolution. She had been a hoyden in her youth, and a skilled lover in her prime. She had taken a number of *cher ami* into her bed on the condition they take her on their adventures.

The Yorkshire countryside of her birth had been quite dull for someone with her appetites and intelligence, and to escape a proper marriage with a proper gentleman who loved his hounds more than her, she had run away at sixteen with the handsome butcher's son. It was a bad decision, for she had soon discovered that he had loved cards more than her. He had lost her in a roll of dice in a gambling palace in London to a scurrilous pirate, for which she was profoundly grateful.

She'd liked her scurrilous pirate. Until she discovered he liked the sea more than her. A bounder of a French aristocrat had picked her up in Marseilles, where she had washed ashore, and introduced her to the bawdy Bourbon court, in which she had thrived on petty intrigue and decadence until the peasantry began chopping off heads. Her French aristocrat's had rolled in the first round.

Life back at Rylestone Green was quiet by comparison, but occasionally it could be quite interesting indeed. It had not been in the least boring since the young duke had come to call. He was a bit stiff, and a total idiot, but then most men were. He'd taken it into his thick head to manage them all, and had yet to catch on that *he* was the one being managed. Anabel had little doubt that her eldest niece could have him eating out of her hand. But the girl was a bit of an idiot herself. She had no conception of men and their foolishness, and if she wasn't careful, she'd have them all on the streets before she came to her senses.

Anabel intended to help things along. She had learned her craft well. One always got rid of the hard evidence first, to level the battle-field. It had taken some time poking about the duke's possessions before she located the book. It was at the bottom of a chest packed full of cravats. She liked a man who knew how to dress, but a hundred cravats for a jaunt to Yorkshire seemed to be a bit excessive, even for a duke.

A strange calm had descended over the castle premises as she made her way down the corridor toward her private chambers near the north tower. Those two young bucks of Montford's seemed to have managed to get the pig in hand at last. It appeared they *could* do more than drink other people's port. Not that she was complaining. The thin, continental-looking one with the devilish smile could drink all of their port and be as useless as he pleased, as far as she was concerned. It was a pleasant change to have someone like *that* to look at. If she were forty years younger, she'd make sure he looked at her as well and had plenty to occupy his energies besides a bottle.

She hated being old.

She turned into her boudoir and shut the door behind her with her cane. She crept over to the fireplace, where the coals were still smoldering from the morning fire, and she stirred them up with a poker until a flame caught. She added a few more coals for good measure, until a nice fire was burning, then retrieved her contraband from the folds of her gown. She tossed the estate ledger onto the flames. It struck the coals in the center, then bounced off to one side.

"Damn and blast," she muttered. She took her cane and attempted to reposition the book. It fell off behind the fire, and she sighed in irritation and bent down, her old bones creaking.

When had it become so difficult to burn a book?

She reached her hand around the fire and tried to grab the recalcitrant volume, but it was too far away. She reached farther in, caught the edge of a page, and tried to drag it out. The page tore and she cursed again.

Something began to smolder, the stink of singed hair burning the back of her nose. It took her several moments to realize her favorite wig had caught fire. She jumped to her feet—or she would have jumped if she could—and knocked the wig off of her head. It rolled onto the carpet at her feet, and it was more than smoldering. It was a ball of fire.

"Oh, dear," she muttered, attempting to beat out the flames with her cane.

This made the situation worse. Pieces of burning hair floated in the air, landing on the carpet and setting it on fire. Quite by accident, the end of her cane caught the underside of the wig, and as she brought up the cane, she brought up the wig as well, sending it flying across the room. It landed on the draperies covering the windows. The fire spread up them at lightning speed.

In less than a minute, her boudoir was flickering with flame and filling with smoke.

"Oh, *hell!*" she muttered, backing toward the door. She had liked that wig.

And despite her youthful rebellions, she rather liked the castle. Astrid was not going to thank her for this one.

⊷·⊷ ⚔⊹☰ ⊷·⊷

"OH HELL," Astrid muttered, attempting to roll away from the duke and pull the edges of her shirt together. It was a bit cold, for one. For another, the hay was scratchy and poking her in places hay had no right to poke. She wondered that barns and stables were such popular places for seductions. It seemed maids and swains were always getting into mischief in them, as if dead straw piled in a room decorated with livestock and riding equipment was in some way romantic. It wasn't.

Well, perhaps it was a little, she conceded, glancing reluctantly next to her, where Montford lay, looking astounded, his eyes sightless, his extraordinary body still shuddering from what had occurred.

But it was damned uncomfortable.

Montford seemed to agree on this point, for he shifted restlessly, reached behind him, and pulled out what looked to be a tree root from the hay. He tossed it aside and turned his head in her direction and watched her attempt to refasten the buttons on her shirt. His eyes were opaque, molten silver. They seemed to cut directly to the center of her heart and attempt to extract her soul. Those eyes wanted everything of her. Even her body had not been enough, and already that was too much to have given.

She could not regret it. Some things were inevitable. But she could wish she'd never met him. She could wish he'd not taken off his clothes like some brazen tart. She could wish *it* had been a disappointment. She could wish *it* had not felt so perfect and astonishing she would never be the same. For then she could regret it and walk away laughing at them both. She could not laugh now.

He reached out and undid the work she'd just accomplished, his hand brushing over her breasts, drawing a response from her body that was alarming. She was embarrassed by how much she wanted him again. Already. She could not be natural. *This* could not be natural.

She turned on her side. He turned her back toward him and climbed on top of her. He kissed her, his rough beard scraping her cheeks. The weight of his body pressed her into the hay, which chafed and itched at her backside. She was only distantly aware of it anymore, because he was touching her again and doing things to her body she was sure were illegal.

She willed herself not to throw herself into the wild fever that had gripped her the last time. She averted her head so that his kiss landed on her ear. "I think we must stop," she said.

He didn't seem to hear her. He set about making love to her ear.

"Cyril!" she hissed, reluctantly pushing him away.

"I told you, don't call me that," he murmured, tweaking one of her breasts with his fingers.

She yelped in shock and renewed desire. Damn. He was good. "Get off me, you oaf," she cried, punching his shoulder.

He sat back on his heels and glared at her.

She blushed at the sight she must present, sprawled out before him, tangled in her mangled clothes. She felt like a mound of quivering jelly, all bulges and odd angles. She picked a piece of hay out of her mouth and tried to shift her hips for some semblance of modesty. Though it was rather too late for that, she supposed.

He held her legs in place, his glare fading, his molten glance pouring over her body, lingering on the one place she would have rather he didn't see at the moment. He seemed to be fascinated by it, and it was titillating and mortifying all at once. What was so fascinating? Her hair was red. He'd complained about it often enough to leave no doubt that he knew its color. Did he expect it to be different on the rest of her? Blue, perhaps, or striped?

She glanced down at his lap, though she probably should have restrained herself. His breeches were halfway down his hips, and his . . .

his Male Part was as exposed as she was. It was bigger than she would have thought, and at the moment, it seemed quite eager to further their acquaintance. A bubble of pure heat sparked in her belly, and a shiver of apprehension went through her. She didn't see how he had fit the first time. She was certain he would not fit again.

His hand splayed over her stomach, and his expression softened, as if he had read her mind. A flush stained his cheeks, the bridge of his nose. He rose on his knees and pulled his breeches up, fastening them, a look of extreme discomfort flickering over his features.

To her embarrassment, he helped her legs back into her trousers and pulled them up her body. She swatted his hands away and buttoned them herself. She kicked him away and sat up, pulling her shirt around her. She was shivering. He reached out to her, but she shied away, climbing onto unsteady feet. He watched her tuck in her shirt and attempt to tame her hair behind her ears.

"Oh, stop gawking at me," she snapped. She wanted no tenderness. She crouched down, retrieved his shirt and waistcoat, and hurled them at his head.

He stood up, swaying slightly as if drunk, and began to dress in silence. She resisted the urge to go to him and pick the straw out of his disheveled hair. Instead, she slumped back down into the hay and buried her face in her hands. She was aware of him moving about, of him kneeling down next to her. He gathered a clump of her fallen hair in his hands and held on to it.

Her heart was breaking. "I'll not be your whore," she bit out.

"No," he agreed.

"This cannot happen again. This is utter madness."

"*No.*" The fierceness of his voice sent fire through her loins and rage and despair through her heart. She had no idea what he meant, but she recognized that tone. She should jump to the ground floor. She should do anything but let him take her again.

Which was what he intended, despite having taken the trouble to have dressed. He gathered her up in his arms and kissed her until her head swam, and before she knew it, she was in the hay again, tumbling about with him, tugging at his clothes. She was mad. Completely cracked in the head to give in to her desires.

He clutched at her breasts and nuzzled her neck, groaning, kicking her legs apart. He ground his hips against hers, and she gasped and pulled him closer. He was so warm and hard and big and overwhelming. He could make her do anything, and the realization was terrifying. It was unfair that she should love him, while he felt no more than an animal need for her.

And she *did* love him. Stupid child that he was.

She would have ripped off his clothes again, but then she became aware of footsteps beneath them and voices raised in alarm. Montford lifted his head from her breast in a daze when he heard his name being called.

He rolled off of her with utter reluctance and began straightening his clothes.

"Your Grace! Where are you?"

It was his driver, Newcomb.

Montford groaned, crawled over to the edge of the loft, and peered down. "What the devil do you want?"

"Is Miss Honeywell with you?" the man inquired in a harried voice.

"No," Montford replied, affronted.

Astrid wanted to vanish into the hay in mortification.

"You sure, Your Grace? For it would be better if she were! Not that I'll notice if she *is*, mind!"

"What are you blathering on about?" Montford demanded.

"If she ain't with you, then she might be in the castle!"

"Yes, that's where she is," Montford said quickly.

"Then we're in a heap of shite, because the castle is on fire!"

Astrid leapt to her feet. "What?" she cried, coming to the edge, modesty bedamned.

Newcomb had the good manners to avert his eyes. "The castle's up in flames! Don't tell me you've not noticed!"

Astrid ran to the nearest window and looked out, her pulse leaping, her stomach sinking. A chaotic horde of people milled about the yard and gardens staring helplessly up at the flames and smoke that leapt out of every available opening in the old structure.

Montford came up behind her. "Hell and the devil!" he muttered. "What next?"

Chapter Twenty-Six

In Which All Hell Breaks Loose. Again.

SEBASTIAN SHERBROOK rounded the edge of the castle, his eyes burning with the cinders floating through the air, his lungs clogged with smoke. He found Marlowe, grimly puffing his cheroot and bellowing out orders to a line of servants throwing buckets of water from the stable well through the windows of the castle, to little effect. If the pile of rocks could be saved, Marlowe would find a way. Though the chances were slim from where Sebastian stood. The castle was an inferno.

Sebastian had been slightly tipsy before the incident with the pig. Now he was stone sober, and his skin was prickling with dread. He couldn't find Montford, and he feared his friend was trapped inside. Sebastian didn't know what he'd do without the old bugger. Montford meant as much to him as Marlowe. He'd be lost without him.

He was growing sentimental, which was a very bad sign.

The two urchins who had unleashed the pig on them came running around the corner, nearly knocking him from his feet. Their strange garments and faces were blackened with ash, making their terrified eyes look enormous. Marlowe moved quickly to intercept them, grabbing their robes and giving them his sternest stare. The viscount had two hellions of his own and knew how to handle them. "You two pests stay put."

"We can't find our sister!" one of them sobbed. Tears streaked the ash on their faces.

Marlowe patted their heads. "Don't worry. She'll be found." He glanced at Sebastian, his expression belying his encouraging words.

Sebastian shook his head. He'd seen no sign of Miss Honeywell either.

Or Lady Katherine, for that matter. But he'd not become hysterical over *her*.

He glanced around him. Araminta was over by an old crumbling stone wall, awkwardly comforting the old lady in the ancient dress, her wig now nowhere in sight. He started over to them. "Where is your sister?" he demanded of Araminta.

The girl lifted a trembling hand and pointed toward the castle.

His heart sank as he followed her gesture. Lady Katherine *was* still inside? He broke into a cold sweat, and his nails dug into his palms. He told himself he'd feel the same for anyone stupid enough to get caught in a burning building.

But then he spotted her tall, elegant form among a cluster of farm hands. Her sleeves were rolled up her slender arms, and dark splotches of soot covered her dress. She hauled a bucket across the yard and passed it off to one of the men. Then she brushed her fallen gossamer hair off her face and marched toward one of the castle doors.

His relief was short-lived. What in hell's name did she think she was doing?

He rushed across the yard, and without thinking he grabbed her by the arm. He hated touching people, but he only remembered this after she'd turned to him, her fine emerald eyes wide, a slash of ash running down the length of her arrogant patrician nose.

"What the devil do you think you're doing?" he demanded, translating his wild thoughts verbatim. "Do you want to get yourself killed?"

Her serene face betrayed nothing but slight surprise, but he could see the flare of fire flash through her eyes. He felt a measure of gratification in ruffling her feathers, however slightly. "No. But the pig is still inside. You locked him in the kitchen. I thought I might . . ." She trailed off and looked away from him, her mouth tightening. "I thought I might save him."

"You're going to risk your life for a pig! I should be amused if it weren't so damnably stupid!"

Her back stiffened. When she gathered herself to her full height, she was not but an inch or two below him, which was most off-putting for a female. She stared at him contemptuously. "It is not stupid to feel compassion, Mr. Sherbrook. Even for a . . . a pig."

This was the most absurd argument he'd ever had. He just gaped at her.

She sniffed and swished her skirts, moving around him, heading toward the kitchens once more.

He stepped in front of her. "You shall do it only to vex me!"

She stared beyond him. "I assure you I do not regard you enough one way or another to wish to vex you."

Ouch. That would have hurt if he regarded *her* one way or another. But he didn't. She meant nothing to him, other than as a fellow human bent on an idiotic folly.

"Nor do you have any authority over me, so I suggest you move aside," she added. She had her chin lifted haughtily, a stubborn gleam in her eyes. She met his gaze nearly at eye level, refusing to back down.

She attempted to move around him, but he stepped in front of her. She moved the other way, and he moved with her.

"You'll not do it," he said.

She clenched her hands into fists. "It is the principle of the thing."

"I hate it when people start speaking of principles. It is ever so tiresome," he drawled.

Her shoulders stiffened even more. He watched a mote of ash land on a strand of hair falling down her neck, black on white. He itched to reach out and brush the ash away. But he did not. He dared not.

"It is a living creature. It does not deserve to suffer any more than we do," she said softly.

"Everything living suffers, and most things die suffering. In pain or hunger or outrage."

She looked back at him, a mixture of frustration and something that looked very much like pity in her eyes. He hated her even more for it. "Do you really believe that?" she asked.

He rolled his eyes. "Of course. And if you do not, you're naïve. There is nothing pleasant about death, and rarely anything pleasant about living. But that is a digression. The pig was probably destined for slaughter soon enough. Perhaps we'll find him later, nice and smoked and juicy, ready for a feast."

"You are despicable." She paused. "I want that pig for a pet, not for the table."

"You can't have a creature like that for a pet."

"I can, and I will," she averred with steel in her tone.

"Oh, for pity's sake," he said, throwing up his hands. She was not going to give this up. "I'll go," he said, regretting the words as soon as they were out of his mouth. He lowered his hand and spun around. "Stubborn woman," he grumbled, stalking toward the kitchen door, which was smoking out of the top and bottom.

He'd not have her dying on him over a pig. He didn't like her—how

could he like a woman who threw in her lot with a man like his uncle?—
but he was not entirely a scoundrel. His honor as a gentleman forbade
him from letting her perform suttee like some Hindu fanatic—and all
over a pig. Though he'd not been honorable or a gentleman in any useful way for years. And he probably wouldn't be for much longer, considering the flames shooting out of the upper stories above him.

But he had no real fear of death. He would prefer it not be entirely
painful, of course—being burned alive was *not* the way he would have
chosen to go—but if it had to be now, then that would be fine by him.
He would be sorry to distress Marlowe and Montford, for those two
were the only ones besides his valet who'd miss him, but they'd understand. He'd never expected to last this long anyway. None of them had.

Besides, there would be a certain ironic humor in having died during the rescue of a male pig named Petunia. He hoped the tale was
inscribed on his tombstone.

—◄ ⬥ ►—

LADY KATHERINE had never truly intended to go after the pig. She'd
considered it for a split second before throwing out the idea as nonsensi-
cal folly, but then Sebastian Sherbrook had intercepted her, bullied her,
and so provoked her to anger it would have taken an entire regiment
aiming muskets at her head before she would have backed down. She
had realized about halfway through their argument that at the end of
it she'd be marching into a burning castle and nearly kicked herself for
digging in her heels. The rogue was certainly not worth it.

But before she could say another word, he was stalking toward the
castle himself. He didn't even hesitate as he slammed in the door with
a long leg and charged inside, which showed a worrying disregard for
his own person.

She bit her bottom lip and watched the door that he had entered,
her worry turning to full-fledged panic as the minutes passed and he

did not emerge. He couldn't die, because she would blame herself for the rest of her life, and that would be *most* unfair of him.

"Where the devil is Sebastian?" the viscount demanded, loping up to her side in his strange attire, bedraggled and drenched, a damp cheroot hanging from his mouth. She'd not expected Marlowe, of all people, to have organized the servants and raised the alarm. It was most heroic of him, if a bit useless. The castle was so clearly lost.

"He went inside." She pointed toward the kitchen door, which had fallen off its hinges.

The viscount threw his cheroot down to the ground, his face paling. "What?"

"He's gone inside to fetch the pig."

"The devil you say!"

She winced. Marlowe started forward, then stopped. His face creased in anguish as he turned back to her. "What have you done? You put him up to it, didn't you?"

She squared her shoulders and raised her chin. "I did no such thing. He rushed off before I could stop him." It was not entirely the truth, but it was close enough.

"You've no idea what you've done! He has no regard for himself. He'll walk straight into the flames if you let him."

"Surely not!" she scoffed, rather startled by the fierceness of his tone.

"He is not right!" Marlowe cried. He pointed to his brainbox as if to illustrate his point.

"Whatever do you mean?"

Marlowe looked as if he wanted to shake her or worse, but with a jerk, he turned away from her, growling like a bear, and started toward the kitchen door. She followed after him, truly panicking now. Even Marlowe, the most feckless man in England, was concerned over Sherbrook's lack of judgment. That was *not* a good sign.

They both stopped in their tracks as the doorway in front of them collapsed, flames leaping from the fog of smoke and dust. Marlowe cried out. So did she. She'd killed the Singlemost Beautiful Man in London! Her heart sank to her toes, and moisture burned her eyes.

But then a now familiar sound captured her attention behind her: the high-pitched squeal of a pig throwing a tantrum. She turned with Marlowe to find Mr. Sherbrook sprinting through the garden, leaping over a wall in order to evade the pig, which barreled after him, intent on murder. He was coated in ash from top to toe, coughing into his handkerchief, the only splash of color left to him his piercing blue eyes. They gleamed like jewels in their new ebony setting.

He waved to them and flashed a grin in their direction, his teeth blinding white. "Got your damned pig. Hope you're happy."

She heard Marlowe sigh in relief. "Bloody damn fool," he muttered, fumbling inside his robe for his cheroot tin. He extracted one from the tin, went over to the collapsed doorway, and lit it in the smoldering embers, grumbling to himself.

Katherine had to go and take a seat next to her sister, her nerves shot.

But the drama was far from over. She spotted Astrid Honeywell running toward them in her scandalous trousers, her shirt gaping open at the top. Her fiery hair was speckled with straw and streaming down her shoulders. She looked, in short, as if she had been rolling in a haystack.

Katherine had thought it only a metaphor—surely the chit hadn't *truly* been rolling around in a haystack—but then she saw the Duke of Montford trailing behind her. He was missing his jacket, and the ends of his lawn shirt were tucked out of his breeches. His waistcoat had been buttoned up unevenly, and his hair was standing up on end. He was also covered in straw.

It did not take much brainpower to deduct that those two had been rolling around in a haystack *together*. Which was scandalous. And very interesting.

Things had, apparently, not ended well between the lovers, however, for when Montford attempted to comfort Miss Honeywell, the chit jerked her arm away and kicked him in the shin. Then she turned her attention back to the castle, falling to her knees in the muck, looking devastated.

The duke looked equally devastated, but he was staring at Miss Honeywell, not the castle.

For some unfathomable reason, Katherine found herself glancing at Mr. Sherbrook, who'd made his way to her side with no sign of a pig in pursuit. He was wiping the soot off his face with a lacy handkerchief, to little effect. When the resources of that bit of fabric were exhausted, Katherine offered him her handkerchief.

After a moment's hesitation, he took it.

There was nothing to smile about, but she found herself giving him a wry grin. She couldn't help herself. "Is your life always like this?"

His eyes went wide. The barest ghost of a smile twisted his beautiful, ash-coated lips, but he didn't look at her. "Disastrous? Of course."

"I thought so."

⊶ ⬩⧓⬩ ⊷

"I THINK it's burning out," Flora said, half an hour later, touching Astrid's shoulder, her face grim and worried. Astrid had been sitting in the mud, watching the castle burn, oblivious to the rest of the world. Oblivious to him.

Montford stood behind, watching Astrid and feeling helpless. He could offer her no comfort, nor do anything to stop the fire. He suspected she would end up blaming him for everything.

"It hardly matters now," Astrid murmured. "There's nothing left."

"The castle's walls are still standing . . . somewhat," Montford said dubiously. "We can renovate it."

Astrid didn't even look up at him. She picked up a clump of mud and lobbed it at his knees.

She was mourning the loss of her home, he told himself. He would *not* be angry.

He heard the sound of a carriage rolling up behind them. He turned and groaned. It was the baroness's barouche. She'd returned. With the stuttering vicar. Oh, this was all they needed.

The vicar gaped at the smoking castle as he descended the barouche. Lady Emily eyed the ruin through her quizzing glass. She was looking smug, and Montford had the urge to plant her a facer, female or not.

She turned her quizzing glass on him. He scowled blackly at her, and her smug smile faded.

"Oh, d-d-dear h-h-hea-heavens!" the vicar cried, rushing to Astrid's side, helping her to her feet with Flora's assistance.

Astrid looked pale and weak and utterly forlorn, and Montford's heart cried out. He wanted to go to her, comfort her, take her in his arms and make all of this go away, but he knew she would never allow it.

"What happened here?" Lady Emily demanded as she descended from the barouche. "What has she done now?"

Sebastian and Marlowe stepped forward, inserting themselves between Montford and the old bag, as if sensing how close he was to murder.

"How nice of you to return, madam," Sebastian said charmingly, his smile all the more potent from the soot dusting his skin. "We need extra hands hauling buckets. You look a stout sort, madam. I'm sure you won't mind."

Lady Emily sniffed contemptuously at Sherbrook's needling and turned her attention to Astrid. "I knew one day something of the sort would happen. You are careless, gel. Don't expect *me* to pick up the pieces of this latest disaster. It is justice, as far as I'm concerned, for leading my boy to ruin."

"M-m-my l-l-lady! P-p-p-please reconsider your h-h-harsh words!" the vicar exhorted.

"Yes, do stop acting an ass," Sebastian drawled. "Before my friend here calls you out."

Lady Emily was outraged. "*Really!*"

Sebastian turned to Montford. "Shall I stand second for you, old boy?"

"I'm obliged, but no. Should I feel the need, I'll inform you." He continued to glare at Lady Emily. She had the good sense to back up a few paces, out of his reach. "If you speak one more unkind word against Miss Honeywell, I shall put you in the stocks. Do I make myself clear?"

"You have a great deal of concern for my niece," she said, studying the hay on his person through her quizzing glass.

"You take *no* concern. I suppose you won't wish to receive her any longer after this."

"Certainly not. It is plain to anyone with eyes what you and she have been up to. No one of good breeding could *possibly* receive her now."

"I am glad to hear your decision. Of course you must understand, under such circumstances, that *we* shall not be able to receive *you*. No one with such a low opinion of my wife shall be welcome under my roof!" he said with all of his most chilling ducal austerity.

It took a moment for his words to sink in. Lady Emily's quizzing glass dropped from her eye, and her jaw went slack.

Astrid pushed her way free from her helpers and stalked forward, trembling with rage. "I . . . I am not marrying you!" she hissed.

"Yes you are."

"No I'm not!" She thrust her hand in the direction of Araminta, who was standing next to her sister, rumpled and distraught. "*She's* marrying you. In a week."

The marchioness patted her sister's arm and gave them all a serene smile. "I'm sure some arrangement can be reached. In fact, now that you mention the subject, Montford, it is one of the purposes of our visit. Well, tell them, Minta, for heaven's sake."

Araminta's mouth worked, but no sound came out. The events of the last few hours had struck her dumb, apparently. Montford squinted at her, wondering what he had been thinking to have engaged himself to such a . . . *boring* specimen.

The marchioness rolled her eyes when Araminta remained speechless beside her and barreled on herself. "My sister does not wish to marry you, Montford. She never did. She is running away with a Mr. Morton. You don't know him, but he fancies himself a poet and is quite the romantic. He's wooed my sister with his verses quite effectively. I am told poetry is a fine way into a lady's affections. It seems to work much better than ordering them about and telling them what they are going to do without waiting for their agreement." She gave him an arch look and glanced Astrid's way as if to emphasize her point. Canny woman. "I am sure Minta shall be quite happy with Mr. Morton. He is not quite as rich as you, but then who is? Have you any objections?"

Montford shook his head mutely.

Marlowe chortled, another cheroot plummeting to its hasty demise. "By gad, that's what I call a coup. Why didn't you just say so in the first place, Lady K? Wouldn't've been so churlish to you about you coming up here, would we, eh, Sherry?"

Sebastian just stared at his step-aunt with an inscrutable expression.

"Araminta, is this true?" Montford demanded.

The chit finally found her voice. "Er . . . yes. Quite. It was Father's idea for us to wed. But I'd rather not. Though I'd like to be a duchess, I think having a husband who loves me shall be much better. At least, that is what Katie says. She's usually right."

The marchioness nodded and patted her sister's arm. "Of course I'm right, dear."

Astrid snorted. "Well, this changes nothing. I'm still not marrying you." She gestured toward the castle. "Look at what you've done!"

He'd known it was coming. "Me?" he cried. "I did not burn the damned castle down!"

"You kept me away, when I might have done something."

"That is the most absurd reasoning I've ever heard," he said contemptuously.

"Well, it's all your fault. Somehow," she returned.

They stared each other down, oblivious to the discomfort of their companions.

The vicar broke the silence by gasping and gesturing wildly toward the castle. He tried to force some words out, but his mouth could not reach past the first syllable.

Everyone swiveled toward the castle, and Marlowe and Sebastian began cursing indiscriminately. So did Montford. The north tower, already on its last legs, had succumbed at last to gravity, one stone followed by another tumbling down onto the castle keep. The impact sounded like cannon blasts, sending puffs of smoke and debris up into the sky.

The falling stones ceased, and for a moment all was quiet. They breathed a collective sigh of relief. But then a great groaning sound rent the air, like the bellow of a newly awakened dragon. The tower began to stagger about, then pitched over in a dead faint, right into the center of the castle.

Montford stopped his ears against the terrible sound. The ground beneath them quaked as the entire castle collapsed in on itself in a chaos of fire, smoke, splitting oak, and rubble.

Araminta fainted. The marchioness rolled her eyes and bent over her sister, fanning her face.

Marlowe's new cheroot dropped, unlit, to the ground.

Astrid looked at him briefly, her mismatched eyes filled with shock . . . and desolation. Damned pile of rocks. She cared more for that bloody castle than for him.

Not that he could blame her, precisely. He'd behaved like a total arse from the moment he'd clamped eyes on her, rutting around in a muddy garden with a pig.

His heart ached. It was as if a surgeon had cut him open, sliced off a piece of it, then sewn him back up and expected him to muck on. He couldn't muck on. Not without Astrid. She owned that piece of his heart.

He breathed out at last, but it was a hoarse, ragged sound, as he waited on tenterhooks for what she would do next.

But as usual, it was nothing he could have predicted. She began to laugh, her cheeks pinkening and her eyes overflowing with tears. She laughed so hard her body shook all over, until she was forced to lean against his chest for support. He didn't mind it one bit, enjoying the feel of her in his arms once more and relieved she'd not resorted to hysterics, as most sane people would have done at the loss of their home. But then Astrid wasn't sane, was she? She was delightfully cracked in the head.

Soon everyone was laughing—aside from Aunt Emily, of course—because what else could they do?

"I told you that damned north tower was crooked," Montford said through a chuckle.

She lifted her head, and her eyes flashed with heat. "Shut up, Cyril. This *is* all your faul—"

He stopped her mouth with a kiss before she could say one more ridiculous thing. Somewhere in the background he heard Lady Emily gasp, the vicar sputter, and Marlowe and Sherbrook whistle, but he was beyond caring. He was not going to let the virago in his arms get away from him so easily, now that he'd made up his mind to keep her.

He'd never know another moment's peace without her. He'd never know a moment's peace *with* her, either, but he longed for the delicious, madcap tangles she plunged him into. The arguments—God, the arguments were thrilling, arousing! He even longed for her to throw things at him. And the very sight of her made his blood sizzle and his body burn. She was so very wrong, what with her corkscrew hair and mismatched eyes and convoluted scheming, but she was utterly perfect for him.

And as he came up for air and gazed dazedly around at the small throng of onlookers who'd turned their focus from the imploding castle to his rather bold display of passion, he caught sight of Lady Emily's vacant barouche and had a brilliant idea.

A way to bind this woman to him forever. And as quickly as possible before she could come to her senses.

He took advantage of her kiss-induced disorientation, bent down, heaved her over his shoulder, and made for the barouche.

Chapter Twenty-Seven

In Which the Duke and Miss Honeywell Negotiate a Truce

IT TOOK Astrid a moment to figure out what had happened to her after being kissed into incoherency and then unceremoniously thrown over a hard shoulder. A tumult of emotions bombarded her, what with her entire life in literal ruins, but foremost among them at the moment was indignation. She'd had enough of the duke's high-handed behavior.

"Put me down this instant, you beast!" she roared, balling her fists and thumping them against his back. She squirmed on his shoulder, but he only tightened his hold with one arm and then thwacked her on the backside with the other.

The thwack left her at sea. It infuriated her, but at the same time she felt warm all over. Dear heavens. He'd spanked her like a child, and she had been . . .

Aroused.

"How . . . how dare you . . ." she sputtered, a bit less emphatically than before. "Let me down."

"Not on your life," Montford said next to her hip.

"Beast! Churl!" she snarled.

When she realized his destination was Lady Emily's empty barouche, her stomach sank. What the hell was he about? She lifted her head and glared at the crowd who gawked at them yet made no move to intercede. Even Lady Emily seemed too shocked to raise the hue and cry.

Truly, it was distressing to have so many obliging accomplices to her kidnapping.

"Help!" she cried. "You must help me!"

"Ignore her," Montford said tersely. "Miss Honeywell and I have matters to attend to. We shall return in . . . well, a fortnight or so."

A fortnight?

He climbed inside and hauled her onto the front seat before she had time to properly digest his last statement. She guffawed with indignation when he began to bind her wrists with his soot-stained cravat. Of all the high-handed, unmitigated gall! Tying her up like some piece of livestock! As if she could go anywhere. If she tried to run away, she had a feeling the unsympathetic onlookers gathered outside would simply thrust her back into Montford's keeping.

He glowered at her, took her trussed hands, and secured the ends of the cravat to the driver's seat. This hindered her movement even more, but she still managed to kick him in the shin. He wrangled with her for a few more seconds, as she was determined to cause him as much bother as possible. Finally, he took her feet and sat on them so she could do no more damage, then took up the reins and flicked the team of horses forward.

And *still* no one made a damned move to stop him.

"Good luck, Your Grace!" Flora called, beaming at them, one arm wrapped around Roddy, her other arm hugging Ant and Art close.

Mr. Sherbrook and the viscount just smirked at each other and gave Montford a jaunty salute of approval.

As they put the castle and all of its chaos behind them and once again set off along the North Road, she turned to glare at her kidnapper, who handled the reins of the barouche like the rank amateur he was. He clearly had as little grip on the proceedings as she did. All of Montford's legendary composure was gone, stripped away, revealing the man beneath. And that man was a dangerous beast in need of a good shave and a good meal, judging from the wild, hungry look in his eyes.

That, or he was in need of some other sustenance only she could provide.

Oh, he looked like the very devil, with his glinting silver eyes and grim-set jaw.

Or at least, he would if he hadn't been covered in hay.

"Well, that was bang out of order," she muttered. She wriggled her torso in an attempt to rearrange her top, which had twisted during her kidnapping. But it was hard to do with her hands tied.

His eyes followed her every movement, she noticed with some satisfaction, when they weren't focused on the road. But his intent, predatory gaze made her satisfaction melt away into the sudden inferno of lust. She tried to keep her head. She tried to resist the lure of those eyes, the promise of pleasure hidden within those depths. "What do you plan to do with me *now*?"

"Isn't it obvious? I'm abducting you. To Gretna Green."

Well, it was about bloody time! Her heart sang with joy at his threat.

But she would settle for nothing less than all of him. It was the only way she could see being married to the Duke of bloody Montford. She needed some leverage, and his heart seemed like a good place to start.

And, damn and blast it all, she so very much wanted him to love her as much as she loved him.

"You cannot be serious!" she said haughtily.

"Oh, but I am. Very. Serious. You're not leaving this carriage until I get what I want."

She laughed. "Then I'll stay here forever. And make you very sorry for it."

He turned from the road and grinned broadly at her. And it wasn't in the least mocking. She was very worried and very, very aroused. He'd smiled like that on one other occasion. Right before he had chased her up the hayloft.

"Oh, I doubt that, Miss Honeywell. I could never be sorry for that."

"And just what is that supposed to mean?"

She gasped out loud as he leaned in closer to her face. There were stray bits of hay, she noted, caught in his eyelashes. She leaned in toward him involuntarily. If she could just flick out her tongue . . .

"I said," his lips said, not an inch from her mouth, "I should not be sorry if you stayed here forever. Tied up in the barouche. In fact, it would please me very much."

She sucked in a shocked breath, just for show. A little tremor of pleasure shot through her spine. "You'd never get away with it."

His grin deepened. "Won't I? It seems I already have."

"You're cracked in the head, Montford," she said, squeezing her eyes shut to distract herself from his eyelashes. And lips. Damn, he was making it very difficult to think straight. "It really was not well done of you to kidnap me. There is much to sort out about the castle. Not to mention running Lightfoot to ground. And Aunt Emily will dine out on this tale for years, the old goat. You've ruined my reputation, you know."

"I know." He grinned. "I may have finally succeeded in ruining mine as well."

"Piffle. You're Montford, remember?"

He smiled again, that predatory smile that made her burst into flames. "Thank you for reminding me."

"As if you could ever forget," she grumbled.

"Oh, but I do. Every time I think of you. Every time I touch you." He brought his free arm behind her back and pressed her against his hard chest, nuzzling into her neck.

She moaned and struggled against her bonds. She wanted to touch him, to run her hands down his shoulders, underneath his clothing. "Untie me."

"No. I rather like this. I can do exactly what I want to you."

Her entire body vibrated with wicked delight, and she groaned in frustration. How very little it took for him to make her lose her mind!

He leaned his forehead against hers, his breath catching. The last of Astrid's good sense fled her as she snuggled against him as best she could. *He* was the impossible one, to make her burn so despite her intentions otherwise. To make her love him, even when he had her tied up in a moving conveyance.

She tilted her head so that her lips touched his, and kissed him, tasted him. He went still, then surged forward, devouring her mouth, thrusting his tongue inside as if he couldn't get enough of her. He finally broke from her with a gasp. "Stop that, or I shall pull this vehicle over and take you now," he murmured against her temple.

"Were you planning on waiting?"

He laughed hoarsely. "You shall kill me yet. You make me lose all sense of propriety."

"I think it is safe to say propriety parted ways with us around the time we entered the stables this afternoon."

He cupped her face and stared down at her with a serious expression. "You deserve a bed. My bed. Our bed."

She snorted. "I've not agreed to anything that would lead to us sharing a bed."

His eyes went wide. He pulled back. "I swear, Astrid, if we drive all the way to Scotland and you *don't* marry me, I think I might internally combust."

Her heart jumped out of her chest in fierce joy. It was exactly what she had wanted to hear from him—sort of.

"But I can't marry you!" she breathed.

He looked so angry and hurt, for once not bothering to hide his emotions, and her whole body ached for him. He led the team over to the side of the road and pulled them to a stop before turning back to her. "Why the bloody hell not?" he demanded.

"You are a duke, a very rich, important duke. I could never be a proper duchess."

"I don't want a duchess!" he roared. "I want a wife. I want you."

"You say that now because . . . for some reason you desire me . . ."

He barked out an incredulous laugh. "I love you, Astrid!"

Her heart began to beat wildly with hope. Her wheedling, it seemed, had paid off. "Really?"

"Yes, really. Really, truly, utterly. I don't think I was alive until I met you. You make me so damnably happy! And miserable. And irritated. And insane. You drive me to distraction, but it is the loveliest sort of distraction I've ever known. I love you, I love you. Shall I say it again?"

"Yes," she said.

He kissed her madly, then drew away, his expression stern. "I love you." His stern expression slowly faded into a smile. "I love you." He kissed her cheeks, her eyelids, her chin. "I love you."

"I think I get the idea," she said with a dreamy sigh. A warm glow spread through her at his words.

He gave her a sheepish look between kisses. "Do you love *me*, Astrid?"

She decided not to let him have such an easy victory. She didn't want their marriage to get off on the wrong foot and have him think he could just make her capitulate with a few declarations of love all the time. "Does it matter? It seems you'll have your way, whether I like it or not," she sniffed.

"*Do you love me*, you little monster?" he growled, tightening his arms around her.

"I might," she hedged.

"Well, do you?"

He'd begun to sound genuinely worried, so she decided to put him out of his misery. She wasn't *that* cruel. "Of course I love you. Even if you *are* Montford."

He glared at her without heat, having seen through her ruse. "I'm afraid I'm stuck with the bloody title, Astrid. Much good it has done me. And I'm not going to give away my wealth, if that is what you want. *And* we must spend at least a few months in London every year. I have a country to run, you know. I'm sorry, Astrid, but we cannot be poor or common. You must be a duchess."

Well, when he put it like that . . .

"Can my sisters live with us?"

He looked at her in exasperation. "Of course. How could you think otherwise?"

"And Aunt Anabel?"

"If she keeps her wigs out of my way."

"I want to rebuild the castle and live there."

He grinned. "Done."

She had not expected such an easy concession. She tried her best to contain her shock and pushed him for more while his defenses were down. "I want to continue to run the brewery. My way."

His grin slipped a little. "Fine," he said rather grudgingly.

"I want you to submit a bill to the House to give women the vote."

His mouth flattened out. "We'll see."

She beamed at him. She knew by that noncommittal answer that she had conquered him utterly. He would have *never* so much as entertained such a radical thought a week ago. Oh, she was going to have such fun with this man.

His mouth turned down in a frown at her glee. "You're trying to provoke me."

"Is it working?"

He shook his head. "Damn it, Astrid, are you going to marry me or not?"

"You have hay in your eyelashes."

"Do I?"

"All over your clothes, in fact."

His eyes turned opaque, and his expression made her blood simmer. "What are you going to do about it, then?" He inched closer to her, until she had only to crane her neck forward to reach his lips. He pulled his head back abruptly and regarded her severely. She cried out in frustration. "Not until you agree to marry me."

She pouted. "You are cruel. Are you going to be such an ogre all the time?"

"Not all. Most."

"Well, then, I suppose I *must* marry you. Someone must protect the rest of the country from your black moods."

"Is that a yes?" he demanded gruffly.

"Yes."

He hesitated. "You aren't going to change your mind, are you?"

She scowled at him. "Never."

"Good." His expression softened. He grinned at her like a giddy schoolboy. Then he lowered his head and kissed her and kissed her, until they both forgot everything outside the circle of their hot, frantic embrace. Or rather, *his* hot, frantic embrace, since she was trussed up like a sacrificial offering.

Which she didn't mind in the least.

"God, how I want you," he murmured, and then he proceeded to show her just how much, propriety be damned. His mouth was on her neck, then her throat, and his hands were everywhere, caressing her until she was certain she would die from unfulfilled need.

She couldn't use her hands, but she used the rest of her body to urge him on, arching against him, legs wrapping around him greedily as he settled his weight atop her. His hands encircled her upper thighs, just as they had that day in the library when he'd seduced a book out of her pantaloons. He didn't find a book this time, but something infinitely sweeter.

Her senses fractured. So did his, apparently, until a sudden, inconvenient realization intruded into this perfect moment, and she went still beneath him, staring up at him in amazement.

"What is it now?" he groaned, pausing above her, reining in his desire with a visible effort. His breath was little more than a ragged pant. His eyes were glazed, his hair stood up on end, and his shirt gaped open, revealing an expanse of naked, chiseled male torso. He was quite the most delicious, ridiculous, lovely sight she'd ever seen.

The Duke of Montford was nowhere to be found, and Astrid couldn't have been more pleased.

What was it she wanted to say? Oh, yes. "I just thought of something. We're in a carriage, and you haven't cast up your accounts once."

He grinned and hugged her close. "How could I? You have cured me, Astrid. Body and soul. I was a wreck of a man before I met you."

"And now . . . ?"

He laughed and nuzzled her throat. "Now I am an even bigger wreck. Thank hell. I love you, Astrid Honeywell. Though you may very well drive me to Bedlam."

"Then take me with you."

"Oh, I intend to," he said, resuming his seduction. "Just give me a moment, will you?"

ABOUT THE AUTHOR

 MAGGIE FENTON is an avid reader, reviewer, and scribbler of romance in between her work as a professional musician. She writes steampunk romance under another pseudonym and has enjoyed some success as a self-published author in that genre. She hopes to enjoy much, much more. *The Duke's Holiday* is her first foray into the historical romance genre, one of her personal favorites. It won't be her last.